MY WILD PET

OLYMPIA BLACK

Cover designed by Rebecca Frank

This book is a work of fiction. Names, characters, places, and incidents either are products of the author's imagination or are used fictitiously. Any resemblance to actual persons, living or dead, events, or locales is entirely coincidental.

Printed in the United States of America

First Printing: February 2025

ISBN: 979-8-9903340-2-1

A NOTE FROM OLYMPIA ABOUT TRIGGER WARNINGS

Thank you for being here. However you found your way to this book, through curiosity, word of mouth, late-night scrolling, or cosmic accident, I'm grateful.

This story you're holding isn't easy. It wasn't easy to write. These aren't lighthearted worlds, and these characters aren't heroines waiting to be rescued. They are confused and resistant. Brave in strange and uncomfortable ways. They fight, flinch, submit, survive, and, sometimes, they even fall in love with the very thing that first frightened them.

That being said, I want to talk about trigger warnings. I include them in some of my books. *My Human Wife* opens with a full "Dear Reader" section that outlines major themes like alien intimacy, coercion, and psychological manipulation. But I've learned something important from having that there, that the kind of darkness I write doesn't fit neatly into a trigger checklist. My books aren't stories about kinks dressed up in tropes for mass market appeal. My books are about power, control, and transformation.

So, if I added a few pages of soft disclaimers to each book, I'd feel like I was lying about what I'm offering.

That said, I always welcome DMs. If you're considering one of my books and want to ask about specific content, I'm more than happy to answer. I value that conversation. I just can't promise a sanitized story and I never will.

If you're looking for safe fiction with neat lines between right and wrong, my books probably aren't for you. But if you're here for stories that ask hard questions and blur the lines between freedom and captivity...

Welcome to the Imperial Cage.

Olympia

AUTHOR'S NOTE ON GABRIEL'S LANGUAGE USE

Throughout this book, you'll notice Gabriel occasionally slips into French before repeating himself in English. This is because he hasn't spoken English regularly for years, so he sometimes defaults to French when he's emotional or caught off-guard. But he quickly catches himself every time, remembering that Briar doesn't understand French and restates his words in English. So, if you read a line in French, don't worry, Gabriel will clarify it right away in English. You won't miss any important details.

"It was the darndest thing I've ever seen. It was big, it was very bright, it changed colors, and it was about the size of the moon. We watched it for ten minutes, but none of us could figure out what it was. One thing's for sure, I'll never make fun of people who say they've seen unidentified objects in the sky. If I become President, I'll make every piece of information this country has about UFO sightings available to the public and the scientists."

JIMMY CARTER
  remark during 1976 Presidential campaign

ABBREVIATIONS

- IGC: Imperial Galaxy Court
- IC: Instant Communicator
- UC: Universal Credit

Please note information regarding the IGC's galactic sentience classification system is located at the back of the book.

CHAPTER 1

BRIAR

"Just breathe," I keep telling myself, because quitting isn't an option. I need to hurt. I can still hear my ex. boyfriend's words like a broken record, 'You never let me in.'

If he only knew how many times I *wanted* to let him in, but couldn't.

So here I am—alone on this mountain. The trail is a lot steeper than I thought it would be, but I welcome the silence and the pain.

A breeze sweeps through the pines, and for a second, I revel in the nature that surrounds me. No phone buzzing, no social media, no emails, and most importantly, no ex-boyfriend telling me I'm too emotionally distant.

Right now, I'm just one human alone on Earth.

When the moment passes, I continue going up and manage to reach a small ledge halfway up the trail. I drop my backpack and rest.

Everything is so *quiet*. It's perfect. If I close my eyes, I can almost pretend I've escaped all my problems.

Almost.

But after a minute, my innate nature to punish myself kicks in and I put my backpack back on and force myself to push through the rest of the trail, ignoring my leg muscles screaming in protest. And just when I think I might collapse from exhaustion, from pushing myself too far, a couple of adorable squirrels bolt out of nowhere, making me jump, sending a much-needed adrenaline kick to my body. I watch, panting, while they chase each other around a fallen log. *Even squirrels have companions*, I think jealously.

Long after the squirrels have run away, I eventually make it to the summit. The view from up here is stunning. An endless stretch of green trees and a huge expanse of sky that looks way too blue to be real. I half wish I wasn't alone.

"Wow," I breathe, dropping my backpack on a flat rock. Then I take out my little notebook and start scribbling notes like I always do, just some sketches and random thoughts. Half the pages are filled with things I've never shown to anyone, private moments I keep promising myself I'll share... someday...with someone... maybe.

Just as I'm finishing a quick doodle of the squirrels, I hear a low buzzing noise. It's faint, like a piece of machinery running in the distance. But my gut tells me something's off. I look around, trying to figure out where it's coming from. It feels like it's coming from all around me, and it's only getting louder.

The birds suddenly burst from the treetops, flapping away in panic as the sound intensifies.

If *they're* scared, *I* should be terrified. I need to run.

I turn around to get my backpack and notice there's a strange shimmer in the air above me, like waves of heat rising off pavement. To my horror, I realize whatever is making the noise is also blocking out the sun. My shadow has disappeared because I'm standing under something much larger than a tree and the mechanical noise is deafening now, making all the rocks around me vibrate.

Not waiting to see what happens next, I grab my backpack and bolt back the way I came. My boots pounding the ground as I run blindly down the trail. I look back, half expecting to see some giant drone, but there's nothing, just that thunderous mechanical vibration and the shimmering.

Then, suddenly, I freeze dead in my tracks. Not because I choose to, but because my whole body has locked up from an outside force. I can't move. A blinding white light surrounds me.

I try to scream, but I can't make a sound. Then I feel myself being lifted off the ground.

Below me, I spot my notebook and backpack lying in the dirt. My last thought as I'm lifted far above the ground is, *No one will ever know what happened to me.*

My own teeth chattering wakes me up with a start. I'm completely naked. My whole body is quaking from the freezing cold. I try to sit up, but I can't. My wrists and ankles are strapped down to a metal slab underneath me that feels like an ice block.

I crane my neck around, but all I see are weirdly shifting shadows and strange pulsing orange lights. There's no door, no window, and no exit. There are just glowing patterns everywhere.

I breathe in and notice the air reeks like old fish and salty ocean water. I close my eyes, silently hoping, *This is a dream.*

But I know, it's a nightmare.

Suddenly, a piercing sound I've never heard before breaks the monotony of silence in the room and I watch as part of the wet organic wall literally melts away in front of me.

Figures emerge—creatures? Aliens? Their skin gleams like liquid metal under the orange glow, and they move in false-starts, like an amateur stop-motion film, and it's unnerving to watch them.

If I'm screaming, I don't even register that I am because I've never been so terrified in my whole life.

One of the creatures makes an awful clicking sound that sends goosebumps rippling over my skin.

A slick, clammy tentacle slithers around my neck. My stomach lurches. I vomit in my mouth.

A futuristic gadget scans me from head to toe with a bright-blue beam. More clicking. More frantic tentacles touching me everywhere.

I realize with dread, I'm a lab rat on their examination table, which is exactly the kind of "first contact" scenario I never wanted to experience.

Some feeling comes back to my throat and lips, probably thanks to all the stomach acid in my vomit and I manage a weak whisper. "Please... don't...."

But the creatures don't even pause to look at me. The clicking just gets louder and the tentacles begin to move more frantically over my body.

That's when I see the surgical tools, silver, shiny, and definitely sharp, gleaming under the pulsing orange lights. Then like lightning, a brilliant flash hits me full-on. My muscles seize, and suddenly I'm sinking into unconsciousness. I catch one last glimpse of those instruments hovering above me, and my brain screams a silent prayer: *Wake up, wake up. Wake up from this nightmare!*

But then darkness swallows me whole.

I wake with a start. I'm no longer shivering, but my skin is coated in a thick, slimy, foul-smelling oil. I want to break free, but my wrists and ankles are still tied down.

The air around me is overwhelming my nostrils with a chemical tang I can't place and I gag.

Before I can fully process what's happening, something moves in my periphery vision.

And then it comes into focus.

Another creature is looming behind me, its black tentacles gleam under the dim lighting. It's gripping the edges of the table I'm on and is pushing me down a dark hallway.

I feel like I've stepped into a sci-fi horror movie I never wanted to watch, let alone be the star of.

After a few minutes, we reach two transparent glowing orange walls, and I see other humans. A dozen, maybe fewer, huddled together. Relief washes over me.

I'm not alone.

But the relief is quickly replaced by panic. None of the humans make eye contact with me. Their heads hang low, as if every ounce of hope has been wrung out of them.

What is this place?

The alien's tentacles twitch as it examines the two cages. Its large eyes scanning each one as though deciding where I belong.

I watch its movements.

My mind screams, *Put me in with the women!* I can see them in the cage closest to me—all blonde and all hauntingly similar, as if they could be sisters.

I try to point, to gesture, to do anything to make myself understood, but it's no good.

Finally after a long minute, the alien has decided where I belong and shifts its attention to a cage holding three men. It raises a device. A weapon? And shows it to the men.

Without hesitation, they shuffle back against the wall.

I want to protest, but something is keeping me from making a sound.

The alien clicks a series of noises, and the orange forcefield surrounding the cage dissolves with a faint sizzle.

Before I can prepare to be touched again, the alien's tentacles wrap around me, their slimy texture sending a shock of revulsion through my body.

I gag again.

Then I'm lifted like I weigh nothing and dumped into the men's cell with a thud.

I instinctively try to get up and run, but it's useless. The force-field has already snapped back into place, sealing me in with the three naked men.

The men stare at me, their expressions a mix of surprise and something more sinister lurking beneath the surface.

I press myself into the nearest corner.

This isn't just a sci-fi movie anymore.

This might be a hardcore porn.

I don't know why I'm here and why I'm not with the women. All of those women are blonde, like me, but not exactly like me. While their hair is pristine, mine is streaked with pink and purple highlights. Who knew aliens were such fashionistas?

I watch the alien leave and then I turn back to face the men in the cell. I instinctively cover my breasts with one hand and my vulva with the other.

A low, mechanical voice echoes through our cage. It's the clicking alien language. It means nothing to me and if it means something to my cellmates, they don't acknowledge it.

A big man with broad shoulders and a mass of dark hair stands closest to me. His gaze locks onto mine and a twisted grin spreads across his face. "Well, look what we have here, boys."

"You've just stepped into the Devil's den, honey" the smaller man says as if he's been waiting years to say that.

"She's probably a trap," the wiry man mutters from the corner.

The big man turns to the wiry one, raising an eyebrow. "You mean she's *booby*-trapped?" he asks, his tone dripping with mockery.

"I'm just saying I wouldn't touch her," the wiry man replies. "You can't even be sure she's human. It doesn't make sense they'd put her in here with us and not with the other women."

The big man looks back at me, his brow furrowing as if the thought had never crossed his mind. His confusion doesn't last long. He steps closer, his massive frame looming over me, and reaches out to touch my arm. His hand is rough and calloused. His sharp brown eyes never leave mine.

I yank my arm away, forcing myself to hold his gaze. My voice is steady, even though I'm scared of what is going to happen to me in this cell. "Do any of you know where we are?"

He doesn't answer my question. Instead, he turns back to the others, shrugging as if I'm some puzzle he's just solved. "She seems human enough. She's still covered in that oily shit they put on all of us when we arrived."

The shorter man comes closer and grabs at me.

"Get off. Who gave you the right to touch me?"

"Definitely human," the short man says with a laugh. "She's got that whole 'rights' thing down. Only a human woman would think she has *rights* here." He gestures around the cage, his grin widening. "Do you see any cops, sweetheart? Any judges?"

The big man chuckles. He takes a step closer and runs a hand through my hair before I can move away. "Maybe the aliens think she's defective because of her pink hair."

I slap his hand away. My eyes dart back to the other cage. The women inside are watching me with interest, their pale, blonde hair gleaming under the strange light. They look eerily similar, maybe they're clones?

"What do you mean, defective?" I demand, trying to keep my voice strong, trying to make them see me as a person, not an object. But I can't help but wonder if my odds would have been better with the aliens?

The small man laughs, a hollow, humorless sound. "Oh babe, how dumb are you? Look around. It's obvious. We've been abducted by aliens for medical experiments. That's what I think anyway," he shoots a look to the bigger man. "Obviously, they've stuck you with us because whatever they wanted you for, it's finished. They got it. Otherwise," he gestures to the women, "you'd be over there with the virginal blondes."

The wiry man in the corner pipes up again, his voice sharp and analytical. "Or," he says, "it's about sorting. Look at them." He points toward the other cage with a jerk of his chin. "The aliens have no hair, no gender, at least not that we can tell. Maybe they're grouping us by hair color, like puppies or kittens. Purple and brown probably seem more similar to them. Or they're color blind. Or the alien who dropped her off is the office idiot. Who knows?"

I look over at the women in the other cage again, wishing I were there. My hair, once just an expression of my individuality, now feels like a branding, a mark that separates me from the safety of other women.

The big man snorts, dismissing the wiry man's theory with a wave of his hand. "Doesn't matter why she's here. They gave her to us. Naked. And now she's ours."

The words send a chill down my spine. *No,* I think. *I'm not anyone's.*

I try to keep my voice composed to find some common ground, "None of us belong here."

For a moment, there's silence. Then the big man grins again, his eyes narrowing trying to decide what his next move is.

The small man tries to touch my breast and I push him off. "Well then, if none of us belong here, no one will mind if this puppy wets himself in that pussy. Come here, kitty."

The big man grabs the small man viciously by his neck. "Me first. Then if you're lucky, I'll allow you to dip your wick."

"No one is dipping anything in me." I say, trying to give myself courage. "Just because we're in a cage doesn't mean we have to act like animals. Did it ever occur to you that maybe our captors are testing us?"

The men all laugh at the same time.

The big man replies, "You can pretend you've consented, honey. I don't care whether my women are willing, fighting, or unconscious. And," he says pointing to the ceiling, "Those *aliens* don't care either. We've already killed a few men before you who didn't cooperate by my rules. Now are you going to pretend you're willing like the whore you clearly are or do we need to force you? The choice of role-fore-play is entirely up to you."

Think. What can I say to stop this? "I have an STD. I have syphilis!"

"And I have herpes. Come here, I'm going to give it to you."

I address the man in the corner watching all of this, "Hey, are you going to stand by and let him do this to me? Where's your humanity?"

"On Earth," he replies flatly.

"Unbelievable," I mutter. "At least these men are prepared to fight for *something.* Although, I must point out, it's not a fair fight," I say turning my attention back to my would-be attackers.

"Life isn't fair," the big man says as he moves closer to me.

I kick him as hard as I can in the groin.

He doubles over with pain, "You fucking bitch. I'll make you pay for that."

He grabs my ankle and knocks me off my feet. I fall hard on the metal floor. Something catches my eye in the confusion and I look over to see all the women in the cage across from us. It looks like they are screaming, but I can't hear their voices, just see their movements, their hands waving in what looks like, 'No!'

I'm glad I have cheerleaders.

The big man hovers over me. He knocks my head against the metal floor enough times that the room begins to turn, faster and faster. Then he holds my neck with one hand and my hips down with another. I summon the strength to fight back as I feel my breath being cut off and I feel the head of his erect cock at my dry entrance.

"You're going to have to rip me apart," I manage to say while spitting up some coppery blood.

"Open for me, whore," he says through gritted teeth.

I hate this man. I kick at him as violently as I can, thrashing so hard I think I might have sprained one of my ankles. I manage to get a few good kicks in and thanks to the oil the aliens covered me in, I wiggle free, but not before I knee him so hard in the groin he shrieks and moves off of me like I electrocuted him.

My chest tightens painfully as I try to draw breath. Every cough feels like sandpaper tearing through my throat. Bent over, gasping for air, I glance at the other women. They're still waving frantically, yelling something I can't make out.

The sound of footsteps rips my focus away. I turn and see the big man barreling toward me.

I don't have time to think. My body reacts on instinct, adrenaline overriding the pain. I get to my feet and charge at him like I'm Xena Warrior Princess.

I leap onto his back, clinging like a wild animal, and sink my teeth into his shoulder with everything I've got. The taste of sweat and salt floods my mouth, but I don't let go.

His cry of surprise echoes off the cage walls. It spurs me on, and I bite harder and begin to taste copper. He thrashes, grabbing at me with his massive hands, and finally throws me off like I weigh nothing.

I hit the metal floor hard, the impact rattling my bones. Pain explodes through my skull, and the world goes sideways. My vision blurs, the lights above spinning like a merry-go-round.

Through the pain, I watch him. He's stumbling, clutching at his shoulder, trying to reach the spot where my teeth left a deep imprint of my jaw.

"I hope it scars," I manage to rasp.

The big man turns back to me, his face flushed with rage. "So you want to play hard to get? Others have tried that. They're gone now. I'm going to do the same to you. I'm going to fuck you to death. We all are."

I spit, a mix of saliva and blood hitting the floor between us. "You think that's a win? Look around, genius. We're in hell, and you think being king of this cell, population four, makes you something? Handing out death threats to the only woman in your little kingdom? You're fucking pathetic."

His expression shifts, the insult landing harder than I expected. He glances at the other men, as if looking for some solidarity. But they're silent.

The fight drains out of me as the adrenaline fades. I let my eyes slowly close. And if death comes for me while I sleep, at least it will end the pain I feel now.

CHAPTER 2

AEFRE

My console beeps sharply, and the holographic display comes to life. Ira's name flashes across the screen—*Commander Ira of the Imperial Fleet*. I hesitate.

Ira's a busy man—no personal communications are allowed while he's away on a mission, so if he's calling now, it means he's back in Imperial space and expecting me to answer.

I stare at the blinking light. Fifi was a champion, one of the best I ever trained a show pet who never hesitated to please. And now she's gone.

The beep continues.

I brace myself, then reach out to press "Accept."

The screen resolves into Ira's stern face.

"Commander," I say.

"Aefre, the goddesses have not been good to you. I've just seen your report. How could you let Fifi die?"

"It was an unfortunate accident."

"Aefre, listen to me and listen well. You have eight months to find me a replacement for Fifi." Ira says exasperated. "How did she die? Did another pet kill her?"

I take a measured breath and try to explain, "She died competing in the Bond Breaker Challenge."

His gaze sharpens. "Who was meant to save her?"

"Ember."

A flash of something—contempt, disappointment, or both—crosses Ira's face. His tone drops, low. "Your favorite male pet chose UCs over his partner in the Bond Breaker Challenge? Explain how that happened?."

"It was completely unexpected. Ember's connection to Fifi was genuine. Their bond seemed strong enough to predict self-sacrifice. But, clearly I miscalculated. I made a mistake. I won't make it again."

"Tell me every detail of how something like this could have happened. She was a champion. She wasn't supposed to die this way."

The Grand Championships are never streamed for security purposes now that the IGC has made the human pet trade illegal. So, I recount the uncomfortable memory from the week before. "The simulated arena was set to level ten for difficulty. Ember and Fifi had just won their third Grand Championships. They were ready to tackle the Bond Breaker. Ember stood at the starting point and at the far end of the course was the artifact. And restrained on a sinking platform in the center, above a pit of toxic mist, was Fifi."

I pause, the scene replaying vividly in my mind. "I told Ember, 'Retrieve the artifact in the time allotted, and you win the prize UCs.'

"Ember navigated the course with expertise. All the while, Fifi panicked, struggling to break free from what she knew was certain death. She screamed for him, 'Don't leave me! Please!' First, she used Imperial, and then when she knew death was near, she used her human language. Her desperation echoed through the arena but Ember was untouched by it.

"He froze in the last minutes, deciding her fate. His face was pale, his heartbeat and breathing registered on his collar as extremely high. He glanced back at her, his expression a mixture of pain and resignation. Then he said, 'I'm so sorry, Fifi. I can't.'

"He chose the artifact. And by the Bond Breaker rules we couldn't save her even for a disqualification. The last we saw of Fifi were her small hands, reaching out, as the toxic mist consumed her," I say, meeting Ira's gaze through the transmission. "Ember saw the challenge for what it was—an impossible scenario. He didn't know that he should have saved Fifi and they both would have lived. He chose to win the artifact and the UCs."

Ira's lips press into a thin line. "Humans value bonds. Loyalty. He severed his tie with Fifi without much hesitation. No one wants to see *that* from a human pet. You've not trained him as well as you think you have, Aefre."

I keep my voice even while I defend my work, "Ember is adaptable. Resourceful. Unlike the other human pets, he sees the game for what it is. At the moment, he sees loyalty as a weakness in the long term. I just need to find him a partner that he values more than himself. Fifi was special, but she wasn't extraordinary. It was Ember who made her so."

"Well," Ira says, "I suppose that's what I'm paying you for, your so-called expertise."

"That's *exactly* what you're paying me for. Don't I bring you the best return on human pets in the galaxy? Ember and Fifi won the Grand Championships three times which is why they were able to compete in the Bond Breaker for even more UCs. And we all received the payout from their wins, including Ember's solo win. So it wasn't a complete loss," I say, and leave off, 'except for my reputation.'

Ira narrows his eyes but doesn't argue. "*Currently* you are still the best pet trainer in the galaxy," he concedes. "But perhaps Fifi's death is the start of your decline? You better be careful, in my experience, one misstep is usually followed by others."

"This was one mistake, and I never make the same mistake twice," I assure him, though the memory lingers of Ember's hesitation, his pained expression—those weren't the signs of a pet without loyalty. They were the signs of someone who understood he had no choice.

"Did Fifi leave any offspring?"

"We have some of her eggs," I admit carefully. "I was going to sell them."

"That goes against the goddesses. I don't want to hear about it," he snaps, his voice betraying his falseness.

"I'll find a replacement," I say. "One that surpasses even Fifi. I just need time."

"Now, listen here. I'm transferring you two thousand UCs to buy a new pet. I want to win the next Grand Championship at The Celestial Spire. I don't want to sit a year out. That's lost UCs on Ember."

"With all due respect, I don't think I can train a fresh female pet to win in eight months." I keep my tone steady, even as my mind races. Training a new human pet for a competition of this caliber in that time frame is nearly impossible.

"You'd better, Aefre, or I'll invest in another trainer. It was wasteful of you to let Fifi die. Don't let me down. You have the UCs and eight months."

"I understand," I reply, not letting my voice betray my uneasiness with this commitment.

I pride myself on shaping pets to show the best humanity can be, if properly trained. I cannot fail again, but these are impossible odds. Yet my mind is already mulling over what happened between Fifi and Ember for the millionth time. Perhaps it wasn't *what* happened, but rather what *didn't* happen.

Before I can dwell on it further, Ira interrupts my thoughts. "Good. Now I have to get back to defending the Empire. Not all of us get to play with adorable human pets every day. And Aefre, I want regular holos of my pets training. Stop being so cautious about the IGC. No one is really going to enforce the law about pet shows." Then he adds as an afterthought, "But send them to me encrypted. Walk with the goddesses."

His image flashes out as the transmission ends, leaving me alone in the silent glow of my office. I drop my head into my hands.

How am I supposed to train a new pet in just eight months? It's hopeless.

But not entirely unachievable. I trained Fifi's sister in six months and she managed to win two shows—though neither was as prestigious as the Grand Championship.

I cloak my galactic connection and begin searching for upcoming human auctions. An Octopod group is hosting one at the Abyssal Nexus. These auctions are notoriously unpredictable—Octopods don't understand human aesthetics. Their interest in humanity is purely biological: incubators for their young and playthings for their tentacles. So, I usually avoid buying from them, but today, I'm desperate.

I activate the comms to my ship's captain. "Set a course for the Abyssal Nexus."

The hesitation on the other end lasts only a moment. "Understood," the captain replies, his voice neutral.

I close the channel, my thoughts already shifting to the task ahead. I need a plan. But just in case I'm overlooking one of the females I already have, I decide to visit all my pets onboard.

When I enter the pet play area, six pairs of human eyes immediately focus on me. Even after all these years, their attentiveness still pleases me. Good humans, every one of them.

I open the door and call for my two favorites. They run to me, dropping to their knees as they've been trained. I rest a hand on the first, Mags—forty years under my care and still sharp. Then Ember, my prized male, here for ten years and the most impressive human male I've ever owned.

"A new human will be joining us soon," I tell them, my voice firm but calm. "You must help her adjust. Understand?"

"Understand," they reply in Imperial, their accents varied but their obedience clear.

"Good humans." I let a small smile cross my lips. "If you're very good, there will be a treat later."

Mags beams at the promise, while Ember nods, his expression steady. I stroke Mags' fur between her legs and then Ember's. I stop before either of them becomes too aroused and then I dismiss them, and they run back to play. I linger for a moment, watching them toss a ball back and forth.

I look at the other two females. They are the right age and have been trained to the extent of their abilities, but they're not enough. Not mentally or physically capable for the challenges at the Grand Championships. Those games are designed to push both pets and their trainers to their limits.

I observe my two other females for another minute, to assure myself that I'm not missing something in their potential. But, I'm not. They just aren't strong enough and Ember would definitely leave either of them to die in the Bond Breaker. I must resign myself to the idea of a new pet.

I open internal communications. "Kaelin, meet me in the conference room. I just spoke to Ira; we have a lot to discuss."

I see Kaelin in the corridor and we walk together.

"Eight months? That's insane."

"I know." My voice is quieter than I intend, my thoughts already circling around the daunting task ahead. "But Fifi..."

Kaelin studies me for a moment. "Well," he says finally, "we'll just have to pray to the goddesses that the Octopods have something special at the auction."

"I'm sure they will," I say but I can't keep the doubt from my voice.

"It's a pity most body modifications and enhancements are penalized now. A few major adjustments, and we wouldn't have to rely so heavily on finding raw talent."

I don't respond as we make our way down the polished corridors of the ship.

Kaelin matches my pace. "This isn't your first impossible timeline."

"No," I admit. "But this is the first time I've had to replace a champion lost during a Bond Breaker Challenge. What happened affected Ember too, even though humans aren't supposed to remember, some of them do. He remembers and it affects him. And there's no research on what to do, except some pet experts suggest retiring him."

Kaelin laughs. "Most human pet experts are charlatans."

"Exactly."

"Do you think Ira's serious about finding another trainer if you fail?"

"I'm sure of it," I reply. "Ira doesn't make idle threats."

The conference room doors slide open with a familiar hiss, and we step inside. The holographic display is already active in the center of the table. I press a few commands, pulling up a profile of the Grand Championship's arena and the projected timeline for the next eight months.

Kaelin takes a seat across from me. "So, how do we turn an untrained human into a champion in eight months? Assuming the Octopods even have a viable candidate."

I lean forward, my hands resting on the edge of the table. "We'll have to maximize every second of her training. Physical conditioning, language acquisition, obstacle courses, Imperial etiquette—it all needs to start immediately. No time for mistakes on our end."

Kaelin nods. "The obstacle courses will need to be modified before she can begin training with Ember. We can't throw her into level-ten simulations right away, but she'll need to be there within four months. That's going to be tough"

"Even then, Ember will have to bring her up to speed."

"Do you think he'll bond with her? After what happened with Fifi?"

"We will use their collars to force it if we have to. He doesn't have a choice," I reply firmly. "None of us do."

Kaelin leans back in his chair, crossing his arms. "And what if this mystery female is not up to the task? What if the Octopods only have duds?"

"Then I'll make her up to the task," I say, my voice hardening. "Or she'll die in the training. Either way I'll be able to keep Ira as my sponsor."

"Would it really be so bad to lose him" Kaelin asks. I know he thinks I should be open to more sponsors, but more sponsors who each provide fewer UCs is more work and more headaches.

"No, then I'd have twenty Ira's trying to micromanage my training instead of just one." I turn off the hologram. "Prep a collar and training simulations for integration. And make sure Ember is ready to meet his new partner, don't hesitate to use mood-influencers. I don't want him being as angry as he is now when he meets the new female. I don't want him scaring her. They have to bond. We don't have time for them to warm up to each other."

"He's stubborn by nature," Kaelin says. "Let me try punishments before mood enhancers. Maybe he needs to fight his grief out with pain?"

I consider this. "Fine, but not too much."

"I know his limits, Aefre. When you return with the new pet he'll be ready. Good luck at the auction and walk with the goddesses."

I don't believe in the goddesses or fate. I believe in hard work with a tinge of luck. But if I were a religious man, I'd be praying to the goddesses for the perfect human female to appear at this auction.

CHAPTER 3

BRIAR

I wake in the corner of my shared cell. Every muscle screams in protest, and the cold, unyielding floor does little to help with the pain.

I've named the men in my cell; Big, Tiny, and Slender. I don't have enough respect for them to use their given names. They're all terrible in their own ways. Big because he's the bully, Tiny because he's the blind follower of the bully and would be the bully if he were physically bigger, and Slender because he's just feeling sorry for himself, unable to do anything that doesn't serve him. More than Big and Tiny, I hate Slender the most. He's the worst kind of traitor, the kind that refuses to take a side so he can always count himself clean.

At the moment, Big and Tiny are muttering about something. I can guarantee that whatever they're talking about, it's utter nonsense.

Slender sits in his usual corner, avoiding eye contact with everyone, especially me. I watch him, wondering if Big has raped him. Even if Big has, what kind of person just gives up? Especially when there are so few of us? Now that I'm here, it could be two against two.

When Big rapes me, and yes, this is a question of when not if, I won't hold him off forever, he's just too strong, but when he does, afterward, I'm not going to cower in a corner. I'll fight harder. Because this is a fight like any other and Big has made it crystal clear, it's to the death.

But I'll use everything at my disposal to keep bad things from happening to me. What's the phrase? 'Keep your friends close and your enemies closer.' So, the more I interact with Big the better chance I have of outsmarting him. God knows I was lucky yesterday. I don't know if I'll be so lucky today.

I shift slightly, wincing at the sharp pain in my ribs. My eyes land on Big, his hulking frame turned slightly as he talks with Tiny. My teeth marks are still fresh on his back all red and angry. I smile. Well at least that's something.

If he tries again, I'll bite off his ear, I think.

"Hey," I say. The cell goes quiet, all three men turn toward me. "Yeah, you," I say looking directly at Slender.

He points to himself, as if surprised I'm addressing him. Always the innocent victim.

"Where are we?" I ask.

"A spaceship."

"How do you know?"

"Alien abduction," he says, his tone flat, as if I'm an idiot for even asking. "I was in the forest. Next thing I knew, I was here. Humans don't have spaceships, and humans sure as hell don't look like *that*." He gestures toward the empty hallway between the cages, where the creature dropped me off. "Don't you remember how you got here?"

"We're not on a spaceship," Big says, interrupting. "This is just rich people fucking with peons. You're just weak, more susceptible to suggestion," he says to Slender. "That's why you *think* you were abducted by aliens."

Slender faces the wall again.

Then Big looks up at the ceiling, addressing the invisible audience in his mind. "I'm not buying it! I know the truth, and that's why you sent me *this piece of ass*," he says, pointing a meaty finger at me, "to distract me. And you made her hard to get, that was clever. But I'll get her, and I'll get her good."

My stomach turns as his filthy gaze lingers but I meet his beady brown eyes head-on.

"They're watching us," he continues, his voice dripping with paranoia. "They're watching us to see what we're going to do. Probably even betting on how long you can stay away from me."

"But it makes no sense for billionaires to keep us like this," I say, trying to get his mind off raping me. "Without food and water, we'll die."

"Oh, the Handlers feed us," Tiny says joining the conversation.

"Handlers?"

"There are three different kinds of *fake* octopus-aliens," Big confirms. "The leaders have elaborate skin patterns, the officers are big and scary, and the handlers are smaller and thicker. The handlers feed us. I think the billionaires must have gotten some Hollywood makeup artists to set this up." Then looking up at the ceiling where he believes there are cameras, he yells, "It's all very impressive and almost believable."

"But we're all starving except for him," Slender points to Big. "He divvies out the food."

Big defends himself, "I told you. You suck my cock again and I'll give you more food. It's an even trade. There are calories in semen. So I'm actually giving you more food than the others."

I look at Big disgustedly. "Well aren't you a prize example of a homo sapien, obsessed with getting an orgasm from anyone at any time, even when there's only four of us here."

Big takes a few steps towards me and then slaps me hard across the face.

Before the sting can even begin register I slap him back hard.

He grabs my wrist. "Is that the best you got little lady? Do it again and I'll fucking kill you."

My wrist is still covered in the oil from yesterday and I wiggle it free. "I'm already dead if this is all that's left to me. You three and those silent women across from us, watching everything we do, like we are some gladiatorial show in the Roman Colosseum."

"It's those bitches fault that I'm sex obsessed," Big says surprising me by blaming innocent women he can't even talk to for his desire to sexually dominate everyone in this cell. "They're just there... naked. They're not even trying to cover up."

Astonished, I turn to look at the blonde women in the cell across from us. Then turn back to Big. "Are we seeing the same thing? They're just standing there, like us. You do realize, none of us, have any clothing, right?"

"If women really cared about each other they would have tried to cover themselves because it's only making it worse for you. They're doing this to you on purpose. They know if I see them naked and then you're here I'm going to have to rape you."

"Are you trying to cover yourself up for modesty?" I ask Big. Then I turn to Tiny and Slender. "Are any of you trying to cover yourselves? No, of course not, so why should they? Your logic is the most juvenile, man-baby, caveman piece of shit, I've heard in a long time."

"Oh shut the fuck up. You covered your tits and pussy when *you* entered," Slender points out, "because you know it's different for women."

"Yes, because I was thrown into a cage with three naked men and I was trying to avoid being raped." I make eye contact with Big. "Because as a rule, until I speak to men, I always assume they're predators. But those women," I gesture to the blonde women, "have nothing to fear from you, so they, just like you, are in their natural state. And it amazes me that you three can't even look at a naked woman and control your sexual desires."

"I can," Slender says.

"Oh big fucking applause for the pick-me boy in the corner, who did nothing when I was being attacked," I retort.

Tiny laughs.

"It's not my fault," Big continues to defend himself. "Look at them," he points to the naked blonde women. "They're purposely acting like strippers."

"They are fucking naked!" I say losing my temper and feeling bad for all the strippers who actually are good dancers but those skills are apparently lost on men who think that naked women standing in a cell are the same as strippers on poles. "I feel like we are seeing two different things. I see regular women trying to survive. They aren't trying to seduce you. That's all in your mind," I say and give up talking to my cell mates for a while.

After a long stretch of silence, I ask Big, "Have you seen any people leave this place? I mean besides the ones you said you killed."

"Yes," Slender replies. Of course, *he* replies. "Some of the women in the other cell have been led out with leashes. Sometimes a few return, but we can't talk to the women, so we don't know what's happening and they haven't tried to tell us what's going on."

"Have you tried to ask?"

Slender shakes his head.

"Of course you haven't."

"None of us men have ever left this cage alive and returned. That's all we know," Slender says ignoring my observation.

My eyes drift across to the women in the other cell again. Some of them are sleeping, others talking, and some are watching us. I make eye contact with a woman and we hold it for some time. I stand and move as close to the forcefield as I can. I hold up my hands questioning and mouth the words, 'What's going on here?'

She stands and then she mouths a word to me, but I can't for the life of me understand. It looks like she's saying, 'set.' Set? Is she trying to tell me to be ready? For what?

She stops mouthing the word as two handler aliens enter and have what I can only assume is food and water. Just like Slender said, Big takes all the food and the water, hoarding it in the corner. My stomach grumbles as I listen to him smack and slurp.

After he's finished, he gives some to his sidekick, Tiny. When there's only the smallest amount of food left, he says to Slender and me, "There's only food left for one of you. So I want you to fight each other for it."

"I'm not fighting a woman," Slender says and honestly, I'm shocked he has any decency for a fair fight.

"Only because you're worried she'd kick your ass," Tiny says.

"Well, she's not going to get it by default and neither are you," Big replies. "I need some entertainment. You fight her or you starve."

"I don't want it. You take it," I say to Slender.

My comment annoys Big.

"Women! She thinks she can trick us into feeling sorry for her," Big announces. "That's not going to work on me. I know all the little tricks women use to manipulate men."

I laugh because it's so absurd. Even when I've been abducted by aliens I still have a man explaining my actions to me. "Why don't you explain my behavior to me a little more? I'd love to hear your thoughts on women's orgasms, periods, and childbirth," I say, my voice dripping with an invitation to fight again.

Next thing I know, I'm flat on my back after being knocked across the face by Big. My ears are ringing. Everything sounds like I'm deep underwater. I'm in so much pain.

Big is hovering over me. His pungent smell making me nauseous. He kneels on my arms, pinning them painfully to the floor and then puts his stinking erect penis in my mouth.

Having nothing to lose now, I bite down as hard as I can and don't let go. I imagine myself a gator in the bayou. I remember the documentaries I watched about alligators latching on to prey and then taking them down to the dark river bed to drown them.

I am a gator and Big is my prey.

Big is punching my head making my it move, side to side, but it doesn't matter. I'm resolved not to let go.

Tiny starts beating on my legs, but I'm beyond pain. I only grind my teeth to sink deeper into his organ. My mouth fills with hot coppery blood, his or mine, I don't know.

I don't care.

I thrash my head back and forth in rhythm with his shrieks. I'm taking him down to the pit of hell with me. His hot blood is oozing down the sides of my mouth, tickling my throat.

I am the gator.

Suddenly, I'm hit with lightning sharp pain. Again and again, the electricity runs through my body.

My jaw is forced open and his organ is pried off my teeth. Then I'm shocked again and I close my eyes. Maybe for the last time.

When I wake, I'm alone. I can see my former cell mates in the cell next to mine and now the blonde women are diagonal. I stand as close to the men's cell as possible, to see if I managed to bite off Big's penis.

I can't see anything from this angle, but when he sees me and we make eye contact he starts yelling like a madman. Thankfully, there's a forcefield separating us. He looks furious as he moves to the edge of the cell and begins banging against the orange forcefield that just ripples in more static orange waves. My eyes immediately go to between his legs. I can't tell if my teeth marks are still there, but what's left of his penis is maybe a half an inch at best and hardly peeks out over his unruly dark pubic hair.

"Fuck around and find out," I say loudly, even though he can't hear me.

The women in the cell diagonal to mine catch my eye and I turn my attention to them. They're all smiling and giving me a thumbs up. I fake humbleness and take a bow like an actor at the end of a play. This makes Big even more enraged and he starts shouting at the women too.

I watch wondering what leads people to become so detached from society they'd hurt others, even in situations like this, when we clearly have a common enemy. It makes no sense.

But I have to reflect on my own behavior too. I was only here a day, two at the most, and I went from being a normal person to a full-on savage.

I didn't start it, I think, trying to reconcile my actions as I watch Big still shouting at the other women, *But I did fucking finish it*.

The days blend together silently. There's nothing to hold on to, no distractions, except the occasional clatter of food being delivered breaking the monotony. Every eight hours, like clockwork.

I wonder if anyone on Earth is looking for me.

People go missing all the time. And it's very easy to make it look like someone decided to go somewhere else or even disappear off the grid. A few fake texts or social media posts, and in a matter of minutes, the world moves on. Goldfish memories.

I think about my own life. I have no one who would demand answers if I didn't show up for work except my boss, but I'm replaceable and despite being the model employee, I've never been close with him or anyone else. I have acquaintances who might make one phone call to the police, but then never follow up.

I own my own apartment. The bills are paid automatically. I don't have a doorman. I'm not a member of any clubs. There's no one.

I have no family to speak of. My mother died when I was four. Her death is one of my earliest memories. I still remember asking her, while visiting her in the hospital, her body connected to wires and machines, "Are you going up to the sky now, Mommy?"

"Yes, baby girl," she had said, her voice breaking. "I'm going up to the sky now. Be a good girl for Daddy. We both love you."

"Your mommy is going to become a star, Briar," my dad added.

My father became a star himself not long after, leaving me alone with only a sky full of distant, untouchable lights as my only parental guidance from the age of eight. Even now, when I look up at the night sky, I imagine my parents are watching me. I know it's childish, but it's a reassuring habit. It's ironic then, if I've been abducted by aliens and I am in a spaceship among those same stars that always comforted me.

After my father died, I bounced between foster homes. Some girls turn rebellious or self-destructive. Me? I built walls. I learned to rely only on myself, to focus on success and money. And the world rewarded me for it. The mayor even gave me an award a few years ago—*a foster child turned commodities trader, the poster girl for success.* The irony still burns. I didn't do anything to inspire others. I did it because that's how I coped with the card I was dealt with in life.

My ex. boyfriend's voice echoes in my mind, as sharp and cutting as ever. *"You treat me like I'm going to turn my back on you at the drop of a hat. I can't live like this anymore, Briar."*

It still stings. He wasn't the first to feel that way, but he was the only one to say it out loud. No other boyfriend lasted long enough to put it into words, but the signs were always there. I'm not easy to love. I don't know how to trust others.

My eyes drift to the men in the cage next to mine. Maybe this is all some twisted experiment. A study orchestrated by psychologists who wanted to see what would happen if they threw people like us, loners, overachievers, outliers, into this hell. Or maybe it's just a game, some dystopian reality show for a higher species.

Whatever it is, I didn't sign up for this.

The same woman from before catches my eye from the female cage across from me. She's mouthing something again.

I squint, trying to make sense of the word, but it's impossible.

She moves closer to the edge of her cage, her gestures growing more exaggerated as she repeats the word. Her urgency is contagious, but it only makes me feel more frustrated.

I shake my head, mouthing back, "I don't understand."

She presses on, joined by another woman who begins miming motions, pointing to herself, gesturing outward, then pretending to hold something close.

"Bet?" I mutter under my breath. "What bet? What does that mean?"

The second woman shakes her head emphatically and repeats the motions.

"Set?" I try again.

My patience snaps. I throw my hands up in exasperation. "I don't know!"

The first woman's shoulders slump. Disappointment is written all over her face.

I sink to the cold floor, wrapping my arms around my knees. But I can't stop watching her. She leans against her cell wall now, defeated, while the other women murmur among themselves, casting worried glances my way.

"Whatever it is, they know something I don't," I whisper to myself. "And whatever it is... it's not good."

———

Three days ago, Slender was taken from the men's cell and didn't come back. And a handful of the blonde women were led out too, but a few of them returned, so I don't think anyone was being executed. They looked unharmed. No, that's not true. Physically unharmed, but emotionally traumatized.

I promise myself that when they come for me, I'll try to remain calm, to figure out as much as possible. In the hopes that the more I understand about my situation, the better chance I have of getting home.

As the days wear on, I'm still not entirely convinced this is a spaceship and as stupid as Big is, I am starting to believe this might be just other humans messing with us. I've never felt the ship move nor have we seen anything really alien except the few aliens when we arrived. And there are toilets in our cells. How would these kinds of aliens know about human toilets?

CHAPTER 4

AEFRE

The Abyssal Nexus looms in front of me. It's a massive Octopod station shaped like a living creature with bioluminescent tendrils snaking out into deep space. It only reminds me of how much I hate dealing with Octopods.

"Prepare for docking," the captain announces. A faint chime echoes through the *Luminous Arc*, followed by the computer's acknowledgment when the docking is complete.

I gaze at the Nexus, its glowing mass reflecting off my ship's windows. "The auction awaits," I mutter.

I make my way to the exit, where my guards stand waiting. I don't expect trouble here, but this is Octopod territory after all. I motion for them to follow.

We walk along the station's dimly lit corridors with their glowing orange patterns. Breathing in the thick air as our feet move through the faint mist drifts along the floor, which allows the Octopods to glide more easily and the rest of us to slip.

The Octopod Docking Overseer approaches. "Imperial Trainer Aefre. Your arrival has been logged. The auction preparations are underway. Please proceed to the Auction Hall."

"Ensure my transport is secured," I reply curtly, but he's already moved on, issuing orders to harsh handlers who are dragging restrained humans off transport ships further down the hall.

One of my guards grimaces as we watch a group of human men roughly yanked into formation by their tentacled captors. "Those male pets, they're so shattered," he observes.

I say nothing, my eyes fixed on the scene. The Octopods' treatment of humans is crude. Their methods dull the spirit, stripping away everything that makes humans valuable as pets.

We continue through the station, the long, curving corridors shimmering with orange light. The walls pulse faintly with bioluminescent designs, and the mist thickens underfoot. Trainers pass by, some nodding in recognition, others avoiding my gaze.

Just as we near the Auction Hall, the sound of humans crying reaches us. I raise a hand, signaling my guards to stop. Seconds later, a group of humans are led across the corridor, their faces pale with fear and their steps unsteady on the slick floor.

I watch them, assessing their condition. "Those humans are damaged," I say under my breath. "They'll fetch a price, but they're useless. The Octopods have made them compliant, but in the process, reduced them to just living bags of water."

"Do you still want to go in?" one of my guards asks.

I hesitate for the briefest moment, the weight of doubt creeping in. *If this is the quality on offer, am I wasting my time?* But I've come too far to turn back now. "We're already here. We might as well go in."

At the entrance to the Auction Hall, two Octopod guards stop us. "No personal security allowed. Only buyers, Master Trainer," one of them clicks.

I glance at my guards. "It should be safe enough. It makes no sense to murder your buyers. Wait out here," I instruct them and then step through the doors alone.

The Auction Hall is massive, a circular auditorium with glowing orange accents and tiered seating. A notification pings on my IC, directing me to a seat near the front. *Good. They've learned to reserve those for serious buyers.*

I glance up at the floating platforms where the humans will soon be displayed. I hope they'll have better humans on offer than what I saw in the corridors.

I hear my name whispered behind me. "That's Aefre. He turns human pets into Grand Champions."

I turn casually, meeting the gaze of a lesser-known trainer. He nods in recognition, and I return the gesture.

Before the auction begins, a loud, clicking announcement echoes through the hall. Even my superior Imperial translator struggles to smooth out the harsh edges of the Octopod language.

A holographic screen flickers to life above the central platform. The voice continues:

"In accordance with Galactic Trade Law, Section Twenty, Subsection One, all potential buyers must be informed of the first subject's history and character prior to sale."

I lean back in my seat, watching the glowing screen. It's not uncommon for the Octopods to show compliance footage before an auction. Even though the human pet trade is technically illegal now, some are still running their businesses as if the law regarding humans was never passed.

The screen pulses, and I hope the auction will begin soon. I need a human who can replace Fifi. Ideally, a medium-sized female with blonde hair, brown eyes, and the physical attributes that human females are prized for, decently sized breasts, enough to bounce when she walks and ample fur between her legs and under her arms.

But more than that, I need someone who can win.

"Subject Number 427-B designation: human female has exhibited extraordinary aggression in captivity. The following footage demonstrates her actions during an incident within the holding chambers."

The video begins and it's raw footage from one of the human holding cells. There are three males and a female in a cage together.

That's stupid, I think to myself. But then again, Octopods can't always tell the difference between males and females. And to be fair, two of the males in the cell are fat enough to have average size female breasts. But you'd think the Octopods would have noticed their penises between their legs.

I watch with everyone else. Not surprisingly the largest male is bullying the female. We can't hear what's being said, but it doesn't matter, humans don't really have complex languages or thoughts. Then the big male tries to put his penis in the female's mouth.

That hole has teeth, I think.

Shockingly, the female bites down on his tender appendage and doesn't let go, all the while taking quite a beating from the other men. Red blood squirts all over her face and by the time the Octopod guards pull her away from the man, she'd torn off most of the male's penis.

The announcer clicks, "Behold, her capabilities. The subject displays intelligence, cunning, and physical aptitude exceeding initial assessments. However, she also exhibits heightened defiance and volatility, traits that must be managed with appropriate measures."

The camera angle shifts to a close-up of the female in the aftermath with the bitten off penis still between her bloody lips. The screen freezes on this image as the auctioneer continues.

"As per galactic custom, these traits are presented for transparency. Buyers should proceed with the understanding that the subject requires careful handling, but such qualities may also present unique opportunities for those seeking pets of uncommon spirit and resilience."

The crowd murmurs. I hear comments of both approval and apprehension. A few trainers around me lean forward in their seats, clearly intrigued by the footage. I've seen humans at their worst, and I've seen this before, aggression born of survival. A primal instinct, and one that's almost impossible to wield in a human. Only an expert trainer can do it.

The video continues then and it's of the Octopod medics trying

to reattach the male's penis. Octopods have very little medical expertise as they prefer to just let each other die rather than waste time and
energy trying to extend one another's life.

I cross my legs as I watch the Octopods try to reattach the human
male's penis while he is conscious and by the way he's screaming; he
can feel everything. Of course, this fails and in the end, the Octopods
cauterize the wound and now he's a eunuch.

The next scene shows the male back in his cell, his wounds
where his penis was, healing. The back of him shows the familiar red
light of an anus plug for training. No doubt they're going to sell him
to be a release pet for the Imperial infantry, men too poor to have
access to females.

The video skips back to the female in a cell alone, pacing back
and forth talking to herself. Maybe she was mad to begin with?

The video fades to black, and the auction begins. The first human
up for bidding is Wild One.

I sit up straighter, my interest piqued. *Who is going to be the
sucker going home with this gem?*

The auctioneer reminds us that she is considered highly
dangerous and, as such, will be sold at a discount. Their reasoning is
almost laughable, "the auction house lacks the proper facilities to
manage a human like her."

No kidding, I think, suppressing a smirk.

CHAPTER 5

BRIAR

By my calculations, I've been here about fifteen days. I run my fingers over the faint scratches I've etched into the strange clay-like mat I've been sleeping on. Every day is exactly the same.

So, when I hear the energy barrier around my cell power down, I jump to my feet. This isn't feeding time. My pulse quickens as a handler motions for me to come out of my cell. In one of its appendages, I spot the metallic punishment device. I saw it used on Slender and I'm guessing it was used on me when I penectomized Big. Painful isn't the word. It's brutal.

So when the handler motions for me to step out, I obey.

My handler pushes me forward with a cold tentacle in the middle of my back. Despite the alien surroundings, I feel an odd relief at the sensation of another being touching me. *At least this confirms I'm not trapped inside my own head,* I think.

I glance at the women in the adjacent cell as we pass. They're looking at me with pitiful expressions. One woman, the one who had tried to communicate with me before, presses her hands against the energy barrier, creating ripples of orange light, again mouthing that same word.

I shake my head, frustrated. *I still don't understand,* I think, brushing it aside. Whatever she's trying to say, it's not my problem now. I'm leaving for whatever comes next.

The handler doesn't allow me to slow down and pushes me further down the corridor, away from the women. I can hear the slimy shift of its movements behind me. *Am I going to be dinner now? Some fantastic feast at a fancy alien restaurant?* Because no Hollywood special effects artist could ever create something as real as all of this.

As we walk, the pulsating walls and alien hieroglyphs give way to more activity. Other tentacled beings moving about, carrying out tasks. The sight sends chills down my spine. *What happens now?*

We stop in front of a large set of doors. The handler clicks and hisses at another alien, and I stand frozen, watching their exchange like an outsider in my own life. It feels surreal.

Finally, the doors open, and my stomach drops. Beyond the threshold is a theater-like space, massive and dimly lit, except for a harsh light illuminating a central stage. It's obvious who the star of this performance is supposed to be.

"No. No way. I'm not going out there," I say, my voice trembling as I dig my naked heels into the wet floor.

The handler clicks rapidly in response, its tentacles slapping against my arms and back to propel me forward. The force of it sends a sharp sting through my skin, and I stumble onto the stage.

The air is colder here, and I'm painfully aware of my nakedness. In the cage, I had grown accustomed to it, but now, under the bright lights and surrounded by an audience, I feel utterly exposed. Instinctively, I try to cover my breasts and vulva, but my handler grips my wrists with its slick appendages, keeping me restrained. It pushes me to the end of the T-shaped stage, forcing me into the glowing orange circle at its center.

I resist, but another tentacle wraps around my waist, keeping me in place. My heart pounds in my chest as organic material springs from the floor and starts climbing my legs to my calves. I realize with a panic, I can't move.

Satisfied I'm frozen in place, my handler releases me and backs away, leaving me alone under the glaring spotlight.

The aliens in the audience begin to move in closer. I watch them in horror. They come in all shapes and sizes with grotesque appendages, too many eyes, and greedy mouths creating a nauseating sea of movement. Some reach out with insect-like antennae that tap against the forcefield surrounding me, causing it to ripple with orange light.

"This must be the next layer of hell," I whisper to myself.

The platform beneath me begins to slowly rotate, giving the audience a full view of me. I suppress an urge to scream. *Don't look scared. Just... focus. Think.*

The truth slams into me like a freight train, the word the blonde woman was desperately trying to tell me clicking into place in my mind.

Pet.

That's what this is. They're selling us like animals.

My eyes scan the crowd desperately, searching for something, anything, that looks remotely human. There must be someone here, someone who can save me from this. Doesn't Earth have a Space Force? An intergalactic CIA to save trafficked humans?

As if reacting to my anxiety, the lights surrounding me intensify. I feel like an object, a thing, spinning under the gaze of these creatures.

My heart thunders in my chest as I scan the sea of aliens, each one more grotesque than the last, a chaotic tapestry of how wrong biology can go.

Then I see him.

Amid the chaos, a figure catches my eye, a man. Or at least something close to a man. His skin is an ashen grey, but his features are undeniably human. Symmetrical and strong, with deep green eyes and thick, smooth black hair that frames his face.

I can't tear my eyes away from him. Even as the platform slowly rotates, I crane my neck, desperate to keep him in view.

He has to see me. Doesn't he recognize that I'm like him? That we're the same. Doesn't he think, 'I should help her?'

I mouth the word, *Help,* but as the motion leaves my lips, I realize the irony. He probably can't understand me, just as I couldn't understand the woman in the other cage.

If the ash-skinned man saw me, he gives no indication of it.

Panic wells in my chest, and I slam my hands against the forcefield surrounding me, sending frantic orange ripples cascading through it.

My time is running out.

"Come on," I whisper. "Look at me. You're human—I *know* you are. You *have* to be."

Finally, his eyes meet mine, and my chest tightens. For a moment, my hope soars. He's looking at me. I wait, breathlessly, for him to do something. Anything to acknowledge our connection, two humans surrounded by aliens.

But he doesn't do anything to assure me.

I hit the forcefield again, harder this time, then drop onto my hunches, my legs still held tight by the stage roots, my hands trembling as I point to him slowly then point to me. This must have the same nonverbal meaning across the galaxy, *I want to go with you.* I repeat the gesture, over and over, desperately trying to make myself understood. Pointing to him, then to me.

"Please," I say. "Grey sir, take me. I don't want to be here anymore. Take me wherever you're going. Please."

I've gotten the grey man's attention now. His gaze narrows, and I don't move, holding still like a statue under his scrutiny. He's assessing me. Calculating. *Is this what you want?* I think. *Are you one of them? Or are you a buyer of humans too, even though you are human?*

"Come on, do something. Please."

He shifts in his seat, and for the first time, I think I see something flash in his expression. It's concern. But then he straightens, his face hardens, and he looks away.

"No!" I scream. "Look at me! Save me! Oh please, save me! Save me!!"

The booming alien clicking resumes, reverberating through the room as glowing orange hieroglyphs fill the air. My heart sinks like a stone. As the platform turns, I glance back at the grey-skinned man. He's talking to someone else, not even looking at me.

The clicking grows louder, and then I see it. He nods, my grey human man nods. *Is he agreeing to take me?* A spark of irrational hope ignites, and I cling to it.

My handler approaches, tentacles curling around my arms as it pulls me from the T-shaped stage. My feet are sticky now from the substance that was holding me to the stage, but I don't care.

"Did I just get sold to the grey man?" I ask my handler, but the alien doesn't answer. Of course not, my language must sound like a dog barking.

The word runs through my mind again. Pet.

CHAPTER 6

AEFRE

The auctioneer gestures dramatically to the human female on the platform. She stands rigid under the scrutinizing gazes of the crowd, her eyes darting around like a cornered animal. Physically, she's striking, undeniably so, despite her body still bearing the marks of a fight some days ago. Her hair is a captivating blend of blonde streaked with violet and pink at the ends, a feature that would make her a prize under normal circumstances. But these aren't ordinary circumstances.

A faint orange light flickers above the human female's head, cycling through rows of data that scroll too quickly for any untrained eye. Of course, I've studied these readouts for years. They're standard at auctions across the galaxy, even if the specifics vary by species.

Wild One's physical stats appear first. A streamlined display outlines her musculature, bone density, and body composition. A pulsing figure indicates her hormonal balance, highlighting elevated cortisol, which the display interprets as 68% "distress readiness."

A secondary panel shows her reproductive viability. Meddling with fertility is frowned upon in the Empire, but here, in the human pet circuit, that data is simply another bargaining chip.

My eyes narrow when I see an above-average reading on neural resilience, a measure of how quickly her brain recovers from shock. That stands out. Humans are notoriously variable in this regard, and I've learned that a high "NR" index can signal a mind capable of rebounding from trauma. Exactly what I want, someone who can endure A to Z of Kaelin's more harrowing training methods without shattering.

There's a chemical readout on her adrenal function, tinted in a faint red if it's too high or too low. Hers is spiking. This is not surprising for a newly acquired human being sold at an alien auction. Fear is an excellent motivator, as long as it doesn't become crippling.

The scattered indicators of trauma mean she's experienced pain before, but she's still standing. The psychological readout suggests a capacity for adaptability under stress. Combined with her fairly high resilience rating, she just might survive the rigors of the Grand Championships, but she bit off another man's penis. I've seen a lot of aggression from humans in my time, but I've never seen that particular action. Humans love sex. So for humans to attack each other in that way, is not a good sign at all.

"Let us begin the bidding for this remarkable specimen," the auctioneer announces with a flourish. "Subject 427-B, wild, untamed, and ready to be molded by the hands of a capable trainer. Do I hear an opening bid?"

Wild One's green eyes lock onto mine, unflinching. I shift in my seat. *I don't want her.* She'll be notorious. The one who bit a man's penis off. Human teeth aren't even designed for that kind of damage. Only an Octopod buyer might consider her. But even they remain silent.

No bids.

Wild One hasn't stopped staring at me. I'm the only Imperial here. The only one with a face and shape like hers. I imagine she's clinging to instinct, recognizing me as her best shot at survival.

As I watch her, I note that she's not foaming at the mouth or thrashing around like a rabid beast. She's composed, vulnerable even.

Minutes pass, and still, no bids.

She seems to sense her precarious position. If she can't be sold, the Octopods won't keep her. Airlocks are efficient, and I have no doubt they'll use one.

Her desperation spills over as she drops to her hunches, gesturing toward me. Silently begging. Giving the impression we might have met before.

The crowd's attention turns to me. My face heats with embarrassment. "I don't know this human pet," I announce, my voice calm but firm. "I don't want her." She's not what I came here for. I need a show-quality pet, not one with a tarnished past or, worse, unpredictable mental instability.

The auctioneer clicks sharply, clearly eager to make a sale. "Five hundred UCs for the Imperial man," he offers.

I barely suppress a scoff. *Cheap,* I think, but then again, she's "defective." I raise a hand, giving the galactic gesture for: *Not a chance in a blackhole.*

She sees it. Her gaze meets mine briefly, and I catch the spark of realization in her eyes. She knows I've declined. Her eyes narrow, the fire within her unmistakable. A faint smile tugs at my lips. *Yes, Wild One. Keep that defiance. You'll need it if you survive another hour.*

Wild One continues her slow rotation on the platform, her eyes scanning the crowd, but no one bids.

The auctioneer tries again. "Four hundred UCs, and a hundred UC discount on another human."

Now they have my attention. I lean back in my seat, considering. I raise a hand, gesturing for a counter offer.

"Fifty for Wild One," I reply coolly, "and a hundred and fifty discount on another human female."

The auctioneer clicks and hisses in negotiation. Finally, after a few more rotations of Wild One under the spotlight, and no other bids, he agrees to my exceptionally low offer.

It's clear she doesn't realize I've purchased her. As the handler approaches to retrieve her, she narrows her eyes at me again.

Yes, Wild One. Hang onto that spark. I'm not going to be easy on you.

Now she's mine. I'm going to double my odds by training her and another human female I buy today.

———

Before the next human is brought out, my IC buzzes. It's Kaelin.

"Did you really just buy a flesh-eating human?" his voice is sharp with disbelief.

"We'll muzzle her until we know she's safe, and then train her," I reply evenly.

"But why?"

"She's gorgeous."

"And dangerous."

"They were practically giving her away," I counter, hesitating before adding, "She begged me, Kaelin. As if she were almost Imperial."

"What if she takes off Ember's penis with her teeth?"

"I highly doubt Ember is going to forcibly put his penis in her mouth. And we don't know the full context of the video. We'll figure out how to handle her. She might be just the right kind of pet for Ember to bond with, igniting his loyalty rather than smothering it. And she clearly has a mind that adapts under pressure and a physical body that can endure the challenges of the pet games."

"If she eats any of the males' penises on board, it's on you."

"I know," I say firmly. "It's my outfit. My responsibility."

"If I were you I would have held out for something normal."

"Wild One was so cheap I'll buy the best female here as well. Don't worry. We'll train them both."

I close my IC as the next human is presented.

A human female steps onto the platform, her hair is the perfect shade of pale yellow and her cream-colored skin glows magnificently under the lights. But she's small and fragile, her shoulders are hunched over as she stares at her feet and tears are streaming down her face. She's weak. Useless. She could never be a show pet.

The next human is taller, with blonde hair and striking brown eyes. She stands trembling, clearly terrified. But there's potential. Fear can be reshaped. She's exactly what I'm looking for.

The bidding begins, and I find myself locked in a battle with several other trainers. The price climbs higher than I'd like, but in the end, I win.

When the auction concludes, I leave the Auction Hall to pay for my purchases and collect my humans.

My two humans are brought out on leashes, naked and filthy. The standard state for humans in Octopod custody.

I step forward to claim them, keeping my movements deliberate, calm, and assertive.

The auctioneer hands over the restraints, and I take them. The smaller human, who I've already begun calling Yellow One, keeps her gaze fixed on the ground. I lift up her chin with my finger, forcing her gaze up. She has the most exquisite brown eyes. Then I cup one of her breasts with my free hand. It's perfect. I slap it to see how far it'll move and it's just the right size. Then I caress the fur between her legs, running a finger over her inner fold there. She's completely dry. Yellow One is frozen and all I see is fear in her eyes. The perfect human pet to mold. It's better when they're like this to begin with.

"Soon you'll crave my touch," I tell her. Then I turn my attention to Wild One. She's looking at me curiously.

I tilt my head slightly, considering her demeanor. Then, for the first time with any pet, I activate my external translator. In a perfect human language, I reply, "Listen to me now, as this is the only time you will hear me speak in your tongue. I don't expect submission, Wild One, I expect strength. And you will give it to me. I am your master now."

I turn to the auctioneer. "I'll need a muzzle for Wild One."

"That'll cost you," the Octopod replies, clicking lazily.

"No, it won't," I counter. "I'm doing you a favor by taking her off your hands."

The auctioneer considers this for a moment, then produces a muzzle. As expected, Wild One resists the Octopod's attempts to restrain her.

"Give it to me," I say, extending my hand. The auctioneer hesitates, then relents, handing me the device. I pass Yellow One's leash to a guard and focus on Wild One.

I pull Wild One into my arms with firm control. At barely 170 centimeters, she doesn't even reach my chest. Holding her tightly, I cradle the back of her skull, gripping her long hair at the nape as I begin to fit the muzzle around her face, but I pause.

My external translator is still on. So I ask her, "Do you know why they fear you?"

She's momentarily caught off guard. "No one fears me. I'm treated like an animal."

"That's incorrect," I say, holding her gaze. "They fear what they can't understand. And what they can't understand, they can't control. That's why they left you to me. Not because you're especially dangerous. You're just a little thing, but because they lack the will to forge strength from fire. But you're mine. And now I will hammer you into something useful or you'll die in the process."

I don't wait for her response. I fit the muzzle into her mouth and activate it, silencing her.

Wild One immediately tries to pull off the muzzle, but it's futile. Only someone who can read the access code on the back can remove it, and humans can't decipher anything but their own crude languages.

I retrieve Yellow One's leash from the auctioneer and lead my new pets out. My guards fall into step behind us, but I keep the punishment taser in one hand and the leashes in the other. Experience has taught me to always be prepared.

Sure enough, as we near the docking bay, Yellow One tries to bolt. Without hesitation, I deliver a quick shock with the taser, dropping her to the damp misty floor.

She looks up at me, her brown eyes wide with shock.

Yes, I think, *you have a lot to learn.*

My guards haul her to her feet, and when she refuses to walk, I swat her backside with my hand. "Walk Yellow One, Walk," I command, knowing she doesn't understand the words yet. But there's no time like the present to begin her education.

———

We join the disembarkment line, a tedious affair that stretches longer than I'd like. My new humans aren't ready for this level of patience. I don't want either of them embarrassing me by urinating here. Humans can be unpredictable when stressed.

I spot a human play area, a pitiful little enclosure with basic obstacles and toys. It's poorly maintained, but it will serve my purpose. I lead my pets inside and secure their restraints to a central tether. I notice there are a few male pets also here, but I think maybe it'll calm Yellow One if she has a male inside of her so I don't bother putting a chastity device on her. I look at Wild One and decide the muzzle will keep the males away. Then, I leave them to their own devices while I handle the bureaucracy of disembarkment

By the time I've worked my way through the line, presented my documentation, and cleared the formalities, I'm the last one to collect my humans.

The play area is quiet as I step inside, save for the faint sound of whimpering. My stomach tightens. *Wild One.* She must have frightened Yellow One, perhaps even attacked her.

I stride toward the back, past the miniature obstacle course. Yellow One is huddled in a corner, tears streaming down her cream-colored cheeks. Wild One stands at a distance, still restrained and wearing her muzzle.

Yellow One's distress is problematic. I crouch in front of her, studying her carefully. She's not injured, but something is clearly wrong. I reach out to soothe her the way I've found humans often respond to, by stroking the patch of fur between their legs. Instead of calming her, she swats my hand away.

Annoyed, I slap her breast firmly but not harshly, a reminder of her place. Still, she cries harder.

"Enough of this," I say, more to myself than her. I try again, running my hand through her fur gently, this time, I allow my fingers to slightly enter her folds and I briefly touch her clitoris with my thumb, but once again, she pushes me away.

I frown, confused. "What's wrong with you?"

Out of the corner of my eye, I see Wild One approaching. I motion for her to come closer.

When she reaches me, I stroke the fur between her legs to test her reaction, fully expecting her to lash out. Instead, she stares at me, her green eyes wide with what I can only describe as bewilderment.

This isn't what I anticipated from her. No anger. She just has a strange curiosity in her expression, as though she's trying to decipher my motives. For a brief moment, I'm fascinated.

A loud hiss breaks my focus. I whip my head around to see Yellow One sprinting toward the airlock, her body lit by the flashing orange emergency lights.

"Stop!" I shout, my voice echoing through the space, but it's too late.

Her small hand slams against the blue release button. The airlock begins to open, and the sudden vacuum pulls at everything in the room. My heart lurches as loose objects are sucked into the void.

Without thinking, I grab Wild One and pull her against me, holding her tightly as I activate my gravity boots. The suction is fierce, threatening to tear us apart, but the boots hold firm, anchoring us to the floor. Wild One clings to me instinctively, her naked body trembling against mine as the airlock completes its cycle.

Three long seconds pass before the alarms stop blaring and the room begins to pressurize. Warmth and oxygen flood back in, but it's already too late for Yellow One. She's gone, her body lost to the emptiness of space. The only thing left of her is the part of her leash still attached to the tethering bar.

As the air stabilizes, I loosen my grip on Wild One.

She looks up at me. Her green eyes frantic.

"What happened?" I ask rhetorically. I know she can't understand me or answer with the muzzle on.

She shakes her head and motions for me to remove it.

"Nice try," I say, ignoring her request.

I take a moment to steady myself, replaying the scene in my mind. Yellow One's actions were impulsive and thoughtless. She likely didn't understand the consequences of opening an airlock. She might have thought her leash attached to the tethering pole would have kept her safe. Humans are ignorant of the dangers that exist beyond their little planet.

I glance down at Wild One. She's watching me closely, no doubt waiting for direction. Some humans have such a short attention span I wonder if she remembers there was another female with her.

I pat her head in reassurance. At least I still have one human to train.

CHAPTER 7

BRIAR

"The word was 'pet.' We are pets," Rebecca says. She's the other woman who was bought by the grey man and the one who had kept trying to explain to me what was going on while we were in the cells.

I adjust my jaw against the muzzle, wincing at the rawness of my skin. Another human pet, clever enough to decipher part of the access code, managed to release the locking mechanism just enough for me to speak, though it's still awkward. "That's not what I got," I manage to say. "I kept thinking... bet, set..."

Rebecca stares at me like I'm the dumbest person alive. "Why would we be saying 'bet' or 'set'? That doesn't make any sense."

I shrug helplessly. "Right?"

She shakes her head and sighs. "But it was justified, I mean, what you did to that man."

I'm confused for a minute. Then I remember, Big. She's talking about him. "He blamed his bad behavior on all of you in the cell across from ours."

"How?"

"Because you were all naked."

"Every human in this place is naked," she says flatly.

"I know. I pointed that out, but he said it was different for women."

Her eyes reflect *exactly* the same way I felt when he told me too. That look that says, 'How is it that some men can live side-by-side with women and still not see us as human beings?'

Then she says, "He deserved what was coming to him. It was God's will."

"I'd call it rage," I reply.

She's looking at me, but it's clear she's remembering something terrible. "Before you, we watched him murder three other men. He made them give him blowjobs and he sodomized them. Then, when they began to refuse to... service him... he killed them. And to my shame, I couldn't look away. Some craving inside me made me want to watch. And I mean, watch everything."

"Did you watch me too?"

"Yes, we did. In our own sinister way, we were all hoping you'd do it—bite it off to protect yourself from that monster." Rebecca looks ashamed.

"I don't think it's sinful to watch. I mean, I'm no expert on scripture, but there's that bit about 'an eye for an eye,' right?"

"True. But it still felt... wrong somehow. Like we crossed a line. I'm afraid I'm going to be punished for it now, by *him*. This grey human looking man who has us on leashes."

I grind my teeth against the muzzle, remembering my mania in that moment. "Sometimes doing the right thing doesn't feel respectable at all, but then again neither does taking out the garbage. You always have to wash your hands afterwards."

Rebecca is not impressed with my attempt at humor and she looks off into the distance ending our conversation.

I break the silence after a few minutes. "I'm grateful to be with someone who at least *looks* human even if he's got grey skin. He could have a lizard tongue for all I know, but at least he doesn't look like an actual lizard. Or an octopus-man. Just a well-fed zombie."

Rebecca doesn't respond. Instead, she turns her back to me, her shoulders shaking as she starts to cry.

I tentatively place a hand on her shoulder. "I wish I could say it's going to be okay," I say softly. "But... I don't know if it is."

She whirls around, her face wet with tears. "We're naked, Briar. With leashes around our necks. We have lost all of our dignity and you're just sitting there, letting it happen to you. This is only going to get worse! Why aren't you worried about what's going to happen next?" Her voice cracks as the words spill out. Then she presses her hands together and begins to pray.

"Pray with me, Briar," she pleads.

I hesitate. "I'm sorry, Rebecca. It's been years since I entered a church." A memory from my time at a Catholic orphanage pops into my mind and I push it down as fast as I can. "And... being here? This only makes me surer God doesn't exist."

Rebecca's hand flies across my face before I can register what's happening. The slap stings, and the muzzle digs painfully into my skin. "Ow! What the hell?"

She looks more shocked than I feel, her hand trembling as she pulls it back. "I'm so sorry, Briar," she whispers. "I didn't mean to, but God exists. We can't lose our faith now. God created the universe, not just Earth. He's testing us. He was working through you when you saved yourself and others from that bad man. Now we must pray for guidance."

"Maybe God wants us to see the galaxy," I say. "Maybe He wants you to meet the aliens He created too."

Rebecca's brown eyes narrow. "God didn't create aliens," she says with absolute certainty, as though the very idea is blasphemous.

"You don't know that," I counter. "Why wouldn't He have created aliens? If He made the universe, wouldn't that include every-thing in it?"

"Because *we* were created in *His* image," she tells me, her expres-sion turning reverent as she bows her head and begins to pray aloud.

"Dear God, if You're listening please, I beg of You—help us.

Don't let us lose ourselves in this place. Give is strength. Strength to survive. And if there's a way out of this, show us the way. Give us a sign, a chance, something we can hold onto. But if there isn't, if this is all we have left, then allow us into Your Heavenly Kingdom no matter how far we are from Earth. Amen." Rebecca looks up at me expectantly.

"Amen," I say for her.

Then, I step away, giving her space. Her whispered prayers continue, her voice soft and pleading.

Now it's just the two of us left here, in this strange little space filled with colorful balls and soft mats. With nothing to distract me, I'm trapped with my own thoughts, and the realization that this is my new reality.

I'm an alien's pet.

Maybe I should be praying too.

The grey man who bought us comes to the back, seeking out Rebecca. I can see it on his face, the concern. I hear him make a strange hushing sound as I slowly join them.

I watch him stroke Rebecca between her legs like he's petting a pet pussy. I smile thinking about that sentence, but my smile turns to a frown when she violently pushes his grey hand away and he retaliates by harshly smacking her naked breasts like a man who has slapped many women's naked breasts and knows how to make it hurt.

She begins crying even louder. I pity Rebecca, she never said so, but I have no doubt that Rebecca has never had a boyfriend and was saving herself for marriage. Now she'll never get that wedding day or the human husband. Instead she's living out another woman's fantasy of being an alien man's pet.

I want to tell Rebecca that it's not that bad, but I don't want the grey man to know that my muzzle has been partially released, so I say nothing. This man who bought us may look innocent enough, but he did just purchase us, and we're naked except for our leashes. *Who knows what kind of punishments he inflicts on pets or slaves or whatever we are if we don't obey him?*

Rebecca is inconsolable, so our grey captor abandons her, and moves to stroke me like a pussy. If I could purr for him I would. This wasn't my fantasy, but neither was getting married and living a traditional life. To be honest, I never had a fantasy. I think I've been stuck in survival mode since my father died.

And so far, this doesn't seem too bad. The more I see of our new master, the more I like the look of him. More than the octopus-like aliens, and he, at least, spoke to me in English, even though he said he was never going to do it again. But he already broke that promise once which speaks volumes to his character, grey skin zombie or not. He has compassion.

I watch him stroke my pubic hair and I want to know more about him. Why he looks human but with grey skin and why he has a leash on us. *Are we his pets for real?*

I don't know. But right now I want to please him so he doesn't return me to the octopus-like aliens. I think about how I might mimic a purring sound as I look into my master's green eyes.

Something passes between us. A spark.

If he were human I'd say it was lust. Or maybe it's just because a man is rubbing my genitals. He's better looking than any of the other aliens and with my survival mode kicking in, I might even be convincing myself that this alien is handsome and that I want him to touch me.

The moment shatters when an alarm pierces the air, and suddenly, I'm being yanked into the grey man's arms.

The airlock is opening.

Loud klaxons blare, but I still can hear Rebecca yelling at me. "God has spoken to me through prayer! Free yourself from that grey Devil and join me! We will be forgiven!"

Before I can process her words, the strongest wind I've ever felt rips through the room, pulling everything into the vacuum of space.

The air is freezing, burning my skin with its intensity. I hold onto the grey man, or maybe he's holding onto me. I'm not sure anymore.

All I know is that when it's over, Rebecca is gone. She chose to risk her eternal soul rather than be caressed inappropriately by this alien. *That is true courage.*

The alarms fall silent, leaving only the slight vibration of the ship and the sound of my own breathing.

The grey man looks at me, his expression one of shock, and then he asks me something unintelligible, I assume he asked, "Why?"

I stare at him, incredulously. *Seriously?* I want to scream at him, 'Gee, I don't know. Maybe she didn't want to be your naked pet in space.' But I keep my mouth shut. Instead, I motion for him to take off my muzzle.

He ignores me.

My gaze drifts to the small window in the airlock door. Rebecca is out there, frozen in place, her face serene, like some kind of macabre Sleeping Beauty.

Rest in peace, I think, swallowing hard. Despite not being religious, I mentally pray that she's in a better place. I should have noticed she was suicidal, and said something more comforting. But then again, I was honest with her, because I don't know what's going to happen.

The grey man follows my line of sight, then quickly shackles my wrist to his, tethering me so I can't make a similar choice. He pulls me away from the airlock and leads me back to the area we were in before.

The bustling crowd of aliens is gone. Now, only a few remain. Three grey men and some of those awful octopus aliens, their tentacles moving sluggishly as if nothing unusual just happened.

As we walk, the shackle around my wrist rubs uncomfortably against my master's. His skin feels human, almost familiar. But he's an alien. Or is he a human that's just grey. I glance out another window, searching for Rebecca, but she's gone. It's like she never existed.

Did that really just happen?

I close my eyes and force myself to breathe. It was real. I know it was. I wish it weren't.

Rebecca chose to end her life rather than live with a complete loss of dignity. And all while I imagined I was having a "special moment" with our new owner.

What does that make me?

CHAPTER 8

AEFRE

When we board the *Luminous Arc,* my second is there to meet us.

Kaelin's gaze goes beyond me and Wild One. "Where's the other one? The good one."

"We only have Wild One and not enough UCs or time to buy another at another auction."

"This one?" Kaelin says pointing at her. "We can't take her on as a show pet. She'll be disqualified for biting the other pets."

"We have no choice, Kaelin. We will have to train *her,* but just imagine if we can pull this off, it'll be our greatest achievement yet."

Kaelin looks at me in disbelief. "You think she'll rise from the bloody ashes?"

"I think," I stress my words, "If we can train her, she'll be the best pet we've ever had. She's beautiful, clever, strong, and brave."

"All I see are those nice white teeth," he says, not convinced. "She's dangerous."

"Only when provoked."

Kaelin shakes his head. "One male lost his penis and a good female went out an airlock. This one's lethal."

"I don't know what happened with the other female pet. She might not have been right in the head." I pat Wild One. "This one on the other hand might have just been unlucky in her captivity with the Octopods."

Kaelin sighs, resigned. "Well, we can start by making her hair all one color. She won't win any competitions looking like this." He spreads her legs apart and, surprisingly, Wild One obeys and he rubs a hand over her fur and parts her nether lips. "At least she's attractive. Her labia is even," he says as he runs a finger over her. "Good lubrication." He brings his finger to his lips and sucks. "Not bad, but has a tinge of Octopod filth. She must have been on their ship for at least a month if not more."

"They reported two weeks so we can double that," I say, evaluating her hair. "We shouldn't hide her. We should let her reputation precede her. Dye all of her fur to match the ombre violet and pink of her hair." I run my fingers through the vibrant ends, as soft as silk. "We should indulge her wildness. Then we can say we tamed Wild One from the Abyssal Nexus."

"If that's how you want to play it..."

"It is," I say decisively. As I remove the muzzle from her face, I notice it's partially undone. Someone from the Abyssal Nexus human play area must have tampered with it. Perhaps a pet who could read enough Octopod to meddle. A mistake on my part; I should've been more vigilant. *What damage could she have done if it had been removed entirely?*

"Get the collar," I order.

While Kaelin retrieves her pet collar, I grip Wild One tightly. When he returns, I steady her head with both hands, my thumbs pressing gently against her ears as Kaelin attaches the smooth, metallic collar.

The moment the collar connects to her neck, Wild One screams, a raw and piercing sound. She claws at her throat, her panic unmistakable as the collar syncs with her nerves and brain stem.

"Good human," I murmur in Imperial, trying to infuse my tone with reassurance, though it does little to calm her.

She thrashes, desperation written across her face.

I tighten my grip as Kaelin begins the synchronization of her collar to our rings. The device lights up, displaying her vital signs in a shifting metallic purple.

Kaelin finalizes the connection, and our rings glow in unison. Then, without warning, he administers a full-body punishment.

Wild One convulses in my arms, her muscles contracting violently as she screams silently.

"You will learn, human," Kaelin says coldly. "Obedience is survival here."

"That's enough," I say sharply after a few seconds.

Kaelin reluctantly ends the punishment.

We hold eye contact. I don't need to tell him I thought that punishment was unnecessary. So I let the feeling hang between us for a few seconds.

He breaks the silence by asking, "What are we going to call her? Wild One? It's a bit of a mouthful, and 427-B is uninspired."

I study her. "Tell me, Wild One, what do you call yourself?"

Her green eyes meet mine, but she's silent. Clearly she doesn't understand, how could she?

I point to Kaelin and say his name. Then, I point to myself and say my own name. Finally, I point to her and ask her her name. I've done this a thousand times with a thousand humans. Most of them understand on the first try.

Wild One straightens her shoulders and then says, "Briar."

It's unfamiliar and uses a human combination of sounds that I don't like. "No," I say, my voice laced with finality. "That won't do." I don't explain to her because it's fruitless without Imperial, but I speak my thoughts out loud for Kaelin and myself, "No, Wild One, you're a fire contained, smoldering in the ashes of what you once were... Ash. That'll be your name."

Kaelin looks at me. "You don't think it's too obvious. Ash and Ember?"

"Not at all. I think it suits her. Look at her," I turn my gaze towards Wild One and point to her. "Ash. You are now Ash."

She blinks, quiet for a moment before she replies in her human language. She says a phrase I don't understand because I turned off my external translator, but her tone makes her meaning clear: *I have a name and it's Briar.*

"I don't understand you," I say bluntly. "You must learn my language. I will not speak or listen to yours. Human languages are a weakness, a disease that slows the mind and leads to insanity."

"Briar," she says again, proudly, pointing to her chest.

"Ash," I repeat, pushing her back with a calculated gesture.

"Briar," she insists.

"Ash." I raise my ring and press it, sending an intense wave of pain through her body. I watch as she writhes. "Names reflect truth," I say coolly. "You may cling to your old one, but in time, you will see the truth in mine. Ash is your name."

When the punishment ends, she slumps in my grip. I point to her chest again. "How are you called?" I ask and then point to Kaelin, and say his name, and then I point to her.

She hesitates, then whispers hoarsely, "Ash."

I touch my ring again, and she flinches, expecting more pain. Instead, I flood her system with endorphins, watching as confusion replaces her fear.

"Ash," I repeat softly, allowing the word to settle over her. She understands now. I can issue both pleasure and pain.

I turn to Kaelin. "Feed her and have her washed. I'll keep her in my quarters in the normal way."

"Don't you worry she'll bite you?"

"No. She's behaved no differently here than most other fresh pets. Unless I see any deviation, I'll consider what happened with the human male on the Octopod ship an anomaly. No doubt brought on by how Octopods keep humans. Perhaps that's what Yellow One was suffering from too. Such a pity."

"We should never buy pets from Octopods."

"No kidding," I agree. I pet Ash between her legs. Her fur is slightly wet from Kaelin's stroking and I assume from our little disagreement about her name. This bodes well. Humans who are aroused by domination make for excellent show pets. I look into Ash's curious green eyes and say, "We saved you Ash, and now we're going to make you a champion show pet."

CHAPTER 9

BRIAR

I'm led onto another spaceship by my new master. Immediately I feel that this ship is different. The air carries a faintly sterile scent, clean and familiar in a way that contrasts sharply with the acrid, oceanic tang of the previous alien ship. Visually, it's more human-like too, or how humans imagine our spaceships would be in science fiction movies, a seamless blend of elegance and utility, where every surface gleams with purpose. Gone are the organic, pulsating walls and alien orange hieroglyphs of the octopus-like aliens. Here, everything is clean and dry, precise and calculated. The only real differences from anything humans would make is the lighting. It's too dark, it feels like I'm in a bar. And it's cold. Not cold enough to kill me, but cold enough to remind me I'm *very* naked.

Another grey-skinned man with jet black hair and large eyes approaches us. He and my master begin speaking in their strange, alien language. Both of them look so human, strong builds, symmetrical features, the only difference is their ash-grey skin.

Although, their language is nothing like anything I've ever heard before. Not that I'm a linguist, but I took a few years of Italian in college and this is nothing like that. Their words are complex, long and guttural like German, yet strangely melodic and tonal, almost like a song. It's hypnotic, and for a moment, I try to listen, to pick out patterns or familiar sounds.

But after a few minutes, my brain gives up, overwhelmed by the alien rhythm, and I zone out entirely. My eyes wander over the ship's interior again, technology way more advanced than I've ever seen is everywhere. I don't even know what most of what I'm seeing does. No wonder they think humans should be pets.

And that realization terrifies me. I think about our own history, how humans treated each other when one group had a large technological edge over the other, and it was even worse if different skin tones were involved. Those situations on Earth never ended well. Now I'm the one outclassed, and I can't help but wonder, *What will become of me here?*

I zone back in when the other grey man begins to part my labia. He runs his finger up and down my slit and I can't help it; I become aroused. Surprising myself, I stand with my feet apart to give him more access. Maybe I've been drugged or maybe after what I've just been through I've subconsciously decided to completely give myself over to these grey human-like men because I would prefer them over the octopus aliens. For the moment, anyway. And what other options do I have? Go out the airlock? I don't have the courage for that. Not yet.

Curiously, I watch my master's face expression as the other man inspects me. He's not looking at me with sexual desire. That's good.

The man with the big eyes stops touching me and removes his fingers. I turn to him and watch as he sucks on them, sucking up proof of my arousal.

Then, the two grey men continue speaking calmly in their alien language. I don't understand a word, but I think their tones shift from clipped and professional to something more intense.

My master gently cups my head in his hands. His touch is gentle but firm, and I tense, unsure of his intentions. He begins undoing the muzzle on my face while the other man approaches me with a round metallic device.

I don't know what's happening until it's too late. The moment the device clasps around my neck, a searing wave of pain radiates through my body. It feels like a thousand needles stabbing me from the inside out, pulsing from the collar that now binds me. I scratch frantically at it, my nails hopelessly grazing the smooth metal.

The man with the big eyes says something to me. I don't need to understand the words to feel the venom in his tone. His voice is cold and cruel. Then the pain comes, worse than what I felt from Big and Tiny's punches. It shoots through me like fire, leaving me trembling uncontrollably in my master's arms even after it subsides.

My master speaks then, his voice softer than Kaelin's, but no less commanding. "Kaelin," he says, pointing to the other man. Then, gesturing to himself, he says, "Aefre." His green eyes lock onto mine, and for a brief moment, I think he's trying to establish something, trust, maybe? Then he asks me my name.

My throat is dry, and it takes several tries to swallow enough to even form the words. My fingers curl around the hated collar as I say hoarsely, "Briar."

Aefre and Kaelin exchange a few words in their alien language. Then Aefre points at me. "Ash," he says firmly.

My blood runs cold. *Oh, hell no.* I point to myself defiantly. "Briar," I say louder.

Aefre calmly raises his hand, the pink glow of his ring catching my eye. Before I can react, he presses it. Pain crashes through me like a storm, overwhelming every nerve in my body. My limbs jerk uncontrollably, and I can't even scream. It's like being electrocuted; every fiber of my being consumed by agony.

When the punishment finally stops, I'm left gasping for air and my body shaking from the punishment I just endured.

Aefre points to me again.

I swallow my pride and force the word out through clenched teeth. "Ash."

Inside, I make a vow. *When I get out of here, and I will get out of here, I'll be Briar again. My name is the only thing I have left from my parents.*

But Aefre isn't done. He hovers his finger over his glowing ring once more. I barely have time to panic before he touches it again. But this time, instead of pain, a wave of intense warmth floods my body. It's pleasure so strong and sudden, that it leaves me breathless and confused. My muscles relax involuntarily, and I fight the urge to smile. I don't want to give him the satisfaction.

Aefre pats me on the head like I'm an obedient dog. My humiliation is complete when he attaches a leash to my collar and hands it to Kaelin.

Is he selling me to Kaelin? No. No, I can't go with *him*. Kaelin's cold demeanor terrifies me. Aefre, for all his control, feels less cruel. I pull against the leash as Kaelin tries to lead me away.

I manage to break free and sprint back toward Aefre. Without hesitation, I throw myself at his booted feet, wrapping my arms around his legs.

"Don't sell me," I beg. "Please, don't sell me to him. I want to stay with you."

Aefre pries me off of him with the help of Kaelin. Then Kaelin throws me over his shoulder my ass high in the air.

I protest. And for that he smacks my ass a few times as we're walking away from Aefre. My butt cheeks sting but it still doesn't' stop me from yelling, "No!"

Kaelin smacks me again.

"Aefre!" I say, my hands outstretched as if I might catch him again. But I can't see him anymore as the doors have hissed closed.

Once it's clear that I have to stay with Kaelin, I stop struggling. Whatever is going to happen to me, I don't want to make it any worse.

Kaelin carries me into a room and the delicious smell of food hits me first. My stomach growls. Spotting chairs and a table, I resist when he directs me to sit on the cold metal floor instead. I glance at the chairs, but my hunger proves stronger than my dignity. Resigned, I settle onto the floor.

Kaelin produces a bowl filled with what looks like rice and meat, and the sight and smell of something so delicious and familiar overwhelm me.

But he holds it out of reach, speaking in that harsh, alien tongue.

All I want is the food.

I watch him closely, trying to guess what he wants me to do. Should I bark? Meow? The thought sparks a flash of sarcasm, and I say, "Feed me!" Wrong move.

He swats my backside, hard enough to make me gasp. Apparently, English isn't allowed with Kaelin either, which I find strange because wouldn't English be my "pet" language? Like a cat meows.

Kaelin repeats a single word over and over, expecting me to parrot him.

I try to shape the alien syllables, but hunger makes it difficult to concentrate. After what feels like a hundred attempts, he nods in satisfaction and hands me the bowl. I grab it with both hands and then begin shoveling the food into my mouth as though it might vanish at any second.

Then, without warning, Kaelin snatches the bowl away.

My protest dies in my throat when he sets it on the floor and forces my wrists behind my back.

The bowl is right there. I hesitate. Am I going to eat like an animal? Hunger crushes my pride, and I lower my face to the dish, each mouthful a searing reminder of my humiliation.

When I finish, my throat feels like sandpaper. I gesture for water, so Kaelin hauls me over to a gigantic hamster-style water dispenser in the corner. My frustration spikes as he holds the metal spout up to my lips, clearly expecting me to lap at it. Again, thirst wins out over dignity. With my arms pinned behind me, I swallow the trickle of water. Each gulp carves a deeper sense of shame.

Just when I think I've reached my limit, Kaelin reaches for the muzzle.

I shake my head, whispering a frantic, "No, no, no," but he's by far bigger and stronger. The strap clamps around my face, painfully tight. All I manage is a muffled grunt, echoing in my own ears, a sharp reminder of how powerless I truly am.

As Kaelin adjusts the straps, my thoughts drift bitterly to what Rebecca told me. She said I bit off Big's dick. Clean off. The aliens had to pry it from my mouth. *So, it's no wonder these aliens are worried.*

I glance at Kaelin, heart hammering as I wonder what his next move is. Another cell with more humans? Or is this going to be my life. I will be muzzled, bossed around, and forced to eat off the floor like some kind of animal? The image of Rebecca mouthing the word 'pet' comes to my mind again. *Oh poor, Rebecca.* But only time will tell which one of us made the best decision. Door number one or door number two.

Kaelin tugs on my leash and leads me into what can only be described as a high-tech spa. The walls are smooth and metallic, lit by soft, shifting lights that fade from cool blues to warm whites. The air is warm and a little humid, carrying a scent that's half floral and half medical, like some alien version of lavender. Two young, grey-skinned male attendants drift by, their silver uniforms blending in so perfectly they almost look like part of the walls.

I swallow hard, suddenly aware of all the slime and muck still clinging to me. You'd think I'd be relieved at the thought of finally getting clean, but I'm too on edge to enjoy the luxury.

Then I spot her, another human woman, older but looking surprisingly fit. She's being washed by the attendants under a large shower. Our eyes lock, sharing a silent understanding of what we've both been through. I nod in greeting, the muzzle keeping me from speaking.

The other human woman just continues to stare at me and then purposely turns away while the two attendants touch her all over her body as they *wash* her. It's the most bizarre thing.

In some ways, it's quite pornographic as there's no question of the men purposely caressing her most sensitive areas with their fingers under the water, but at the same time, *Why?*

Then, as if it's part of the cleaning process, the young attendants bring her to a clitoral orgasm in front of Kaelin and me. One rubs her clit in small rhythmic circles while the other pulls on her nipples and kneads her breasts. I look up at Kaelin, he seems unmoved. My gaze shifts back to the attendants. They too have the demeanor of people just doing their jobs. *What kind of place is this?*

I watch as the older woman thrashes with erotic enjoyment under the water. The only sounds are her moaning and the water running. Her orgasm goes on for at least a minute while the attendants work her body. When she's got no more left to give, they rinse her and dry her. While she just stands there, like a good pet.

After the woman is dried, she's dressed in a small leotard number that exposes her underarms, breasts, and her vulva to her anus. They also do her hair in a strange way with a silver bow. Then they attach her leash to her collar and hand it over to Kaelin. She immediately sits at his feet and doesn't even look at me.

Not even a friendly dog-to-dog sniff or a bark of recognition. *Disappointing,* I think. *I am going to be so lonely if this is my only human companion.*

I try to get the woman's attention, but Kaelin yanks on my collar and says something unintelligible. Clearly, he doesn't want me interacting with the older woman. Then he hands me over to the attendants and the last I see of Kaelin is him leading the old woman out of the room.

The attendants take me in their arms, as if I'm a scared puppy, and remove my leash and muzzle. It's clear from their manner and actions they don't look at me like I'm a person despite our common appearances. The only difference is I don't have grey skin.

One of the attendants gently takes my arm, his touch firm but not rough, while the other adjusts the stream of water pouring down from a hovering, oval-shaped shower head. The water is warm, almost too warm, and smells faintly of the same lavender-metallic blend in the air.

Their movements are quick and efficient. One pours a thick, glowing soap into his hands and begins lathering it over my skin, the soap warming instantly as it touches me. The other focuses on my hair, untangling the strands and working another type of liquid through it that tingles. I try to hold onto some shred of dignity, trying to cross my arms over my chest, but the male attendants gently guide my arms away.

There's no malice in their actions, but there's no kindness either —just routine. I glance at their faces, trying to gauge if they feel anything about what they're doing, but they're unreadable, their focus unwavering.

When they finish washing me, they blast me with a stream of warm air, like standing in a desert breeze. I'm relieved that they didn't make me orgasm like the other woman. I don't think I could have taken that kind of humiliation today.

When I'm dry, the attendants dress me in alien garments clearly designed to highlight every inch of a female human body. And despite being clothed, I've never felt more exposed. My breasts, my most private areas, even my underarms. Everything is on display.

Next, the attendants guide me onto a chair that molds itself around my body, holding me in place. I feel completely helpless but I think, *Maybe they're going to wax me.* So I don't freak out when they grab smooth, silver instruments as they talk casually in their own language. But when I catch a glimpse of amusement on their faces, I begin to worry.

"What are you going to do to me?" I ask.

They ignore me and continue talking like I'm not even here.

Then one of them starts running the silver tool between my legs.

It's warm, absurdly smooth, and I flinch on instinct. The attendant pauses, glances at me, and then goes right back to work. Meanwhile, the other attendant uses a similar device on my underarms. I assume they're removing the hair in those places

After a few minutes, I notice a reflective surface across the room and scream. In the reflection, I watch as my pubic hair grows thicker and longer, as if fed by some invisible energy, taking on an unnaturally groomed shape. Then its color shifts from subtle pink to a vibrant, almost neon gradient. It's so deliberate, so artificial, like an alien version of a salon dye job. The hair under my arms is made to grow long and unnatural too. So when I put my arms down you will still be able to see tufts of pink hair.

As if that weren't enough, when the attendants finish, they add a big pink bow on my head and a smaller one in my newly "styled" region between my legs. I've so much hair there now you can't even see a hint of a mound or labia. And with the stupid bows, I look like a poodle fresh from a dog salon.

I'm also given little pink booties that are little more than textured socks. Clearly, I'm an indoor pet. I guess that's a silver lining.

The attendants step back when they're done, giving me one last inspection.

I glance at my reflection in a mirror-like surface along one wall. The person staring back at me is now a polished, pink, human pet. And the only reason this isn't my worst nightmare is only because I never thought of it before.

Once groomed, I'm put in a cage with a little blanket. I watch from between the bars wondering what's going to happen next.

But nothing happens. The attendants talk to each other in their strange alien language and I'm completely forgotten.

However, it's not long before the melodic sound of the alien language puts me to sleep and I curl up with the little blanket in my cage.

I'm woken up by the door to the shower room opening with a hiss followed by someone yelling, shattering the sterile silence. Two young male attendants wrestle a human man inside, a near-giant of toned muscle, clad only in metallic briefs that leave little to the imagination. He's soaked in sweat, fighting like a cornered beast, and all I can do is stare in disbelief. *Who is* he?

They try to force him under the shower, but he's too strong, thrashing and twisting with pure power. Then his eyes, a stunning molten amber, lock onto mine. The look in them goes beyond fury—there's pain there, or maybe even grief. I don't know. But whatever it is, it gives me goosebumps.

He shouts something in rapid-fire French. Unfortunately, my French ends at 'bonjour' and 'oui,' neither of which he seems to be saying. Sensing my chance to finally speak, my muzzle's off, I call out, "Bonjour, Frenchman! I have no idea what you're saying!"

He freezes for a heartbeat. His jaw tightens, and I half-expect some powerful declaration. Instead, he just spits, "American," in a thick French accent before hurling himself back into the struggle with the attendants. He almost overpowers them, but one whips out a taser-like device and jams it into his side. His whole body seizes, all resistance draining away in an instant. Those intense eyes lower, and he's dragged under the water. They strip away what little he's wearing as they start to bathe him.

I want to look away, but I can't. Soap bubbles spread over his golden skin, flowing down a body that looks like it was sculpted from living marble. He's breathtaking, like some ancient statue of a European barbarian brought to life, his wavy hair dripping water down broad shoulders, a full, rich brown beard and chest hair as if an artist had painted the perfect man. Yet all that beauty is caged by total humiliation.

The attendants work with cool detachment, scrubbing him as though he's just another chore. It makes me wonder at the variety of humans kept here: the older woman I saw earlier, and now this gorgeous, wild-eyed man. He's nothing like the beaten-down souls I was once caged with. This man is pure masculine rebellion, refusing to yield.

I'm torn between fear and a strange rush of hope.

CHAPTER 10

GABRIEL

I'm thrashing, throwing kicks and punches, desperate to feel something other than helplessness and grief as les garçons try to wrestle me into the shower.

I'm caught off guard by the sight of a new female pet. She's breathtaking, blonde hair tipped with violet ends. Our eyes meet, and for a moment, I forget the pain, forget this damn place. Then another blow sinks into my gut, driving the air from my lungs. She calls out something in an American accent, and reality rushes back.

I lurch forward, fighting les garçons with everything I have left, until one jabs me with a needle of calming fluid, the other with a taser. Merde. My body grows heavy, the drug washing over me in waves. I struggle to keep my eyes open, half to keep sight of her, half out of sheer defiance, but the darkness creeps in anyway.

I know the drill. I'll wake up scrubbed clean, locked in a cage, ready to play the part of the perfect human pet again. Only this time, there's a new face in the menagerie, and maybe, just maybe, one that changes everything.

"Hey!" I hear as my mind slowly begins to come out of my drug induced stupor. "Hey you."

I know I'm still in the cleansing room by the sickly sweet smell of lavender soap before I even open my eyes. But I don't recognize the voice that's woken me up. It's not Mags. She's been in captivity so long that she refuses to use any human languages. She probably can't even remember them.

I remember now. The American, the English speaker, she must be in the cage next to mine. I glance around quickly to ensure les garçons are nowhere in sight. The room is dead quiet. They're likely eating their evening meal, or perhaps it's late enough that they've gone to bed and we've been accidentally left here.

Satisfied that the coast is clear, I take a deep breath and, for the first time since Fifi died, I risk speaking in my native tongue. I keep my voice low. "Parles-tu français?"

A pause. Then her response comes cautiously, "Sorry, I don't speak French. Only English."

I switch to English, clumsy from years of disuse. "Okay," I say. Using the reflection in my water jug, I catch a glimpse of her, blonde hair streaked with purple and pink. So I wasn't imagining that. "Are you sick?" I ask.

"No. Why?"

"The ends of your hair... they're purple," I explain, unsure if it's a mutation or some alien interference.

"How can you see me?" she asks, and I hear the rattle of her cage as she shifts.

"Barely. Through the water jug. I see your colors." I pause, struggling to find the words in English. "Where are you from? Another Imperial ship or have you just arrived from Earth?"

"*Of course*, I've just arrived from Earth, minus a few weeks with some octopus-looking aliens." Frustration tinges her words. "Where am I now?"

"Écoute bien, Américaine," I reply, settling into an explanation. "This ship is called the *Luminous Arc*. It's an Imperial vessel. Our owner, Aefre, trains human pets to compete at the highest levels of human pet competitions. He's one of the best trainers in the galaxy. Kaelin, his assistant, is crueler than Aefre with the physical punishments but lighter on the mental stuff. But no matter what, always remember they both only want what they think is the best for us."

She's so silent, I wonder if she's still listening. I wouldn't be surprised if she didn't hear me anymore. The only memory I have of my first days here are scattered nightmares at best. Everything's a blur in the beginning of pet life.

After a few minutes of silence, she says, "None of this makes any sense. How can we be pets to men who look almost exactly like us? They're just... grey humans. Why are they doing this to us?"

I sigh, running a finger along the familiar cold metal corner of my cage. "Je me demande ça depuis des années. I've been wondering this for years," the bitterness in my tone is unmistakable. "And I'm still no closer to an answer."

She begins to say something, but then abandons it, and asks instead, "How long have you been here?"

"At least six years," I reply. "Imperial years, they're longer than Earth years. But during the first years I didn't count." I pause then admit, "It took me awhile to accept what had happened. That I really was... *here*."

"How old were you when they took you?"

"I was sixteen," I say. A thought strikes me. "What year is it on Earth?"

"My last day on Earth was September 29, 2024, and that was about a month ago."

I do the math in my head. "Then I'm twenty-eight. Earth years old."

"I'm twenty-eight too." A silence, and then, "What's your name?"

"Gabriel," I tell her. "It's my human name."

"What's your alien name?"

"No. I refuse to introduce myself that way. You'll learn soon enough. What's your *real* name?"

"Briar." Before she can elaborate, I interrupt.

"I also don't want to know what they've named you. No matter what they do to me, I'll always call you Briar."

"They'll hurt you for calling me Briar?"

"They'll shock us by our collars for speaking any human language, even just our names. Aefre and Kaelin are very strict about that. They believe using our native languages makes us stupid and that it gives them brain damage to even listen to it."

She's quiet again.

"Briar, did I scare you with the truth?"

"No," she says softly. "I was just thinking... wondering how I ended up in this nightmare."

"I'm sorry you're here."

"You didn't do it," she says. "Did you?"

I chuckle despite myself. "Non."

"Were you being punished for calling someone by their human name when you were dragged in here?"

"No, I misbehaved in a different way," I hesitate, then elaborate, "C'était pour me sentir vivant—to feel alive. To remind myself I'm still human. That my body is still mine, not theirs. But now that you're here, I'll gladly take a beating every time I call you Briar."

"Don't do that. Just call me—"

"*Non!* Don't tell me your pet name. I'm happy to take the punishment if it means keeping the smallest bit of humanity alive between us. Our names, they're all we have of our past lives when we were free."

Her voice softens. "Okay. Is there something I can do for you?"

"Tell me about the last day you had on Earth," I say. "Not the aliens—the part before. What were you doing?"

Leaning against the cold bars of my cage, I close my eyes as she begins describing a sunlit mountain trail, squirrels darting through the underbrush, and the small red notebook she used for writing down her thoughts. There's a musical quality to her voice, a soft lull that carries me far from this metallic prison, back to a world of fresh air and open skies. I feel such a connection to this stranger...

"Gabriel?" She speaks my name quietly, snapping me out of the daydream.

I blink, focusing on her blurred reflection in the water jug again. "I'm here. Désolé, it's just... been a long time since I've spoken English. Most of the other pets speak Spanish."

"And French?"

"Not so much French. But you have replaced a French woman. Her name was Fifi."

"What happened to her?"

"My English isn't good enough to explain," I lie, unwilling to share the truth yet. Briar has already heard enough horror stories for one night.

"Do you speak the grey men's language?"

"Imperial. Yes. You'll learn it too. It's not so hard, after you get the basics, but getting the foundation laid is brutal, unfortunately."

"Why would *I* want to learn their language? Are we pets or are we people? On Earth we don't train our pets to talk unless they're parrots."

"We have to learn their language to compete and to survive in the world of human pet competitions," I reply simply. "Follow the rules, Briar. That's all you can do. There are worse things for a human to be in the galaxy than being Aefre's show pet."

"Are you trying to convince me or yourself?"

"Always myself," I admit.

She falls silent again, and I take the opportunity to redirect the conversation. "Tell me, have you ever been to Paris?"

"Once. It was beautiful. Just a few months ago Paris hosted the summer Olympics. They held some swimming competitions in the Seine."

I let out a groan of disgust. "La Seine? Quelle horreur. Those poor swimmers! Or is it clean now?"

She laughs lightly, it sounds enchanting amidst the darkness. "I don't think so. Some of the swimmers threatened to sue."

"Bien sûr," I reply, grinning despite myself.

I watch Briar try to find my face in the reflection of her water jug. She's still new to all this. Still thinks there's a logical explanation for why we're locked away like exotic animals.

"Gabriel," she asks quietly, "what's beyond this part of the ship? Is Aefre the captain? How many humans are trapped here?"

I let out a slow breath, glancing at the corridor to make sure we're not overheard. "Aefre is just the trainer who owns the ship. There's a whole crew on the other side with a captain. I've heard him talking to Aefre many times over communications. Aefre keeps us 'show pets' separate from the main crew. There are seven pets on this side now, including you. I don't know how many other human pets are on the other side, if any. There's a corridor, a literal boundary line, that divides their world from ours. I've crossed it a few times, but..." I trail off, memories of failed escape attempts surging back. "The other side isn't much different, but there are Imperials everywhere, acting like they own the stars, giving orders, and talking about far-off planets. They've got smaller ships in the hangar, but stealing one isn't easy."

"You tried?"

"Oui. More than once. I was caught each time and punished badly. Eventually, they programmed the computer to lock me out of every security system. They think humans are stupid, or maybe they just prefer to keep us that way by beating us down. They never expected me to figure out their codes or remember the pass-phrases to move freely around the ship after teaching me their language."

"That's good to know."

"They're going to watch you closely, you know. You're the seventh human pet. In Imperial culture, that number means luck. They'll treat you like some kind of omen." My gaze drops to the metal floor, remembering how they fussed over 'lucky' pets in the past. "But none of that changes the way they see you or us when it comes down to it. To them, we're ornaments, spectacles to show off. They don't recognize our sentience. To them, we're just subpar Imperials. A couple steps below them in the evolutionary chain."

"Has anyone ever escaped and made it back to Earth?" she asks.

I hesitate. The truth bitter on my tongue. "Peut-être... maybe. But not Earth. I've heard rumors about safe havens for humans in the galaxy, far from the Empire. But, rumors are the only currency we have in a place like this."

Briar doesn't reply and I let the silence pour in between us. I have no doubt her mind is spinning with all of this.

I hear faint footsteps in the corridor, growing louder. Les garçons.

"We can't talk anymore now. They're returning," I say softly, barely above a whisper. "But I'll take every beating they give me for your name and never doubt that it's worth it to me."

"And to me, Gabriel," she says and her pronunciation of my name ripples electrically through my body as if she told me she loved me.

"I'll bleed a thousand times to taste the humanity of your name on my tongue, Briar."

She tries to respond, but I cut her off quickly. "Chut! Don't ruin our beautiful conversation with the pain they'll bring us both if they hear."

The door hisses open, and les garçons stride in. Aefre follows behind them with that signature, measured grace of his. His sharp green eyes lock onto mine through the bars of my cage.

"Ember," he begins, his tone oddly conversational. "Why do you insist on these outbursts lately?"

I know better than to answer.

The calm in his voice is just a mask. I know, my punishment has already been decided. He straightens, hands clasped behind his back. "No treats for the rest of the week," he says. "No playtime."

I meet his gaze, forcing my face into a blank mask. He doesn't want the truth—that I'm not some mindless creature. He wants me to uphold the fantasy that I'm just a pet. To survive, I have to play along.

"I know you were talking to Ash in a human language," he adds casually.

Ash. The name scrapes at my ears. I press my lips together, then figure I have nothing more to lose today. "Why do you call her that?"

He arches an eyebrow. "Why do you care?"

"I care because it's a dirty name," I say. "She's anything but a burned out fire."

"Why I chose that name for her... well, Ember, it's a delicate topic. I'm not sure it's appropriate for humans to know."

"D'accord. I can handle delicate."

Aefre lets out a low, condescending chuckle. "You've always been curious, Ember. One of your better traits. But don't let it blind you to your place. Human pets are fragile, emotionally and otherwise."

Fragile. I can almost taste the insult. *Tu es fragile,* I think. *Not me.* Still, I don't argue. There's no point. My gaze slides to Briar's cage, but she wisely keeps her head down.

Aefre leans in. "Ash suits her. Look at her, she's a flame contained, smoldering in the ashes of what she was. I will forge her into a superior human. And the perfect partner for you, Ember."

My blood boils. "Briar suits her better."

Aefre's eyes narrow. "You will call her Ash, or you'll be punished."

After a few seconds, I dip my head in a show of submission I don't feel.

As he turns to speak with les garçons, I sneak another glance at Briar. Fear shines in her wide green eyes. Tiens bon, I silently urge her. Hold on.

"Open Ash's cage," Aefre orders. "I'm taking her now. Kaelin will fetch Ember later."

Les garçons yank open the cage beside mine, and I press up against my own bars to get a better look at Briar. Her long blonde hair fades into violet at the ends, but it's the blonde to bright pink ombre mass between her legs that slams into me like a punch to the gut. The alien "styling" is such a violation. It's a grim reminder of how they see us as accessories to be groomed and trained, not people with dignity or choice.

My gaze travels upward. No obvious changes beyond her underarms, thick with dyed hair.

My eyes catch on Aefre and I recognize the glint in his eyes when he looks at her full breasts with large rosy areolas. And I can guess what he has planned for them tonight.

Guilt sinks into my gut. I didn't warn her because I thought it'd already been done.

I watch as Aefre leads her away, her attractive bare backside on the verge of disappearing through the door. Suddenly, I can't hold back. "See you later, Briar!"

Aefre pauses mid-step, touches his ring, and a spike of pain rips through my body. By the time it subsides, I'm panting. But I smile. Saying her name was worth it.

CHAPTER 11

AEFRE

I guide Ash down the corridor with her leash firmly in hand. Until she's properly trained, she'll be sleeping in my quarters, not in the communal pet area. It's safer this way, especially with Ember's unpredictability lately. *Managing two wild cards is hardly ideal*, I think as I tighten my grip on Ash's leash.

Ash follows quietly, her little boots tapping against the floor and my thoughts drift to what she did to that other human male. It's unsettling when humans refuse sex, they're typically mindless creatures obsessed with it. They build entire technologies to chase that physical pleasure. Matriarchies across the galaxy call humanity an evolutionary dead-end, blaming the absence of female leadership for stunted development.

Personally, I think it's simpler: humans are non-sentient by nature, driven by base instincts. Something went wrong in their evolution, and it has nothing to do with women being absent at the helm. Their brains just stopped progressing. Rumors crop up occasionally about meeting a fully sentient human from Earth, but it's rare. Usually, if humans attain any real intelligence, it's because they were raised in the galaxy and have Imperial DNA spliced in. That's why I avoid mixed-heritage pets, no matter how human they may be in appearance.

Ember is the only exception I've ever encountered, he's almost sentient. Or so I sometimes tell myself. More likely, he's just perfected Imperial speech and body language enough to mimic my own thoughts. It's easy to mistake a talented copycat for genuine intellect, but deep down, I know it's just a polished reflection of me.

I guide Ash into my quarters and directly to the bathroom. So far, she's proven more compliant than most new pets. She hasn't urinated on herself, which is a common mishap in the beginning. I show her the toilet and demonstrate how to use it. Her green eyes track my every movement, and I can't help but note they match my own Imperial shade. Perhaps that explains why she seems more attentive than the average human.

Once she's finished, she presses the flush button.

I pat her head. "Good. Clever pet." Then I lead her by the leash into my bedroom, removing the tether so I can inspect her more thoroughly. I tell her to stand with hands behind her head and legs apart. She doesn't understand me so I have to guide her hands, and I tap the inside of her thighs to get her to stand with them open, but she doesn't resist.

The cleansing attendants did a remarkably convincing job dyeing her body fur to match her hair, it appears almost natural, as though it grows that way on its own.

I run my fingers through the fur between her legs, purposely trying to see how many strokes it takes for her to become aroused. I make a mental note of about twenty full and strong strokes, which is average for a human woman in her prime. I bring my fingers up to my nose. Kaelin was right, she smells good. Better than I thought she would, given the state I bought her in.

Leaning in, I take in the scent of her underarms. There's an earthy warmth there, laced with the faintest notes of salt and citrus. It lingers despite the soap used to scrub away any trace of Earth.

I move my hands to her breasts. I roll them and weigh them out.

They're larger than most females who compete in pet shows, but still quite firm. I bounce them up and down. I don't think they will hinder her too much. Aesthetically, her nipples sit high and her areolas are large meaning the nipple piercings will even look more exquisite once fitted.

I absently rub one of her rosy nipples while I think about the jewelry I'll put here to show her off. Long silver pieces that will connect through her legs, perhaps? I bet she'd like that, a little chain that rubbed her labia and pulled on her nipples simultaneously.

I make eye contact with Ash as I think about all these things. Her eyes show the unmistakable signs of desire. I check Ash's collar readout and note the subtle spikes across her vital stats, elevated heart rate and a slight uptick in dopamine. Also, the flush in her cheeks is equally telling. She's aroused, plain as the readouts and her own body language confirm.

I watch her as I pull on her nipple. She slightly opens her mouth as I do. "Good girl," I say. Then, I run a finger across her bottom lip. "Open for me," I say automatically even though I know she can't understand me.

But she seems to know what I want and she opens her mouth. I look at her teeth which look clean and straight. I get her to show me the length of her tongue by tapping on it. I tentatively put my finger in her mouth to see if she'll bite me.

She doesn't. Not even a nibble.

My door chimes and I verbally allow the doctor in.

"Is that wise?" he asks upon viewing the scene.

"I don't think she's as feral as they made her out to be. I don't think we know the whole story of what happened in that cage."

The doctor shakes his head. "Aefre, I think you're so anxious about replacing Fifi that you'll believe anything that'll give you hope right now."

The doctor may be right. I am worried and I do need Ash to be the perfect human pet. If Ash doesn't do what I need her to do, Ira might find another trainer to invest in. Then not only do I lose my ideal sponsor, I lose face in the pet circuit.

"We'll see," I reply positively as I watch the doctor remove his tools to pierce Ash's pink nipples.

"Just the nipples," he asks. "Not the labia?"

"Not the labia. Her fur speaks for itself. Look at it." I run my fingers through the long fur between her legs causing the little bow to fall out.

"You don't think it's too much? With the color, I mean?" he asks absently as he readies his tools.

"No. All the other trainers will have heard I bought her. I might as well use her fierce reputation to my advantage. We've got no other options but to train her, unless you have a secret show pet you've been hiding at the medical center?"

The doctor smiles as he positions Ash to pierce her left nipple. But as soon as the needle begins to prick her sensitive skin, she pulls back with an adorable yelp.

"Ash, be a good girl."

She doesn't look at me as I say her name because she's too busy glaring at the doctor.

"Perhaps you should punish her, Aefre."

"No, no. She must know this is not punishment. This is for a purpose. To enhance her beauty. To mark her as owned." I want to give Ash the opportunity to understand. "Try again, Doctor."

The doctor hesitates, but says nothing.

Ash speaks in her human language.

"Do you understand what she's saying?" the doctor asks.

"No, I rarely indulge humans in their languages."

"Good, because as you know, it causes brain rot. I've seen many good trainers lose their minds over listening to their pets in their human languages. They become obsessed and deranged. They begin to believe humans are sentient. When in fact humans just repeat what they have heard because they're incapable of independent thought."

I don't answer the doctor, but speak to Ash in a calm tone. I know she can't understand my words, but perhaps she'll understand my tone. "This is a symbol of status and of belonging. It's not meant to degrade, but to elevate."

"She doesn't understand. If you want this done. Hold her. I have to see Ember after this. You know he got into quite a fight in the showers."

"I heard," I say not taking my eyes off Ash. "But he's calm now."

"After he slept it off chemically. He's still physically hurt."

I put my hand in the middle of Ash's back and push her forward. And surprising me and the doctor she doesn't resist.

I nod to the doctor and he moves toward her, his tools gleaming faintly in the light.

Ash stiffens as the doctor reaches out to take her left breast in his hand.

She takes a step back again. Although this isn't perfect, I'm pleased to see she doesn't try to bite him.

I catch her eyes and hold up my ring connected to her collar.

Immediately, she takes a step forward into the doctor's waiting hands.

"Good, you will endure this. And when it's done, you will see that strength lies not in resisting, but in mastering what I give to you."

"Goddesses Aefre, she's a wild animal or are those instructions for me?"

"Do your job," I say quietly. "And I'll do mine."

I can tell the doctor is nervous that she'll attack him. I calm him too, "She won't bite. She doesn't want to be punished by her collar."

"The bruises on her body suggest that pain doesn't necessarily stop her."

"Don't show fear then. Don't let her think she can best you."

"I prefer humans after you've trained them," the doctor says as he pierces her left nipple.

Ash lets out a sweet whimper and I step forward to stroke the abundant fur between her legs. "Good girl. One more my new pet."

The doctor pierces Ash's other pink nipple and I watch Ash as she holds her breath again. "See she's cleverer than the others," I say to the doctor. "She didn't attack."

"Maybe she's a human who likes pain. We've seen our fair share of those."

"No, this is different," I say studying her as she investigates her new piercings. "If she liked only the pain, she would have wanted me to issue it through her collar."

I run my hand gently along the curve of her thigh, up over her small hips and then cup her breasts looking at the piercings. "Good girl."

Her lips part, and she attempts to repeat me, but what comes out is garbled nonsense. "Gooo gill," she says, her brow furrowing in concentration.

"Good girl," I say again, enunciating the word clearly.

"Good gurl," she manages this time.

"That's good enough," I say, a smile tugging at my lips. I produce a small human treat, one of their favorites, from my pocket and hold it up for her to see. "Good girl," I repeat, letting the scent of the treat catch her attention.

"Good gurl," Ash mimics, her eyes fixed on the treat with a mixture of curiosity and hunger.

I press a single finger to her lips, and she opens her mouth, waiting. Then, I place the treat on her tongue.

Her expression shifts as the taste registers, her green eyes lighting up with recognition and, dare I say, approval.

"You like that, don't you?" I ask rhetorically. "If you're a good girl, you'll get more. But if you're a bad girl..." My voice drops slightly. "You'll be disciplined. And my punishments can be as vicious as my rewards are sweet."

Ash doesn't understand the words, not yet, but I say them anyway. It's a ritual, a way to formally begin her training.

She watches me closely, her gaze unwavering. "Good gurl," she says again, opening her mouth expectantly.

I decide she's earned one more treat. "Good girl," I say, placing it gingerly on her tongue. She chews quickly, clearly savoring the taste, but when she looks at me again, I've already tucked the treats away. She'll learn that rewards are earned, not begged for.

"Hands on the back of your head," I instruct, guiding her into position for the next procedure.

She complies, hesitant but obedient, and I take out the custom tail—a masterpiece of craftsmanship. Its long, silky strands perfectly match her blonde, violet, and pink hair. I run my fingers through it, the texture smooth and luxurious, before handing it to the doctor.

He steps forward, holding the tail against Ash's lower back, evaluating its placement. "It'll take a moment to get the alignment just right," he says as we deliberate on its positioning.

Finally satisfied, the doctor begins the procedure. The surgical attachment is quick, precise, and seamless. He steps back to admire his work, running his fingers lightly through the tail. "It'll be as if she's always had it," he remarks. "Though I thought this sort of modification was against the new regulations."

I shake my head. "This falls under piercings and hairstyles. Technically, it's cosmetic. Most trainers avoid tails because they can slow pets down during obstacle courses."

"You're not worried about that?" he asks.

"No," I reply confidently. "The aesthetic points she'll gain and her reputation as a wild, untamed pet will far outweigh any minor disadvantages."

I gesture for the ship's computer to produce a mirror, allowing Ash to see her transformation. Her reflection materializes, and she steps closer, her green eyes wide with amazement. The tail sways slightly as she moves, blending perfectly with her hair and fur between her legs and under her arms. She looks extraordinary now, like a creature from a myth brought to life.

I run my fingers through the tail, admiring its softness and shine. "You're truly something special now," I say quietly, more to myself than to her.

The doctor begins packing up his equipment. "I'll leave you to it, then. If there's nothing else?"

"Not right now," I say, glancing at Ash, who is still captivated by her reflection.

"May the goddesses help you," he says, his tone half-sincere, half-joking.

"They are with me," I reply, giving the standard response with just enough respect to keep him loyal. He's skilled, and I don't want to risk losing him to another ship.

As the door hisses behind him, I watch Ash in the mirror, her fingers hesitantly brushing against her new tail. She's still assessing her surroundings, and that curiosity speaks volumes about her intelligence.

"Good girl," I say again, watching her closely.

CHAPTER 12

BRIAR

I don't recognize myself.

I'm looking at my reflection and trying not to freak out. I'm in a purple ombre jumpsuit, but my armpits, breasts, and vulva all the way to the top of my ass are exposed and now I have a blonde and purple ombre tail that looks like it's made out of human hair growing out just above my anus and falling down to the back of my knees. Oh and my nipples are now pierced and I'm wearing a pet collar. *What in the name of an alien pet version of Alice in Wonderland is going on?*

Aefre looks so pleased with himself. I want to scream, 'I'm not a pet!' But what good will that do? Is there any way out of here? I'm on a spaceship as Rebecca made abundantly clear when she went out the airlock and froze to death. I don't even know how to get back to Earth even if I knew how to fly a spaceship. I know three words, 'food,' 'good,' and 'girl.' That's not going to get me home. Gabriel speaks their language and even he's trapped here. There's no hope for me but to submit for now.

I close my eyes and try to keep myself from yelling out of frustration and anger. I open them again when I feel my master moving my nipple piercings back and forth. It hurts and I explode. I push his hands away, "Don't touch me! That hurts!"

He looks surprised then annoyed. He moves closer to grab my wrists but I back away. Aefre doesn't give up though and he's much bigger and stronger than I am. He corners me next to a wall and takes both of my wrists and puts them behind my back. Then he attaches them together with some kind of handcuffs I didn't even know he had. Next he puts something around my ankles that allows me to walk but I can't put my legs together. Finally, he reattaches my leash and leads me out of his quarters.

I hobble behind him. After a few minutes we're in a room with lots of grey men just hanging around. Aefre starts talking to them and then they all look at me.

I feel helpless. I want to run away, but I can't. I'm at their mercy.

When I look toward the door, the man who pierced my nipples comes in and Aefre says something to him in a determined tone. I don't think it's nice because the other man now looks irritated.

I resist as the other man reaches out to put some kind of alien gel on my nipples. They already hurt. I don't want him touching me again. But he holds me to him and suddenly my nipples don't hurt at all anymore.

Aefre gives me a nod and I feel relieved. But then I think, *How was I supposed to tell you they hurt if not by my actions?*

I say, "Good gurl." Hoping that this will get me released from my handcuffs or at least another delicious chocolate treat.

Aefre says something and since he's not moving to release me I assume that word means 'no.'

Then Aefre turns his attention to the men in the room. They are dressed like the attendants in the shower room. Soon they all surround me. They begin tentatively touching the bars running through my nipples and kissing and licking my breasts. Some of them are saying things in hushed tones, but I don't understand because none of their words are 'good girl' or 'food,' which makes up almost the entirety of my vocabulary. Their grey hands are running all over my body, even their fingers through my new tail.

My master looks on.

What am I supposed to do?

Aefre says something unintelligible to me. His demeanor is calm.

I try to weigh out the situation.

None of the men come close to even looking like they are going to take off their clothing or even put a finger inside of me. It's just caressing, like people would a new puppy, but it continues until I'm on the verge of orgasm. They must know what they're doing.

But right when I want these men to continue touching me, continue playing with my nipples and pulling on my tail, Aefre tells them something and then they disappear. I'm left with my hands handcuffed behind my back unable to bring myself sweet release.

This was my punishment for resisting the piercings, I realize. Damn.

Aefre escorts me back to where we were before and I wait and watch as he extends a stool out from the wall. He bids me to sit there and I do out of curiosity. Then my handcuffs meet a stud on the wall. I try to break free but I'm stuck and the same with my ankles around the stool's legs. I'm spread eagle now. My labia and clit engorged just hoping the right amount of breeze is going to trigger my orgasm. I wiggle around on the stool in an effort to do the trick but women's bodies and my body in particular, just doesn't work that way. I need more friction to send me over the edge.

A neck and head rest extend from the wall to hold my head in place. Apparently I'm going to be like this for a while. Great.

"Good gurl," I say to Aefre, hoping to be let go.

Aefre turns and says the word 'no' again firmly and then something else I can't understand.

I watch him as he goes into the bathroom and then emerges completely naked. He looks human, but with grey skin. He hasn't got an ounce of body fat on him and so he looks more muscular than most humans, and his penis has more girth than I've ever seen, but that could just be Aefre's personal endowment. We make eye contact and then I notice, his penis twitches. He's turned on by seeing me this way.

"Do you want me?" I ask, but immediately regret it because he comes over and hits my breasts hard. I know I'm not supposed to be speaking English, but I don't say 'good gurl' again in Imperial because that might just annoy him further. If I knew how to say 'bad girl' I'd say it and hope that it'd drive him over the edge and he might accidentally hit my clit and give me the release I need.

Instead, I stay quiet and watch him get into his bed across the room, turn out the lights and go to sleep.

So I guess I'm staying here like this all night.

This is so strange. I can't see anything. There are no little lights or anything in Aefre's bedroom, but I can hear him breathing.

As time goes on I start to wonder where I am. In the other cell, with the octopus aliens there was always a light. Here, I could imagine I'm back on Earth.

I try to sleep but I'm too aroused. I want to orgasm so much. I try to think of the sexiest things I can, but nothing works.

In the what must be the middle of the night, the lights go on and Aefre gets out of bed, and comes over to me. Shockingly, he begins sucking on my nipples and moving my new piercings back and forth with his tongue. It's erotic. Excitedly, I think he's going to bring me to orgasm any second now, but instead he stops right when I'm on the cusp. Then he gets back into bed, turns out the light and goes back to sleep.

This is agony.

I doze on and off against the wall. Almost too aroused to sleep.

In the morning, Aefre rises, showers, puts on his clothing and then releases me from the wall. He leads me into the bathroom, watches me pee and poop. He reminds me to hold up my tail, which is unnecessary because I realize to my shame, my tail is prehensile and just goes up on its own. I'm a real life human kitty.

After I've used the toilet, he puts my leash on and we go out. We head toward a dining hall where I sit at his feet while he eats.

I'm so hungry, but I obey because he hasn't tied me up or muzzled me. I'm sure I'll be fed later. He needs to keep his pet alive.

Next thing I know he's standing up and he's allowing some of the other grey men to pet me again. I try to angle my body so they'll rub up against my clit and bring me orgasmic release right here in this dining hall, but none of them do and Aefre holds me back from rubbing myself up against their legs to make myself orgasm when they get too close.

After being denied an orgasm again, I'm led into an area of the ship I haven't seen before. It's vast, streamlined, and filled with gym equipment that looks straight out of a sci-fi movie. A training area.

Of course. I'm a pet for pet competitions as Gabriel said. Tricks and obedience. It's degrading, but at least now I know where I stand. Not that I'm looking forward to doing anything without a sports bra or underwear, but at least I'm not alone. I see other human women running through some exercises, their breasts fully displayed and bouncing like basketballs being dribbled at an NBA game.

And just as if my imagination had conjured him, I see Gabriel. His skin glistening under the soft lights as he pulls himself up on some futuristic gym equipment, muscles taut and defined. He looks even more striking than he did yesterday. His chin reaches the top of the bar, and he freezes, his piercing amber eyes locking onto mine across this strange gymnasium.

His expression is cold, unyielding, like he despises me.

It's no picnic for me either, buddy, I think, as the leash tugs me forward. Unless he has multiple personalities, I don't think he is directing his annoyance at me. It's something else.

CHAPTER 13

GABRIEL

Aefre leads Briar into the training center, and I catch my first glimpse of her new "enhancements." The matching tail, swaying with every step, and the nipple piercings—it's all so blatantly designed to arouse an Imperial man, not a human. But damn it, it *works* on me too.

Mon esprit et mon corps, tous les deux empoisonnés, I think bitterly. The Imperials have twisted me so thoroughly through their conditioning that I find a human dressed up like a pet more appealing than a natural human woman. Their collars, commands, and punishments have etched themselves into my mind.

I grip the pull-up bar tighter, ignoring the strain in my arms.

I can't keep my eyes from Briar as Aefre parades her around pleased with himself. The sight of her sparks something deep inside me, some instinct that I've never felt. *She's mine.* It's not a rational thought. It's raw and primal. *It's my last bit of humanity,* I think

I pull myself up one more time, desperately hoping the motion can calm the storm inside me, the attraction, the arousal, the frustration, and the desire to claim her. But it doesn't.

Aefre leads her closer, looking smug. I want to punch that look right off his face, but I can't afford to show open disobedience. Instead, I leave my station to greet Briar.

"Ember," Kaelin warns, "don't walk away. You're not finished here."

I ignore him, I know Kaelin would rather have five things to punish me for rather than just one, so I walk toward Briar.

Aefre blocks me from seeing her face-to-face. "Return to your training, Ember," he snaps.

"I just want to welcome our new pet," I say. "Especially since she'll be taking Fifi's place."

"I think yesterday's little greeting was enough. And she'll replace Fifi eventually, but today, we have endurance tests to run. You'll only distract her."

I step to the side trying to get past Aefre, but he cuts me off, and summons Kaelin with his hand.

Kaelin yanks me back with the threat of punishment and mentions Briar's rumored past of hurting another human pet. "She'll bite your penis clean off with those teeth. It's not safe until she's properly trained, Ember. Come on now."

It's obviously Imperial gossip, but it rattles me. "She wouldn't do that to me."

"I'm sure that's what the other man thought as well," Kaelin replies. "Now he's a eunuch serving the Imperial Infantry. You don't want the same to happen to you. You're so good looking; they'd probably dress you as a woman too."

I dismiss this. A pet is a pet. It wouldn't be nice being ass fucked every day but it's also not a dream come true being a show pet and having your partner die. "Briar," I call over Aefre's shoulder. "They're going to test your limits today. This will be..." A shock rips through me, courtesy of Kaelin's ring. My lungs seize, but I force out the rest: "...your toughest day. Don't die."

Briar quickly moves to the side of Aefre and mouths a quiet "Thank you" in English.

My heart beats faster at her words.

"For that," Kaelin says, "you'll run the obstacle course until I say stop."

Aefre doesn't object, so I have no choice. We usually only run that thing once, maybe twice a week because it's ruthless on the body. But I've learned something today, *I'm not as dead inside as I thought.*

Briar has awakened something in me. Suddenly, I'm asking myself all the questions I've ignored for years: *Why am I here? What have I been doing for the last decade? Just parading around as Aefre's prized pet?*

Mon Dieu, I want more. I want Briar. And to have Briar, to truly have her, I must be free.

And if it means putting her above all else, then so be it. Elle est à moi. *She's mine. My humanity. My sanity. My freedom.*

Kaelin conjures the obstacle course in a holographic section of the gymnasium. I draw a shaky breath and head toward it, wiping away the last of my tears from that jolt of punishment. *It was worth it,* I tell myself. Worth it to warn her.

The obstacle course in front of me is a nightmare of shifting platforms, glowing walls, and mechanical traps, crafted to test body and mind until you break.

"This is what you get when you disobey," he says. "Speaking to her in that primitive tongue, you know better, it rots your brain. You speak Imperial almost perfectly. If it were safe to remove memories on pets, I'd have the doctor strip you of your human languages, to protect you. Instead all I have are punishments at my disposal," Kaelin says as if he's doing me a favor.

I grit my teeth as the platform tilts beneath me and I begin making my way through the obstacle course. Behind me, I hear the drones approaching. Kaelin is really pulling out all the stops today. I begin to move faster reminding myself that the drones won't fire unless I stall.

I'm not even half way through and my lungs are burning. I notice the wall up ahead is too smooth and too tall to climb, but still I try. But suddenly it cracks open, spewing freezing mist that burns my skin.

I press on, as the stinging subsides, swinging from a spinning column slick with foul-smelling blue slime. By some miracle, I land on the next ledge, knees trembling.

"We haven't got much time," I manage to say, my mind unable to subdue my thoughts of Briar, "if she's replacing Fifi. It's best we train together."

"Focus on yourself, Ember. Leave the training to Aefre and me. You're just a pet. You can't grasp the complexities of it."

I glance over my shoulder and immediately regret it. A drone zips closer, flashing its lights before zapping me in the thigh. I cry out and stumble onto my hands and knees.

"Keep moving," Kaelin says. "Or shall I use punishment to encourage you?"

I bite back a retort, forcing myself upright, and forcing my legs forward.

Kaelin's voice follows me like a bad dream. "She's not worth it, you know, she won't survive. We'd still have a better pet if Aefre hadn't bought Ash. She's dangerous. She'll bite your penis off if you get too close."

I freeze for half a second, then blurt, "Have you had sex with her?" Drones shock me again, sending agony piercing through my body, but I must know.

"No," Kaelin replies, lifting his ring to shock me even more.

I collapse under the double assault.

"And you shouldn't be thinking about that, either. But, I understand. Her faux tail stirred your human instincts to mate. Maybe if you're good, we'll let you breed her, supervised, of course, and with a muzzle. That is, if she survives today."

Rage floods my veins remembering the last time I was rewarded with sex under their watchful eyes. Both Aefre and Kaelin held our leashes as they coached me through it just like they do in my training. There was no véritable passion. It was choreographed physical sex with an audience with Fifi. And instead of bonding us closer together, it drove us further apart.

That's not what I want with Briar. I want so much more. I want to feel something real. With her, it could be different.

But another part of me is already aroused by the thought of having sex with Briar tied up with a muzzle on. And I hate myself for it. For wanting her, even if Aefre and Kaelin arrange it and were watching, holding our leashes, and instructing me how to plunge in and out of her body. I am ashamed of what they have made me, a grateful human pet.

I push to my feet, ignoring the flare of pain, and hurl myself at the next ledge with all my rage. My fists clench around the smooth platform edge, but my determination flares.

"This disobedience sets a poor example for the other pets," Kaelin says.

A cruel smirk tugs at his mouth. *Quel salaud.* Bastard. I refuse to concede for him today. The platform cracks beneath me, forcing me to dive for another ledge. My knee hits the hard edge, pain shooting upward, but I keep moving.

At last, I collapse on the final platform, my body throbbing, and drenched in sweat.

Kaelin steps up, his smug expression unchanged. "Better than I expected. But you'll do it again. Understand? You don't train humans, we do."

My glare says it all, but he waves me off. "Back to the start, pet."

Va te faire foutre, Kiss my ass, I think, but I don't dare speak it.

"Faster, Ember. Or is your fixation on that female pet draining all your strength?" Kaelin taunts.

I don't answer. I focus on the course. Another series of spinning pillars awaits, glistening with that awful blue substance. I jump to the first one, gripping it desperately. A sudden jolt of pain hits my groin.

Kaelin's little setup, no doubt. I let out a strangled curse in Imperial, letting him know I see through this.

"Ah," he says, voice full of fake sympathy. "We wouldn't want you to become a eunuch, would we?"

My mind flashes to the human eunuchs I've seen before, the memory forced, possibly by Kaelin's ring. I almost lose my hold on the pillar, my body shaking with the effort.

"Remember those eunuchs," Kaelin purrs, stepping closer. His ring twinkles, and I realize he's planting these thoughts and images in my mind.

All at once the obstacle course vanishes and I fall to the ground. The forced memories still running at full-blast through my mind. Men without penises forced to urinate through machines. Their purpose to serve the poorest men in the Imperial fleet. I'll never forget the horror. A fate worse than death.

"Get your injuries checked, then report to the attendants for cleaning, before I reconsider and send you to solitary," Kaelin barks.

Every muscle in my body quivers as I stand and limp off the platform. I ignore the curious stares of the other pets. I've never been so furious, but at the same time, *I haven't felt this alive in years.*

I pause at the exit, the door already open, but I can't leave without checking on Briar. My eyes sweep across the busy gymnasium until I spot her at the far side, chasing a shifting platform, sweat drenching her skin, that damned tail plastered to her legs. She's almost lost her footing twice in the last minute.

Normally, I wouldn't risk another punishment for stepping in. But watching her struggle like this, I refuse to stand by and say nothing.

Aefre stands at a central console, tweaking the course.

Briar stumbles again, nearly falling off the platform, something that could be fatal if she was unlucky with how she fell. I've seen more than a few pets die on their first day of endurance training.

"She's had enough," I call out in Imperial, my voice echoing through the gymnasium bringing everyone to a halt. Pets and trainers stare. Not good for me, but for some reason I don't care.

Aefre glances up at me. "Ember, you may speak my language, mimic my mannerisms, but don't forget you're only pet. Return to your training, unless you want further punishment."

"She's exhausted!"

A faint trace of curiosity crosses his face. "She's stronger than you think. We did the same to you once. Maybe you've forgotten."

"She's not some animal you can push until she drops dead," I say.

Kaelin starts to shout something at me, but Aefre lifts a hand to silence him. "What would you have me do, Ember? Coddle her? Stop challenging her? Do you think Ira would accept second place at the Grand Championship? Ash can do this."

"Let her at least breathe. You're pushing her too hard."

Right then, Briar collapses, knees hitting the platform hard. I rush forward instinctively, but Aefre's voice cuts me off.

"Don't you dare touch her. We wouldn't be in this mess if you hadn't let Fifi die during the Bond Breaker."

The ring on his hand glows, and suddenly I can't speak. My throat locks. He's silenced me by my collar.

"Ash will learn to be a champion pet," he continues. "She'll thrive under my hand, just like you did. Look, she hasn't cried once. She's stronger than most human females who would have been sobbing in a corner by now. And not once has she fallen off the platform. Trust my methods."

Aefre forces my head toward her with that cursed ring, and I see the defiance in Briar's green eyes, tired, but still burning.

"If you want to protect her," Aefre says, "then leave her alone. She doesn't need a crutch. She needs to be pushed to rise."

I clench my fists but step back.

Briar pushes herself upright. I can't read the expression on her face. She sees me but says nothing, just goes on, stumbling yet determined.

Against my body's instincts, I can't help thinking *maybe* Aefre's right.

I look at Kaelin then, we make eye contact. *Is he planting thoughts in my head?* Did Aefre sense it too, and that's why he hasn't punished me more for this? I've never openly questioned his training methods even when other pets died.

CHAPTER 14

AEFRE

I watch Ember stalk away, noting an evident shift in him. He rarely fraternizes with other pets, certainly not in a forbidden tongue, yet he chose to speak to Ash extensively in the cleansing room yesterday, and now he's publicly challenging my methods. Perhaps her untamed nature has captivated him.

Ash continues the obstacle course, and I turn my gaze to the collar's readouts hovering beside her. They provide real-time statistics on her physical state:

> *Heart Rate: 168–172 bpm and climbing*
> *Oxygenation: 95% RBC saturation*
> *Lactic Acid Threshold: 43% above baseline*
> *Cortisol & Adrenaline: Elevated*

Her heart rate and temperature are inching toward dangerous levels, as lactic acid is building in her muscles. Her stamina is impressive for a first day, better than the typical human directly from Earth.

Ember sees only her exhaustion and failures, but I recognize her determination. She refuses to give up to me or let the course best her.

Ember doesn't realize that without my interventions, he'd be a pale reflection of what he is today.

Stepping over to the console, I increase the difficulty. Platforms tilt, drones hiss closer, and lights strobe like a living maze. Ash falters, sweat cascading down her shaky arms, but her collar feed shows she's still pushing her aerobic capacity, and that pleases me. The same fire that caused her to harm another human is what is keeping her legs moving when any lesser pet would fail.

Ember doesn't see what I see: *potential.*

My hand hovers over the console, instinct urging me to flood her body with regenerative nanites, but I hold back. I want to see if she will rise on her own.

Slowly, Ash pushes herself to her feet, unsteady but upright. Her body is a trembling testament to her effort. As I brush damp strands of hair from her face, I allow myself a rare moment of softness. "That's enough for today."

"Today," she repeats in her heavy accent, her voice barely above a whisper.

"Yes, today." I attach her leash as I lead her to the gymnasium exit, steadying her as she wobbles. "Good girl," I murmur.

Inside the cleansing room, I hand over Ash's leash to the young attendants. "Keep her away from Ember. He's... drawn to her."

One of them nods. "Yes, Master Aefre."

Satisfied, I leave to find Kaelin. We need to discuss Ember's behavior and what it might mean for the training ahead.

CHAPTER 15

BRIAR

My body feels like it's been dragged through hell. Every muscle screams and every joint aches. But the worst part isn't the pain. I'm no stranger to pushing my body physically, I was a regular gym rat, but it's the memory of the gymnasium itself.

I've never seen anything like it. The whole obstacle course felt alive, shifting under me like it was testing me, pushing me harder, waiting for me to fail. Platforms tilted and spun without warning, walls rose and fell, and those damn drones, they hummed and circled like vultures, waiting to strike the second I hesitated. The shocks weren't enough to knock me out, but they were enough to remind me who was in control.

Aefre stood at the console the entire time, his voice calm and his words incomprehensible.

It only took me about an hour to realize that the course wasn't just about strength. It was about breaking me. About seeing how far I could go before I gave up, and I got it into my head that if I gave up to Aefre and let the course best me, then I also gave up on myself and I couldn't do that.

I was prepared to die on that course today.

Ironically, I did exactly what Aefre wanted. And if I had the extra energy, I'd feel upset that I was tricked. But I don't even have the energy to be angry.

I close my eyes, leaning my head back against the cold surface of the shower wall. The metallic lavender smelling water stings where it hits the cuts on my knees, the bruises on my arms, and the raw blisters on my palms. The attendants work silently around me, their hands scrubbing my body, leaving no part untouched.

They even move the new piercings in my nipples back and forth. For their pleasure or for mine? I don't know. I derive pleasure from it. Then I wonder then if they're going to make me orgasm like they did the other woman? I had almost forgotten my state of arousal until now. But as tired as I am, I still want to orgasm. And the vision of Gabriel almost naked in the gymnasium flits through my mind. I look at the attendants and wonder how I would ask for a happy ending.

The attendants don't look me in the eye as they massage the excess hair around my vulva or shampoo my god forsaken tail. I hate that thing. I hate the way it swishes around. I hate how Aefre and the doctor just added it to my body as if I should have always had it.

But still my body wants sexual release and so I grind my hips against one of the attendants hands, wondering how old he is. Telling myself it doesn't matter because he's an alien. But then that makes me just as bad as these grey men owning me. What should our skin color have to do with it?

But already I'm confusing myself. It does matter.

I grind my hips harder against his soapy hand. I'm almost there. Just a little more. *Oh it feels so good. Just a little bit more.*

But then the attendant removes his hands from me and when I try to reach down and touch myself. Suddenly, both my wrists are locked on the shower wall.

"No!" I say as I'm left underneath the running water, unsatisfied.

Crushed, I close my eyes and imagine that I'm back from my hike. That I wasn't abducted by aliens and that none of this is real. The sound of the water is steady, rhythmic, and is drowning out the reality around me. For a moment, all of this almost feels normal. *Almost.*

But then the memories rush back, abrupt and unrelenting.

The UFO.

Tentacled aliens.

Big.

Small.

Slender.

The auction.

Rebecca.

Aefre.

Kaelin.

Gabriel.

The tail.

The obstacle course.

What's next?

I fight back tears. I must not give this nightmare currency or the pain will break me.

My mind refuses to let go, so I focus on the least unnerving thing from this last month: Gabriel. Of all the horrors I've endured, he's the most bearable, if only just.

He surprised me today. I didn't expect him to speak to Aefre as if they were equals. We're all pets aren't we? Or is this a 'some animals are more equal than others' situation? I don't know. And although, his words were a mystery to me, his tone was unmistakable.

I thought at first, *I don't need you to protect me,* but after a few seconds of hearing him speak up in this alien language, it did something to me.

All at once, I was reminded of the warm, but odd conversation, we shared last night, and yeah, maybe he came off a bit too passionate, but that's probably what ten years in captivity does to you.

But his thoughtfulness today, it gave me more strength than I thought I had in that moment. It shows he really does feel that in this situation, it's *us* against *them*. And that's the most reassuring thing I've felt in a month.

As the attendants release me from my shackles and I step out of the shower, I catch a glimpse of the cages beyond and my heart skips a beat when I see Gabriel.

He's sitting in one of the cages, leaning back against the bars with his arms draped over his knees. His head is tilted slightly, the soft glow of the cleansing room's dim lighting casting shadows over his sharp features. His wavy brown hair falls messily over his forehead, his full beard well-groomed and thick, and despite everything he endured today. He still looks... stunning.

Then as if he can feel my eyes on him, his head lifts, and our eyes meet. There's something in his amber gaze. I don't know, maybe relief. But it makes me feel better all the same and I stand a bit taller as the attendants run their hands over my naked body.

Gabriel continues to stare as I'm dressed in another outfit that reveals my breasts, underarms, and vulva all the way back to my lower back so my tail is included too. It's so damn embarrassing to have a tail. I took note that none of the other humans have one. I feel singled out and I can't help but wonder if it's a punishment because of what I did to Big. A sign that I seriously injured another human pet that I'll have to live with forever like a scarlet letter.

After I'm dressed, one of the attendants takes me by the collar and leads me towards the cages.

My heart is racing but I don't know if I'll even get a chance to say anything to Gabriel because the exit is also near the cages. But more than anything, I want to talk with him. To thank him for today.

Gabriel shifts slightly, as he leans forward. The movement is subtle, cautious, but it's enough to tell me he's waiting, watching, and hoping for the same thing I am—a moment between us. Just one.

"Are you okay?" he mouths, his lips barely moving. His eyes search mine.

I nod, a small, quick movement, even though it's a lie. I'm not okay. I don't know if I'll ever be okay again.

As we near the cages, the attendant leading me, places a hand on my shoulder, then latches a leash to my collar and pulls me toward the exit. I glance back at Gabriel.

He doesn't move or call out, but then, at the last moment, I hear him say my name, my real name, like a prayer through soft noise of the hissing automatic door "Briar."

Our one last bit of humanity. Our human names. The memory of what he said yesterday sweeps through my mind, 'Our names—they're all we have of our past lives when we were free.'

I don't say his name out loud as I'm led through the dark corridors of the ship, but I think it like a chant I can never get enough of. *Gabriel.*

CHAPTER 16

GABRIEL

The cleansing room is quiet, the air thick with humidity. A faint hum from the lights blends with a distant drip of water. I'm in my cage, knees drawn up and the cold metal beneath me a familiar companion.

The door hisses open, and I can practically feel Aefre enter before I see him. "Ember," he says, voice calm. "Why did you disobey Kaelin and me today?"

I don't answer. I just stare back, keeping the façade of a stupid human pet.

"Speak," he commands, his finger hovering over his ring. "Why did you disobey?"

I stay silent because admitting the truth, what I feel, what I fear, would only please him.

"You think I don't notice how you look at Ash?"

"Briar," I snap, refusing to use the name he's assigned her. "Her name is Briar."

Aefre crouches, bringing himself to my level. "Ash is her name now."

"No," I say firmly. *Je ne l'appellerai jamais ça.* I will never call her that.

His smile vanishes. "You think you're protecting her. But you're weakening her." Aefre moves closer, just the metal bars between us now. "And I know this isn't about Ash at all. This disobedience is about Fifi."

My chest tightens at the sound of her name, and I look away.

"You failed her," Aefre continues, "and now you see another female pet and you think you have to save her."

I can't bear to face him. The guilt swirls, suffocating me.

"Now that I've told you what you're suffering from, Ember, I expect you to reign in this bad behavior and stop fighting me," he says, unlocking the cage. "Remember your place. You are not her protector. You're my pet. Go to your bed and sleep."

He walks away but his words are still ringing in my ears.

Do I feel this way about Ash only because of what I did to Fifi?

CHAPTER 17

AEFRE

I sit at the desk in my quarters looking at the holographic interface before me debating whether or not to step up security with Ember. With a decisive tap, I message Kaelin. He's praying for the next hour and unreachable, but I want to do this before I change my mind.

The display confirms the line is open. "Kaelin. I need you to watch over Ember tonight. He's... unsettled, as you well know. He's still processing what happened with Fifi and the wound has reopened in unexpected ways with the arrival of Ash.."

I pause, measuring my next words. "There's more. His attachment to Ash isn't entirely organic. I've taken steps to deepen their connection, subtly, through mind control sequences. I've adjusted his memories of Fifi. He still feels the guilt of leaving her, but the bond's intensity has been redirected toward Ash. *She* is now his purpose and reason to win. Should they compete in the Bond Breaker challenge, I'm confident Ember won't repeat past mistakes."

The faint glow of the recording icon flashes across my fingertips. "If properly bonded, I believe Ash and Ember could surpass what

Ember and Fifi achieved, but it must feel genuine to them. They cannot suspect my influence."

I lean toward the console, lowering my tone. "Do not interfere with their development, Kaelin, just monitor them. If Ember displays any sign of psychological distress, notify me at once. Their bond must remain convincing, regardless of how... artificially it began."

With a final tap, I dispatch the message. The holographic display winks out. The weight of my own manipulations settles in the silence, but I brush aside any doubt. The stakes are too high for regret. I tell myself that manipulation is just another instrument in my arsenal.

I rise, smoothing my jacket, thinking, *There's no room for error. Ash and Ember must win.*

In my bedroom, I open Ash's cage. She doesn't come out immediately. "I'm not going to hurt you." I know she doesn't understand all my words yet, but I speak slowly and evenly for her to learn. "Come on, Ash."

I know she recognizes her name and the word 'come,' so she tentatively looks up at me with her expressive green eyes and gingerly comes out of the cage. I'm going to have to give the cleaning attendants a talking to as they should have dressed Ash in a purple or pink outfit before they went off to have the evening meal. Instead they put her in a red color more suited to Mags. I curse under my breath as I find a purple outfit for Ash and put it on her myself.

After I dress her I can't help but play with her nipple piercings. Today while she ran, I thought about how beautiful she would look running with gorgeous jewelry to swing with her movements. The perfectly adorned human pet.

She moves her body closer to mine. She's still aroused. The fur between her legs glistening with her desire. I grab her right hand and bring it up to my nose. She's been touching herself.

"You've been a bad girl," I tell her. I know she wants to orgasm, but I won't give it to her because it's part of her training.

It doesn't stop her pressing her body next to mine, trying to straddle my thigh, as I push her away I notice she's left my trouser leg wet.

I turn her around and swat at her cream rear, the skin turning red. I realize after a few strokes that I should check her collar and sure enough, her collar's readout shows an abrupt spike in adrenaline, norepinephrine, and dopamine levels. Classic signs of arousal in humans.

I need a different tactic. I turn her around again, so she's facing me. I lightly tap her inner thighs to open her legs wide and I stroke her between her legs just for a moment. "Good girl."

"Good girl," she repeats. Then adds, "I am good girl."

"Good, Ash. You're learning." I take my hand away. Knowing she's at a very heightened state of arousal that won't be met. I will just casually keep her on edge for days.

I attach her leash to her collar and lead her into my quarter's dining room.

It's quiet except for the soft clink of the metal bowl against the floor. Ash kneels before me, her hands hovering uncertainly at her sides as she stares at the food I've placed in front of her. Her green eyes look up to me for approval.

She's learning.

"Eat," I say simply. I know she knows this Imperial word from Kaelin. She must be starving. "Eat," I say again.

Ash hesitates for just a moment longer before leaning down, her blonde and purple ombre hair brushing the edge of the bowl as she takes her first bite with her face in the bowl. There's no grace in it, no dignity, and that's the point.

I can tell she resents this, but she complies because she must. Because she understands, on some level, that this is her reality now. Performance pets must obey their masters on every level. If I allowed her to eat at the table like sex ship pets, then she may think she has some leverage with me, when in fact she has none.

Ash finishes her food quickly and lifts her head to meet my gaze. I know what she wants, but she can't have it. I've only got eight months to train her. "No more."

Ash gets on her knees, her hands clasped above her perfect breasts, pushing them together sweetly, and looks up at me pleadingly. She says the only words she knows well, "I am a good girl."

I know this is the human version of begging. "No." Then I grab her stomach. "No," I say to make it clear what's going on. However, she may not know *why* she is unhealthy. I can't understand why she would choose to be this way if she knew. But then again, I don't know how well humans can avoid the toxins in their food. It's all irrelevant now. She's mine and I'll make her healthy.

For a moment, I think she might continue to plead. But she doesn't. Good. Obedience.

I gesture for her to follow me. "Come."

She rises slowly and follows me into the bathroom. I turn toward her, gesturing toward the toilet.

"Use the toilet, empty your bowels," I instruct slowly, hopefully she'll remember the Imperial words, watching as she hesitates.

After a few seconds she remembers and steps past me to sit on the toilet.

"Pick up your tail," I remind her, but she doesn't understand my words, so I move behind her and grab it.

She tenses at the sensation and then looks up at me with annoyance.

I put her tail in her hand. And then take a step back watching her.

She lets go of her tail and it rises on its own behind her. It's the cutest thing I have ever seen. But then we hold eye contact and wait.

I glance at the timer displayed on the interface of my control ring. Too much time has passed. Ash is testing boundaries again, though I suspect she doesn't think of it that way.

To her, it's a way to cling to the fragments of control she imagines she still has.

To me, it's a teaching moment.

She will dislike this, but it's effective and this lesson, though unpleasant, is one she will remember.

I press the command on my ring, and her collar pulses faintly. I watch as Ash feels it.

Her green eyes widen in surprise as her bowels empty in a seconds.

"You will submit your entire body to me, Ash."

She glares at me standing up. "I am a good girl."

"You will be."

She doesn't understand my words yet but my tone is clear.

I step closer, reaching out to adjust the collar around her neck. "This isn't punishment, Ash," I say softly. "It's preparation."

I lead her to my bedroom and to the little pet bed in the corner. I gesture for her to go to it. "Lie down, Ash," I say. "Lie down and you'll be a good girl."

At the sound of 'good girl,' she complies, lowering herself onto the little human bed.

"Stay," I command her and use my hand to indicate she shouldn't move.

Ash looks up at me suspiciously as I retrieve the small chastity device from the console nearby. It's designed with the same precision as the control collars and is both functional and symbolic. A reminder of the control I must maintain, and the discipline she must learn.

"Open your legs."

She looks at me confused. I bring my free hand down to her thighs and gently stroke them open. I know she's still aroused. There's not enough training in the world that would make a human body forget about sex.

I stroke the abundant fur between her legs and then spit on the blonde and purple ombre curls before I sink my whole mouth over her labia. Surprised, she moans with pleasure, but just when she's wet enough for me to attach the device, I quickly mount it in place. It locks with a faint click and then adjusts automatically to fit her body. It's integrated with the collar and will ensure she remains unable to orgasm until it's removed.

Ash's hands reach between her legs as she tries to remove the device. "No, no, no..." she says and then tries to get to her knees to beg.

I stand. "There will be a time and place for your pleasure, but you must understand the boundaries of your existence now. I control your body."

I activate the forcefield around her bed. It's a seamless barrier, undetectable until touched, and it'll hold her for the night.

She tests it almost immediately, reaching a hand toward the edge only to recoil when the faint shimmer crackles against her skin. Her green eyes meet mine.

"This is for your safety," I tell her. "And mine. I don't want to have to muzzle you. And you worked hard today, so you deserve a good night's sleep."

I move to my own bed, sitting on the edge for a moment as I watch her settle into the space she has been given. She shifts slightly, testing the limits of the force field again.

"Rest now my new pet. Tomorrow will be just as demanding."

She doesn't respond. But I don't need to check my control ring to know her mind is racing, as it always is.

I wake up during the Watching and check on Ash. She's still asleep. I put down the forcefield and wake her gently by caressing her back. Humans need more physical attention in the beginning of their training, so I move her to my bed. She wakes up as I put her under the blankets with me. My hands roam her body from her toes to her scalp. She jumps sweetly as I touch the bottom of her feet and even laughs a little. "You'll get used to me touching you everywhere," I tell her.

I drag my fingers up her legs, in between her thighs, over the chastity device, just to play with her, I'm not going to remove it. When she tries to angle her body toward me, I push her back on her back. "No, Ash. I touch you." She must learn to take what I give her and be grateful for it. "You are my pet. You obey me. My commands."

I'm pleased that she does as I say. She lies still on her back while I continue to touch her. And after I've stroked her entire body countless times, I run my fingers around her large breasts, outlining them and then her areolas. And finally the piercings. I hold up the blanket and wonder if I should pierce her labia too, but I think it'd take away from the aesthetic of her fur and her tail.

I turn her over and caress her back and play with her tail. Everyone likes a human with a tail.

When Ash begins grinding her hips against the bed, I pick her small form up and move her back to her little bed. And then I try to go to sleep myself. But after a few minutes, I realize that's impossible, touching Ash made me aroused too. So, I call a slave artist to my room.

When she arrives she goes directly to Ash's bed. "Oh a new human pet. She's adorable. Look at that purple ombre hair. Can I stroke her, Master Aefre?"

I let down the forcefield for the Imperial woman to stroke Ash's tail.

"Will you take off her chastity belt? I would enjoy watching a human pet orgasm."

"Not tonight." I put the forcefield back up. "I'm the one who needs your attention."

"It's no wonder if you've been training that adorable pet all day, Master Pet Trainer." She moves closer to me and runs her fingers expertly along the length of my penis that comes to life under her touch.

"I'm glad you understand the situation. I can't have her yet. It's too soon, so I need you."

"I can put a tail in my anus if it helps?"

I think about her offer. Then I look down at Ash's bed. She's awake and watching us. "It's not necessary as long as she's watching."

The slave artist looks down at Ash. "Do you want her to watch to know how to have sex?" she asks incredulously. "I thought that was the one thing humans *did* know how to do."

I smile and then kiss the Imperial woman, my hands reaching inside her green shirt to find one of her nipples to gently tug on it. "Oh she knows about sex. It's just that she just needs to unlearn the barbaric human way of doing it. She needs to know how I want it done and that when she has sex with me, it's the ultimate reward."

"Oh," replies the woman surprised. "I'm new to your ship and don't know much about your profession except that it's lucrative."

"Profitable because it's difficult," I answer and then groan as she expertly strokes my penis again.

"Well, I'm happy to be here. I came from a warship. So many military men with their rules. I was tired of it."

I remove her shirt exposing her small taut grey breasts, her small nipples pierced and adorned with large jewelry that glimmers in the low light. "Good," I say as I pull on the jewelry stretching her nipples until I hear her sharp intake of breath. "Good."

"Are you going to do that to my clit too?"

"Is it pierced?"

"In a manner of speaking, yes," she says as I quickly begin unfastening her green skirt.

I reach between the folds of her labia and find the small silver chain and I gently pull. The Imperial woman lets out a small moan and I urge her on her back. With one hand I hold the nipple jewelry and with the other, the one attached to her clit. As I lean down to investigate, I see that it's more of a ring surrounding her clitoris, attached in several places. I drop my head and gently lick it. "Pleasure and pain then?"

"Yes," she breaths out. "I'm happy to be on a ship where I'll be better understood. That's how you train the human pets I hear."

"Yes. Pleasure and pain. I'm glad you've joined us," I say. "A lot of artists only want to be on the best military ships where all the glory of the Empire is. But the money they make here, although just as good, doesn't compare to the excitement on the front lines," I say in between long licks of her hairless sex.

"Not me. I don't want to die in space," she confesses.

"Then we have that in common," I say as I begin to move a finger in and out of her lubricated vagina. Slowly bringing her closer to climax, her scent of desire filling the bedroom.

"I'm excited to serve the Empire on your ship and see how the rich live in the galaxy. All the fancy hotels and cosmopolitan stations that host human pet shows," she trails off with a whimper. "Yes, oh goddesses, do you do this to your pets?"

"Only the good ones. Now orgasm for me," I command the artist as I move my fingers expertly in and out of her tense body. Her silver jewelry making a faint jingle with my actions. When she doesn't come instantly, I continue the same pace with my finger, but grab her clit chain again and swing it around in a circle. Almost immediately she begins trembling and then her body releases into a strong orgasm.

"You know women's bodies," she praises me afterward.

It's not her words that get me aroused though, it's the idea that Ash is watching all of this and is wearing the chastity belt. She must be in erotic agony. It's such a good training moment. Because sex with me will be the reward that will allow me to push her to her absolute physical limits, beyond anything she ever imagined she could do. It's one of the oldest and most foolproof human pet training methods.

The slave artist takes my cock in her hands and then urges me onto my back. She hovers over me on her knees, putting both of the long silver strands connected to her nipple piercings in my mouth and says, "Control me with them on as I ride your cock for your pet to watch. I assume you'll instruct her to do the same."

"Only if she's a *really* good girl," I reply before I begin sucking on the silver strands, so the ends are tight against my teeth.

Then she slowly impales herself on my aching penis, enveloping me. It feels incredible.

I watch her as she begins to expertly ride my body and I use the silver strands in my mouth to control how fast she goes and her position by moving my head up and down, right and left. She obeys my every direction.

"You're a real task master. I wish I were wearing a tail."

It's an erotic thought. The idea of this woman donning a tail, but after looking at Ash's human body all day, this thin Imperial woman is serving only my physical needs. She rides me and I like it, but what I really want is Ash riding me with her pink tail swishing on my thighs and her large breasts bouncing while I try to contain them with the same kinds of nipple jewelry leads.

I orgasm into the slave artist's core and then release the silver strands of jewelry from my mouth. She slowly stands and licks my penis clean of all the semen.

Then we make eye contact and she smiles as she licks her lips. "I can't wait to explore the galaxy with you, Master Aefre."

"Welcome to the *Luminous Arc*," I say as she puts on her clothing unnecessarily. It's the Watching, the middle of the night where everyone is up praying, working, or relaxing, but unlike during the day, it's acceptable to be naked anywhere on the ship.

The slave artist looks at Ash. "I hope I gave her something to look forward to as well. Good bye for now, little human pet."

CHAPTER 18

BRIAR

I'm so confused. I just watched Aefre's girlfriend come over and have sex with him after he woke me up in the middle of the night and touched my whole body.

And what's even more strange, or erotic if I'm being honest, is that he kept looking at me the entire time he was having sex with her.

I mean, I'm thrilled that none of the men here have tried to rape me. However, I'm not excited by the way they're touching me and then leaving me aroused without giving me any release.

This is the longest edging of my life. And I'm beginning to wonder if it's possible to die from lack of an orgasm?

And now I have the sensual visuals of Aefre and his girlfriend to play over and over again in my mind. It's amazing how *real* life seems without a phone to scroll or television to watch. Every interaction I have, I think about it, and review it in my mind's eye for entertainment over and over again. I don't even know how many times I've thought about Gabriel tonight and replayed our few interactions.

And now I have a detailed memory of alien sex to think about. It didn't look unlike human sex, except for while Aefre's girlfriend was riding him, he had her long nipple jewelry in his mouth, guiding her movements like a horse and a rider.

While I watched, I pinched my own nipple jewelry, wishing he was doing that to me. However, I just tortured myself more because this chastity belt device won't allow me to orgasm. Not that I've ever orgasmed from touching my nipples, but given what I was just watching, I thought it was certainly a possibility. And I got so close, but it only ended in erotic agony because this chastity belt won't let me orgasm.

When his girlfriend left, Aefre looked at me again and said something. It might have been as simple as 'goodnight' but in my fantasy, he said, 'You're mine tomorrow if you're a good girl.'

Now, as I lay in the darkness, it occurs to me that pets on Earth must watch their owners have sex all the time, so why would this be any different?

It's different because I wanted to be her. I wanted him to have my silver nipple jewelry in his mouth and have him whip me with the silver strands until I rode him until completion. Then, I wanted to lick the excess semen off his hairless grey body around his alien dick that's surprisingly ridged, the only real difference I've seen in his anatomy from that of a human. That and he and the woman had no body hair. And I don't think people's pets on Earth watch their master's having sex and think, 'I'm next.'

I close my eyes and will myself to have such erotic dreams that if I'm lucky, I'll orgasm in sleep.

Aefre wakes me by caressing my back. I turn, open my eyes and legs wide for him. He runs his hands over my lower abdomen and then releases the chastity device. When the cold air hits my sex I moan. I lift my hips up to him, but he's already walked away putting the device back where it came from. All he says is, "Bathroom."

"Buuthroom," I repeat the word back as I sit up.

"Correct," he says and then points the way.

I go directly to the toilet and he tells me the word for tail again. Even though I don't need to make sure my tail goes up when I use the toilet, it happens naturally I do grab it and make sure it's out of the way just in case.

I make eye contact with him. I wonder what he's thinking. He's naked and the visions of his girlfriend on top of him last night run through my mind. I'm naked now too. The chastity device is off.

I pee and then try to get up.

Aefre shakes his head and says something I don't understand. But then he motions to his ring. I don't want him to force me to empty myself entirely again. That was painful.

So I force out poo while he watches.

When he's content with my toilet activities, he brushes my teeth for me with a laser. Apparently human pets are not skilled enough to manage this by ourselves. But I don't mind, he's standing behind me and his muscular body against mine feels good. And I relax against him hoping that after this he'll allow me to orgasm.

But the next thing he does is brush my pubic hair. I suppose it is long enough to brush, but it's odd. I watch as he runs a small brush through my hair between my legs and I realize suddenly that if he continues this, I will orgasm.

However, he must have noticed this too so he says something I don't understand then stops brushing. *Damn. So close.*

After we are both finished in the bathroom, I follow Aefre into his walk-in closet. The space feels more like a showroom than a closet, sleek but dimly lit like the rest of the ship. The walls are lined with racks of clothing, each piece hung with meticulous precision. There are shelves stacked with items I don't recognize and drawers that hold who-knows-what. It's an unsettling mix of luxury and alien practicality.

Aefre dresses himself in a nondescript tunic and trousers similar to what he always wears and then he moves with his usual method-ical steps looking for something else. I'm assuming it's something for me. His green eyes scan the options in front of him, as though choosing the perfect outfit is some grand decision. The only hint that he's pleased with whatever plan he has for today is that he's tapping his finger on his thigh.

I glance at the clothing in what I would call the 'human pet section' of his wardrobe. Most of it isn't clothing, not really. The pieces look more like costumes, tight, shiny, elaborate, and impractical. Pieces designed to accentuate and to display.

Aefre finally pulls something off the rack, holding it up for a moment as he inspects it. It's small and shimmers faintly under the soft light. I catch glimpses of straps and what looks like metallic accents.

Whatever this is, it's different from what I wore on the obstacle course yesterday. That was somewhat functional, meant for running and climbing and falling, minus a bra and underwear. This... isn't. It's something different.

"For you, Ash," he says, and doesn't look at me as he sets the outfit down. Then moving to another section of the closet, he selects a pair of black booties, small, soft-looking things, nothing I could run in. He sets them next to the outfit, then turns to me. "Come," he says.

My heart pounding as he dresses me. I'm hoping he will touch me between my legs so I can orgasm. I purposely move so that the fabric briefly touches my clit, but it's not nearly enough.

Aefre's fingers move without any sexual intent. They're soft and controlled as he finds my nipples and lines up two small holes in the outfit. Then he does the same for my vulva, exploding with pubic hair, and my stupid tail. Next he puts fitted silver suspenders on me that go between my legs and accentuate my breasts with a hook or something at the back. It's like I'm going to be attached to something. There's no mirror in here but I imagine I look like some kind of Shein Barbarella with my boobs and dyed pink pussy exposed.

This can't be good, I think as he finally attaches my leash and leads me to the pet center for breakfast.

CHAPTER 19

GABRIEL

Briar steps into the pet feeding area right behind Aefre.

Mon Dieu. Yesterday's endurance tests pushed her too far, that much is obvious, but I worry there's more. Did Aefre have sex with her last night? Already? The thought boils my blood.

Then I notice it. The silver harness strapped tightly across her chest and through her legs, pulsing faintly with Imperial tech. The *harnais linguistique*. My throat tightens. Memories I've buried for years resurface. And I swallow hard, pushing down the nausea associated with that, the language harness.

Efficient. Effective. Brutal. It forces the wearer to learn Imperial through direct neural stimulation, bypassing natural cognition and creating artificial pathways in the brain. It's the Imperials' favorite way of making humans "civilized." But it's torture. And now, it's wrapped around Briar.

Her green eyes scan the room. For a moment, they meet mine. She knows something is off. She can sense it.

Every pet here recognizes the harness. We've all endured the barbaric device.

Kaelin's voice breaks the silence. "Focus on your bowls, all of you. Or you'll go hungry."

The others obey instantly, their heads dipping into their food. But I can't look away from Briar.

I know exactly what awaits her. The disorientation, the nausea, and the pure, unrelenting agony in the language harness. Stumbling over words never heard before, meanings that haven't had time to settle in the mind. And through it all, Aefre will watch, impassive and detached, as though this is just another day of training. All the while, the pressure in the skull becomes unbearable, like the brain is being blown up and then stitched back together again.

I grip the edge of my bowl. I want to warn her.

Her gaze meets mine.

This time, I force a smile. It's small, reassuring, and completely empty. I hope she can draw strength from something I don't even feel. Sois forte, Briar. Be strong.

Kaelin's hand clamps down on my neck, shoving my face into my own bowl. The wet food covers the whole lower part of my face. "Focus, Ember."

I bite back a retort.

When Aefre leads Briar out, every pet in the room looks up, their eyes filled with pity.

Kaelin doesn't miss it. "Eyes down!" he barks, and when we hesitate, he shocks us all for good measure.

Pain rips through my body, but it's nothing compared to the pain I know she's about to endure.

CHAPTER 20

AEFRE

The language harness is an ingenious device. Humans could never grasp our language without it. Their minds, their neural pathways, are too limited. But this harness bridges that gap, reshaping their brains with precision.

I position Ash in the center of the room. Her arms are crossed, her green eyes darting from the harness to me, suspicion and unease written all over her face. It didn't help the other pets took one look at her clothing and looked at her with fear.

"Sit," I command, gesturing toward the small seat mounted on a pole in the center of the room.

Slowly, she lowers herself onto the seat.

I move to the console to begin the set up. The harness clicks into place on Ash's back, its metallic straps locking over her shoulders, her chest, and through her legs. The buzz of its systems activating fills the room. Tiny tendrils of tech climb up her, molding to her body, connecting to her spinal cord and collar with a soft, mechanical hiss.

She flinches at the sensation and looks over to me with terror in her eyes. I check her collar:

Heart Rate: 142 BPM.
Adrenaline: Elevated.
Cortisol: Spiking.

She's paralyzed by fear, her pupils are almost fully dilated. She's ready. Her terror will serve as a potent accelerant for what the harness is about to teach her. Imperial linguists say, the more terrified the human the faster they learn.

"Have courage, Ash," I say. "The Imperial language is not something humans can grasp naturally. This device will give you what your mind cannot achieve on its own."

"What?" she asks, her voice shaky with fear.

"It bypasses your natural limitations," I explain even though she can't understand me, yet, while adjusting the settings on the console nearby. "It replicates the sensations a child experiences when learning a language—fear, love, excitement. It forces connections in your brain where none exist, embedding the language deeply and permanently."

She stares at me. "Ash is a good girl."

I pause before starting the first lesson. "Yes. Ash is a good girl. This isn't a punishment."

The console notifies me that I've forgotten to equip her with something to catch her bodily fluids. Humans, when placed in this state, often lose control of their bodily functions. The fear and disorientation overwhelm them. So I retrieve the small discreet device and attach it beneath the harness. It connects seamlessly to Ash's groin. I make sure that her tail is above it and she shifts uncomfortably.

I kiss each one of her nipples and say, "It won't be as bad as that."

Now she's confused. I answer her silent question, "To prevent unnecessary interruptions."

The console beeps softly, signaling that the system is ready. I turn back to her. "Let the language system guide you."

She doesn't respond because she doesn't know what I've said. *Poor Ash*, she so frightened, she's trembling in the harness. "Zzzz," I comfort her. "You're safe. I will always take care of you."

Then, I activate the language harness and its tendrils begin to glow faintly.

She gulps as the first wave hits her and her body jerks against the straps.

"Stay focused," I say, serenely. It's important that I stay calm, no matter how uncomfortable it is to watch my pets go through this, it must be done. "This is the Foundation Course. Commencing in three, two, one, now begin."

Her breaths come in uneven pants as the device begins its work. The harness moves her subtly, her muscles twitching as it guides her body into the rhythms of speech, and the patterns of movement associated with the Imperial language.

I step back, observing her carefully as the session progresses. Her body stiffens, relaxes, stiffens again. Her mind is fighting it, resisting the unfamiliar sensations and the forced linguistic connections. This is the most difficult part watching her and not being able to coach her through it.

I've put more than two hundred human pets through this process, but I've never felt this concerned about any of them before. There's something very special about Ash. When I bought her I knew she was a fighter, what I didn't realize was that her fight comes from determination to win, which is a good quality for a show pet, but even more than that, she's curious, and sensual. She's going to have a good long life with me and I may even breed her myself. I've not had children since Mags bore me a child twenty years ago.

CHAPTER 21

BRIAR

The silver straps are cold against my skin, locking me onto the small stool like I'm on an alien amusement park ride. My heart is pounding so hard I think it might explode, and I can't stop shaking.

Aefre stands nearby, calm and composed, his green eyes fixed on the glowing console.

I don't know what's coming. Is this a punishment? My mind spins with possibilities, each one worse than the last. The looks the other pets gave me made me think that whatever was happening today was going to be horrendous. Even the smile Gabriel tried to give me revealed this as something to fear.

"I am a good girl?" I ask out of desperation.

Aefre looks momentarily surprised by my question, but then answers me, assuring me that I am a 'good girl,' although he doesn't even glance in my direction. The rest of what he says I don't understand.

Relief floods through me that this isn't a punishment, but it's short lived when the harness tightens even tighter around my body. Its artificial tendrils wrapping around me like a robotic cocoon.

And then the nightmare begins.

My brain begins to throb. It's unbearable, sharp and electric, making my vision blur and my ears ring. I scream from instinct, the sound tearing out of me, but the harness doesn't care. It presses on, tapping into my brain, forcing connections so fast, I can't begin to comprehend them.

Then the room around me shifts. The stool, console, Aefre... they're all gone. Replaced by darkness. Suffocating darkness. I can't see and I can't breathe.

Then *they* appear.

Gigantic tarantulas, their black hairy legs clicking against invisible surfaces as they scuttle toward me. I freeze, my body locking up in pure terror as one of them lunges, its massive mandibles snapping inches from my face.

"Run," a voice whispers in Imperial.

I don't know where the word came from, but it burns into my mind like fire. *Run.*

My legs move before I can think, but I'm not really running. The harness is moving me, dragging my limbs through the motions, forcing me to comply.

The huge tarantulas chase me. I hear their clicking behind me. *Run.*

"Jump," the voice commands, and I do. My legs bend, and I leap over one of the glowing webs, landing hard on the invisible ground. My knees buckle. I hear the words, *Fall.* But my fear pushes me up and forward to keep running. *Run.*

The spiders close in, their wet mandibles clicking. One of them lunges, wrapping me in its glowing web. The sticky strands tighten around my body, and I fight against them, sobbing as the Imperial voice whispers,

"Die."

"No!" I scream and I think I pee myself. Maybe I throw up. I don't know. It's all a blur, the darkness closing in until there's nothing left but the fear and the Imperial voice, whispering commands over and over.

"Run. Jump. Fall. Die."

It's endless. Relentless. Each word sears itself into my brain, tied to these horrifying experiences. The harness forces my body to move, to respond, even as my mind cries for it to stop. I don't know how many times I die.

And then, just as suddenly as it started, it ends.

The spiders vanish, the darkness recedes, and I'm back in the room. My body is shaking uncontrollably. Sweat soaks my skin, mixing with tears, urine, and vomit.

Aefre steps forward. He wipes my face gently with a cloth that smells like unfamiliar flowers. "Ash is a good girl," he says, his voice calm, like I haven't just been through hell.

I can't respond. I can barely breathe. My hands grip the edges of the stool as I stare at the floor. The dim room feels too loud and too real. My mind spinning with the Imperial words. *Run. Jump. Fall. Die.*

Aefre puts a finger under my chin and makes me meet his eyes. His eyes are the same color as mine and when he's this close, I don't see his grey skin. I see another human. "Why?" I ask. And I surprise myself as the word I spoke which I didn't know before was Imperial.

"Good girl," he says. And then reaches into his pocket and shows me a piece of chocolate.

I want that chocolate. My eyes follow it as he moves it slowly.

"Run. Jump. Fall. Die," he says still holding up the chocolate.

"Run, jump, fall, die," I say as fast as I can then open my mouth expectantly.

Aefre puts the chocolate on my tongue and I relish in it. It's rich with a buttery undertone. I let the taste settle into every corner of my mouth. It's both comforting and electrifying after cheating death from the spiders. I hope this is the end of this particular challenge today.

Aefre nods to me and says, "Again."

A fresh wave of terror rips through me, and I bite back a sob.

The room and Aefre fade away again, but this time instead of cold, warmth floods my veins like a gentle fire. My heart pounds harder and faster, matching each little surge from the harness.

Then I see Gabriel or someone who looks a lot like him. He walks up to me, wet from somewhere, maybe a shower, his skin is warm and he says, "You're okay. I'm here. You're safe." His words touch me so deeply. A wave of euphoria overtakes me.

He reaches down and kisses me so gently. I want nothing more than for him to hold me in his arms forever. His skin smells so clean and his strength so inviting. He whispers the Imperial words in my ear, "Devotion, cherish, and beloved." Each word resonates with a heightened sensation coursing through me, as if my brain is imprinting them in direct connection to the feeling of this rush, this profound affection. My cheeks flush and my sex tingles.

When the simulation ends, it fades like a fast-passing dream. My pulse stutters, trying to recall that fleeting, blissful feeling. The voice ceases, the warmth ebbs, and I'm left trembling, wanting and aroused. I whisper the newly learned words in Imperial and look at Aefre with hopeful eyes. *Please Master, make me come.*

He comes over and strokes my pussy. "Good girl."

"I repeat the words again: devotion, cherish, beloved." He's not taken his hand away so I open my legs wider for him. *Please keep touching me.*

"Yes," he says, rubbing me even faster between my legs. I watch him. This isn't cold for him. He actually wants to see my orgasm. I'm turned on by watching him watch me.

"Devotion, cherish, beloved," I say again breathlessly. I just want to make sure he doesn't stop. I spread my legs even wider for him. I'm so wet the friction is creating an erotic slapping sound in the room. I don't want him to ever stop touching me. His touch is perfect and consistent. As if he knows exactly what to do and when.

Through my own loud heartbeats I hear him say, "Orgasm now, my pet," Aefre as he expertly brings my body to a complete meltdown. Then he grabs on of my nipples and pulls hard. I can't help but think about him and his girlfriend and how I want to be her.

I come so hard, I close my eyes, and I can't think of anything else but the pleasure electrifying me throughout my body. Every part of me is tingling with pleasure. And Aefre keeps rubbing me, urging every bit of the orgasm out.

And now I understand more of his words, it's sexy as hell. "That's a good girl, come for me Ash."

When he finally finishes his ministrations and I open my eyes again, I watch as Aefre is wipes the tears from them with his thumbs. I smell myself on his fingers just before he puts his two fingers in my mouth.

"Suck them clean," he commands.

I obey. Holding eye contact as I suck my desire and urine from his fingers.

"Good girl," he says and pats me between my legs sending an after-orgasmic wave through me.

Then, I stare as he reluctantly walks back to his console.

I want him to come back. To touch me again. I want him to have sex with me right here.

Ultimately, I want the pleasure he gives me. And if it means doing another level in this language course harness, I will do it.

CHAPTER 22

AEFRE

I stand behind the console as I review the data. Ash's vitals spike erratically across the screen. Elevated heart rate, shallow breathing, and cortisol levels through the roof. All expected. All necessary.

I double-check the data feed, ensuring the parameters are set correctly, a carefully calibrated simulation of intense emotional states, each meant to plant Imperial vocabulary and grammar in the pet's mind.

I've done this countless times with other pets—fear, triumph, humiliation, desperation. But in all my years, I've rarely used the "love" setting. It's notoriously complicated to replicate, but it's important that I push the bond between Ash and Ember. So, I've programmed the harness to replicate a human male who looks and even smells like him.

My console flashes green. The harness pulses, and Ash's expression shifts, pupils dilate, and her dull cream cheeks flush with the mild euphoria the system induces. A swirl of words in Imperial hover in the air, each linked to the harness's emotional feed: devotion, cherished, beloved.

As the program progresses, tears begin to form at the corners of her eyes. I check her stats. There's nothing to worry about. She's experiencing the sensation of "love" that the harness is conjuring. Dopamine and oxytocin levels are spiking. She breathes out something between a sigh and a whimper, whispering the new words in Imperial. If I let it, the moment might stir something emotional in me too. But I can't afford that. Why should I be jealous of a holographic Ember? She's my pet and this is a training exercise, no more, no less.

I step closer as the program ends. Her eyes open when she senses my approach, and for a moment, she seems shaken, caught between the illusion's afterglow and the reality of my presence.

Her body shivers as the simulation's warmth begins to fade. She's breathing faster now, scanning my face for some kind of explanation. I keep my expression neutral, glancing at her collar readouts once more. All satisfactory. All good.

Ash stammers a few of the Imperial words again, as if testing them on her tongue, and maybe even wanting to show off her new skill, "Devotion, cherish, beloved."

A small part of me notes the near-perfect pronunciation. "Good girl," I tell her and stroke her between her legs. Her pink fur is soaking wet from urine and desire.

She looks into my eyes pleadingly. Her pupils are still dilated, her cheeks still flushed, the readout on her collar shows high levels of arousal. I feel my own arousal straining beneath my trousers and against my better judgement, I decide to deny her no longer. I part her legs with my hands, and then run my fingers up and down the folds of her labia, gently teasing her into what's to come. I watch as her mouth opens slightly and the sweetest little moan escapes her lips at my slight touch.

"Yes, pet. This is what you want," I say, as she tries to move her hips closer to my hand and open her legs wider. I begin rubbing her faster, never taking my eyes from hers. "It's me giving this to you, Ash. Remember that. You're mine now and I control every part of you."

I know I'm risking intermingling her connection to Ember from the language training with my own role as trainer, but there's something about Ash that makes me not want to share her with anyone. Not even another pet. It's mad. It's frightening, but I can't control my jealousy right now and my need to dominate her.

I expertly work her body into a sexual frenzy. She's moaning so loudly now that it's echoing off the walls as I continue to stroke her and tease her little sex. Finally, when she's on the edge, I command her to orgasm for me, and when she doesn't, I pinch one of her pink nipples hard, twisting it with my free hand, using the friction of the nipple piercing to get her attention.

Now I have what I want, her eyes meet mine, I command her again. "Orgasm for me Ash."

And she does.

Good. None of her bodily functions are hers anymore. She is mine. Every part of her. She must submit herself completely to me. She will become my perfect human pet just like Ember. "Good girl." Then I tell her to, "Suck." And I put my wet fingers in her mouth and she hungrily sucks her lubrication and urine from my fingers.

When we have completed the last program in the Foundation Course I tell her, "Tomorrow, we will begin Unit One."

"Please Master," she says in accented Imperial.

"You must, Ash."

I step away from the console and unlatch the harness from her, the metallic tendrils retracting with a faint hiss.

Her breathing is shallow and her pale skin is glistening with sweat. Even if I hadn't had access to her stats, it's obvious her body has reached its limit.

"Ash is a good girl," I tell her.

When she tries to move off the stool, she's too weak to stand.

I catch her and lift her into my arms. It surprises me how light she feels. It's ridiculous that I should even reflect on this. I know her exact weight. But her personality makes her feel heavier, like a force to be reckoned with and a secret weapon no one in the pet circuit is expecting. *My pet. My weapon.*

I walk her to the medical center and as the doors slide open a familiar voice calls out from behind us.

"Briar?!"

Ember. He must have passed us in the corridor. His face is flushed with anger.

"What have you done to her? You monster!" he accuses me. But his outburst is predictable given the circumstances and a good sign that I was successful in manipulating his own emotions to bond with her.

I shift Ash in my arms so that if I need to, I can hit my ring to issue a punishment. "She's just tired, Ember." I assure him calmly. "The process is necessary for her ability to speak Imperial. You know this. Go to where you're supposed to be or I'll have your privilege to come and go on your own revoked."

I see the conflict in his eyes, the resentment, the protectiveness, the helplessness.

I hand Ash to the medics and turn my attention towards Ember. I stroke his head. "It's okay," I say. And for a moment, I see my gorgeous obedient pet again. But then his mood changes back when Ash makes a small whimper as they lay her down on a medical bed.

"It's okay," I say again, caressing him in a way I know he likes and usually calms him. I run my hand back and forth over the back of his muscular thighs. Hinting that if he is a good boy there'll be a sexual reward for him.

But he steps away from me. His golden eyes meet mine and for the first time in years, I see defiance there.

"Remove him," I command the guards in the medical center. "Put him in solitary confinement."

The guards step forward.

Ember resists at first, but he does not fight long. He knows better than to challenge them outright as they're armed. Still, his words linger in the air as they drag him from the room. "You monster."

I walk over to where Ash is being hydrated and given some sleeping aids. She's not broken. Far from it. Ember's dramatics are unfounded, fueled by the connection I planted there. If I didn't have so much riding on Ember bonding with Ash for the Grand Championships, I'd attempt to reverse some of what I did. But, it's too late now. We all have to let this run its course.

CHAPTER 23

GABRIEL

Solitary confinement is a living nightmare. The room is just a cube of cold metal. If I stretch out my arms, my fingertips touch both sides. If I raise my hand, my knuckles graze the ceiling. I'm stuck in this cold, silent, dark box that amplifies all my thoughts, doubts, and fears.

Of course, I've been here before. Especially in my first years. Every time I resist Aefre. I mean, *really* resist him. This is where he puts me. It's meant to break me, to make me question everything. And mon Dieu, it's working.

Why do I care so much about Briar? Why did I explode like that, knowing exactly what Aefre would do to me? Why did seeing her, so exhausted, ignite something uncontrollable in me? I've seen others pushed to their limits before. Je suis passé par là moi-même. I have been there myself, but this? This is different. She's different. Or maybe... I am different?

My mind flies to the thought of Fifi and I hold back a shudder.

I lean back against the cold wall to calm myself. My collar vibrates faintly, a constant reminder of the control they have over me. It's not just a tool. It's a weapon. And Aefre wields it like the master trainer that he is. He can control my thoughts, warp my emotions, make me question what's real and what's not, all with a subtle pulse from this damned thing.

And now I can't stop wondering, what if what I feel for Briar isn't real? Est-ce que je peux me faire confiance? Can I trust myself to know what's real?

I bite the inside of my cheek, trying to stop myself from thinking about Fifi again, but this time, it's no use. Unbidden, the memories flood in. Fifi. My steadfast partner who I left behind. The one I failed.

I shake my head violently. No. Briar isn't a replacement. She's not a second chance. She's different. She's... elle-même. She's mine.

And I think I love her. We've barely spoken, just a few stolen glances and whispered words. And yet, when I see her, it's like I've known her forever. Like she's a part of me I lost long ago.

Or are those feelings only Aefre's manipulation?

I slam my fist against the wall. Merde. Pain shoots up my arm, but it's nothing compared to the chaos in my mind.

"Briar," I whisper her name into the silence. It feels real when I say it.

But Aefre has made me completely reliant on his version of reality. I know this. I see it in the way he controls other pets and I'm no different.

But in my heart, I can't believe that this isn't real. It's just too... too real to be an illusion.

I love Briar.

When I saw her in the medical center, something broke inside of me. And it wasn't about Fifi, or Aefre's manipulations. It was about *her*. That jealousy and anger can't be faked by any collar. Love doesn't work that way.

I don't think.

I press my forehead against the cold wall and say her name like a prayer for transparency in all of this, "Briar."

CHAPTER 24

BRIAR

The Imperial language simulation still haunts me, even after all these months.

I hated it, but I can't deny that I learned. The grammar, the vocabulary, and the subtle semantics, they all still surface in my head almost as naturally as my own mother tongue.

Occasionally, when I speak these words out loud, I'm back in those simulations for half a breath. The fear, the love, the humiliation, the pure desperation... you name it, Aefre put me through all the paces of life to force the language in. But now I understand a lot, enough to use it and easily pick up new words and grammar.

And now I also understand what Gabriel meant when he said, "It could be worse." Every now and then, new pets arrive for a short amount of time. Apparently, Aefre does some side consulting.

Most of these transient pets on the *Luminous Arc* only speak Spanish or Imperial so I communicate with them in the alien language.

Not long ago, I spoke with a woman who'd been captive for so many years she'd lost count. She told me she'd spent most of that time on military ships until her master couldn't afford her anymore, so now she's been sold again. Her new owner is a different class of Imperial man and she struggles to know what he wants. He's some kind of galactic trader and says that she's been sent to be trained by Aefre because he wants her to be "better behaved in public."

When I asked her what that meant she told me that he has a fetish of wanting to parade her around naked and allow all kinds of aliens to touch her. "And I don't like it," she said. "Grey hands, okay, but not tentacles or mandibles. An Octopod put its tentacle up my ass and I screamed like I was dying. It was so disgusting and humiliating. My old master would have never done that."

So Aefre was going to use the *Luminous Arc's* holographic training center to retrain her.

And this woman wasn't even shocked by it. She was resigned to it. Gabriel was right, some fates are worse than being a show pet. But it's cold comfort all the same.

Just last week, Aefre began training me with Gabriel. And I'd be lying if I said, I wasn't excited by this. Just to be next to him makes my heart beat a little faster and my eyes linger just a little bit longer on his perfect muscular body and the golden hair covering his chest. Sometimes I imagine him, holding me, or pumping into me, that hair against my breasts. It's a fantasy. But one I hope someday I'll be able to make a reality. For now it's all training.

Aefre's voice brings me into the present, "Ash, pay attention."

I nod and focus on the holographic obstacle course ahead of us, towering walls, swinging ropes, shifting floors, and dizzying drops. We've already tackled it once, and I'm exhausted both physically and mentally. I don't want to do it again. And apparently this is only Level Two and Aefre wants me to get to Level Eight.

Aefre hovers on his flying pedestal off to the side, silently observing. At least it's him today and not Kaelin. Kaelin never hesitates to use his ring to issue a punishment of jolting pain through my collar whenever I make a mistake.

Gabriel stands beside me. He's so focused and ready.

Even though we're not allowed to chat, I've gotten to know Gabriel better through his interactions with me and our trainers. For starters, his grasp of the Imperial language is perfect, better than his English. But is it really a surprise? He's spent his entire adult life in this alien world, for which I pity him. But I can't tell how upset he is by it because on the day-to-day he seems mostly content. Nothing like the man I met on my first day here.

Next, his patience. Despite being an expert show pet and now my partner, he never races ahead. He not only waits for me, he reassures me with small words of encouragement in Imperial, but he's stayed true to his word about my name. It makes me wonder how many other female partners he's had in his show pet career.

And he never has ever called me Ash. And that just makes him all the more attractive to me. He calls me Briar if he must use my name and Aefre and Kaelin punish him for it every time with their rings.

We are in the middle of the obstacle course now. Gabriel is showing me how to handle the next challenge: a rope swing over a gaping drop. If I fall, I'll die.

Aefre calls out rapid-fire commands. Imperial words I recognize, but they're unintelligible to me right now, looking at that long drop, I'm so scared of falling.

Gabriel, seeing my confusion, murmurs each phrase again, slower and quieter, his tone gentle, so different from the artificial voice of the language harness or Aefre's commanding tone.

"Climb," he says in Imperial. Then, in a much softer tone with his accented English, "You can do this, *mon cœur*."

I'm not sure what that French phrase means. Gabriel's English is infused with French and I wonder sometimes if I spoke French I'd know him better. But there's hardly any time to convey basic information, let alone have a language class.

I watch him jump easily, the rope swinging with effortless grace, and he lands on the next platform like it's the simplest thing in the world.

Aefre's voice commands me to move, "Ash. Jump. Swing. Release."

Gabriel motions to me, repeating the Imperial commands more slowly.

I grip the rope and jump. It vibrates causing me to almost lose my grip. Panic rips through my body. I'm so focused on holding on I don't even realize I've made it to the other platform.

Until I hear Gabriel's voice, "Release! Release!"

I let go just in time, stumbling onto the platform, losing my balance.

Gabriel quickly grabs my arm and holds on to me so I don't fall off. Our eyes meet as he helps me up and for a moment, I can't look away. There's no disapproval in his eyes, only relief. It makes the entire course feel a little less awful.

"Again," Aefre commands. "You're too slow. Ember, work together faster. And, Ash, speak Imperial. The judges will want to hear you. If you're silent we will lose points."

Gabriel and I exchange glances. I'm not sure how I'll ever match his skill, or how I'll speak Imperial clearly under so much pressure.

"Next," Aefre says and we move to the next challenge.

"Breathe," Gabriel says, his voice barely audible as he switches briefly to English. "You're overthinking it."

I nod. I'm not sure how to just *stop* overthinking. We've barely finished scaling a slick wall, and my legs feel like they're made of rubber. But to be honest, I can't tell if it's from exhaustion or from the way Gabriel is looking at me right now.

"You did well," he murmurs, stepping closer so Aefre won't hear.

But his closeness, the heat radiating from his sweaty body and his masculine scent, is sending my body into lusty overdrive. Despite being warm myself, a tingling spreads through my body and my nipples become taut yearning for touch. Which is embarrassing because my breasts are exposed. He and Aefre can see the signs of my arousal.

Gabriel brushes a strand of hair away from my face, letting his hand linger. A shock of heat ripples under my skin and between my legs, and it's not my tail.

His amber eyes lock on mine, and for a heartbeat, the entire course, the commands, the weight of our surroundings... it all vanishes. His gaze drops to my lips. My heart pounds so loud it's all I hear.

"Enough!" Aefre commands.

I draw back, but Gabriel refuses to move.

Aefre repeats himself, louder this time, raising the hand with his ring. Before I can even shout a warning, Gabriel goes down his face in agony. There's a buzzing sound coming from his collar, from what I've come to recognize as a high-voltage shock.

"Stop!" I say.

"Do not interfere, Ash."

When Aefre finally lets up, Gabriel staggers, breathing hard. He straightens, and his eyes find mine again. No anger, just something steady and shockingly authentic. So real in fact a chill runs down my spine.

"Back to the course," Aefre orders.

But his words are background noise to us. Something just happened between Gabriel and me. Something that can't be controlled by Aefre. I think it's love. I search my feelings. I've never been in love nor loved by anyone. So I'm unsure...

Gabriel doesn't move at first, still watching me, like whatever connected us in that moment hasn't quite broken.

Aefre barks another command in Imperial, something I don't catch.

Gabriel exhales, his voice low. "Je ne veux pas que tu souffres.

He's furious and I don't want you to be punished. Let's finish this, okay?"

I stare at Gabriel. He's gorgeous. His amber eyes meet mine with determination. It makes my pulse roar in my ears. I don't know if I can finish the course. My body feels wrecked and the memory of his lips nearly meeting mine lingers like an unspoken promise. *He almost kissed me.* Even now, as we force our way through the remainder of the obstacle course, I can't stop my gaze from drifting to his mouth, his strong lips, wondering if the next time he leans closer, Aefre won't interrupt us.

Gabriel glances my way again, *I think I'm in love.*

***

The water hits my skin in a blistering rush. The attendants work in brisk, practiced motions, scrubbing every inch of my body without a shred of tenderness, as though I'm nothing more than a piece of equipment that needs cleaning.

Gabriel stands across the room, watching me. When our eyes meet, his gaze is steady, neither leering nor indifferent, just tender in a way that makes my body burn with desire.

The old me would have shriveled up and died inside at the thought of anyone, let alone a man like Gabriel, seeing me stripped bare and bathed publicly by male hands. But I'm not that woman anymore. Not since Earth. Not since I became an alien's pet with a tail that swishes behind me and more body hair than I ever asked for. I learned quickly there's no room for shame in the human pet world, but what surprised me most, was how quickly I shed it.

As Gabriel watches me, I wonder if he sees a mutilated human woman or a prized Imperial pet? And if it's the latter is that why he's attracted to me? I reckon I would rather have it be the latter, I wouldn't want him to want me out of pity or desperation.

He shifts, stepping a little closer as the attendants step back. I see the faint glimmer of satisfaction in his gaze, not lust, exactly, more like... delight?

Shockingly, the attendants just walk out of the room, leaving us alone and uncaged for the first time.

My heart thumps hard. *Is this a trap?* I can't tear my eyes away from Gabriel's. I hope he's going to finish what he started on the obstacle course.

CHAPTER 25

GABRIEL

The room feels smaller now that les garçons are gone. Briar stands across from me, her emerald eyes darting to the door as if she expects someone to burst in at any moment.

"Détends-toi," I say softly, stepping toward her. "Relax."

Her eyes narrow, suspicion flashing in their depths.

"Did you get them to leave?" she asks, her voice low and cautious.

"Oui, I bribed them," I admit with a small shrug.

Her brow furrows. "You... have money?"

I smile faintly. "Pets don't get much when we win competitions, but respectable trainers like Aefre don't take away what we earn. It goes into an account we can access through the database. It's in the eating place."

"We can't even choose when or what we eat," she murmurs, shaking her head in disbelief, "but we're allowed to access money?"

"Aefre's a galactic-class trainer—part of showing off his wealth is letting his pets have credits, too. Most save their UCs in hopes of buying freedom that never comes. Or..." I fall silent, leaving the rest of that bitter truth unspoken.

Her fingers fidget with the edge of her towel. I can see the uneasiness in her. I force my gaze up away from her body and even further up from her lips. I meet her eyes. "Briar," I say gently. "I'm not going to hurt you. That's not why I asked them to leave."

Her shoulders loosen just a fraction. "I know..." she says those two words and they mean so much more.

Does she want me to kiss her now? So suddenly? I don't know. I don't know how to be a human man with a woman. I abandon changing my initial plan.

"I just wanted to talk," I continue. "After everything you've endured, the language harness, the endurance tests, the obstacle courses, I thought you should hear it from someone. You're strong, Briar. Stronger than anyone I've seen come through this place."

She blinks, her expression changing to one of surprise. "You used your precious money just to tell me that?"

"Oui. Don't you think it's important? I think it's important. You should know. Aefre is tough on you, but it's all for a purpose."

She smiles in reply and it warms my whole body.

Then she does something I am completely unprepared for. She opens her towel, like wings of an exotic bird, exposing her naked body, clean now from the shower, and says, "I liked the way you watched the attendants bathe me. But, Gabriel, I'd like it even more if you touched my body in a way they can't."

I take a step closer to her. I feel like I'm living out a fantasy I've imagined so many times. I tentatively reach out a hand and rub my thumb over her bottom lip. She opens her mouth slightly. Her green eyes are dark with desire. I feel like I never want this moment to end. So I stare into her eyes and memorize the feel of her soft skin against my fingers.

"What do you see in me?" she asks quietly.

I swallow hard, my heart pounding in my chest. "Je vois quelqu'un... quelqu'un de courageux," I say, my voice thick with emotion. "I see someone brave. Someone who hasn't let this place break her. Someone who's worth every risk I've taken just to be standing here."

Her cheeks flush and it's breathtaking. I move my head closer, but slowly. I want to relish this moment. This may be my only time alone with her, ever. I won't rush it.

"Briar," I whisper, barely audible. My lips brushing hers as I speak, "Puis-je t'embrasser?" May I kiss you?

She hesitates, her breath catching. "Yes."

It's as if the entire universe has narrowed to just the two of us. When our lips finally meet, our kiss is soft, hesitant at first, then deepening into something electric. Her hands tremble as they touch mine, and this feels real. And I know that my feelings for Briar are my own and not the conjuring of Aefre and his collar.

I put my arms around her and pull her naked body against mine. The coolness of her nipple piercings pressing against my chest. I run my hand over the small of her back, finding her tail and running my fingers through it as my tongue charges into her mouth with purpose.

Just then, the door hisses open, shattering the moment.

"Enough! Barbaric pets!" Aefre yells. Then a low-level shock follows through our collars.

I pull back slowly, frustrated. But I don't take my eyes off her.

Briar stiffens as her eyes go to Aefre.

"Ash, back to my quarters now. Ember, clean yourself and go to bed," Aefre commands. "You must not give in to your base human instincts. If you want to mate, you ask me for permission."

Briar looks over her shoulder at me as she's being led away on a leash.

Ce n'est pas fini. This isn't over.

Not by a long shot.

CHAPTER 26

AEFRE

I knew something was wrong the moment the attendants returned earlier than expected. Their excuses were flimsy and their behavior uncharacteristically fidgety. They didn't need to explain, there was no way they could have completed both Ash's and Ember's evening routines in the time allotted. Whatever they had done, whatever deal had been struck, I would find out soon enough.

It didn't take long.

When I arrived at the cleansing room, the answer was already waiting for me. Ember's head bent toward Ash, his lips on hers. The scene was almost absurd in its simplicity—two humans finding solace in each other amidst the chaos of their existence. Solace, or perhaps rebellion. Either way, it didn't matter.

I separated them with a slight punishment. Both were compliant.

And now I'm here, standing in the silence of my quarters, considering my next move.

I activate the communication console, the glowing blue screen pulsing faintly as it connects to Kaelin. His face appears a second later.

"Kaelin," I begin, briefly startled he would answer while a slave artist is riding him. I can see the curve of her hip and ends of her silver nipple jewelry on his naked chest. "We have a situation. Ash and Ember —there's been a physical incident."

Kaelin raises an eyebrow, reluctantly sitting up and I hear the Imperial woman move off of him somewhat annoyed. "What happened?"

"Ember kissed Ash in the cleansing room. I intervened before it went further."

"How do you want to deal with this?"

"I told Ember to bathe himself and then to bed," I say. "As for Ash, her training will proceed as planned. I'll begin tonight to strengthen the intimacy between trainer and pet."

"And Ember? Do you want me to discipline him?"

"Yes, but carefully," I warn. "Lay off the harsher physical punishments. He's teetering too close to the edge of pure infatuation. We can't risk them trying to escape or worse, dying in the attempt. It would be disastrous for them and for us."

"Understood. What if he—"

"Trust me in this," I interrupt, cutting him off. "For now, Ash's progress is paramount. She must be tied to me before Ember interrupts the natural bond between trainer and pet."

"Fine. Anything else?"

"Not at the moment," I say. "I'll inform you if anything changes."

"Aefre," Kaelin says while he motions his Imperial woman back to him, "remember she bit off another man's penis while at the Abyssal Nexus. Don't assume that she's not going to try it again. I don't need to tell you that even the best trained humans can be unpredictable."

"I'll be vigilant," I say with a small smile.

The screen dims, and I exhale slowly, turning my attention to the holographic schedule still open on my desk. Training regimens, performance assessments, dietary adjustments, it's all there in meticulous detail, a roadmap to what I hope will be success.

But the weight of the situation lingers. Pushing the bond between Ash and Ember has proved more difficult than I first imagined.

Humans are so emotional, so irrational, and so prone to acts of rebellion that defy all logic, I must be careful now. I remember Yellow One going out the airlock. Managing Ash and Ember must be done delicately.

Tomorrow, the training will intensify. The challenges will grow more complex, more demanding. And Ash and Ember will face them together, under my guidance and under my control. Because in the end, it is not only about their bond. It is also about mine to them.

I stand, already aroused, thinking about the next phase with Ash.

She's on her little bed in my bedroom. No doubt aroused as well. She was naked and Ember was holding her close, kissing her. His hands running through her tail.

In some ways, his actions and my interruption came at the perfect time.

CHAPTER 27

BRIAR

As I wait for Aefre in my little bed, I can't get my mind to settle down.

I keep replaying the kiss in my head, over and over. Gabriel's warm hand on my back, the way his lips felt against mine, soft and sure, like he'd been waiting to kiss me his whole life.

I have never been kissed like that. Like I mattered.

It's the only moment in this place that hasn't felt controlled. But now, lying here, half-afraid, half-curious, I wonder what my punishment will be. But, no matter how Aefre punishes me, I am sure Gabriel's kiss was worth it. It's the kind of kiss a woman can live off of for the rest of her life.

Finally, the door slides open with a soft hiss, and I sit up straighter, my heart pounding.

Aefre steps inside, his movements calm, as always.

"Ash."

I just watch him. I don't respond. I've noticed he prefers that unless he's asked me a direct question.

Aefre walks to the edge of my small bed and stands there for a moment, looking down at me. "Did you initiate the kiss," he asks, his tone measured and his words slow so that I understand, "or did Ember?"

I open my mouth, then close it again, unsure how to answer. The truth? A lie? I hadn't considered it before, but since these pet collars show everything about us to our trainers they probably show when someone is lying too.

"It was... mutual."

"Mutual," he repeats, his tone thoughtful. "And how did it feel?"

My cheeks flush. "It felt... nice," I admit reluctantly. "I don't know."

"You don't know? Was it comforting? Exciting? Did it make you feel safe? Desired? Did you want more from him?"

His questions feel invasive, calculated, like he's trying to dissect the moment piece by piece and then reshape it. "I don't know what you want me to say."

"I want you to be honest. I want to understand you better, my pet."

I swallow hard. "It felt... good," I say finally. "It felt awakening."

His expression doesn't change, but he leans down so he's at eye level with me. "And what about me?" he asks, his voice smoother now, almost curious. "Do you feel the same when you're with me? Do you still long for my penis inside of you or only Embers?"

I can't answer. *Is he offering me sex?* Or am I so aroused I can't even concentrate on his words. "What Master Aefre?"

"You like it when I touch you, yes?" he asks.

The question hangs in the air between us. Part of me wants to shout *no,* to tell him that he's nothing like Gabriel, that I could never feel that way about him. But another part of me, the part that wants to be an obedient girl and a winner, hesitates. He's Master Aefre to me. He's in control of everything. He controls when I eat, pee, poop, dress, sleep, and exercise. The only moments I have to myself is when I'm asleep or the few minutes I'm in my cage forgotten in the shower room. And I have fantasized about having sex with him so many times. I often revisit the memory of the grey woman riding him and her nipple jewelry in his mouth. I want that too. And he knows it. Every night he touches me until I orgasm to help me go to sleep, but never anything more. I can never touch him, but he can see it in my eyes. I want him to fuck me, to dominate me, to make me ride him like that with reigns on my nipples. To tell me how to fuck him, play-by-play, just like he guides me through the rest of my life.

"I..." I begin but can't bring myself to finish.

"You don't have to answer," he says, his voice low. "Your body can answer for you."

I let out a shaky breath, unsure whether to feel relieved or terrified by his answer.

Aefre lifts me out of my little bed and sets me on my feet. Then he leads me by holding my collar over to a plain area of the wall in the bedroom. He puts my palms against the wall and as if the wall can read his mind, shackles come out and hold my wrists. Then Aefre pulls my ankles back so I'm bent over, my ass up in the cold air. My tail hanging between my legs.

Aefre swishes my tail and then secures it firmly between my butt cheeks. Then without saying a word begins smacking my bare ass. *Is this my punishment?*

"Does it hurt?" he asks taunting me. Just what the doctor said in one of the language challenges, so the phrase carries some traumatic weight to it.

"No," I reply honestly and Aefre increases his pressure. Now his hand hitting my skin is making a loud smacking noise.

"You were a bad girl kissing Ember. What would have happened had I not come in? Do you know?"

"I don't know..." I answer as Aefre takes a break and plays with my tail running the end of it up my thighs. The sensation of his hand moving through my tail is erotically electric.

"I can tell you're lying. Your collar betrays you. Would you have wanted Ember to rut you like an animal?" Aefre asks, his hand now pulling on my tail just enough to tilt my ass up even further. "Or would you have bit off his penis? Was that your plan?"

"I ..." I stumble with the question. I've not thought about Big in months. I almost had forgotten I did that. It seems like it was another person. But it was me. "I would never do that to Ember.... Or to you," I say wanting to keep all my options open. I've never been so horny in my life as I am right now.

And confused. Do I want Gabriel or Aefre?

"Do you think you're allowed to have sex with another pet?" He asks as he begins smacking my ass again. His strikes are hard but they don't hurt. They feel good. Erotic. A warm tingling is spreading between my legs.

"I don't know the rules." I honestly don't know if pets are allowed to have sex with one another. "I know all the other pets sleep in one room. There are women and Gabr.. Ember."

"Do you think Ember has sex with those female pets?"

I had never considered this before. *Does he sleep with them all?* Is that the reason he's the only man with all these women? Like a rooster in a hen house.

"I don't know," I pant out between the spankings.

"No, of course, he doesn't," Aefre says as if I should know this and relief washes over me. "Pets cannot breed without the owner's consent. Did either of you have my consent?"

"I don't know that word, Master Aefre."

"Did you ask permission from me?"

"No, Master."

"That's what makes you a bad girl," he says and stops smacking my ass. Then he lifts my tail up again and runs a solitary finger from the top of my vulva to my anus, his finger caressing my folds, finding his way through all the pubic hair that must be soaked with my desire. "But it's understandable, you're human and you've not had sex in a long time. I think you'd have sex with anything you could put in your hole right now. What do you think?"

I don't know what to say. This feels like a trick. He's made me sleep with the chastity device on every night so I haven't been able to orgasm unless it's by his hand. And sure he touches me every night before bed, making sure I'm sated before he puts on the chastity device, but I swear the constant orgasms with no penis may be worse than having no orgasms at all. And with the chastity device, I can't even have dream sex or orgasm in an erotic dream. Is he making it clear that it's not Gabriel who I really like, it's any male or even worse anything I would fuck. Or maybe it's really just him. Maybe I just really want Aefre?

No. That's not possible, is it?

I'm so confused.

Aefre smacks my ass again but this time while still holding up my tail erotically. "My precious little pet. How am I going to fix this?"

"I don't know."

"Another lie. I see it on your collar. Tell me what you want. How do we solve this? We can't have you going around trying to mount any male or anything that looks fuckable." He swats me again and it feels so good. I wonder if he's aroused by this as well. The thought of his girthy grey dick getting hard over spanking me makes me even more aroused.

"Your collar tells me everything and your level of arousal is as high as it gets and it's from my hands. Not Ember's." He smacks me a few times again.

I want him to pull down his trousers and enter me. I can hardly think of anything else.

"What do you think that means, Ash?"

I hesitate. What does he want me to say? Then I remember the medical vocabulary from the language harness. "Please Master Aefre, I want your penis inside of my vagina."

"Good girl. Honesty." Aefre rewards me by putting one of his fingers inside of wet core and I can't help myself. I moan with wanton desire even though it's by far not enough to fill me.

"Yes. Inside of me," I breathe.

Aefre removes his fingers and begins smacking my ass again. "Human pets are so sexual. You can't help it. Humans love sex. You have to have it. So now I'll give you two options. The first is that I pull down my trousers and take care of you myself, the old-fashioned way, between pet and trainer. The second is that I call the doctor to relieve you with a medical device. I know the doctor would prefer the second. He loves putting his devices on pets and making them orgasm over and over again."

"Not the doctor," I can't say it fast enough.

"Fine, if you want me to relieve you of your sexual frustration you need to convince me that you really want me, an Imperial man, your trainer and not another human or a different kind of alien inside of you. Prove to me that you want me."

How did this turn into me convincing him? Did I translate his words correctly? He repeats himself and I arrive at the same conclusion. How am I going to convince him with my limited Imperial? And chained to the wall with my tail up in the air? I look nothing like the Imperial woman he was fucking. I think for a minute and then say, "My body has answered your first question. I'm slick and ready for you as I have been for months. It's you who brings me to climax every night and you who controls my chastity. I'd do anything for you to be inside of me Master Trainer Aefre."

The shackles on my wrists disappear and I would have fallen to the floor if Aefre hadn't caught me by my waist, pulling my naked hips into his where I can feel his hard erection through his trousers. A bout of wetness drips out of me with the contact.

"I long to have my penis between your furry folds. To feel your barbaric body grinding next to mine," he says roughly in my ear and I feel like I might orgasm on the spot. He pushes me back from him then and says, "Get on my bed. On all fours, I want to see that tail swishing between your legs and that red ass high in the air."

All thoughts of Gabriel have left my mind I'm sorry to say. It's all about obeying Aefre to get what my body needs. I get on Aefre's bed, a place he only has me on as a reward for being a good pet, and wait for what I've wanted for months now. My physical body is almost exploding with giddy anticipation. I can't believe Aefre is finally going to fuck me like the animal I feel like.

Aefre returns to the bed naked. He rubs his hands over my back, buttocks, and thighs. Then he grabs my tail and hoists my ass up. "After I make you orgasm I'm going to put my dick inside of you and fuck you from behind holding your tail to remind you you're still my pet and it's I who allow you to orgasm."

"Yes, Master Aefre," I say obediently just like on the obstacle course. I'm so aroused by this. All I want him to do is enter me with his hard dick.

I feel his hand reach between my legs and then he flips me over on my back. One hand still inside of me.

"Open your eyes," he commands me. "Look down. Watch me. My superior grey hand pleasuring your barbaric wet human sex. Does it feel good?"

"Yes. Don't stop," I say. I'm riding the tip of an orgasm that's been building for hours.

But then he stops.

Did I miscommunicate? Did I say the opposite of what I meant?

"Master?"

"Sit up halfway and watch me, my face in your fur and my tongue lapping up your desire."

I can't sit up fast enough. I watch as he parts my folds through my copious pink pubic hair to find my labia and my clit. Then he begins licking me like a wild animal. It's like nothing I've ever felt before and I let out a moan. His tongue must be extra textured compared to a human man's. It feels like hundreds of little sparkly bubbles are exploding all over my sex. "Oh don't ever stop."

"Open your eyes and watch me."

I force my eyes open but it's so hard. It feels too good.

Aefre looks up at me, takes both hands, one for each nipple piercing, pulls my nipples out hard stretching them and orders me, "Orgasm now, pet. Orgasm for as long as you can until it hurts."

And I do as he says just like I do in the obstacle course. But instead of him pushing my physical limits or my psychological ones, he's now pushing my erotic ones. I come so hard and for so long I can't even remember where I am. There's nothing but this physical gratification and all I know is that I want more and I want it to never end.

Aefre sucks and pulls as if he's milking me of all my pent up sexual energy that he's been torturing me with these last months. Has it only been months? Not years? Not an eternity?

When the muscle contractions have subsided, when his face is covered with my shiny lubrication, Aefre flips me over on my stomach. "On all fours, pet."

"Yes Master," I obey. My body greedy for more sexual pleasure. For what he promised me.

"I won't be gentle. You don't want that. I know what kind of human you are. You want me to use all my strength to pound into you." He grabs my tail firmly in one hand and the hair on my head in another. I feel his penis hovering at my entrance. "Are you a good girl Ash?"

"Yes Master. I am a good girl."

"And what do good girl's get."

I can't think. What does he want me to say? "Good girls get fucked by their Masters." I say hoping that's the right answer.

It must have been because then I feel his large girthy organ push its way into my tight and wet vagina. His penis is so ridged I can feel each peak as he moves inside of me. It feels both pleasurable and painful at the same time.

"That's it, Ash. Take me in. You're so small. It's all that training. You're so tight, but you'll take me. Good girl."

My body immediately reacts to him calling me a good girl and dopamine rushes through me. I want to be his good girl. I want to take him all the way into me. But he's so big and the ridges are scraping the inside of me ruthlessly.

Aefre begins to move in and out of me faster and faster. Harder and harder. He's pulling my hair and tail so much, I know that if he weren't fucking me, it would hurt. But instead it's erotic, like being fucked by a caveman in *Clan of the Cave Bear*. He's just taking me.

Giving me exactly what I want without me asking for it. I would never have said I wanted this on Earth, but now it's all I want.

When I don't think I can take the fast and hard pounding of his penis anymore, Aefre groans loudly and I feel his body tense. Next I feel my core being filled with hot semen, there's so much it overflows onto my thighs. He rolls me to my side and then positions me near his penis still twitching. "Lick up all the semen, human pet. This is your treat."

I know this is part of the Imperial sex act or at least from what I saw with Aefre and the other Imperial woman, so I open my mouth and lick his penis and balls clean. It's a mixture of my own desire and his semen.

He watches me, putting his head on my hair, guiding me just like he does with some of the more complex motions on the obstacle course. "Good girl," he says in the exact same way.

It makes me feel good.

"You're such a fine pet, Ash."

When there's no more semen between his legs he looks at my body messy with our sex and picks me up to take me into the bathroom. I've never had a shower in Aefre's room before and it makes me feel special. He turns on the water and bathes me himself. Something that he's also never done before.

I watch him as he meticulously goes over every inch of my body with soap, making sure that I'm thoroughly clean.

"You're a stunning human," he says as he lathers up my pubic hair. "And your vagina is so tight."

His words and then his hands moving to cup my breasts makes me want him all over again.

"What's your sexual fantasy, Ash?" he asks as if reading my mind. But then I remember he can see my level of arousal from the collar.

I don't lie but it's difficult for me to describe my fantasy in my limited Imperial. "When you were with the other woman. I want her," I motion to my small nipple jewelry. "Then I want to be on top."

Aefre chuckles. "Like a real Imperial woman." But then he says more seriously, "If you're a good girl I will arrange that for you. No more kissing Ember. Understand?"

"I understand."

Aefre turns off the water and dries me. Then he puts me back into my little bed on the floor and activates the force field.

I fall asleep almost immediately. My body is so tired but also now sexually satisfied for the first time in a long time, even from before I was abducted by aliens, and I almost feel content.

Maybe I've misunderstood this whole situation? Is being Aefre's pet so bad?

CHAPTER 28

GABRIEL

The metallic door slides shut behind me with a hiss, sealing me inside the human pets' sleeping quarters. I sit heavily on the narrow cot assigned to me. I run my fingers through my hair, hoping to dispel some of my frustration.

Briar, ma douce Briar, my sweet, Briar, Aefre's with her now. What is he doing? What is he saying? Is he... touching her?

"Merde!" I spit, slamming my fist into the wall beside me.

I know the only reason I'm not in solitary is because Aefre is going to have sex with Briar tonight. I'm furious with jealousy but there's nothing I can do about it. And what makes me even more angry is that I can't even masturbate thinking about her without asking permission.

I lean forward, resting my elbows on my knees, and try to breathe. Focus. Think. I need a plan. A way to take her far away from him, from this place, from all of it.

The UCs. I have them. They're my only card to play, my only shot at freedom for both of us. But how much would it take to bribe a guard? To steal a ship?

I've seen the patrols, the security systems. It won't be easy. I've tried before and my voice is already locked out on the *Luminous Arc* so Briar's Imperial would have to be good enough to trick the codes. The ship only responds to native speakers. Even if I could somehow get us past the guards, past the cameras, and onto a ship, where would we go? The galaxy isn't kind to humans. We're not just pets. We're prey. Everywhere, there's someone stronger, smarter, with better tech. Even if we found a place to land, who's to say we wouldn't be sold back into this hell or something worse?

I close my eyes, forcing myself to think. The credits I've earned, it's not a fortune, but may be enough to pay for passage to some distant, forgotten corner of the galaxy where humans aren't just commodities. But where?

A memory sparks, a rumor whispered among the pets; Fifi was always talking about it. A hidden colony, Haven, a place where humans live free. A fantasy, most likely. But isn't that all I have now?

The image of Aefre fucking Briar crosses my mind and I hit the wall again. The other humans look up at me cross.

"Ma chère," I whisper. "If there's even a chance, I'll find it for us."

Aefre thinks he's in control. But he doesn't know how far I'm willing to go to get her to myself. And he may have Briar's physical body, but he hasn't got her heart. Not yet.

The lights are on. It's the Watching. My body aches for sexual release. Watching les garçons bathe Briar's body, kissing her sweet lips, and her warm body pressing next to mine has been playing on repeat in my thoughts for the last four hours.

I open internal communications to Kaelin from the pet sleeping quarters.

"Ember, what is it that it couldn't wait until the morning?" he asks annoyed.

"I want to masturbate." I find it only mildly degrading now to have to ask and be monitored, but it's life as a human pet.

"I'll arrange it and come by and get you. Control yourself until then."

I go back to bed. There's some grumbling among the other humans that I woke them up, but I don't care. It's the Watching, the lights are on. We aren't supposed to be sleeping, although most of us pets do sleep during this time.

I lie under my covers and stare at the ceiling. My mind races thinking about Briar and what Aefre is probably doing to her right now. I can't help but remember the first time Aefre had sex with me. I'm not attracted to men, but I was attracted to him then. There was nothing more that I wanted than to have him dominate me. So I understand if Briar just gave herself over to him willingly. He's trained us to do that. To do his bidding. To love him and to be obedient to him in every way.

The day after Fifi died, he came to me and I welcomed him. His closeness. How he comforted me then. How he mastered me.

I shake my head to displace the memory. What I want now is to masturbate thinking only about Briar. Thinking about our kiss in the cleansing room. Thinking about where that might have gone if we'd had the full hour alone.

Whatever she and Aefre are doing right now it's only physical. When I make love to her it'll be human to human, lover to lover. I'll be so gentle and attentive, nothing like sex between trainer and pet. Someday, ma chère Briar, we will have our time.

It seems like an eternity before Kaelin arrives. As soon as he's at the door, I walk out, but he stops me.

"Wait Ember," he says as he attaches a leash. "I have to use this now after what happened with Ash earlier."

I don't reply. I don't care. I just want sexual release.

Now that I'm all leashed up we begin walking toward the medical center. Human sperm is never just thrown away. As we enter, the doctor greets us, and I'm taken to a small room, not unlike solitary, except in this one the two other men join me.

I don't wait for Kaelin to release me from my leash. I just pull my clothing down, my erect penis springing forward, surrounded by copious hair. I don't even know if all of my pubic hair is my own. I was only sixteen years old when Aefre bought me and those first months were so traumatic, I don't remember many of the details.

I remember the magic cross piercing though. A horizontal and vertical piercing through my penile head. It's supposed to bring more pleasure to the women I have sex with. Although I'm rarely allowed to have sex with anyone. Aefre likes to keep me on a tight leash sexually.

Kaelin turns on the computer. "I have a holo of Ash running, her tits bouncing like crazy. It's only a minute long, but given what happened today..." Kaelin says. He knows exactly what I want as the doctor does. We've all been together on the *Luminous Arc*, playing these roles for the last twelve years. These men have watched every sexual encounter I've ever had and sometimes even participated. Except for my kiss with Briar. Everything else has always been orchestrated by them.

"One minute will be enough," I reply. I don't even care that they are watching it too. Sometimes the doctor's extra commentary on human body hair annoys me. But, when all three of us begin to watch Briar running, her breasts bouncing and her tail swaying behind her, I don't even care what the doctor says.

"She's such a beautiful human female. From her scans her vaginal canal is just long enough for the average human male, so she'd be a tight fit for any of us, and especially you Ember. Your dick would be so squeezed inside of Ash... I rarely envy Aefre, but lately when I see that human pet, I do."

I stroke myself while I watch the holo of Briar running, trying to block out their conversation. I concentrate on her big breasts swinging as she sweats and runs in the video. The tail that matches her hair swishing erotically behind her. I think someday, she'll be mine. If even for only a day. I imagine having sex with her in the cleansing room under the running water. Pinning her to the side of the shower and entering her as I kiss her. Now that I have the doctor's extra information about the size of her vagina, I can add it to my fantasy. My dick pushed inside of her so tightly...

"When she's fully trained I hope that I'll be able to experience sex with her," the doctor says. "I'd love to fuck her holding that tail."

"I prefer her defiant spirit," Kaelin says, "I don't care about her body. It's her heart. She's so rebellious you can see it in her eyes. No doubt she'd love a strong hand. Spanking. Being tied up. Being dominated. I'm sure that's what Aefre is doing right now and I envy him."

Unable to block them out all I can think is, *This is what makes me different.* I don't want her for either of those reasons, *Mon Dieu,* Je l'adore, truly. I adore her. Thinking about that, it's not long before I'm coming hard into the doctor's vial which he holds for me.

"That's it, Ember. Stroke it out. You know how to do it. Good boy."

I look down as the clear medical container seals automatically with my sticky white semen in it. I don't ask what the doctor's going to do with it. I never do. The truth is I don't want to know. The less I know about genetic testing or children I've inadvertently fathered in the galaxy, the better. It's not that I don't care, I just want to be able to sleep at night.

"Should we wait?" the doctor asks, meeting my eyes.

I take a deep breath. *Do I need to masturbate to her again?* "Yes. Again."

"I thought so," says the doctor. "Those breasts are pretty amazing and you see her every day, bouncing."

"You like her defiance too, don't you Ember?" Kaelin asks me.

I nod. I don't want to discuss what I like about Briar with these men. She's mine in my mind even if she's not yet in reality.

"Do you want the same holo?" the doctor asks me. "Or we could get the feed from Aefre's room. You know he keeps it open to track his pets' progress."

Do I want to see Aefre fucking Briar? I'm so tempted. I meet the doctor and Kaelin's eyes. I know they want to watch it.

"If we turn that on," Kaelin says, "I'll have to relieve myself too."

"Same," says the doctor. "But there's nothing stopping us from watching it." The doctor checks something on his device that gives a readout of all the pets' health. "He's definitely had sex with her. There's semen in her vagina, mouth, throat..."

"I want to watch it," I say before I can think about it too much. I want to know. To torture myself. To see if she really loves him or to see if it's the same pet to trainer sex I had with Aefre.

The doctor and Kaelin share a smile. Three more vials for semen appear and the doctor begins the holo when the two other men have pulled down their trousers. This is new for me. Usually they're just watching me, but now all of us are masturbating together while watching Aefre and Briar. It's almost like we are worshipping Aefre in a strange god-like fashion, our semen the offering.

But I don't think about it too much because watching Aefre spank Briar reminds me of the sex I had with him.

"Oh grab her by that tail," the doctor says while pumping himself.

As I watch, I'm relieved that it's the same trainer to pet sex. There's no love or passion. It's all physical. All the way to the end when Briar licks all the semen from his grey body. She never looks at Aefre the way that she looks at me.

After we've all orgasmed our semen into the vials, I ask the doctor, "Can I keep the holo of her running?"

"No, but you can see it again if you behave. And that means no more talking to Ash in your human language or paying off the attendants for privacy. You can talk to her in Imperial or not at all."

I reluctantly answer, "Understood, Master Kaelin."

"And Ember," the doctor says catching my attention as Kaelin begins leading me out by my leash. "There's a high possibility that Aefre will want to breed you and Ash if you win the Grand Championships. So I have something more to look forward to. I know I'd love to watch you rub your furry genitals together. Humans, half-Imperial, half-beasts," he smiles at me.

"Good" I say as convincingly as I can. I've been bred before. It was my second sexual experience after Aefre trained me. The first was with Aefre and the second under his watchful eye a year later with a human woman. I didn't even know her real name. Only her pet name, Fawn. She had brown skin and dark brown hair. She was gorgeous and more than willing. She told me I was the most handsome man she'd ever seen.

All of our trainers were there, including the doctor. I wasn't even allowed off my leash because human males couldn't be trusted in breeding situations. Aefre dictated everything I should do to her and I did it. Was I aroused by the sight of Fawn. Yes. Did she like me? I think so. Did we both orgasm? Yes. She orgasmed twice. First I licked her between her legs exactly how Aefre told me to. It was embarrassing that I didn't know how to bring a woman to orgasm then. Next, I entered her with my cock. I'd never had sex like that before and I came quickly. Finally, I massaged her clitoris to make sure she orgasmed again for a better chance of pregnancy. She kissed me on the cheek afterward and told me I was sweet, but it wasn't as real as kissing Briar. It wasn't even as real as masturbating to a holo of Briar running.

How is that possible? I might have even fathered a child with Fawn and I don't even think about her or that experience often. But Briar is always on my mind.

My thoughts are interrupted as Kaelin pauses in the hallway. "We need to return to the medical center. There's one more thing I forgot."

Immediately, we turn and return. The doctor is waiting.

"I knew you'd forgotten," he says to Kaelin. "Ember," the doctor says to me, taking off my leash and guiding me toward the holographic room. "I'm glad you came to masturbate tonight. Your cortisol levels have been too high, and your lack of appetite and irregular bowel movements are classic signs of stress. So I've arranged a pastoral feeding session for you. It was supposed to be tomorrow, but since you're here now..."

I'm ushered into a room with a holographic human woman. She beckons to me. And I go to her. I sit next to her as she opens her shirt and takes out her breast. She offers it to me and I take it. Sucking the milk from her nipple. The woman is a holograph but the milk is real. Donated from someone somewhere in the Empire. A human or an Imperial woman, I don't know. But these feeding sessions are mandatory to alleviate stress in all males, human and Imperial alike. Another reminder that even though men command my life here, women command theirs, and hence these strange habits they have.

There was a time when I found this repulsive, but now it's a fact of life. I revert to being a baby again. I suck both of her nipples until there's no milk left as she gently combs her fingers through my hair. It's so comforting and safe.

As I emerge from the feeding room, feeling completely relaxed now, I hear the doctor assuring Kaelin that physically I am where I should be now. "Mild increases in oxytocin and endorphins, and reduced cortisol. His heart rate and respiration have also stabilized." When he sees me he asks, "Do you want to masturbate again? I know how breastfeeding can trigger that."

"No," I say. "Not today."

Kaelin attaches my leash and leads me out. We're both quiet as we walk through the corridors. When we reach the pet sleeping quarters, he undoes the leash. "You should sleep very well now, Ember."

I don't reply but just enter, and quickly slide into my bed, the cool sheets a stark contrast to the heat of my thoughts. As much as I want to mull over my feelings for Briar, I let sleep take me. Perhaps, in my dreams, I'll find the clarity I crave, un moyen d'éclaircir ce chaos dans ma tête, to clear the chaos in my mind.

CHAPTER 29

AEFRE

Ash and Ember stand at the starting line, fully aware that I've changed today's parameters. They always sense when I do, and they know exactly why. Time is ticking away and we don't have much time before the Grand Championships.

I watch from my elevated control pedestal. The first few obstacles are familiar: physical endurance tests designed to force them into cooperation.

Despite their little incident in the cleansing room, they work together better than I anticipated. Ember's recent insolence has tempered under the prospect of winning the Grand Championship and the expectation of breeding with Ash. In the meantime, I tolerate his awkward human affections to reinforce their partnership. And Ash, in turn, clings to him for human connection, but looks to me for sexual gratification. It serves us all. But it's a precarious balance.

At the halfway point, I shift the program. The atmosphere changes noticeably, and I see Ash and Ember realize something's off. She backs away worriedly and he hesitates, scanning the altered course.

Good.

A towering spider materializes in Ash's path, its legs covered in bristling hairs, its mandibles glinting with simulated venom. She freezes instantly.

"Move forward," I say, my voice deliberately calm.

She doesn't budge. Her heart rate spikes on the collar readout.

Ember steps in front of her, shielding her from the hologram.

"Briar," he says, it's an immediate transgression. I send a minor shock through his collar for using her human name. "It's not real," he tells her in pristine Imperial. "You can handle this."

She wavers, but ultimately takes a shaky breath and steps closer to the spider. It mirrors her movements, forcing her to pass directly under its form. She hesitates again, uttering something in her human language. Another spider appears behind her, and she screams.

"I can't! It's too scary!" she shouts in accented Imperial.

My fingers hover over the console, prepared to cut the simulation short, but I'll give Ember one more chance to calm her.

"It can't hurt us," he insists, voice gentler than I expected. "I promise. I won't let anything hurt you, Briar." Another jolt for him for repeating her human name.

Amazingly, Ash pushes forward, taking halting steps until she crosses the edge of the hologram. The spider dissolves into light, leaving her trembling, but triumphant. That's progress.

Ember faces his own trial next, in an instant, the holographic arena shifts into a savage battleground. Towering spires of rock jut skyward, and the floor beneath him rumbles with hidden machinery. Emerging from the darkness is a massive, four-legged beast, snarling, muscled, and bristling with bony spines. An artifact is tucked behind the creature, perched on a ledge. It's clear that retrieving it will be Ember's task.

"Retrieve the artifact," I command. "Prove your strength."

I watch the readings on his collar. Initial spikes of adrenaline, surging cortisol, and traces of fear despite him knowing it's not real. But it can still kill him, hologram or not, if he loses and I choose not to stop the program.

The beast roars, pounding the ground with its forelimbs.

Ember hesitates, scanning for weak points as his breath tightens. He tells Ash to stay safe in a corner and she obeys him.

Then lunges forward for the beast.

The creature swipes with razor-sharp claws, but Ember dodges them effortlessly, rolling to the side. He counters with a sharp kick at its hind leg. Pain flares in his collar readout. He's gotten too close and taken a hit.

Driven by the urgency of my command, he feints left, then scrambles behind the beast toward the artifact's ledge. The creature roars again, furious, but Ember ducks and with another burst of speed, he jumps, snatching the artifact before the beast can react.

As soon as the prize is in his hands, the holographic beast dissolves.

Ember collapses to his knees with the object clutched tightly to his chest.

Ash and Ember regroup near the final obstacle, both breathing hard, their coordination still intact, and they manage to finish together, just as required.

It's adequate, but far from flawless. The Grand Championships will present far harsher challenges and exploit much deeper vulnerabilities. These were elementary.

I watch them from my elevated platform. I sense complacency lurking beneath their exhaustion.

"Ash, Ember. Today was acceptable," I say, voice echoing through the gymnasium, "but hardly worthy of Grand Champions. You're capable of more, far more. And I expect it. Tomorrow we will train harder."

I let those words settle before motioning for the attendants to take them to the cleansing room.

CHAPTER 30

BRIAR

In the dim light of the cages in the shower room, I lean as close to the bars of my cage as I can. Gabriel is in the cage next to mine, his face barely visible in the half-light. His voice is low, barely more than a breath, but in his words, I can hear the trance of something I can't quite articulate. *Hope?*

"I'm telling you, he's real," Gabriel whispers, his words slipping through the tiny gaps between us. "Gael the Returner. Half-Imperial, half-human. Il existe. He's rescued human pets before."

"You don't really believe that?" I whisper back. "It sounds like something other pets would make up to keep from losing our minds."

"It's not just a story," he insists, his voice firm but still soft enough that no one else can hear. "I've heard about him from others. During the competitions, all the pets are put in one area, le centre des animaux, and that's when we have free time to talk. He's out there, Briar."

I want to believe him, but I can't. I've not been here long, but I don't think the galaxy is a place where miracles happen. We're property, nothing more. And even if someone like Gael does exist, the idea that he'd swoop in and save us from a ship like this... impossible.

And as much as I don't like certain aspects of this life, there are others I do. To my shame. I enjoy Aefre touching me. I enjoy performing for him. I enjoy my talks with Gabriel. And maybe this is the best that I can hope for for the rest of my life. I know what it's like to lose, I lost my parents and then I lost Earth and now I'm afraid to lose what little I have here.

"How would he even know we're here and want to be rescued?" I ask, my voice sharp despite my attempt to keep it quiet. "We're on one of the most secure Imperial ships in the galaxy according to you. Aefre isn't going to send him an invitation."

"Gael has his ways," he says. "He has contacts. Imperials who are sympathetic, who help him. There's always a point of contact at the Grand Championships."

"And how does he get past security?"

Gabriel hesitates, and for a moment, I think I've won the argument. But then he exhales slowly, his fingers tapping lightly against the bars. "He doesn't do it alone," he says quietly. "He has a crew. Humans, Imperials, hybrids. Ils travaillent ensemble. They work together."

"And then what?" I whisper. "Even if he could rescue us, where would we go? What would we do? We're... we're pets, Gabriel. That's all anyone sees us as. I have a fucking tail that's stuck into me like it's natural." I hold back the tears. "I'm an animal."

He speaks in a low, soothing tone. "Briar, I understand how it feels wrong, mon Dieu, I do. But there are so many species in this galaxy with tails, some that stand equal to or above the Imperials. They're not seen as animals or lesser beings."

"Humans don't have tails!" I cry harder.

"Ma chérie, listen to me. You're more than any physical trait they force on you. You're clever and fearless. I've seen it and I've felt it. C'est ça that's all that truly matters, not whether or not you have a tail."

"You think I'm fearless?" I wipe my eyes.

"You're... magnifique, Briar," he whispers, slipping my human name past his lips like silk. "And I promise you Gael and his crew will not see you as an animal. For Gael we are people who have the right to freedom. Survivors. He doesn't just rescue us, he gives us a chance to live again."

The word *freedom* lingers on the humid air in the cleansing room. I want to believe Gabriel, but freedom feels like a dream too distant to reach right now, like the stars, like my parents. Just a word for something I'll never have again.

"I don't know if I want to risk what little I have here," I admit.

I glance at Gabriel through the bars again, his jaw set. He believes this. He really believes it. And he's frustrated I don't.

Aefre comes to collect me from the cleansing room well after Kaelin took Gabriel away. He puts my leash on and leads me back to his quarters. Once we're inside he says, "I have a treat for you, good girl."

I look up at him expectantly. From a nearby table he shows me two long silver pieces of jewelry. "For your nipples. Should I put them on for you?"

"Yes, Master Aefre," I reply and watch as he takes out the small bars in my nipple piercings, which feels so strange to have removed and see the large holes in my nipples, and then fills those holes with the ornate silver pieces that hang down past my belly button. The memory of the Imperial woman riding Aefre replays in my mind like a tidal wave. "This is *my* fantasy."

"I know," Aefre says as he puts my other nipple studs somewhere safe. When he returns to stand in front of me, he picks up the ends of the nipple jewelry and leads me into the bedroom, tits first.

At first it hurts to have my nipples pulled so hard, but soon, the pain turns to pleasure and then anticipation.

"On your knees," Aefre demands.

"Yes Master Aefre," I obey. I watch him as he takes off his clothing slowly putting it away. Then he goes into the bathroom for some time. He even showers while I'm still here on my knees. But I don't' move. I just wait.

When he comes back into the bedroom he has another silver object in his hand. I'm worried it's the chastity device.

"Calm yourself," he says, and pushes me forward so I'm on my hands and knees. "Today is your reward for being a good girl."

If I were a cat, I would be purring. But I'm a woman so my core is preparing itself for penetration. However, I tense when I feel Aefre's deft fingers circling my ass and then he spits into it as he circles it some more. I don't want to be ass fucked. I want to have sex with him. But I worry if I say 'no' now he'll put the chastity belt on me.

I decide to wait. But as he continues to rub around my anus I become worried.

He spits again into my ass and then inserts something. It's not as big as his cock nor is it too much. It's warm and it feels, strange but not unpleasant. I feel... full.

Aefre slaps my ass a few times and says, "It's to increase your enjoyment. I know you don't understand, but trust my decision, Ash. I know what all my pets want."

I don't answer. This is one of those times he doesn't want me to. He likes to pretend I don't understand half of the time.

Aefre takes my nipple chains in his hands. "Stand up. Now jump as many times as you can with the heels of your feet touching your ass."

This is one of the training exercises he makes me do. It's strange he's making me do it now. But I do it. My breasts bouncing not as wildly as usual because he's holding my nipples tightly with the silver chains. And the butt plug making my movements seem strange. I look at Aefre's face as he watches me. This is *his* fantasy.

"Stop," he tells me and I immediately do so, out of breath. I must have been doing that for five minutes as I watched his girthy ridged grey dick become erect. I think he's going to tell me get on the bed now, but he surprises me by saying, "Stay."

I do and wait, pushing my thighs together, thinking about riding him with the silver jewelry on my nipples. Even now I love the erotic way the chains tug on my nipples and fall against my stomach.

Aefre returns with a rectangular box that turns into a low table with different size dildos on it. He uses the silver chains attached to my breasts to lead me to the first dildo in the row. "This is a Lyran penis," he says as if that means something to me. "Impale yourself on it."

I want to be a good girl so I get my prize of riding Aefre so I hover over the dildo. It looks a lot like a human man's penis, except with a little more texture. I hold Aefre's green gaze as I lower myself onto it. Suddenly it warms and comes alive, the whole little table begins moving up and down. I'm shocked and try to move my body off it but I can't. Then prickles come out from the dick and scratch the inside of my vagina. I scream. Then the dildo lets go.

I rub between my legs, wishing I could rub the inside of my vaginal canal. I feel like my vagina just walked through a briar patch.

"I'm sorry," Aefre says. Then before I can say anything else, he has the doctor on the comms.

"No," I try to interject. "No doctor."

"The doctor is on his way."

I'm sure he is.

Minutes later the doctor enters. Aefre explains the situation and the doctor has me lie down on Aefre's bed. Aefre stands to the side as the doctor unnecessarily touches every inch of my body and then uses a polymer to heal the inside of my vagina.

"Good as new," he says. Then he looks at Aefre and asks, "I know this is presumptuous but may I stay and watch?" He adds, "For professional reasons."

I want to scream 'No!' I want to ride Aefre. This is my treat. But I say nothing. Aefre wouldn't like it.

"Not this time, Ash is still shy," Aefre says and I'm relieved.

The doctor packs up his equipment and leaves clearly disappointed.

My attention turns back to Aefre. He picks up the nipple jewelry and says, "Now where were we? Oh yes the table. I had it programmed for the wrong species. Clearly you're human."

"What is this?" I ask.

"At some of the competitions there are informal side games for female pets. This is one of them. Perhaps it's not for you. The other two females like it."

It occurs to me then that he has sex with them too. Probably in the same way he has sex with me. And I don't know why, but that doesn't bother me. Most likely because I'm the only one with him here now and we're so close to having sex again. And I want his cock inside of me so much. "Please Master Aefre, I want to ride you," I say directly, risking his annoyance. He doesn't like it when I ask for things.

"Yes, but I want you to work for it first. That's *my* fantasy tonight."

"What about with Ember?" I say and I hold my breath as I wait for Aefre's answer. His face is unreadable.

But don't ask don't get.

CHAPTER 31

GABRIEL

The doctor comes unannounced to the pets' sleeping quarters. "Ember," he says, "get out of bed. You're wanted."

I obey without hesitation.

However, when I grab my clothing, the doctor says, "You won't need your clothing."

As I exit the room naked, he attaches a leash to my collar. I don't ask where we are going but it's obvious to me after a few minutes in the corridor that I'm being taken to Aefre's quarters.

We enter and I'm surprised to find Aefre and Briar in the middle of what I can only assume is foreplay because Aefre is also naked and Briar is wearing magnificent silver jewelry in her nipples with chains long enough for her to be lead around by. I know the sex pets on military ships often wear these but a pet here has never had them. I didn't think Aefre had such fantasies. And it worries me he's playing them out with Briar.

"Ember," Aefre says, "Ash wanted you here."

My eyes fly to Briar in surprise. *Why would she want me here like this?*

Aefre motions to a table full of dildos. I've seen that many times before and what he makes female pets do. Fifi hated that. She said that at the competitions there would always be an informal private event between the female pets and they'd have to orgasm on each dildo to win.

"Ash doesn't want to play with this," he gestures to the table. "And suggested we play with you instead."

My mind can't process this, but my physical body is already aroused by the idea.

"And I thought it would be a good test for her. We know she bit off a human man's penis when she was with the Octopods, but since she's been here, she's shown no signs of aggression. And so I thought, why not test her with you."

I find my voice and ask, "What do you mean, Master Aefre?" As far as I know, sucking on a man's penis is forbidden in the Empire. No one has ever put their mouth on me like that. I imagine it would feel good...and having Briar do it. On her knees before me... the mental image makes me so hard. I don't even care that there's a crowd here. Nothing I do is ever private.

Aefre takes the ends of Briar's silver nipple jewelry and jerks on the chains so her nipples are seductively stretched and dragged as she follows with slow steps.

"Goddesses, I never get tired of seeing that," the doctor says. "Those nipples being pulled."

"On your knees," Aefre says to Briar and she obeys. "Open your mouth wide." Then Aefre looks at the doctor, "Use the leash and bring Ember forward."

I stand still looking at Briar with her waiting open mouth. "This is forbidden," I say.

"Not for humans," the doctor laments. "You have no souls so you can enjoy this sinful act. You'll never go to the Afterlife as a pet. You have nothing to lose. Let her suck on your cock, Ember. Just look at you. You're already ready for her. I rarely see you so aroused. And it'll be a much better memory for you to masturbate to, then a holo of her running."

I look down and make eye contact with Briar. "Yes," I mouth the word. Then say softly, "I touched myself thinking about you."

I can't read Briar's expression. *Is she disgusted?*

The doctor interrupts my thoughts and says to Aefre, "Just so you're aware, Ember's penis is much larger than Ash's mouth. If he fits his entire penis in, it will go down her throat and she may vomit."

"I understand," Aefre says. "But this is a treat for Ash and I know humans love this. I've seen it many times in the play areas around the galaxy. But I've never allowed Ember to partake because..."

The doctor interrupts, "Because you coddle him sexually. Look at him now, he's confused. He doesn't understand, but his body reacts."

And the doctor is correct. I'm baffled but aroused. My penis is erect and when the doctor tugs on my leash I step forward. Then Aefre says, "Ember, show us that you trust Ash and put your penis in her mouth."

I put my hand at the base of my cock, but I hesitate as I look in her green eyes. Did she really bite off a man's penis? Can I really trust her?

"Come on, Ember. She's made her decision either way. And I'm ready to reattach it just in case." A whole minute passes. "Do you trust her or not?" the doctor says, husky anticipation lacing his voice. I've known him long enough to know that the next words out of his mouth are, "Nothing better than watching furry humans fucking like animals."

I'm a human show for them, just like she is. I look down and make eye contact with Briar. *Does she want this?* There's no question about my wanting her to do this. But if she doesn't want it, I'll resist. I can't figure it out, so I ask, which I know I'll receive a punishment for. "Will you put me into your mouth, Briar? If not, I'll fight this."

"Don't speak in your human language," Aefre says his words are predictably followed by a shock through my collar.

Briar doesn't speak but I watch as she sticks out her pink tongue and licks the tip of my dick. Words cannot describe how wonderful that feels. Then as if she were reading my mind, she puts her whole mouth around me and begins moving back and forth.

Somewhere in the background I hear the doctor say, "Humans love this barbaric stuff. Look at her tail sway. That's how it moves when she's happy."

"Watch them closely to make sure she doesn't bite him," Aefre says. "Ash, put your hands on the back of your head and move in and out more. Ember, touch the back of her throat with your penis."

Before I can question this, Briar puts her hands over mine and leads them to the back of her head. She looks up at me, my penis in her mouth, desire consuming her and I begin moving my hips, thrusting my hard organ in and out of her mouth. I can feel my piercings touching the back of her throat and I have to use all of my control not to orgasm right now. This whole scene and all the sensations are so overwhelming. But I know I'm not allowed to come until Aefre allows it.

"Faster, Ember," Aefre commands me.

"Yes Master Aefre," I obey. This feels like a breeding session, but it's different because I'm with Briar and as far as I understand it, she wants this too. And she's allowing me to fuck her mouth which is apparently a very human thing. I love this. And I don't know much about sex, but I don't think anything can be breed this way, except maybe teeth?

Then when Aefre tells me, "Orgasm now," I do it. I groan and clutch Briar's hair as I come hard into her mouth.

And when he says, "Suck all of that down, Ash." She milks the semen from me like it was the water of life and I watch her like she's a goddess. Believing in this moment that she's the most wonderful creature in the world. And relieved when I come back to my senses that she didn't bite my penis off when she had the chance.

"Well done, Ember," the doctor says to me. "You're very brave putting your penis in her mouth after what she did. The way you were enjoying yourself I don't think there was any way you would have withdrawn even if she bit down."

Aefre pats both Ash and me on the head and says, "You're truly bonded as a team now. I'm glad to see it."

"Now my little pet," Aefre says to Briar, pulling on her silver nipple chains, "You're going to lay on your back, on the edge of the bed, your legs open and make yourself orgasm for all of us to watch. I'll hand your nipple chains over to Ember as a reward for him being so brave."

Briar positions herself on the bed like Aefre said and I hold the chains to her nipples. I want to pull and play with them, of course, but I don't want to hurt her either.

Aefre stands beside me and coaches me through it. He instructs me how to pull and release to give her the most pleasure. And then when Briar orgasms for us, she's only looking at me and without thinking, I rush between her legs and lick all of her desire up. Lapping it up like an animal.

The doctor pulls on my leash and Aefre punishes me with the collar, but they're going to have to drag me off of her. With my face between her legs she orgasms again and then the two of them manage to drag me away.

"Human men," the doctor says as if that explains everything.

"C'est différent. J'aime Briar. This is different I love her."

CHAPTER 32

AEFRE

It was a brilliant idea to bring Ember here. It allowed me to strengthen the bond between him and Ash and at the same time let Ash believe I'd given her something special. It was also convenient to test whether or not Ash is still a danger to human males. Now, I know I don't have to put a muzzle on her every time she's in a human play pen with males. I will use the chastity device though. The way she just orgasmed with Ember proves her preference for human men.

"Now for your treat, Ash," I say to her. "On your knees."

She gets on her knees, excitement in her eyes, and then I lay down on my back. "Impale your furry human sex on me, pet."

She of course looks at Ember.

"Don't look at Ember. Look at me. This is what you wanted. Ember, will enjoy watching you and learning."

Neither Ash nor Ember replies. But I feel something silent passes between my pets. And why not? If I were Ember, jealousy would be raging through me. And that's the point. I'm the one in charge and they both will obey.

I pull and swing the silver chains to get her moving. "Ride me, my sweet human pet. Slowly at first. That's it." I watch Ash as she moves her hips slowly over my own. Then I begin to use the chains more forcefully, pulling hard on her nipples, when I want her to increase her speed. "That's a good girl. You like this don't you? You're so tight and wet."

As I get closer to my own climax, I'm directing her hard with the chains and am satisfied with her desire to please me, especially in front of Ember. It's necessary for her to separate her relationship to me as her trainer and her human relationship to Ember as his partner and then feel how we all work together.

After I orgasm, I move her off of me and say, "Lick me clean, Ash."

She obeys while all three of us watch her. The only sound in the room is her pink tongue and mouth cleaning my body.

I think this is going to be the end, but then the doctor says, "May I make a request?"

I nod as I watch Ash lick the last remaining drops of semen from my body.

"I'd like to see the human pets have sex. Look at poor Ember, his penis is fully erect again."

I glance over to Ember and the doctor's not wrong. I think this through as the doctor continues talking. "You know there's nothing more adorable than seeing furry humans match their bodies up together. Their fur rubbing against each other. And they've been working so hard. I know this would be good for Ember's mental health. His hormones still aren't where I'd like them to be."

"*They have been working hard,*" I agree. "Maybe it's better they do this with supervision now in case something goes wrong," I say, imagining Ash's pink hairy sex against Ember's golden fur. I, like the doctor, also find it adorable the way humans look together. And I'm confident that the bond between myself and Ash is stronger than hers to Ember.

"Ash do you want Ember to put his pierced penis inside of you?" I ask.

She looks at me with surprise and a red color spreads over her cheeks.

"It's natural that you'd want that," I tell her. "You're human."

"Tell us what you desire, Ash," says the doctor.

She doesn't take her eyes off me. *Good.* She knows who's in charge.

"Look at Ember. He wants you badly," I say. When she doesn't look at Ember, I force her head over and direct her gaze between his legs.

"Look at her collar light up with arousal. It's so primal," the doctor says enthusiastically.

"Ember you can have Ash. She doesn't need to vocalize it."

CHAPTER 33

BRIAR

I didn't realize that when I suggested Gabriel join us, that *this* was going to happen. That Aefre was going to test my reputation of biting off human men's dicks. But what really touched me was that Gabriel was willing to risk serious punishment rather than take from me what I wasn't prepared to give. And that he didn't believe what the aliens had said about me, even if it was true. I did bite off Big's penis. But that feels like it happened in another lifetime or in a dream. I can't imagine ever doing that to any of the men here. But then again, none of them are threatening to rape me either. Coercing me, maybe.

But it was a nice touch, reminding me of Gabriel's personality, because I was more than willing to give him a blowjob in front of the doctor and Aefre. To show them how much I prefer Gabriel to their alienness. That I'd do anything for him. And that I was turned on by seeing his large, pierced human penis and imagining it in my mouth.

After Gabriel's penis had been thrusting and pushing against the back of my throat, I longed to feel how that piercing would feel going in and out of me. A much more satisfying hole, I'm sure.

I meet Gabriel's golden eyes, hoping that he doesn't care about sloppy seconds, but given how the *Luminous Arc* is run, I highly doubt it.

A part of me wishes we were alone. But another part of me, the new Briar, enjoys this uncomfortable newness in my life.

The constant gaze someone always has on me. Someone is always looking out for me. I'm well taken care of. I'm a beloved pet.

And Aefre is always thinking about me. Monitoring my physical and mental life. Why should I feel embarrassed that he monitors this too? It makes me feel... safe. Loved. Protected.

I never felt this on Earth.

I lean back in my master's bed and open my legs wide in Gabriel's direction.

He stands between Aefre and the doctor. His large, erect, pierced penis is surrounded by copious amounts of amber hair, while his eyes, fully dilated are fixed on me.

I want him to take me like the barbarian he looks like. I want to play out the human fantasy for these aliens.

Aefre unleashes Gabriel like he's a wild animal, "Go get her Ember."

Gabriel steps toward me quickly like I'm the prize in one of his challenges. He growls as he pulls on my ankles to shift me into a position that he can easily pick me up from and in the next second, I'm being held so tightly in his strong arms, my feet dangling off the floor, I can hardly think.

Gabriel kisses me roughly, his mouth pulling at my lower lip as if he might devour me, then, the next second, his tongue in my mouth, mimicking the rhythm of his hips against mine. His large, calloused hands are everywhere, taking turns, one holding me under my arm, the other fondling my body frantically caressing me like he may never have another chance at this.

I can hear myself moaning. *This is nothing like sex with Aefre. This is real. This is animalistic passion.*

Gabriel makes a small growling noise again and pushes me up against a wall. Then he quickly finds my used and wet entrance with his fingers and thrusts his large, pierced cock inside me with one strong push.

I whimper loudly with satisfaction. It's so big and at this angle with the piercing both pleasing and enticing I feel like I'm going to come again.

I let out a gasp as he pounds into me at a steady rate. "Yes," I say in English unable to speak any other language now, not wanting him to stop or do anything differently.

Gabriel whispers something French in my ear, "Tu es ma lumière dans l'obscurité."

I have no idea what he said, but I never want him to stop fucking me like this. And even if I wanted to ask him, I can't because I cannot form a word this feels so fucking good.

I hear the doctor in my periphery, "That's it Ember, fuck her like an animal. Without any preamble. Take her like the barbarian you are."

Gabriel's holding me against the wall, his mouth on mine his hard cock pumping into me searching for release. Finally, he groans and grasps my breast hard which brings on my own orgasm and we tremble together against the wall.

"Good show," the doctor says.

"Well done," Aefre says with the same tone as when we've done well on the obstacle course.

Gabriel pulls back a little and makes eye contact with me. His amber eyes speak volumes about everything that just happened.

Even when we are having sex, we are show pets. Nothing is private here.

He gives me one last kiss with his eyes open, his lips pulling my bottom lip slowly as he sets me on my shaky feet.

I look up at the doctor and Aefre and say in my best Imperial, "I forgot you were here."

I hear Gabriel laugh a little behind me and then we both get shocked by our collars, but the jolt of pain only intensifies the trembling from my last orgasm. The real orgasm. The all-encompassing one. Or rather the only one that really mattered to me.

Aefre then orders me, "Ash on your knees and lick Ember clean. You may have fucked like humans, but you'll still finish up like good Imperial pets."

I get to my knees, look up at Ember, and then take his whole penis in my mouth again. It touches the back of my throat and I push my thighs together wishing it were somewhere else.

He closes his eyes and leans back.

Aefre shocks me on the collar. "Bad girl. Not like that. Lick it up. No sucking."

I release Gabriel from my mouth and lick as he, Aefre, and the doctor watch me. And I'm enjoying myself. Is this what captivity has done to me? Or have I always had these tendencies?

The morning begins like any other training day, though I wake up feeling off. There's a dull ache low in my abdomen. I push it aside. Pain isn't new here, it's as constant as the collars around our necks.

Aefre dresses me in the same kind of thin leotard that reveals my breasts, underarms and sex like he always does, but today I feel like it's tighter than usual.

Kaelin is already waiting in the training area when Aefre drops me off. He's leaning against the console, scrolling through something on his data pad. When he glances up and sees me, he says, "I heard you got a big treat last night, Ash. I hope that doesn't mean you're going to be lazy today."

I don't reply. He doesn't want me to.

"And you didn't ask for me to join?" Kaelin asks with a tone that makes me uncomfortable.

I pretend like I don't understand him. "Where's Ember?"

"He'll join us later. He's with the doctor now."

I mull over that briefly. What could he be doing with the doctor? "Is he sick?"

"No. But it's beyond your understanding, Ash. Now come on. It's time to train."

The training course today is another maze of shifting platforms, glowing obstacles, and drones. My body already feels heavy as I stretch, the ache in my stomach sharper now, radiating down into my thighs. It's not until I take my place at the starting line that it clicks.

My period.

Fuck.

Of course, it all makes sense now. I was so horny yesterday and not just from Aefre's methods or Gabriel's handsome looks, but my own biology. I'm always not quite myself the day before my period, but it's difficult to track because I've always been so irregular. And obviously here without a calendar or my phone, there's no tracking of anything. All the days are the same. If Aefre's culture recognizes weekends he doesn't take them.

"Begin," Kaelin commands.

I take off and I can already tell I'm slower than usual.

The first set of platforms shifts beneath my feet, and I struggle to find my balance. The drones zip toward me with precision. I dodge one, but the second one grazes my shoulder, sending a jolt of electricity through me. I stumble, barely catching myself before I hit the ground.

Kaelin's voice booms through the training area, "Focus, Ash!"

I push forward, ignoring the sudden cramping in my abdomen. If I had any hope the blood would wait until after training, that's gone now. I can feel the wetness on my thighs. *Damn. I thought I'd been exercising so much my body had stopped menstruating.* A fairy tale. And I'm worried about how these aliens will deal with my female bodily function.

The course shifts again and the platform tilts sharply. I jump to the next one, landing awkwardly. I feel blood everywhere on my thighs. I glance down at my larger than life pubic hair and the pink tips are soaked in red blood.

Kaelin yells, "Stop!"

I freeze mid-step, my chest heaving. The room goes silent except for the buzzing of the drones.

Kaelin steps onto the training floor, his eyes narrowing as he approaches me.

My blood runs cold, no pun intended, as I watch his gaze drop to my vulva and upper thighs.

"You're bleeding," he says unnecessarily.

I swallow. *No shit, Sherlock.*

"You should have reported this."

"What?"

Kaelin steps closer. He reaches a hand between my legs and runs his fingers through the bloody hair bringing them back up to his nose and inhaling. "There's nothing more sensual than a woman menstruating." Then, as if he's fucking Count Dracula, he puts his finger, wet with my blood, into his mouth savoring the taste.

"Ah, I remember," Kaelin says, probably noticing my expression of horror. "Humans don't know. Menstrual blood is powerful. So much so, the doctor will want to collect it."

"For what?"

"Stem cells, immune cells, platelets, exosomes, and hormones. Women are the givers of life in all regards," his voice almost sounds reverent when he says the last sentence.

I'm shocked, but who am I to question their medicine? They fly around in spaceships and have technology beyond my comprehension. I double-over then with a fresh wave of cramps.

"Come with me Ash. We need to go to the medical center."

Kaelin doesn't wait for an answer before he hoists me up into his arms. Once we enter the medical center he doesn't wait for any of the medics, he takes me directly to an area that's more private, and dare I say, almost comfortable. Then he lays me down on a bed in the middle of the room that looks like it's got many functions. After pressing a few buttons to my right, my feet are up in the air and I'm spread eagle. Not waiting for the doctor, he attaches something inside of me.

"This menstruating bed is the same kind Imperial women use," he tells me, as if that's supposed to make me feel special. "You see here on the panel," he points to my right, "you can adjust the heat and massage functions. I know you can't read, but if you want something ask me, I'll activate it for you." I'm surprised Kaelin is being so thoughtful, it's a complete one-eighty from how he usually acts. "This bed is specifically designed to collect your blood, but may I lick what has already been lost along your furry folds and down your legs? I promise to make you orgasm at least once to help with the cramping. I can see you're in a lot of pain from your collar's readouts."

I knew he wasn't being kind without an ulterior motive.

I want to say, 'no,' but after last night I feel like what's the difference now if I let Kaelin eat me out? If he wants to lick all the blood off my body, he can go ahead and do it. And he's not wrong about the orgasm. I am in pain and that would help. But of course I'm going to be thinking about Gabriel the entire time.

Once Kaelin begins, lapping up the blood like a zombie, loudly licking his lips and groaning with pleasure, I must admit, his ministrations feel really good. This may be the best celebration of my period I've ever experienced and that thought makes me laugh a little. *Who is excited by period blood?*

Aliens.

I lean my head back with a smile and let him go at it. I'm so sensitive right now, so I moan when he puts his strong hands under me, grabbing an ass cheek with each hand to gently hoist my hips up to get the blood that crept up the back.

In this new position, I can feel the collection device inside me, lightly sucking. Like the air at the dentist's office.

Kaelin groans again. "You taste so good, Ash."

This is so wrong, but it feels so good.

"Orgasm for me. That's it. Good girl."

I come so hard and Kaelin makes growling noises of pleasure as he licks up all the blood.

When my muscles have settled, Kaelin looks up at me and a chill goes down my spine.

He looks exactly like a zombie from *Night of the Living Dead*, his grey skin, his big grey eyes delirious with desire and my blood all over his face and in his mouth. "You're divine, Ash. You know all women taste differently."

Not only does he like the strawberries and cream he's a fucking menstrual blood connoisseur.

I sit up to check the lower half of my body, I was covered in blood twenty minutes ago, but now Kaelin has licked me clean. And there's a tube like device running into my vagina.

"How long does this take?" I ask indicating the machine.

"A day or so. It's a delicate process and one that can't be rushed. Those stem cells are important for your health. You know if you were to have a nasty fall from one of the obstacles, your own blood could heal you better than any artificial technology."

I'm momentarily stunned by this revelation. Humans have been going through so much trouble getting stem cells out of bone marrow when it was in period blood all along. I guess this is one of the differences between a matriarchy and a patriarchy. Women's bodies in the Empire were probably studied first.

My thoughts are interrupted by Kaelin, "Aefre will want a taste of you too, that is, if he can convince the doctor to give up some of your blood. It's about the quantity. And since we've been working you so hard you haven't had your periods. But, mmm, you're truly exquisite in every way, Ash. So I'm sure some UCs will be exchanged today. A bribe from Aefre to remove the collection device for thirty minutes so he can have his taste."

CHAPTER 34

AEFRE

I've adjusted the obstacle course, raising the difficulty to simulate what they'll face in the Grand Championships, which is only two weeks away.

I tap a sequence of commands on the console. The floor shifts, revealing contoured platforms, metal beams, and a steep vertical climb that dominates the far corner. The overhead lights dim and then refocus on the newly exposed obstacles.

"Begin," I say.

Ash and Ember exchange a glance, silently deciding who will go first. Ember nods, taking the lead. He's an expert at this. Ash, on the other hand, struggles, still uncertain how to anticipate the obstacles or Ember's intentions. My instructions have been explicit, *You must function as one mind, or you will fail.* The challenges are too fast even for a moment's hesitation.

The first few obstacles go smoothly. A timed sprint over moving platforms, a tandem swing where they must grab onto a hanging bar in unison, and a coordinated dodge through low-level drones that fire at regular intervals. They stumble only slightly, with Ember offering a hand or a whispered Imperial cue each time Ash's hesitation threatens to slow them down.

I can't help but feel a small, private satisfaction. They're good. Almost good enough to be champions. If I can push them just a little bit more... they'll have it.

They arrive at the Tandem Wall Climb. It's a harsh, vertical structure with built-in grips that rotate unpredictably. Ember scales it quickly. He times each grip's rotation perfectly, seizing the best angles. Ash follows, but her eyes dart back and forth, and I notice the slight tremor in her leg. Her attention is split between the rotating grips and Ember's position above her. She's overthinking it.

"Just move, Ash," I instruct. "Ember is almost at the top. Don't lag behind. You're losing points."

She shoots a brief glance up at Ember again.

Foolish, I think.

In a blink of an eye, she misses a grip's rotation and is now hanging by one hand from the obstacle. She's panicking. Her hold is slipping.

Ember notices immediately and shimmies back down, leaning over to grab her hand. He pulls her upward, but the climb sequence is thrown off. The automated system registers this misalignment and ramps up the difficulty, a quirk of Kaelin's programming I left in place.

"Now!" I call out. "Both of you, jump to the ledge! Now!"

Ember, recognizing the tone of my voice, executes the maneuver quickly and flawlessly, hooking a hand on the top edge. Ash hesitates as she tries to mimic him, and her foot misses the rotating grip. Ember reaches down and barely catches her wrist. Now she's swinging in his grip. He attempts to anchor them both, but the sudden shift in weight triggers a mechanical fail-safe in the platform. It drops a fraction, then a fraction more, until the entire mechanism is tilted forward.

"Help me, Gabriel!"

"Pull her up," I say in a tone sharper than usual.

Ember braces, pulling with everything he's got, but Ash's fingers slip from his grasp. He tries again, lunging downward, but it's too late. She's lost her footing completely.

I leave my console as she tumbles down, hitting one of the lower outcroppings with a sickening thud before landing on a partial safety net. Her momentum bounces her off, and she slams into the side rail, rolling onto the floor. The net saved her from a lethal fall, but not from serious injury.

Ember yells something in his human tongue, an anguished sound that echoes in the gymnasium.

I grit my teeth. Kaelin or I would have shocked him for such an outburst under normal circumstances, but I have bigger concerns now. Quickly, I use my IC to summon the medical drones and direct them to the accident site while I hurry to Ash.

I'm worried as I see her crumpled on the floor, barely conscious.

Before I can reach her, Ember leaps down the structure without a thought for his own safety, dropping the last ten feet. He rushes to her side, gathering her limp body in his arms.

Ember glares at me with a rage I've not seen in him in years. "You pushed her too far. She's not ready!" he says.

I meet his eyes. "Put her down and let the medical drones attend to her."

Ember does as I say.

Then I say to him, "Ash fell because you two still haven't synchronized. You tried to save her, yes, but your bond is not strong enough. If you can't act as one, accidents will happen."

He looks like he's ready to lunge at me, but his attention turns to Ash when the drones finish stabilizing her and begin transferring her onto a hovering stretcher.

Ember and I both go to her side as she's elevated. I become concerned when I notice that her skin has gone pale, I check her collar's diagnostic display, and the numbers cascade in alarming red across the holographic screen:

Heart Rate: 192 bpm (critical)
Blood Pressure: 90/58 (borderline hypotension)
Cortisol: 600% above baseline
Adrenaline: nearing maximum tolerance
Shock Index: borderline, verging on collapse

A grim realization settles over me as I take in these readings.

The medical drones whisk her away and Ember dashes after them.

I follow as my mind races through contingency plans. If she can't pull through, if she's too injured to compete—No, that's not going to happen. Ash doesn't give up and she's strong.

When I arrive in the medical center, Ash is surrounded by the doctor and his assistants. Her readouts show erratic vitals.

Ember stands in the periphery watching everything, his own collar flashing red, but not from injury. When our eyes meet, I half expect him to charge. But he doesn't. Instead, he glares in silence, barely holding back tears.

It's not his connection to Ash that's the problem. It's hers to him. I realize as I watch the scene before me.

The doctor mutters something about "internal bleeding" and "hairline fractures." Another medic injects a coagulant, while a third stabilizes her spine. For a brief moment, I fear this might slip beyond their ability to repair, but then the monitor shows a stabilizing heartbeat.

I put my hand on Ember's shoulder. "I need to see you succeed," I say softly. "Both of you." My voice is calm, but each word carries undeniable seriousness that I know reaches him. "Her failing to keep up, your failing to protect her... all of it stems from a lack of true partnership. Blame me if you want, but unless you two become one, accidents like this will only continue as the obstacle course becomes more difficult."

The doctor interrupts us, "She's stable and will make a full recovery, but we'll need to keep her sedated for at least a day."

I tilt my head in acknowledgment, then shift my focus back to Ember. "When she's recovered, you'll return to training. She must learn to trust you."

He doesn't reply, simply turning his back on me to stand vigil at Ash's bedside. The medical attendants begin to move her to a recovery pod, and then the hum of machinery encompasses the room. The faint beeping of her heart rate monitor mirrors the tension in the room.

I linger for a few minutes and look at Ash through the window of the medical pod. *I could have lost her.*

Kaelin comes up behind me taking in the scene. The medics have dimmed the lights around her, creating a faint halo against her pale skin.

"Should I take Ember away? I don't know if it's good for him to see this," Kaelin says.

"Let him stay a little longer."

"I watched the video of what happened. Once she missed that first time, they would have had to move very fast to not have had the whole platform turn."

I nod. Replaying the whole thing in my mind. *Am I pushing her too hard?*

As if reading my mind, Kaelin says, "You've grown very attached to Wild One." He uses her old name when he wants to point out that she's just a pet. A human I bought. This isn't the first time he's noticed that I look at Ash differently.

"She is a pet, no more."

Kaelin arches an eyebrow, unconvinced. "You treat her even better than you do Mags."

I glare at him until he looks away, acknowledging my unspoken command to drop the subject. But his question refuses to be silenced. *Do I treat Ash like she's more than my pet?*

I exhale, forcing my expression into composure. Whether Kaelin is correct or not, I can't allow sentiment to derail our goal.

Yes, the course was difficult, but nothing beyond what they'll face in the Championship. If Ash can't manage this level, perhaps Ember needs to learn how to guide her more effectively.

CHAPTER 35

BRIAR

I hear the faint beeping of monitors before I open my eyes. My mind feels foggy, but slowly I begin to remember the accident. The moment my fingers slipped from Gabriel's grasp. I feel like I'm falling again in bed remembering it and I hold my hands around myself to make the memory stop. But I'll never forget the look on his face. Or my fear in that moment.

I thought I was going to die. *But clearly I didn't.*

Modern alien medicine. I bet they used some of my stem cells from my period blood. Thankfully Aefre didn't take it all.

The door slides open, and Aefre walks in flanked by two medics. None of them talk to me. Why would they? I'm a pet.

Aefre checks the monitors above my bed. My heart rate picks up involuntarily, the memory of him watching me fall still too fresh. Surely he could have done something.

"You're going to make a full recovery," Aefre says.

I almost died and you aren't even going to acknowledge that? Before I can form a response in Imperial that won't come with punishments from my collar, he nods to the medics behind him. One of them taps on a console near my bed and the collar around my neck tightens. My skin prickles, and a surge of warmth flares through my body.

Before I can ask if the doctor should be administering whatever I've just been given, Aefre assures me, "It's medicine to ease your suffering and speed up your recovery. And by the way, Ember would like to see you, if you want to see him that is? He, of course, blames himself."

"I want to see him," I say. I'm angry that Aefre is acting like this is all Gabriel's fault. It's not. Aefre created the obstacle course that was too difficult. But I'm afraid of being punished and still in shock after almost dying, so I say nothing about it.

"I'll leave you alone for a little while. I suggest you use this time wisely," he says and leaves the room.

A few seconds later, Gabriel appears in the doorway. He walks in quickly, stopping at the edge of my bed, his hands hovering over me as if he's unsure if he's allowed to touch me. "I'm so sorry. I couldn't hold on. I tried, but—"

"I'm okay. I know you tried your best." My heart beats faster and a strange warmth intensifies throughout my entire body. I wonder if it's the medicine Aefre just gave me or the relief of seeing Gabriel.

His fingers brush mine. "If I'd reacted faster—" His beautiful amber eyes are shining with guilt.

"It was me, I froze. I... I'm the one who miscalculated and lost my balance." My voice wavers, and I realize I'm on the verge of tears too.

Gabriel and I hold eye contact for a long time without saying anything. His eyes are full of emotions that I feel as well. Then he squeezes my hand, and a sudden wave of affection surges through me. Am I awake? *Is this real?* It feels real.

"When you hit that net—"

I squeeze his hand in return, that eerie sense of warmth returning and coursing through my veins. "I'm okay," I say again, though I'm not entirely certain that's true. I feel so... strange. In a good way, but not myself.

"We must train harder and Briar, you must trust me. I won't let this happen again."

"But how can we prevent it?"

Gabriel doesn't answer me.

In the corridor beyond the glass partition, I catch a glimpse of Aefre standing with Kaelin. I can't hear their conversation, but it looks tense. Kaelin's gaze is directed toward us for a second, and then he says something to Aefre, and Aefre shakes his head, looking worried.

"Gabriel," I say, using his true name under my breath. "Do you ever wonder if... if our feelings are our own?"

His expression darkens. "Mon Dieu, of course," he admits. "But I also know how I feel when I look at you. Even if they are messing with our minds, ma chérie, part of it must still be real. No alien technology can override human emotions for such a long period of time. I know when I look at you what's real. And if they could make me love just anyone then they would have done that before now. I've been here so long, but I've never loved anyone before you."

A tear slips down my cheek at his words. "Not even Fifi?"

It looks like I've stabbed him by asking the question, but I have to know.

"I didn't love Fifi the way I love you. She was my companion. When they forced us to breed... it drove us further apart. But when I was having sex with you, I think it made us closer."

"You had sex with Fifi?" Then I try to backtrack, "I mean it's none of my business."

"We did it as we did everything Aefre commanded us to do," he says.

I wish we weren't having this conversation. It's not as if we're talking about an ex-girlfriend. This is dark and strange. "Was it for breeding?"

"I don't know. Possibly. They called it that. But they call a lot of things that aren't for breeding, breeding. Or Aefre thought it would bring us closer? Or the doctor wanted to make a holo to sell to other doctors? You know Aefre doesn't tell his pets his motives for anything."

"But it didn't bring you closer?" I say reiterating what he said as I understand the situation much better now.

"Non," he says and takes a deep breath. "It made us..." he searches for a word. "Ça nous a éloignés...distant."

I don't understand all of what he's said but I definitely understand how one becomes distant after having sex with a friend or colleague. I myself had an incident at the company Christmas party and I regretted every day afterward. "I'm sorry. I won't ask you about it again."

Gabriel leans in and gently brushes a thumb along my temple. "Rest now. I'll stay until they make me leave."

I nod and close my eyes. All I feel is Gabriel's fingers around mine, holding on to me so I won't get lost in my nightmares.

Just as I'm almost asleep, I hear him murmuring something in French, "Je reste avec toi, ma chérie," words I don't fully understand, but the tenderness in his tone speaks to my heart. "Don't worry," he adds in English. "I'm here. I'll always be here."

CHAPTER 36

GABRIEL

Briar is asleep and she looks so peaceful. As I watch her slowly breathe I think about our lives on Earth. I wonder if we would have ever met if we both were still on that planet. And my mind drifts to the conversation we had just twenty-four hours ago.

I told her about my upbringing in Paris, how my parents wanted me to study German, but I picked Spanish instead, ironically making me fluent in the language most human pets speak. If my parents saw me here... it makes my heart break to think about it. It's better they think I died.

I told Briar things I've not spoken out loud in years, about the simple pleasures I took for granted on Earth. My music. I was talented. And I enjoyed it. And oh, how my parents nagged me to practice, but I always ran away from my piano, sneaking out to the park with my friends because I was a teenage boy too. Now, I'd give anything to feel real ivory keys under my fingers again, to let a haunting melody from Chopin or Debussy fill that room in my parents' house. And how I miss real French food, fresh baguettes, warm croissants, pungent cheeses, and the sweetness of a macaron. Things I never imagined would be taken away from me forever.

Likewise, Briar told me about her own life, which was very different to mine. She'd grown up in foster care after losing her parents. Throughout her childhood, she was uprooted from one home to another, never truly settling until she went to university. Then, after graduation, she got a job and learned how to trade commodities. She said she made a lot of money and had acquaintances, but never anything more because from a very young age she'd learned to rely only on herself.

It was difficult to listen to her. I have my childhood to remember. My happy memories. She has nothing. It didn't sound like her work, although lucrative, fulfilled her life. And now she is here in a cage, owned by aliens. It's rare that I pity another pet on the *Luminous Arc*, but I pity Briar.

"Then, unexpectedly there's you," she said. "You're the only light in this darkness. In my whole nightmare of a life, actually."

I doubt she realized how powerful her words were to me. It felt like she reached into my soul and acknowledged every lonely hour I've spent here as an alien's show pet.

I wipe away my tears as I watch the subtle rise and fall of her chest, and I hope she's dreaming of something better than this alien pet world we're trapped in.

I run my thumb over the back of her hand lightly. "Je te protégerai, Briar, I will protect you," I whisper.

Today is Briar's first day back after the fall. Aefre has put a countdown to the Grand Championships above our readouts. I don't know if that's for him or for us. I've been to three Grand Championships at the Celestial Spire, not once has he ever done this.

Briar is standing beside me at the starting line. There's something new in the way she carries herself, she's not pacing like she usually does.

"Begin," Aefre's voice booms.

The course shifts ahead of us, obstacles forming with precision, the path revealing itself in fragments, changing and shifting before our eyes. I take the lead, but glance back briefly, something I wouldn't have done two days ago.

Briar is right behind me. She doesn't hesitate as I kneel to give her a boost over the wall, her hands gripping the top as she pulls herself up. For the first time, she's not overthinking this.

"Good," I say.

She nods and we continue. The next section is a series of swinging ropes, their movement timed to throw off our rhythm. We've failed here before. I jump first, the rope swaying wildly as I land on the platform on the other side. I turn, holding the next rope steady, and meet her gaze.

"Now," I say in Imperial.

Briar doesn't hesitate. She jumps on my command. I watch her body move with an ease that surprises even me. She lands a little unsteady, but not enough to have points detracted from our score.

"Together," I say, pointing to the next set of ropes.

We move in tandem this time. I don't know what's changed, but Briar is more confident today, not what I expected after her fall.

The wall climb comes next, and I feel the tension rise in her again. This is where her hesitation cost her a fall. I step forward, my hand already outstretched to guide her.

"Trust me," I say in Imperial.

She looks up at me and for a second I see doubt in her eyes.

"Trust me, Briar," I say in English and receive a small shock from Aefre. But it's what Briar needed to hear in front of the same obstacle that almost killed her.

She takes my outstretched hand and we climb together, one right after another. I don't let her out of my periphery vision.

When we reach the top, I turn and extend my hand again. She doesn't hesitate. She takes it, and I pull her up.

"Good," I say as we head toward the final obstacle.

A narrow bridge over a simulated valley. This is where trust is everything, where we have to move as one. I step onto the bridge first and she follows close behind.

"Left," I call out in Imperial, guiding her to shift her weight.

"Left," she repeats in her accented Imperial.

"Forward," I say, and she mirrors me perfectly.

The bridge sways beneath us. Step by step, we cross together. When we reach the other side, my heart is pounding, not from fear, but relief. Briar has definitely leveled up. Maybe Aefre was right?

"You were much better," I say, my own breath coming fast.

She nods, wiping the sweat from her forehead. "I had a lot of time to think in the medical center and I realized that I didn't want to die from hesitating...I want to at least die trying," she admits.

"For the first time that was satisfactory and would earn you a place in the Grand Championships," Aefre says interrupting our tête-à-tête. "You're improving, but there's still more work to do. Let's do that one more time."

CHAPTER 37

AEFRE

I watch from my console as Ash and Ember cross the final obstacle. Their movements are almost synchronized now—almost.

Still, they've improved and I have no doubt this is because Ash has a closer bond to Ember, thanks to my latest intervention. I flooded her system with Neural Bond vX: Synthetic Oxytocin 50 IU per while she was in the medical center just before Ember walked in.

Most medical facilities would only administer a quarter of that. But for my plan to succeed, Ash needs to trust Ember and it was taking too long for it to happen organically.

I step away from the console, descending the staircase to meet them on the gymnasium floor. The sound of the holographic generator fades as the course resets itself, the obstacles retracting into smooth metal.

"You're improving," I say. "But, the Grand Championships will not wait for you to find your rhythm," I continue, my gaze shifting between them. "Your movements must be seamless. Your trust in each other, absolute. Tomorrow, we will increase the difficulty," I say.

As I turn to leave, I glance back briefly, catching the way Ember leans slightly toward Ash, his voice low as he murmurs something I can't hear. She doesn't pull away. Instead, she nods, her expression softening just enough to show that she's listening.

Good. Their bond is growing strong. I just hope the artificial foundation is robust enough to hold it.

I stand in the ship's strategy room, the holographic interface glowing faint blue as it displays the Championship course. The layout is vast, intricate, and unforgiving. A maze of shifting obstacles, deceptive holograms, and calculated distractions designed to exploit weaknesses and test pet and trainer bonds alike. Every turn, every challenge, every trap is deliberately engineered to reward exceptional pets and punish mediocre ones.

Ash and Ember's profiles are displayed beside the course, their biometrics and performance metrics updating in real time. Their progress has been steady, but not without its flaws. But today they both made tremendous progress.

I adjust the course simulation for tomorrow, overlaying the specific challenges that will require their synchronization. The tandem rope bridges, the shifting walls, the mirrored corridors that distort perception. Each one demands perfect timing, unspoken understanding, and absolute trust.

The holographic interface shifts, displaying the other competitors, human pairs from across the galaxy. The contenders from Callix Prime are particularly concerning. Their statistics are higher than Ash and Ember's, their movements are flawlessly choreographed. Will Ash and Ember be good enough to win?

It's dark and I'm almost asleep, but then Ash calls out to me. "Master?"

"Yes?" I say curiously.

"What's going to happen at the Grand Championships? I mean," she hesitates, searching for the Imperial word. "What's the schedule?"

"First, we travel to the hotel," I say. "The Celestial Spire is one of the finest in the galaxy. You'll see human pets and trainers from countless worlds, some more competent than others." I pause, letting her absorb that. "Once we're there, you'll have a week of orientation and practice to get used to the arena and to slot you into the proper heats."

"And... Ember? He's reigning champion, right?"

"Indeed. I expect you both to be placed at prime times, performing during the highest spectator turnout. That's how the system works, the better your ranking, the larger the crowds."

"Is that... important?"

"Yes. More spectators mean more bets. More bets mean more credits, for trainers and pets alike."

"After that week of practice... then what?"

"Then the competition begins in earnest, stretched out over several days. Around fifty teams will likely start, but many will fail in the early rounds, some pets will die, others just won't score high enough to advance to the pair challenges. The numbers aren't your concern, Ash. It's complicated for a pet to understand. Don't worry. I'll monitor everything."

"I know about numbers," she says.

"Of course you do," I say, humoring her. "But focus on the events themselves. The order is straightforward: first, a public observation of pets and trainers. Then come the individual trials, followed by the pairs challenges. Finally, if you and Ember win the Grand Championships...You will face the Bond Breaker."

"Isn't that where Ember's other partner... died?"

I hesitate. I don't want to scare her, but I can't lie to her either. Ember or one of the other pets must have already told her what happened. "Yes, Fifi died there. But don't let that trouble you. Ember won't let you die. He was... confused last year, but this time he knows better, and I've trained you both more thoroughly." I can see her collar flash in the dark with anxiety.

I get out of bed, take down the forcefield around her little bed and bring her into my own. I caress her naked body trying to calm her. "You've nothing to fear, Ash," I murmur. "Just do as I say, and remember what you've learned in your training with me."

I slip my fingers between her legs and begin stroking her, rubbing away all of her worries.

CHAPTER 38

BRIAR

The attendants leave us alone, just as Gabriel promised they would. I know it costs him UCs he's earned through competitions and I feel slightly guilty for that, but he always tells me it's money well spent. And I have to agree, if I had money, I would spend it on time alone too. What else is there to buy as a human pet on the *Luminous Arc?*

We sit across from one another, close enough that his knees are touching mine.

And he's looking at me like he's trying to memorize every detail of my face. "I love you," he says quietly. Then as if we were back on Earth and on a date, he leans forward, puts his hands on either side of my face and kisses my lips softly. "Tu es tout pour moi."

"You know I don't speak French, right?"

He replies by kissing me again. This time his tongue enters my mouth, igniting my desire. I respond by drawing him closer to me. Soon his hard muscular body is covering mine.

"What if we're caught?"

"We should have an hour and I'd spend days in solitary confinement to have you alone like this. With no one watching."

"I'm sure the doctor is watching. He gets readouts from our collars. They will know if we orgasm. He probably has an alarm set to go off."

"No. They're at the evening meal and it's an Imperial holiday. They're all drunk. That's why it was easy to pay off the attendants today. Now kiss me. Let me make love to you the way I dreamed about it."

"I didn't mind the way you did it last time," I admit. We've never had a chance to talk about what happened in Aefre's room.

"I wasn't going to take you on anything that belonged to him. Tu es à moi, Briar."

"What does that mean?"

Gabriel leans back an inch so I can look into his amber eyes. "You're mine, Briar." Then he doesn't wait for a reply before taking down his trousers and placing his erect penis at my entrance. "You've always been mine." He thrusts into me. I put my hands around his large shoulders. "And when I escape the *Luminous Arc* and this pet life, I will take what's mine with me." He pushes into me again, stretching my vagina. The piercings scraping through my desire.

I feel so full both emotionally and physically, so much so, tears begin to stream down the sides of my face.

He wipes them off with his thumbs and tries to move off of me.

"No," I hold his large shoulders. "I'm crying because I'm so over-whelmed with how good you make me feel. It's so different to every-thing else. I don't want this moment to ever end, and I'm crying because I know at the end of this hour, it will."

He kisses away my tears. "I don't understand, Briar."

"I want you to claim me as yours. I want to be yours. Take me."

Gabriel holds eye contact, no doubt trying to work out why I'm crying but am still saying want to have sex with him. I lean in and kiss him. Then I begin to move my hips rhythmically against his.

He needs no more incentive. He begins slowly moving in and out of me again, but taking his time now and maintaining eye contact with me as I fight the urge to close my eyes and be lost in this moment.

"More," I tell him desperately. "I need more, Gabriel."

As he increases his speed, we now move as one, our hips in tandem as he finishes releasing into me. Then he slowly lowers himself to his side, gently taking me with him.

Kissing my shoulder he says, "I want to lick you between your legs, but..."

"But?" I'm thinking he doesn't want to lick his own semen which might be understandable.

"My first real sexual experiences were here as a pet and directed by Imperial men. I don't know if that's what human women like and I want to get it right for you, Briar. This is about us being human together. I don't want to love you like an Imperial man or even worse a human pet. Teach me how to love you like a human man."

His words break my heart. I hold him close to me and run my hand through his wavy brown hair. "Gabriel, you're an excellent human lover. If you were on Earth now, no one would ever guess that you hadn't always lived there and made love like a man."

Now it's his turn to cry. I don't stop caressing his hair. I still have nightmares from my own abduction so I understand. But my experience is nothing compared to his decade long imprisonment here. I can't imagine how he must feel and I feel inadequate that all I can offer him is my body and my sympathy.

When his emotions run their course, he begins kissing my neck, my cheeks, then his lips brush mine with a quiet desperation, as though he's afraid I'll vanish the moment he blinks. I savor the warmth of his mouth, the press of his body, but I can sense his unease.

"Suis-je encore un homme? Ou est-ce que j'agis comme... eux?" His eyes shine with a suggestion of fear. I don't know what he's saying, but he sounds lost. I don't want to ruin the moment by asking, 'What?' so I just hope he'll realize he wasn't speaking English.

I cradle his face, my thumb stroking the line of his jaw, my fingers caressing his well-groomed beard assuming that this is still about his insecurities of not being human enough. "You're every bit as human as I am," I murmur, my own heart pounding. "Nothing about you is alien. Not this." I guide his hand to rest over my heartbeat. "You feel that? It's real, and it beats for you Gabriel."

"J'ai tellement peur d'avoir tout oublié... My life before captivity, before they trained me to act a certain way." He bites his lip, shaking his head. "I worry I can't remember how to be a man, not just a pet."

A pang of sorrow tugs at me. "Gabriel," I say, drawing him close until our foreheads touch, "I've never seen you as a pet, only a man in a bad situation."

"Merci, ma chérie," he whispers, eyes closing in a rush of relief. Slowly, he begins to kiss me again.

It's such a simple act, two humans reveling in a stolen moment of freedom, but for us, it's everything.

"Je t'aime, Briar." The French phrase is ironically one of the only sentences I know in French.

"I love you, too," I whisper, holding him tight.

He replies by kissing my chin, my neck, then my shoulders and then takes my breast and sucks on my nipple, while his other hand cups my other breast, kneading it in his palm.

"I want to taste you; I don't know if this is what human men want as well? But I can't stop myself."

"They do," I assure him. "If they like a woman they do."

"Good," he says kissing his way down to my belly and then my abdomen. "I need this from you," he says in between kisses. "I have to."

I lean back with anticipation as he settles himself between my legs. Then he begins circling my clit with his hot tongue and I already feel my body begin to open to him in a way that's different than sex. As if I'm allowing him this pleasure of tasting me, of bringing me to orgasm.

Gabriel is apt at cunnilingus more than any man on Earth I was ever with, but I would never tell him that. The last thing he wants to hear is that Aefre trained him well in this too. And for a moment, I feel guilty, as this lie is for my own pleasure.

But soon I can't think about anything. Gabriel has my body on a thin wire, just holding me steady on the verge of an ultimate climax.

From between my legs he says, "Tell me you want me to make you orgasm like this."

"Gabriel, please make me come by licking my pussy," I breathe out the words, almost unable to speak.

"Merci, ma chérie," he says quickly and then within seconds has my body writhing against his mouth and hands. Pulling the orgasm through my body with expertise until I have nothing left to give and am completely sated. Afterward, he kisses his way back up to my mouth, aftershocks still coursing through my body and he holds me close to him, caressing my hair.

I look over to make sure Gabriel's still awake and then ask, "Tell me about this Gael the Returner. Fifi told you about him, right?"

He nods against my naked body. "After we won the Championships last year. She wanted to find him."

"Why didn't you?"

"I was foolishly proud. Proud of what we'd done, of the UCs we'd won. Aefre lets me keep them. Not every trainer does that. I believed at the time that this pet life was fine. That it was enough."

"What changed?"

Gabriel doesn't answer right away. His hand goes to his collar, his fingers brushing over it lightly. "I haven't told you the truth about what happened to Fifi," he says, his voice strained. "There was a challenge called the Bond Breaker. We'd never done it before. We weren't prepared. They... the judges made it seem like it was real in the same way the holographs we face in the language learning program are real. Like we were trapped, like she was in danger, but it was all holograms. At least, I thought it was. These things..." He taps the collar.

"They make you feel and see things you'd never come up with on your own. It can be confusing."

"What happened?" I whisper, not sure I want to know.

"I wasn't prepared for the deceptions I'd face in the Bond Breaker," he says, his voice cracking slightly. "I thought it was a trick. But it wasn't. She died, Briar. And I left her to die. She begged me to save her in that arena and not only did I let her die, I was given both of our prize money, but I didn't save her. I should have saved her."

I stare at him, the weight of his words settling over me. "You left her to die?"

"I thought she was an illusion. I thought the real Fifi must be somewhere in the challenge fighting her way out just like I was. But it was the real Fifi in front of me. Do you believe me?" His amber eyes bore into mine seeking forgiveness. But I don't know if I can give it.

Would he leave me to die for UCs? Am I here now with him only because Fifi died in that arena and it's her money we are paying off the attendants with to have sex. That sounds terrible, when I think it. Suddenly, the weight of all of this bears down on me and I look away from him to gather my thoughts.

"I wouldn't leave you, Briar. You have to believe me. I didn't want Fifi to die. I was so confused. This place," he motions his arms around wildly. "This fucking place. Nothing is real that Aefre doesn't say is real."

"Am I real?" I ask.

"You're the only thing I know that *is* real, Briar. You're so fucking real, and that's why I want out," Gabriel says, drawing me into a kiss. I taste the salt of his silent tears on my lips. "I swear, if you and I ever face the Bond Breaker, I'll know it's you. We have a connection, un lien, Fifi and I never shared. Maybe that's why I failed her in the Bond Breaker. Maybe... maybe I should have known."

I touch his cheek. "You feel real to me too." Hesitating a moment, I ask, "If we win the Grand Championships and earn all those UCs, are you still willing to risk our future with this stranger, Gael?"

"Oui, *Briar.* I want freedom with you. We deserve more than this endless cycle of training, collars, and cages. We deserve to decide what is real and what is not."

I pull back slightly, memories of my time with other aliens swirling in my head. "I'm afraid," I admit. "Aefre is... predictable. Safe, in his own way. He's never *really* hurt me. Out there, everything's uncertain."

"Nothing about what we've lived through is truly safe. It's just... familiar. We can do better than familiar. We can have a life that's our own. But I understand, I was where you are last year, so I'm asking you to be brave and trust me."

I close my eyes. "I... I'll try to be brave."

His hands find mine. "Nous le ferons ensemble," he promises. "We'll do it together."

CHAPTER 39

GABRIEL

I can see the Celestial Spire ahead of us. Its crystalline towers catch the pale lavender light of the twin moons, refracting it like a living, breathing entity. As we get closer, the whole place seems to pulse with the excitement of the Championships. This will be my fourth time here, and I never get used to the sight.

The grand staircase leading up to the entrance is a monument. A performance piece. A reminder of when humans were first yanked from Earth and paraded around as novelties in this galaxy. The steps are beautifully carved with statues of humans who fought in those first pet challenges, but they're also a grotesque testament to the horrors of countless human lives lost. Pets dragged here as entertainment for aliens and the ghosts of their suffering still haunt every last stone on every step up to the hotel's lobby.

"We're here," Aefre announces unnecessary.

I glance at him. He's in his element.

The transport hisses open, and Briar steps out first. She moves tentatively, as she takes in all the people, the towering spires, and the impressive staircase. She doesn't carry the weight of this place the way I do. Not yet. She has nothing but curiosity on her mind now.

I follow her, but I stop when I hear the roaring alien crowd. It hits me like a punch to the stomach.

"Ember" Aefre's voice pulls me back into the here and now. "You can do this."

His words are meant to steady me. But they don't.

I nod anyway, without looking at him. My gaze is fixed on the staircase. Memories flood my mind unbidden, the alien crowds, the adrenaline, the victories. Fifi. Her laughter, her determination, her absence. The crushing realization that I killed her.

I hate this place. I hate what it took from me.

A small warmth against my hand pulls me back to reality again. I look down. Briar's hand is in mine. Aefre is walking in front of us and doesn't see, or doesn't want to see.

"We've got this," she says in accented Imperial.

The simplicity of her words disarm me. Her green eyes meet mine, and for a second, the weight of this place eases. *I'm not alone here.* And I won't let Briar die. I'll die first before I let that happen to her. Still, I think, *Forgive me, Fifi. I swear I didn't know.*

I squeeze Briar's hand. "Merci," I whisper, expecting a shock from my collar, but none comes.

Aefre notices us from the corner of his eye, but he says nothing. As if we were free for the last two minutes.

Suddenly everything feels different than it did before. As if the lighting changed from pale lavender to bright white. I climb the stairs and am detached from its history. It's both freeing and frightening.

The inside of the Spire feels like stepping into a dream, gleaming corridors stretch endlessly, their intricate designs shifting and shimmering under a soft and unnatural light.

We're led to our quarters, a streamlined and compact room. The bed in the center is much larger than what I have on the *Luminous Arc.*

Aefre stands in the room with us. "You'll be monitored at all times," he says. "Do not forget that." Then he unfastens the leashes from our collars.

"Am I to stay here too?" Briar asks.

"Yes. It's tradition. A little perk for competing in the Grand Championships," Aefre confirms.

Briar tries her best to hide a smile, but fails.

"However," Aefre continues, "you will wear chastity devices when you're alone in this room. Both of you."

Briar frowns.

It's clear that our bodies, and by extension our intimacy, still remain under Aefre's strict control. He never demanded this with Fifi, but then again, Fifi and I were only intimate when Aefre and Kaelin made us.

I watch with unease as Kaelin enters and retrieves two metallic cases from an unmarked trunk. Inside each case rests a small device with tiny glowing indicators that shift from green to blue with a steady pulse.

"These are standard chastity devices in the Empire. They'll ensure you both focus on the tasks at hand with no distractions," Aefre explains as he holds up the devices like an auctioneer.

The device for me is shaped to fit around my most intimate parts, with a flexible alloy band that secures around my waist. The interior is lined with a soft padding so it can be worn long-term.

Briar's device is similarly form-fitted, a small shield that cups between her legs, angled to lock with a slim harness around her hips. It looks uncomfortable, especially when Aefre demonstrates how it snugly seals with a quiet electronic click.

"Any attempts at forced removal will trigger a fail-safe," Aefre says. "It'll emit a low-level shock strong enough to deter tampering. A built-in sensor will report your vital signs, heart rate, blood pressure, cortisol levels, relaying the data back to our pet rings just as your collars do," Aefre and Kaelin both hold up their rings just in case we are stupid humans and forgot how they issue the punishments through our collars.

"If you become too aroused, the device will tighten and restrict blood flow," Kaelin adds.

"How will we clean ourselves?" Briar asks.

"Each device can detach or open partially for cleaning at set intervals, under direct supervision, of course. But beyond that, you will remain inaccessible to each other sexually when you are in this room."

Kaelin beckons me to him, with the device in his hands. "Remove your clothing Ember."

I obey.

When I'm naked, Aefre comes from behind me and begins stroking my penis. I don't know why I feel embarrassed. He's done this every week for the last twelve years, but I don't want Briar to see me like this. To see Aefre making me orgasm for him.

"Ember," Aefre says. "Is it nerves?"

Briar and I make eye contact. Her face is unreadable and then she looks away.

I close my eyes and pretend I'm somewhere else. I concentrate on the orgasm Aefre wants me to have.

"That's a good boy," he says as he finishes me. I shake uncontrollably in his arms as Kaelin collects the semen. And then attaches the chastity belt.

The metal is cold at first, then warms to my body temperature. The harness band clasps around my waist with a final click, echoing in the silent room.

"Your turn Ash," Aefre says and kneels before her. Kaelin stands behind her, holding her chastity belt. "Open up for me. Ah you were aroused watching weren't you. Don't worry, now it's your turn."

I want to look away but I can't. I watch as Aefre licks Briar's pussy, his face deep in the pink hair between her legs. She doesn't look at me and I'm glad she doesn't. I don't want her to see how aroused I am by watching this.

Kaelin begins to bounce her large breasts in his hands and tugs on her nipples and the nipple rings. "I know how you like that Ash. You like it when we play with your tits like this."

My chastity belt makes a sound and both Aefre and Kaelin stop what they're doing and look over at me. Then look at each other and smile before returning their attention to Briar. No doubt, it was a signal that I was aroused.

I continue to watch as Aefre and Kaelin bring Briar to orgasm. She makes the most erotic sounds which makes it all the sweeter to watch. After she's come, Kaelin hands the chastity device to Aefre and he secures it between her legs.

"Better than the muzzle my good little pet," he says rising and then stepping back to admire the devices on us. "Now you both should be sated for tonight. Try to get some sleep and remember, no unauthorized physical contact. Ash don't let any of the male pets near you. Ember I know *you* know better. Understand?"

I'm so angry because I thought I would have this time alone with Briar, but I say in unison with her, "I understand, Master Aefre."

Briar meets my gaze and her eyes reflect her own humiliation.

Aefre and Kaelin leave us without another word. The door seals shut behind them with a faint hiss, leaving the room unsettlingly quiet.

Briar lies down on the bed as soon as Aefre leaves, curling up into a ball.

I join her on the bed and try to comfort her. "It's not forever."

"Why didn't you tell me he was going to do this?"

"I didn't know."

She turns to meet my gaze. "But you've been to the Grand Championships before."

"I told you it wasn't like that with Fifi. He didn't do this. Obviously he knows we've been having sex on the *Luminous Arc*. And this is more about his reputation than ours. He doesn't want the other trainers to think his pets have special privileges."

"He could have just asked us."

"No he couldn't have. He thinks we are animals unable to control our sexual desires."

Briar can't help herself and she smiles.

I hold her close to me and kiss her shoulder. The metal of our belts collide against one another.

"This room is nice." Briar says, changing the subject which I'm grateful for. I hate these belts as much as she does, but we can't do anything about them now.

"It's a galactic hotel," I tell her. "One of the better ones I've seen. Sometimes they even have a token human working at reception."

"A human pet working the front desk?"

"Not a pet. A human from Earth. It's an anomaly. Apparently after the IGC passed the law making it illegal to own pets," I hold up my hand. "Before you get too excited, I don't know if that law is true because all of this," I motion around the room, "but that was the reason for having a free human there, to act as a representative for us in case there was a raid. But I don't know how true that is. I mean she could be half Imperial and just pretends to be a human from Earth."

I have Briar's full attention now. "Did you see this mysterious human receptionist when you were here last time? Did you talk to her?"

"Yes."

"Did you talk to her?"

"No. She was working. I only saw her when she came to watch some of the events. She was given a special seat far away from any pets."

"Do you think she's really from Earth? How could a human see this and not do something to help?"

"What is she going to do? As far as I can see she's a prisoner like the rest of us."

Briar thinks about this for a second. "You're probably right."

Then she changes the subject, "I've been thinking about tomorrow. I'm nervous Gabriel. What if we ..."

I put a finger on her lips to stop her from continuing. "No, you must not even think it. I've been here three times before and survived. And you will too. But I'll not lie to you. This place... it tests you. You'll feel like you're losing yourself. Like there's no way out. But you won't lose me. We're here together." I leave off saying, 'We'll either leave together or die together.'

CHAPTER 40

BRIAR

The bed is too big and too small at the same time. I'm used to the small bed on the floor in Aefre's room and the plush material beneath me now is softer than anything I've felt in months, reminding me of where I am, and how high the stakes are.

Gabriel is lying on his side, his naked back to me, his breathing even, but not deep enough to suggest he's asleep. I'm on my back, staring up at the soft, glowing ceiling, trying to will my body to relax.

The chastity belts.

The Celestial Spire.

The arena.

Gael the Returner.

The Grand Championships.

I can't shake the feeling that no matter how hard I try, it won't be enough.

"Can't sleep?" Gabriel's voice is quiet.

I turn my head slightly. He's so gorgeous in the dim light. "No. Too much to think about."

He shifts, rolling onto his back so we're both staring at the ceiling now. "Same."

The silence stretches between us. It's strange, sharing this space with him. We've trained together, had a secret passionate tryst, whispered our hopes in the quiet of our cages, but this is different. If we weren't wearing the chastity belts we could imagine we were free here.

"What was it like the last time you were here. You don't have to tell me if you don't want to," I tack on the last sentence in a rush.

He's quiet, and after a while, I wonder if he'll even answer. But then he sighs, and says, "It was... overwhelming. It felt like the entire galaxy was watching, waiting for us to succeed or fail. And when we won..." He pauses. "It felt incredible. Like we were invincible. Aefre and Kaelin were so proud. I was proud..."

I can hear the shift in his tone, the weight that follows. "And then?" I prompt.

"And then it all fell apart. Fifi... the Bond Breaker... realizing what I'd done. What I let happen. It wasn't worth it."

I reach out and take his hand in mine.

He doesn't pull away.

"That won't happen to us," I say. And when he doesn't respond I squeeze his hand and look over at him.

His lips twitch into a faint smile, and he squeezes my hand back before letting go. "Je t'ai déjà promis, ma chérie. We walk out together or not at all."

"Okay," I say, wishing I had something grander to say in the face of love and death, but I don't. I'm American. I don't need to be flowery. My word is my word. I continue to stare at him. There's nothing I want more than physical contact to seal the deal. Not sex, because we can't, but I want him to hold me.

But I don't push him. He's never had a lover he could share a bed with. Maybe cuddling is a learned behavior. I don't know, but I have to believe that he still loves me even if he doesn't want to touch me now.

Once he's asleep and his breathing is slow, I wiggle my way into his strong embrace and say, "Just hold me like this." I close my eyes and imagine we're on holiday at a fancy hotel.

CHAPTER 41

AEFRE

I linger at the edge of the Starlit Atrium, letting the buzz of conversation and shifting bioluminescent lights whiz around me. Ornate tapestries and polished glass reflect the opulent façade that the Celestial Spire is known for.

I'm at an event for trainers and judges. Maybe it's my own insecurities, but I think I hear my name murmured between false smiles.

"The Wild One," they're saying. "Aefre's lost his mind. First Fifi and now this?"

I catch the sideways glances and sudden excuses people make when I approach them. I hear Ash's name in whispers as I pass. They all know she came from the Abyssal Nexus, deemed too feral, even for Octopods, which is a low bar indeed. They think I'm out of control.

Maybe I am?

A trainer from Callix Prime comes over to me, her glossy attire nearly as distracting as her serpentine grace. "I hear your pairing is... unconventional," she says, voice dripping with politeness. "A wild human from the Abyssal Nexus? That's quite bold even for you, Aefre."

"It's strategic. I knew from the moment I saw Ash that she was resilient. And her bond with Ember more than meets the basic requirement for the Championships." I almost add more but I stop myself. My history here speaks for itself, even if these people want to momentarily forget that.

I can tell that that wasn't what she was expecting me to say. So with another polite word she leaves me to find someone else to fish for weaknesses.

I return to my little area of the room alone. In these circles, revealing too much is a mistake. I watch the other trainers position themselves. *This is the first competition of the Grand Championships,* I think.

I exhale and straighten my posture. Tomorrow, training begins in the arenas. If they want to whisper, let them. I'll show them what a 'wild human' can do and I'll remind them why my name once sparked more than just idle gossip.

I'm poring over a holographic simulation of the competition arena when Kaelin arrives. "You look worried. Has something happened?"

I nod, turning the simulation off. "I'm analyzing... Ash and Ember are good. But this year's line-up is fierce. The Callix Prime team, the Aria-7 hybrids... they're near flawless."

"Perfection isn't invincible. Ash and Ember's advantage is their chemistry."

"Chemistry that might be built on a false foundation," I remind him. "We both know what we did."

"We had no choice. We couldn't create trust out of thin air. Plus we know from experience the hormones only nudge their emotions. Their trust is real. You've seen how they protect each other."

"You're right. I've witnessed that spark between them. There's something genuine there, false hormones or not."

"Enough about that for now," Kaelin says, "We can't do anymore.

We need to decompress. I've heard the best dancer in the galaxy just arrived at the hotel. I could arrange a private performance here."

I almost smile at the idea. It feels indulgent, but maybe that's exactly what I need a momentary escape before the madness of the Championships truly begins. "Hire her. We can set tomorrow's strategy after we've cleared our heads."

Kaelin nods, already reaching for his IC.

She calls herself Kresh of Nara, and she's known across star systems simply as the best. I've witnessed performances from countless dancers, humans, aliens, hybrids, but Kresh is on another plane entirely.

She moves with a fluidity that defies ordinary anatomy. Four slender arms move in perfect synchronicity, each limb adorned with bioluminescent tattoos that shimmer like starlight against her deep violet skin. Her head is crowned with delicate tendrils like hair, but they pulse shifting colors, mirroring the rhythm of the music. When she gazes at me, I notice she has three eyes, each a different hue, lavender, gold, and midnight blue, giving her an aura that is erotically hypnotic.

Her dancing is more than just a dance. It's a fusion of styles from half a dozen worlds, Sedar wave dance, Thae ribbon art, even the subtle floating twirls from the Sasser Nebula tribes. She draws them together seamlessly, stepping beyond mere choreography. Every shift of her hips and every splay of her fingers, is deliberate, drawing me into her trance.

But there's something else. Something about her presence. It's as though she can reach inside my mind and command my attention without a word. Perhaps it's a gift of her species, or maybe it's her own unique talent. Either way, Kresh has my full attention.

As the dance continues she gets on her knees in front of me and begins moving in a sensual way that mimics sex. Then she turns on her side and it looks as if she's aching to be touched, running one of her purple hands up her thigh, bringing the hem of her dress with her. She licks her violet lips looking at Kaelin.

Then she turns her back to both of us and lifts up her skirt and begins moving back and forth as if she's having sex with the air. Slowly she lifts up her skirt more so we can see both of her vaginas and the small tongues inside of them. I've only had sex with a Naraian once, but it was exquisite. The females have a small tongue inside each of their vaginas that can caress and their vaginas have the ability to suck as well. I'm becoming aroused just watching her pump her hips, her holes opening and closing with expertise and desire.

Then she turns around again and slowly removes her shirt, revealing one breast at a time. She has three breasts and she uses three of her hands to pull on her three nipples while she continues to move her hips in a rhythmic motion. The sound of her costume hypnotic. Then she leans back and puts her legs up and down. Her skirt rising and falling as her vagina tongues lick their lips at us. Beckoning us to them.

I look over at Kaelin and he gives me a smile.

Kresh gets on her knees again and gives us her back. This time her skirt is around her waist so we have a good view of her ass which is also covered in tattoos. I know I shouldn't but I can't resist. I reach out and grab a cheek.

She turns around in complete surprise. "No Master Trainer. I'm not that kind of woman." She looks down with all three of her eyes feigning innocence. I know this is part of the show too. To seduce her. It's a man's fantasy in a matriarchy where we ask women for permission for sex.

"Is it your first time?" I ask, playing along.

Kresh gyrates her purple naked hips again making her costume jingle. "Yes. I've never had any penises inside of me. I don't know how it will feel, but I have this aching." She runs two of her hands over her sex and plays with her little tongues in her vagina with her fingers. "My little holes are so hungry, but I don't know how to feed them. Do you? Can you help me?"

I rise and run my hands over the front of her body. Caressing her triple breasts down to her double vagina. Kaelin is behind her his hands on her neck and down her back, grabbing her ass. It's been awhile since we've shared a woman, but we always fall back into it.

"Do you like that Kresh?" I ask.

"I don't know. Is my body supposed to be this hungry for Imperial men? I hear your penises are pointy and large. I'm scared."

"Why don't you try?" Kaelin says in her ear and then takes it into his mouth. She leans back into his embrace and I knead her three breasts, trying to pull them altogether at once and then letting go.

I feel Kresh's hands on my trousers and her expert hands have them off me in seconds. And it's not long before I'm pushing her back on the bed. Kaelin and I make eye contact, silently agreeing on how we're going to do this.

I lay down on my back and Kresh hovers over me. Her first vagina hitting my mouth and then Kaelin hovers over her, he's taking her second vagina and then we begin to kiss them. Our tongues meeting her mini tongues in her sex. They're dripping with her desire and urging ours on.

I moan, almost orgasming myself, with what must be a seductive drug laced in her juices. I meet her little tongue and force my tongue inside her core. Kaelin must have done this at the same time because her body soon begins convulsing in an orgasm. I keep licking until her desire is all over my face.

Kaelin then flips her onto her back and he lies down on his back, pulling her on top of him, His penis ready to enter one of her vaginas. I look down to see the little tongues searching for something to guide in. I position myself at the entrance of her other vagina, her little tongue caressing the tip of my penis, urging me in. I moan, it feels so good.

Then I look at Kaelin and nod. We enter Kresh at the same time. And she feels so tight and good. Her core has latched onto my penis like I have it stuck in a suction pipe with a tongue stroking it up and down. I don't know if I can move without orgasming so I stay still for a minute.

Then I feel Kaelin begins to move and I do the same. Kresh begins to guide my hips with her arms. And it's not long before Kaelin and I are moving in and out of her at a good pace. And just when we are past the point of no return, she says, "Go against the goddesses and orgasm your Imperial semen all over my purple tits."

I don't want to remove my dick from her, but I do it anyway. Kaelin gets to his knees and moves to the side.

"I want to watch you work," she says seductively. "Come on. Put that semen all over me."

Kresh plays with her purple breasts and pinches her three nipples as I spray white hot semen all over them. She rubs it around and then looks at Kaelin. "That's a good boy. Come on."

Kaelin empties himself on to her as well. It looks as if her breasts have been covered in white paint there's so much there. Then she says to me, "Now go get one of your human pets to lick it up."

Kaelin and I make eye contact. Of course we both want Ash to come here. But that wouldn't be good for the bond between her and Ember.

And now I know why Kresh was available tonight. Some of the other trainers are out to sabotage us. Thinking that we would risk the bond between our pets for this erotic night.

"Please, get your human pet. Then you can both fuck me hard," Kresh says and I look between her legs at those little tongues. "My other mouths are so hungry."

Kaelin gives me a look.

I shake my head. "We can hire a slave artist."

"Oh Master Trainer, I want a human," Kresh says. "With a tail."

Kaelin is already on his IC naked ordering a slave artist. I add, "With a butt plug tail." And he nods.

Within minutes a grey Imperial woman shows up with very little clothing and a butt plug tail in pink. "Perfect," I tell her leading her in. I take her to Kresh, and say, "Lick up all of our semen from her tits."

While the Imperial woman leans over to do that. I take off her skirt and move her tail to the side then I begin massaging her sex, finding her clit to bring her to orgasm as quickly as possible. It doesn't take long and she's still licking the semen from Kresh as I enter her. I hold her hips tightly as I guide her in and out of me. Her pink tail moving back and forth. It's not the same as having Ash here but I can imagine it in my mind and I orgasm again.

When the Imperial woman is finished licking up all the semen from Kresh she turns around and licks the excess semen from me. Then she waits for directions, which Kresh gives, "Come here darling, I want to lick all of Aefre's semen from inside you while they give my hungry mouths something more too. That is if Master Trainer is up for it again?"

"With that pink tail, I'm up for anything again," I assure her. "And nothing would please me more than watching you sit on Kresh's face with that tail hanging over her breasts."

Kaelin gets on the bed again and Kresh gets on top of him. Then the Imperial woman sits on Kresh's face and I enter her other vagina. The scene before me is so sensual and erotic. I imagine it's Ash sitting on Kresh's face as she gets her insides filled with my semen eaten out. And as Kaelin and I fill Kresh's other little mouths with more. It's not long before I'm groaning loudly and coming again. It takes Kaelin flipping Kresh over and holding all of her arms back as he climaxes, but it's exciting to watch. Then the Imperial woman licks and kisses the little vagina tongues in Kresh.

When the women have left, Kaelin and I both decide that that was a clever set up.

"And one I almost feel for," Kaelin admits.

"Good thing we didn't."

The next day, during the morning briefings, the conversation shifts to Gael the Returner. His name has become a fixture among the trainers, a ghost that haunts the Championships. The room buzzes with talk of increased security.

"They say he's telling pets about the new law," one trainer mutters with irritation. "That humans can no longer be owned."

"It's absurd," another says. "Most pets wouldn't even want to leave. What would a human do in the galaxy? They're better off where they are."

I listen in silence. The idea of humans being free is absolutely absurd. The galaxy is unforgiving and humans don't have the brain power to survive on their own. "It's only a matter of time before the IGC reverses their decision."

"But the humans did manage to maintain their settlement on one of their nearby planets, as is the requirement."

"A fluke," I say. "We all know one in a million humans has a spark of intelligence, but that's only one in a million. And one of those managed to build something useful, but when she dies, then what? Humans will always be the lesser species. We all know that."

"But the humans don't know that," the trainer from Callix Prime says. "They'd believe Gael's lies and that's the real danger."

She's not wrong.

"You're not afraid your Wild One will run off with a man's penis in her mouth?" The trainer from Aria-7 asks and everyone laughs at my expense.

I shake my head as if the joke doesn't bother me. But, of course, it does and I worry. I've pushed Ash and Ember to their limits emotionally.

Kaelin leans in, and assures me, "They're loyal."

CHAPTER 42

BRIAR

The days in the Celestial Spire blur together with training during the day and talking with Gabirel in the night.

The hotel's arena is relentless and the other competitors feel like Olympians compared to me. Every day, it feels like the obstacles grow harder, like Aefre is pushing us to the brink just to see if we'll break. Sometimes, I think I'm close. But then I see Gabriel's determination to win and it pulls me back.

Every night, we lie in bed holding hands under the blankets talking. I tell him about the life I had before all this and how this life feels more real than anything I had before. No computer screens, no bills, no emails, no paperwork, and yet I have a relationship with Gabriel that reminds me why I breathe.

Gabriel talks about freedom, about Gael the Returner. But what does freedom even mean? Where would we go? What would we do? This life with Aefre isn't what I imagined I wanted in life, but neither was being a commodities trader. It was a job. I wasn't really free. I really only feel free with Gabriel. He warns me that our time together is limited with Aefre and is adamant that we must escape to ensure a future together. But is leaving Aefre behind worth the risk?

The stories I've heard from other pets here terrifies me. What if we escaped and were caught and bought by someone else?

But with our chastity belts fitted tight, it's a constant reminder that we aren't free. We are controlled and it's clear that Gabriel no longer can live like this.

CHAPTER 43

G ABRIEL

We're in bed together. The lights have gone out and I'm holding Briar against me. With the damned chastity belts, it's torture.

"I'm sorry," I say.

"For what?"

"For finding you desirable. For the damn chastity belts. I hate how it chimes when I'm beginning to become aroused."

"And you're sorry for that?" she says, as she turns in my arms. I love the feeling of her soft breasts against my chest.

I pull her closer and lean down to kiss her lips slowly, letting her bottom lip linger as I pull away. I know she's exhausted, she's mentioned it more than once since we returned to the room. But still I tell her, "I wish I could make love to you, Briar."

"Even without the chastity belts, I assume we're being watched," she says.

"Watched and recorded, no doubt," I tell her.

She sits up. Her breasts moving with her motions, her nipples hard and I can't help but kiss one before she moves my head away. "You mean the Grand Championships would record us here and then sell it?"

"Yes."

"And that doesn't bother you? You would still want to have sex?"

"If I worried about these aliens watching every second of my life, I would go insane. We are their pets. We have no privacy. Of course, they want to watch us have sex. In the same way they watch us masturbate, eat, go to the bathroom, or interact with each other."

"Do you think they watched and recorded Aefre putting the chastity belts on?"

"Definitely. We are their entertainment whether we are in that arena competing or here in this hotel room sleeping and everything in between."

Briar is staring at the ceiling now in a daze.

"If we weren't wearing these chastity belts, I would slip under the blankets where they can't see me and lick your pussy until you cried with satisfaction."

I search her green eyes. She's imagining it. Good.

I pull the blanket up over our heads in a grand gesture that makes her laugh in surprise. Then I kiss her and let my hands slowly roam her body. Her device makes a sound now too. And we both smile.

Elle est à moi. She's all mine, no matter what happens to our physical bodies.

CHAPTER 44

AEFRE

Kaelin finds me in the strategy room.

"You've heard the talk?"

I nod. "They're starting to pay attention."

"They're more than paying attention. They're recalibrating. The Callix Prime team ran their last simulation differently, faster and more aggressively. They're trying to match what Ash and Ember did this afternoon."

"Good," I say simply. "They should. I would do the same."

Kaelin folds his arms across his chest. "You're really enjoying this aren't you?"

"Well why not? It's different isn't it? We usually come in as the best, former champions and all. This year not only are we coming in hot with a pet that has not competed before but one that I basically rescued from the Octopods. No one thought this possible." I turn back to the holographic display of the arena. The simulation replays Ash and Ember's tandem leap, their timing nearly perfect. "They've earned the attention."

"You've done the impossible."

"We both have," I reply. Then I change the subject. "What have you heard about Gael the Returner today?"

"Nothing except the gossip from the other trainers. Of course, they've noticed how close Ash and Ember are. They say if Gael gets anywhere near them, they'll run because they're so in love."

It's a risk, of course. The bond I pushed between Ash and Ember is both their greatest strength and vulnerability. "So we must make sure that Gael never talks to them and that they're so happy with their success that they willingly return to the *Luminous Arc*."

"Perhaps you should promise them something? To sweeten the deal."

"They're pets, Kaelin."

"You and I both know Ember is the real liability. He's never recovered from Fifi's death. He worries about his own mortality and now Ash's too. And it's obvious to everyone, he wants to keep Ash like a wife."

I laugh. "Are you suggesting humans could maintain long term relationships, Kaelin? Have you got human mind rot from listening to human languages? Ember will forget about Ash once she is no longer new to him." I leave off saying, 'But I'll personally never let her go. I'll keep her the same way I have kept Mags.' I don't want to tell Kaelin how I really feel about Ash. I suspect he knows already. "But I'll humor you in this because I'm curious, what would you suggest I offer Ember?"

"Their own private quarters on the *Luminous Arc*."

"Outrageous. We would be the laughing stock of the galaxy. They're not our equals."

"Think about it. One of the reasons they'd consider running is for privacy. That's the one thing Gael can offer them that they want and we can easily give that to them."

"Where are you getting these ideas? Humans don't like privacy."

Kaelin sighs. "It's your outfit. I've given you my suggestions."

"You have and I think you're listening too much to the younger trainers who have strange ideas about humans. Oh I've heard them too. Saying things like humans have long-term memories and are capable of so much more then we give them credit for, but I've been doing this for over forty years and not once have I had a human who was more than half sentient, except for Ember, maybe."

"I have been speaking with the younger trainers. They showed me some shocking new studies."

"Imperial?"

"No."

"Then there you have it."

"Have you ever considered that they are traumatized from the experience of abduction? Or that we may not be giving them the chance to show they are sentient?"

"Honestly Kaelin, I'm not sure if your drink was spiked, but I thank you for your suggestions. If we hear more rumors about Gael the Returner or if I hear he's been in contact with Ash or Ember then of course I will try to offer them something more. We have an early start tomorrow. Go and sleep off this whole humans-might-be-sentient thing. I'll see you in the morning."

CHAPTER 45

BRIAR

I wake before the artificial dawn. Today is the last day of training. Tomorrow the Grand Championships officially begin. I nudge Gabriel. "I'm too stressed to sleep. Let's go."

He sleepily nods and follows me out of bed.

Usually, the training arena is alive with murmured chatter and clanging equipment as pets train in a mixture of Imperial and human languages, but this morning, it's eerily quiet.

I notice a lot of small groups of pets speaking together today. But the instant I come near them, they break apart. Maybe it's because they still call me "Wild One," or maybe they don't trust me because I speak only English and Imperial, while so many of them speak Spanish.

Across the arena, I see Gabriel hanging from a pull-up bar, scanning the training area as if searching for someone. I feel like he also knows this secret which everyone else has been talking about. I walk over to him. "What's going on?" I ask in Imperial. "You keep looking around and everyone else is acting... different."

He offers the slightest shake of his head. "I'll tell you later," he mutters, like there's some secret he can't risk sharing in front of the watchful eyes of trainers and drones.

I return to my station, forcing myself to focus on the upcoming drills.

An hour later, a snatch of conversation drifts to me over the clatter of exercise machinery, "Gael... freedom... law." It's an urgent whisper between a pet and an attendant, and the attendant glances around with obvious panic before rushing off. The moment the pet sees me watching, she goes rigid, then pivots on her heel and disappears.

Did I hear that correctly? Gael the Returner? That's why everyone is acting so weird. Is he among us? Are pets escaping right now? I scan the room. It's not obvious anyone is gone. At least not in a large number.

When the day's session finally ends, we're all herded back to the pets' quarters. The moment the door slides shut behind us, I ask Gabriel.

"Is Gael the Returner here?" I ask in English. Trainers don't bother to translate our human languages as they don't think we can articulate higher thoughts with them.

"Yes."

"Have you—" I begin, then pause, uncertain if I want to hear the answer. "Have you spoken with him?"

Gabriel's eyes flick to the door, ensuring we're still alone. "Oui. Je veux la liberté, Briar. I want us to be free." The French slips out first, it always does whenever he's overcome by emotion. "But we must win the Grand Championships to have enough UCs to pay him."

"After the Grand Championships? Not before? We could die tomorrow." I say, devastated.

Gabriel places his hands gently on either side of my face. "Briar," he murmurs, his golden eyes boring into mine. "You won't die. Je ne le permettrai pas. We'll survive, we'll win, and then..." He leans in, pressing a soft, chaste kiss to my lips. "Then we will be free."

I want to believe him. But the fear of dying in the arena, another nameless human pet lost to the Grand Championships, threatens to consume me. But in Gabriel's steady gaze, I see unwavering conviction. He's survived so much already. *I need to trust in him and this plan.* Or what? What if we win and we've not made an arrangement with Gael? Then we have no choice but to return with Aefre.

I close my eyes for an instant, letting the moment ground me. "Okay," I whisper.

A tiny smile curves his mouth. "Nous survivrons, we will survive," he says gently, brushing a stray hair behind my ear.

"So you told him we wanted to go?"

"Once we've won and have the money he will arrange it. He said he can't tell me anything about it in case they use mind control to get the information to catch him."

I want to ask about the mind control but how we get our hands on the money is my first concern. "But how will we get the UCs from Aefre? Don't you think he'll be suspicious?"

"We don't have to. They automatically go into our account. He set that up beforehand and it can't be changed now."

"How do you know?" I ask dubiously.

"It's common knowledge if you have access to the Grand Championship database. Aefre is proud he lets his pets keep their winnings for their own treats."

"Does Aefre know about Gael?" I ask.

"Of course he does. All the trainers know."

"Yet?"

"Briar, they think we're pets."

CHAPTER 46

GABRIEL

I kiss Briar and want to tell her about my doubts, about the guilt that grips me every time I think of escape. How Gael the Returner was all Fifi talked about and I dismissed her and then I let her die.

But I don't want to sound like a broken record. I feel like I've already mentioned it one too many times. And I don't want Briar to think about death. We must win.

"Il faut du courage, maintenant, ma chérie," I whisper with quiet resolve, speaking as much to myself as to Briar. "We must have courage."

CHAPTER 47

AEFRE

"Ember," I say to Kaelin, my gaze fixed on the holographic replay of the training session. "Something's changed."

"He's distracted."

"What do you think is pulling his focus?"

"It could be the pressure."

"No," I say, dismissing that. "This is the fourth time Ember has been here."

Kaelin hesitates. "Gael the Returner. Gossip among the pets has been rife."

"How could *he* believe those rumors?"

"Oh, I think they'd be difficult to ignore. Especially in his current state."

"You mean, someone whose heart and mind are in emotional turmoil," I say, vaguely admitting my guilt about putting thoughts in Ember's mind and artificial hormones in his body. "Perhaps I'll have to take your advice after all and sweeten the deal for Ember. But I'm going to give it another day. Once his mind becomes focused on the Championships and winning, he may forget."

CHAPTER 48

BRIAR

The holographic mirror in the dressing room reflects a version of me I barely recognize. The woman staring back at me is a stranger. A creation of Aefre's meticulous human pet design. My purple costume shimmers and clings to my body like a second skin, accentuating every curve. Displaying every patch of hair, under my arms, my vulva, and my tail. And making sure my pierced breasts are on full display.

Aefre's hands fasten the final clasp at my shoulder. When he steps back, I meet his green eyes in the mirror. For a second, there's a softness in his expression.

When he looks at me like this I want to scream, "Why don't you see us as the same species?"

But I never do. And all he ever sees before him is a human pet.

"You look perfect," he says. "The judges will see it too."

I don't say anything. *Perfect.* The perfect pet.

What happens if I don't win for Aefre? Will he sell me? Will I become obsolete, discarded like a failed experiment? Or worse pushed out an airlock?

"Breathe, Ash," Aefre says, his voice breaking through my

spiraling thoughts. "You've trained for this. You're going to perform fantastically."

I force myself to take a deep breath, holding it for a moment before releasing it slowly. I hear our names announced and I follow him as he leads me to the arena on a leash, I focus on my feet, one in front of the other.

As we enter the arena, lights blaze from every corner, illuminating the space with an unnatural brilliance. The alien crowd's roar fills the air.

Memories of my auction suddenly flash through my mind, the bright lights, the alien faces, and the helplessness.

I stop, frozen.

Aefre whispers, "I can't use the collar to calm you now. Don't give that memory currency. Leave it. I bought you. You're mine." His hand tightens on the leash, pulling me back into motion.

I'm his. He owns me. He thinks this is going to calm me but it's a statement that's a double-edged sword. He keeps me safe now but his statement is also a reminder he can do whatever he wants with me.

We reach the center of the arena, and Aefre stops, his presence beside me solid and commanding. The leash in his hand feels like a lifeline. Like it's the only thing tethering me to reality.

The alien judges sit high above us. Their expressions are cold and their attention is sharply focused on us. I feel like they're cutting through the layers of glitter and fabric to assess the creature beneath. Me.

"Kneel, Ash," Aefre says.

I lower myself to my knees, folding my hands neatly behind my head, my chest out, and posture straight, exactly as I've been taught.

The glaring lights and the alien audience make the terror inside of me bubble up again, but I try to focus only on Aefre's voice as he guides me through the routine.

The command sequences are first. Aefre issues a rapid series of orders: *sit, kneel, bow, roll over*—all in Imperial, expecting me to keep up flawlessly. The slightest hesitation might earn a humiliating correction in front of the entire audience and lose us points.

After Aefre has demonstrated his complete control over me, the linguistic portion begins, and I brace myself as the first question comes.

"State your name and origin," one judge says, their tone clipped and hard.

"Ash," I say clearly, though my voice trembles slightly. "Earth."

"Describe your trainer in three words," another demands.

I hesitate for a fraction of a second before glancing at Aefre. His green eyes meet mine, and I force myself to speak. "Strong. Intelligent. Kind."

The judge nods, making a note on their tablet. The questions continue, each one a test of my fluency and composure. I navigate them as best I can, but one particularly tricky word catches me off guard. I stumble over the pronunciation, my cheeks burning with embarrassment. I glance at Aefre, expecting his expression to harden, but it doesn't. He remains unreadable.

Next is the examination of my body. This is my first pet show so I don't know what is going to happen. Gabriel warned me that it'll be invasive and embarrassing. I don't know what could be more embarrassing than wearing this outfit with all my lady parts hanging out and running around with a leash and a master.

I kneel with my hands behind my head as Aefre stands next to me, waiting for the judges.

I close my eyes not wanting to look at the crowd.

"Open your eyes," Aefre says. "You're doing well."

Aefre tugs on my collar to get me to my feet and usher me into the main judging panel. My heart races as I step onto the elevated metallic ring. All around me stand alien judges, each one more unsettling than the last.

The judges take turns coming closer and investigating my body, their features partially obscured by shadows or intricate headpieces. Some have strange eyes that shift colors as they hone in on me, while others have hard-shelled limbs or antennae that twitch when the spotlight moves. The variety is overwhelming. Nothing on Earth ever prepared me for this melting pot of terrifying anatomy.

I stand in the center, and a hush descends over the crowd. My pulse pounds in my ears as a spotlight pinpoints the augmented tail behind me. Every judge angles their gaze, assessing the forced modifications I've undergone. They also examine the extra pubic hair dyed to match my hair and then they begin prodding me. They open my labia and they investigate my asshole. They even play with my tail to see how naturally it's connected to my tail bone. Then they bounce my breasts and pull on my nipples. My cheeks burn with humiliation.

A judge with slitted nostrils and shimmering, scale-like skin speaks in clipped Imperial. Her voice sounds like a whip cracking through the air. I can only pick out a few of her words, "modifications," "performance," and "human adaptability."

Then I catch a phrase, something like "wild pet" or "exotic specimen," from another judge as he pulls my tail.

One judge puts a tentacle up my vagina, touching my cervix, and says, "unbred human."

I stand frozen although every muscle in my body is screaming for me to run. But there's nowhere to go even if I could run. I must stand here and endure all of this.

When the judges back off and begin entering their appraisals into glowing panels. Aefre strokes me between my legs as is his custom when he's concerned about a pet becoming too anxious.

The judges have now returned to their seats in the arena and I think this means we are finished.

But then Aefre says, "There's one more task. You must show affection toward me."

I look at him blankly for a second. Then before I can ask what I'm supposed to do because I honestly can't think of anything, he steps behind me, his clothed groin hard against my naked flesh, and he begins stroking me between my legs in earnest. He's done this so many times in private. He knows my body better than I know it myself. But this feels wrong. *Is he going to make me orgasm in front of a stadium full of aliens?*

But I can't control my body or his familiar hands. I lean back against him and moan. Aefre knows exactly where to rub me. He's perfected it over these last months. Oh and now he's gotten to the point where he spits to make me more wet and I move my hips up and down creating more friction with his fingers.

"Open your eyes, look at the judges and the crowd. Orgasm for everyone, my pet. Scream out in your human way as I work your body for their entertainment."

I want to say, 'I can't,' but Aefre is touching me so skillfully and the build-up from wearing the chastity belt in bed with Gabriel makes it impossible to resist the promise of an orgasm. But if I could think, I would probably come to some conclusion about that, but I can't think. My body is solely focused on the building tension between my legs.

"Yes Master Aefre," I say, and use all my willpower to open my eyes and survey at all the aliens watching me. After a few minutes, I let myself go and orgasm for them all, like the sexy show pet I am. My muscles spasm and I even squirt a little as Aefre doesn't let up. And the worst part about it is that I don't even mind now. I'm a mindless beast only seeking the pleasure my master's hand brings.

"That's my good girl," he says patting my hairy vulva wet with my own desire.

Despite myself his praise feels good.

"You orgasmed just as fast as you do on the *Luminous Arc*," he informs me as we walk into the waiting area. "You're a born show pet, enjoying the crowd watching your every move."

"You time my orgasms?"

"Of course. The faster I can bring you to orgasm the more affection you have toward me."

That's some fucked up human pet logic, I think. But I say, "You're a good master."

My hands tremble as we wait for our scores. Aefre has me kneeling with my hands clasped behind my back. Every now and then he reaches down and strokes me between my legs. I know he thinks this is calming. And maybe it is, I don't even know anymore.

The numbers flash on the screen above us, incomprehensible to me. I look to Aefre for guidance, my heart pounding so loud I can't hear.

"High enough. You did well, Ash. We scored extra points on how quickly you orgasmed, but lost points on some of your linguistic skills."

I let out a shaky breath. "I... I made a mistake."

"And it didn't matter. Overall, you performed beautifully."

He's pleased. I want him to call me a 'good girl' again. I don't know why but I'm waiting to hear it and disappointed as the minutes pass and he doesn't say it.

Aefre gets me to my feet and begins leading me away by my leash. The murmurs of the crowd and the blinding lights fade into the background. But everything that just happened is still replaying in my mind and the wetness on the top of my thighs a reminder that I orgasmed for everyone in that arena, but that my body still wants more. My life on the *Luminous Arc* has been one of orgasms followed by penetrative sex with Aefre and Gabriel. My body expects it.

Aefre must know this. My collar must read out high arousal levels now. I hope he's taking me somewhere to fuck me. I need that.

We stop at a water jug and he leads me to the little spout. One of his hands plays with my nipple piercing as I drink. My arousal must be off the charts now. I need something inside of me.

Then he leads me into a small room and attaches my leash to a pole. He puts my hand on the bar in front of me and makes me lean over. The next thing I hear is his trousers dropping. Then he enters me with a deep groan of satisfaction. "You're such a good girl, Ash."

Finally, the words I've been longing to hear, 'good girl.' The phrase out of his mouth makes me feel so special. Just like he does.

The way he knows me. The way he knows exactly what I want and I don't have to tell him.

"You did so well." He moves completely out and then in again, slowly. "Such a good, wet, aroused pet. All the judges wanted to fuck you, but you're mine." His ridged penis to subtly pick up speed and soon he's pounding into my vagina as his hand holds my tail, guiding my hips to meet his.

"Yes, Master," I breathe. Not wanting him to stop.

"You're so wet for me, Ash. I bet you wish we could have done this in the pet show too. You're such a performer. Such a human."

I know he means that as an insult. A human, who in his mind, is obsessed with sex. But I am who he has made me to be and in this moment, him degrading me more is only a turn on. "I'm a human pet."

"My human pet," he rasps out.

He continues to pound into me, harder and harder, until he's emptied himself into me. Imperial men always have so much semen it spills out of my vagina and down my thighs.

Aefre unlatches my leash and puts me on my knees, my hands behind my head, and commands me, "Lick it up, pet."

Right now, I feel exactly how he's trained me to feel. I feel like a good pet. And my tail is even wagging.

CHAPTER 49

GABRIEL

From the pets' observation lounge, I see everything, the stage, the judges, the crowd, and Briar. Aefre leads her around the arena like he created every molecule in her body. And I watch nervously as her shimmering costume catches the harsh lights, designed to amplify her most human physical characteristics. She looks like an ideal Imperial pet being led around by her beloved trainer.

I can't block out the whispers around me, "Wild One," they say, "she eats men's penises."

I turn to any other human who will meet my gaze and narrow my eyes. Most of the murmuring stops then.

I focus on the arena again. I see the faint tremor in Briar's hands as she folds them behind her head, She's afraid. Terrified, even. The crowd won't notice, but Aefre does. Of course he does. The way he subtly shifts his stance beside her, steadying her without touching her. *He's not a bad Master*, I reflect.

Being here and seeing the other trainers has reminded me just how bad it could be with another owner. Although I won't mention this to Briar. I still think it's right we try to leave with Gael if possible. That the risk is worth it.

I watch as Aefre leads Briar through the basic pet commands. She jumps, runs, and sits just as Aefre says to do. Her breasts larger than most show pets swaying with all her movements and something about the scene makes me hard. It's almost as if I'm fighting with a fantasy that wants to take form in my mind. My breeding Briar while Aefre holds her leash. I try to dispel it by concentrating on the next task, but my physical body has latched on to it.

The judges begin their linguistic questions and Briar answers in Imperial.

She's good. Incroyablement bonne.

The judges nod, their faces unreadable.

Then they proceed down to the arena floor and touch her body everywhere. She stands like a statue as they prod her and look in every hole. It's humiliating but she handles it well.

Finally, she needs to show Aefre affection. I have no doubt that Aefre has trained her in the same way he trained me for this initially so that she won't say no. I know how his hands feel, how he can bring out an orgasm with the perfect expertise. I remember him whispering in my ear, "Ah you see that's the difference between humans and Imperials, you'll orgasm for anyone stroking your cock."

And he was right. Since I came to live with Aefre he's been making me orgasm for him at least once a week. He does this for all of his pets, even Mags who doesn't do anything anymore but eat, sleep and sometimes throw around a ball.

I watch Briar's orgasm in the arena and hear the crowd cheer. Her wet desire coats the hair between her legs and glistening in the bright lights. I know exactly how she smells and I want her even more now.

Some of the other pets whisper behind their hands and giggle at my notable erection, but I don't care. I love Briar and it'd be strange if I didn't feel this way watching her, wouldn't it?

The scores flash on the screen, and a murmur ripples through the lounge. They're high, higher than most so far, and relief floods through me. She's done it.

I see her glance up at Aefre, the way her green eyes light up with pride when he nods, the faint curve of her lips when he praises her. She's basking in his approval. I know what it feels like to crave that warmth. I know how intoxicating it is, and how Aefre will take her to the trainer's room to reward her even further now. A pang of jealousy runs through me.

Briar, tu es à moi. You're mine, not his.

CHAPTER 50

AEFRE

Back in the strategy room, I pull up the schedule for the next few days' events, my mind already dissecting the challenges ahead.

I glance at Ash's profile on the holographic display. *My Wild One*. Perhaps I should send the Octopods a bottle of their favorite nectar as a token of my appreciation.

Kaelin enters. "High scores today."

"People are talking. Bets are coming in. They think you've done the impossible, turning Wild One into a real contender."

"She's more than a contender," I correct him. "She's a champion. It was obvious she even enjoyed the crowd watching. She was born to be a show pet."

"Yes. You had her under complete control and she adored it," Kaelin says. "The Aria-7 female cried when her trainer made her orgasm."

I flinch. "No one wants to see a human pet cry."

"Unless you're on a military vessel. They love to torture the poor things."

I nod. "It's true. Perhaps if they acquired pets through more established traders and not shady Dulu sellers, they'd have better pets to begin with."

"Some trainers are complaining saying Ash should be disqualified because you bought her at a discount."

I pause, a slow smile crossing my lips. Then I laugh. Kaelin joins in, and for a moment, the tension in the room dissolves into shared amusement.

"They can complain all they like. Ash was purchased from a legitimate seller."

Kaelin nods. "I think a lot of people paid more than they ever have before for humans, given the new law and at that humans are harder to come by. So they're jealous you got Ash for next to nothing and trained her in eight months."

"What can I say? I know what I'm doing when it comes to human pets."

"I was surprised you didn't bring her to the galactic cock fixture? She must have been aching for it."

"You know she doesn't like that," I say. "I dealt with her myself in one of the trainers' rooms."

"Ah," Kaelin replies, and that one sound speaks volumes. He thinks I should have forced her instead of taking the pleasure myself.

"Her bond to me is still fragile."

"You're the expert. Now, I'll leave you to your planning. Let me know if you need adjustments made."

Kaelin leaves and I lean against the console, my gaze lingering on Ash's profile. I recall the look she gave me after today's performance, relief mingled with pride. She wants to prove herself. She wants my approval. And I want to give it to her. Finally, we've settled into a good trainer to pet dynamic.

The comm-line crackles to life. Ira's face appears in holographic form above my desk, his razor-sharp grin all too familiar.

I incline my head in polite acknowledgment.

"Aefre," he begins without any religious preamble, "I heard about Ash's latest triumph. I trust this little success is due, at least in part, to my suggestion that you acquire a new human?"

My jaw tightens, but I keep my expression neutral. Ira has a knack for taking credit, whether it's warranted or not. "Ash performed well today. She's exceeding expectations."

"You see?" Ira leans in. "I insisted you buy a fresh pet, something untamed. You had your doubts, but now look, she's become the highlight of the circuit." He sits up straight again, taking a sip of something from a black ceramic cup, as though our conversation is a casual toast to her brilliance.

"You did suggest I buy a new pet to replace Fifi," I concede. "But my methods shaped her into the pet she is."

Ira waves a hand and I suspect he's drunk. "Of course, of course. Still, I'm pleased my little 'nudge' proved so... fruitful. Everyone loves a good success story, and yours is one of the best this season. Quite a return on investment, wouldn't you say?"

"Most definitely," I answer. "Ash's rise benefits us all, especially you, considering your share in her winnings."

"Precisely," he says. "You'll continue to keep me apprised of her progress? I wish I could have been there. Damn Agnorrians always causing trouble on the border."

"I'll keep you updated."

He lingers a moment. "I want to see for myself the masterpiece we've cultivated and send over a holo of her masturbating, I've promised the crew. And Aefre, do let her know I'll be watching."

"I will," I say, "Was there anything else?"

"That's all, Aefre. Keep up the excellent work." The comm-line flickers then his image dissolves in a swirl of static.

I exhale, rubbing a hand over my jaw. Ira has a knack for making me grit my teeth. Still, he's right about one thing, Ash is shaping up to be quite the show pet. But, she is a testament to my training, not his.

I tell myself it doesn't matter; I can let him gloat. When the final scores are tallied, *I* will be the one standing in the winner's circle with Ash at my side.

My IC chimes. It's Ira,

Send me the video of her.

I search my database for the best video of Ash masturbating. I realize I don't have that many as she's so new I rarely let her touch herself. But finally I find one and briefly watch it before sending it over.

In the video I hear myself saying, "Touch yourself, Ash."

"You mean," she says in accented Imperial. "I can rub myself here and you won't punish me, Master?"

"Yes. I want to watch you."

This human woman has such a hold on me.

I am never letting you go, Ash. You'll be mine forever.

CHAPTER 51

BRIAR

The purple uniform Aefre has chosen for me today clings to my skin, it's different from yesterday's as it's light and streamlined for maximum mobility. I run my hands over it, trying to steady my trembling fingers.

I turn slightly, inspecting my tail, expertly braided so it won't hinder me. My fucking tail. A cruel reminder of how far I've been molded into this version of myself that isn't truly me.

My gaze travels over the thick bush of blonde and pink pubic hair spreading wildly down my thighs and creeping up my backside. I swear Kaelin must have slipped something into my water to make it grow even bushier. But what would be the point of mentioning it? My opinions about my own appearance don't matter. Even the simplest bodily autonomy, like using the bathroom alone, is a luxury I'm not allowed. With the touch of my trainers' rings they can make me pee and poop at the same time. Not even that bodily function is my own.

I run my hands over my braided hair that match my tail and take a deep breath trying to calm myself. Today is about survival. Precision. Performance. I've run the simulations with Gabriel so many times I could do them in my sleep, but this is no simulation. This is the real thing. Judges, audiences, competitors...

If we fail today... Or if I fail... what will happen?

What if I die on the obstacle course?

Pets have already died today. Fallen off the course and that was it. There's no safety net at the Grand Championships.

I glance in the mirror again. I look tired. I have shadows under my eyes. Gabriel and I can't resist talking when we're alone together. Just the two of us, and in those moments, I can pretend this alien pet life, *isn't* our life at all. Instead, I picture us on Earth, in a home that's ours. Then the chastity belts chime and bring us back to reality. But still Gabriel holds me through the nights and I feel safe with him.

However, I'm not in the sanctuary of his arms now. This is the arena at the Grand Championships in the Celestial Spire, and the stakes couldn't be higher.

I force myself to breathe. In. Out.

My hands are trembling again, and I make them into fists, willing the shakes will stop. I stare into my own eyes, hardening my expression, locking away the fear.

Today, I'm a competitor. I don't want to think it, but my mind has already thought the word. Pet. Not set. Not bet. Pet. The memory of Rebecca mouthing that word to me over and over again through the orange forcefield runs through my mind.

What would you tell me now Rebecca? I smile with dark humor, "Save your soul. Walk out the airlock." And part of me wants to do just that. I haven't thought about God much in my adult life, but one thing I know for certain, I don't think He's here with me among these aliens, letting humans be treated like this. Or if he is, I've failed miserably because there's a part of me that enjoys the sexiness of this life.

I hear my name, "Ash from Earth, Master Aefre's Pet," and I leave the female warm-up room. It's time.

CHAPTER 52

GABRIEL

Briar stands tense, her green eyes fixed on the shifting platforms and mirrored corridors stretched out before us.

"Step to the line," Aefre commands, releasing the leashes that bind us.

The obstacle course tests pets and trainer alike.

We move forward in sync. As we reach the starting line, I can see Briar's hands trembling slightly.

"Briar," I whisper, "Look at me."

Her eyes meet mine.

"Trust me," I say. We must win today. She cannot falter now.

She nods, barely perceptible, but it's enough.

The signal blares and we launch into motion.

The first obstacle is a series of shifting platforms suspended over simulated fiery hot lava pits. The heat radiates upward, the air shimmering with distortion. I jump first, landing solidly on the first platform. Briar follows.

"Keep your pace steady," I say in Imperial. "Don't rush."

We move as one, timing our jumps perfectly, until we reach the edge of the platforms. The next section appears ahead, a mirrored maze designed to twist perception.

This part will be hell.

As we step into the maze, the air immediately becomes cooler and the light bends unnaturally around us. The mirrors stretch endlessly in every direction. Every surface reflecting distorted images.

In one mirror, I see myself as I used to be, young, hopeful, unscarred by the reality of pet life. In another, I'm an old man and still Aefre's pet. It's a cruel trick.

"Ignore them," I say over my shoulder to Briar. "It's only a trick. The computer is dipping into our subconscious to find things to confuse and unsettle us."

The maze shifts with every step, the reflections rippling as if they're alive. At one junction, the mirrors show something meant to slow us to a dead stop.

Illusions of Earth and of freedom.

Then in another, a child of two years old with Briar's pink-streaked hair and my eyes, the toddler's collar gleaming faintly in the light.

Briar gasps. "Gabriel, is that...?"

"No," I say sharply, refusing to look at the child for too long. "It's a lie. This isn't thing doesn't tell the future. Keep moving."

The sight of the child unsettles me more than I let on, but I can't let it stop us. I grab Briar's hand, pulling her forward as the maze shifts again, the reflections turning darker and crueler.

Finally, the exit comes into view, the light beyond a welcome relief from the maze's illusions. We step through together, the air immediately warmer, the noise of the crowd crashing back into focus.

The final challenge awaits, a rotating platform suspended high above the arena floor.

I look over at Briar before we climb up the ladder to the platform. She's visibly shaking.

"You won't fall," I tell her before we begin the climb. "Trust me."

She nods, but she's still shaking.

There's nothing I can do about that. "Let's go." I climb first. It's about a hundred steps up. "Don't look down," I call to Briar. I forgot to mention the climb. Aefre never practices this on the *Luminous Arc* and I don't know why. It's terrifying.

Once we reach the top the obstacle begins moving. Briar and I must move according to Aefre's commands or we risk being pushed off the platform to our deaths. And if Aefre is wrong or too slow we will also be pushed off the platform and die.

Aefre's voice comes through the speakers, issuing rapid commands in Imperial.

"Ember, step left. Ash, move forward."

We obey, our movements controlled as the platform tilts beneath us. The glowing markers shift faster now, testing our reflexes. Briar stumbles once, her foot slipping off her marker, but she catches herself before the platform tips too far.

"Focus, ma chère," I murmur. "We're almost there."

The last sequence is a blur of jumps, spins, and perfectly timed steps. My muscles burn, my heart is pounding as Aefre's commands come faster, pushing us to our limits.

Finally, the markers stop glowing and the platform steadies beneath us. The crowd erupts into cheers.

I glance at Briar. Her exposed breasts moving up and down with her heavy breathing, her green eyes shining with relief. I reach out, brushing her arm lightly. "Bien fait, Briar. You were incredible."

For a moment, the arena fades away, the roar of the crowd nothing more than a distant sound. And it's just us in the whole galaxy.

I want to tell her that it's our destiny to be free but I can't say that here. So instead I just hold her gaze and we both bask in the praise of Aefre telling us we are 'good pets.'

CHAPTER 53

BRIAR

Gabriel and I slip into the pet observation deck, adrenaline is still coursing through my veins after the obstacle course. Other pets mill around, pets who've just competed, or who are preparing for their turn. There's an undercurrent of tension in every corner of the room.

A woman with a shaved head waves us over. At first, I hesitate, but Gabriel nudges my elbow in encouragement, "I've spoken with her before. She's kind."

We wind our way through the crowd, collapsing onto a pair of soft cushions.

"You two did well," the shaved-headed woman says in halting Imperial. "Scored high enough to keep your trainers off your backs for a while, huh?"

"Seems like it," Gabriel replies, forcing a polite smile. I don't think he'd ever describe Aefre as being 'on our backs.' And it makes me wonder what her pet life must be like.

"Where are your masters from?" I ask not recognizing the markings on her collar.

"Callix Prime . My mistress looks like a lizard woman."

"Oh," I say. I have no idea which one she's talking about. Quite a few of the trainers look like lizards. "Have you been with her long?" I ask, and Gabriel gives me a look. Apparently, I'm making some human pet faux pas, but I don't care. I'm curious.

"It's okay, Ember. She's new and I don't mind telling her what I can. I've been with my mistress for six years now. She's not good or bad. She is what she is."

"And do you sleep with her?" I ask, holding nothing back.

"Oh no, definitely not. We have cages that are stacked like coffins in the gymnasium."

Now I know why Gabriel didn't want me to ask any questions. "I'm sorry to hear that."

Another pet on the other side of the woman nods in agreement, tugging at the edge of his collar. "It's humiliating," he murmurs, glancing around. "They make us do demonstrations. Parades in front of high-ranking officials. We're fitted with gear that... emphasizes our humanness. And they like body modifications." He trails off, face burning with shame.

I swallow hard, recalling the bizarre augmentations I've heard rumors about. Extra limbs, tails, ridges. My own tail flicks behind me, and I feel a jolt of sympathy. *At least my tail could be considered cute.* Weird as fuck, but cute. If I ever make it back to Earth, I'm sure I could make a lot of friends in Japan with this tail.

Suddenly, a slight woman with long blonde hair comes over to join our group, but her focus is squarely on Gabriel. "Is it true," she asks quietly, "that your master has set the date for you and me to breed after the Grand Championships?"

My body goes rigid. I glance at Gabriel, and he looks just as stunned as I feel. "I... haven't heard anything about that," he mumbles, color rushing to his cheeks. Even so, the woman's eyes spark with lust.

"Well," she says, "if you're interested in getting a head start, maybe you and I could go over in that corner? I don't mind if the other pets watch. I'm not shy." We all look to where she's gesturing. There's a little bed in the corner. It's empty, but no doubt it's free for pets to use, *As long as it's televised throughout the galaxy and monitored by a trainer*, I think.

As the words of her suggestion sink in and Gabriel's lack of response lingers, a surge of jealousy I'm not prepared for rips through my body. "He's not interested," I say for Gabriel.

She arches an eyebrow but shrugs, unfazed. "You must be *new*. Fresh from Earth. Let me give you a tip, there are no relationships here. You don't get to call dibs on anyone and no one gets to call dibs on you. We are at our master and mistresses' mercy and if we happen to *like* what they decide for us then we should make the most of it. Ember is a champion and good looking. He's also known for being a good lover, why would I not want to have him as many times as I can? God knows there's precious else good that comes from being an alien's pet." Then she looks at Gabriel, "What do you say Ember? I hear your dick is pierced for her pleasure as well. It makes me wet just thinking about it." She licks her lips.

I dive for the woman. *I'm going to strangle her.*

Gabriel pulls me back before I can do any real damage. And then says, "I'm sorry. I don't think I'm ready for anything now, but I look forward to a future meeting with you with our trainers."

My cheeks burn at the thought of it all, Aefre orchestrating Gabriel's "breeding," and the casual way these people discuss his body like it's just another commodity.

A hush settles over our group, and the shaved-headed woman clears her throat. "You'd be better off trying to find Gael the Returner," she whispers to us. "Word is he's here today."

Gabriel and I exchange a glance. "Where?" I ask.

"No one knows. He's keeping a low profile. Some say he's disguised as a trainer; others claim he's hiding in the ventilation systems. But if he picks you as a candidate for freedom..." she stops speaking and lets her face expression say the rest: *You might get out of here alive.*

A whisper of hope passes through me, warring with the fear that it's all a trap or even worse just a rumor. I notice the woman who propositioned Gabriel eyeing me with a mix of curiosity and resentment, like she's sizing up whether I might overshadow her chances with Gabriel. It's frightening, how quickly trust dissolves among humans.

Before any of us can speak further, an attendant's voice crackles over the intercom, calling my name and Gabriel's in Imperial. Time to return to our quarters, presumably. We stand, and the small group disperses.

As Gabriel and I head for the corridor, I can't shake a sudden certainty, *We can't let them decide our fate.* Aefre, Kaelin, the doctor, Ira, the Empire—they all see us as nothing more than exotic playthings. We have to find Gael, if he's real, if there's even a chance at a future together.

Gabriel catches my hand briefly, giving it a small squeeze.

Tomorrow might bring another victory, and I'll be momentarily satisfied with my accomplishments and feel good hearing Aefre praise me for being a good girl, but one thing's certain, I can't live like this for long, with rumors of breeding dates and showpieces overshadowing my humanity.

One way or another, I vow silently as we pass under the watchful eyes of a drone overhead, *we'll find a way out.*

CHAPTER 54

AEFRE

I stand in the center of the observation deck, arms folded behind my back. Around me, half a dozen trainers are gathered together, sharing the usual gossip about upcoming auctions, pet shows, and legal and illegal human pet modifications. Over all of this, there's a question that hangs in the air and one that comes up more often now than it ever has in the past, since the IGC made it illegal to own humans as pets: Are humans sentient? It's been scientifically proven that they are not, but the discussions with other trainers who doubt Imperial science always leave a bitter taste in my mouth.

"All I'm saying," proclaims Marath, a lizard-like alien with shimmering jade scales from Callix Prime "is that these humans can't be so different from the rest of us." She flicks her serpentine tongue. "They breed humans into Imperial lines, don't they Aefre?"

I clasp my hands more tightly. "The Imperials have always allowed crossbreeding if it strengthens the gene pool," I say, keeping my tone measured. "But that doesn't mean humans are fully sentient. They simply share enough baseline DNA to produce viable offspring."

A few of the non-humanoid trainers exchange glances. One of

them, a floating organism encased in a translucent shell, quivers in a way I recognize as disagreement. "They stand upright, they speak languages, they have culture," it clicks through an external translator. "That sounds sentient to me."

A silence follows, thick and uncomfortable. I feel all their eyes, biological or otherwise, on me. I've spent forty years as a human pet trainer, climbing the ranks and perfecting my methods. I've brushed up against this question time and time again: *Are they sentient?* But I've always answered with a steadfast "no." Humans exhibit limited capacity for higher reasoning, failing to plan for the future, easily forgetting important details. They're practically children with adult bodies. They have short memories, get confused by complex instructions, and can't handle technology beyond the simplest of gadgets. If that doesn't define partial sentience, then I don't know what does.

I calmly meet the floating organism's gaze. "They are... close to us genetically, but that doesn't make them fully sentient. They're missing certain... attributes. Long-term thinking, for instance. The ability to retain knowledge from one generation to the next without outside influence."

I can sense the tension rising. One by one, the other trainers find reasons to drift off, someone goes to check a com-link, another starts fiddling with an IC. Only a handful remain. Marath crosses her arms over her slick chest, her tail coiling around her ankles. "You do realize the IGC, which is mostly made up of Imperials, passed a ban on human ownership, yes?"

"I'm aware," I respond briskly. "But it's never been enforced. The IGC—"

"They still could enforce it," she interrupts, her eyes gleaming in the artificial light. "Everyone but Imperials and other humanoids, see humans for what they are, an intelligent species, just unfortunate enough to be technologically behind everyone else in the galaxy and physically adorable. Let me cut to the chase, is the IGC going to enforce this law? Are you going to recognize that humans are probably genetically yours? What's that religious myth your zealots go on about? The Lost People?"

I clench my jaw, a surge of discomfort rising. I've heard the religious myths, how some factions believe humans might be Imperials who evolved differently, their skin pigment shifting to adapt to Earth's environment. If there's even a grain of truth to that, that humans are, in fact, our genetic cousins, then my entire career has been built on the subjugation of near-equals. It's an idea that nags at me especially more lately with Ember and his reaction to Fifi's death. But whenever it creeps in, I remind myself of all the other humans I've trained and how I know, beyond a shadow of a doubt, that they are not fully sentient.

I force myself to answer Marath with composure, "I don't pretend to be privy as to why the IGC actually passed this law. As I've mentioned to others here, some humans, one in a million show signs of intelligence and sentience. I believe that's what's happened now with humanity's sudden burst of technology, but like with everything with humanity, it will be merely a blip and then they will destroy it themselves because they will have forgotten why it was important in the first place. A truly sentient culture never behaves in this way. I personally am not worried about the IGC, they are always slow to act when the laws come about these ways... by default, but not reasoning. And many of the humanoid races would never tolerate losing their pets. It's an industry woven into our culture."

"So, you're content to keep enslaving them and ignore the possibility they might be more like Imperials than you'd like to admit?"

My throat tightens. I shift my weight, letting my gaze drift to the staging area where a young human is being put through her paces. She looks pale, trembling slightly, her collar blinking with the newest compliance tech. I see the fear in her eyes, intelligence—maybe not enough to pass an advanced Imperial exam, but enough to register her own situation. "I'm not ignoring anything," I say, forcing a calm I don't feel. "They have no real technology, no real civilization and they have had more than enough time to build something substantial, but choose to fight amongst themselves instead. They scavenge Earth's resources with minimal efficiency. Earth is on the outskirts of the Milky Way, practically a backwater. A sentient people would have thrown everything into technology to learn about the galaxy they live in. Humans instead, have chosen to create technology for the promotion of their most base carnal and violent desires. Would you call that a truly sentient society?"

One of the other trainers, a spindly-limbed insectoid with glistening black eyes, pipes in. "I visited Earth once," he chirps, mandibles clicking. "For scouting. They have art, music, and architecture. And it's true, they are behind in star flight, but they exhibit all the hallmarks of a developing civilization. Perhaps if they weren't abducted so regularly, they'd have advanced further by now. But so it is with many of the losers in the galaxy. We take what we want from them for our own pleasure and entertainment. For me, there's no question of humans being fully sentient. They are. But I don't want the laws to be enforced because I enjoy my little pets as I think we all do. You, as an Imperial, Aefre, genetically similar to humans, have more to lose with this. The mighty Empire is such a proud place and a proud people, imagine if it were discovered that there were Imperials who chose to live as uncivilized as humans?"

Some of the other trainers chuckle at this, which is irritating, but not uncommon. I know they think humans are sentient which is part of the reason that the IGC invoked this law. They believe humans would willingly choose to be their pets, which makes every Imperial uncomfortable as it begs the question if humans were sentient and chose to be pets to these other aliens, then would Imperials choose to do the same? Of course not. We are not the same as humans.

A hush lingers among us, each alien lost in their thoughts. Then Marath strides off to oversee another training session, her tail flicking in agitation. The floating organism drifts away without another word. I'm left alone, staring at the labyrinth course below. My heart pounds in a way that reminds me I'm not as young as I once was. Forty years in this business, and I've never truly doubted the basis of it, until recently.

I recall my earliest days as a trainer, full of righteous confidence, reconditioning humans to be obedient showpieces. They were and still are so... childlike in their curiosity, easily frightened and easily bribed with treats or gentle praise. And I was proud of my skill, proud to have turned so many unruly creatures into model pets. But now, as I watch the trembling girl in the staging area, a prickle of uncertainty nags at me.

"Is it possible?" I murmur under my breath, thinking about Ash and Ember. If humans are in fact sentient then I've spent my entire adult life enslaving people not so different from my own species. The shame that thought conjures is too big to face, so I shove it away, forcing myself to recall every instance of a human failing to follow directions, every meltdown, and every short-sighted decision.

My mind drifts to the IGC's ban, enacted but unenforced. I rely on that limp piece of legislation to assuage my conscience. If the IGC truly considered humans equals, they'd be enforcing the law.

Off in the distance, an alarm sounds, indicating another batch of humans is about to run the next challenge. I straighten my posture, smoothing the front of my trainer's uniform. In the end, it doesn't matter what Marath or the insectoid or that drifting intelligence believes, my livelihood depends on treating humans as partially sentient pets. The day I acknowledge otherwise is the day I destroy everything I've built.

CHAPTER 55

GABRIEL

Briar and I are talking when suddenly the door hisses open, and Aefre steps in, his green eyes scanning the room.

I'm stunned. Aefre is not a man who makes unannounced visits. He comes at the set times to watch us shower and relieve ourselves. I'm worried. Did he turn on his translator and listen to us speaking English? Is he going to punish us for talking about Gael the Returner?

"Your connection to one another is close, but it's not enough. Tonight, I'm going to remove your chastity belts and we are all going to bond together. We need to tighten the bond between pets and trainer alike."

I glance at Briar. I can't tell how she feels about this.

"You need to work on your bond," Aefre continues. "Trust each other. Understand each other and trust me. The final challenges will demand more than skill. They will demand unity from all of us."

I meet his gaze.

"Ember, I'm giving you permission to have sex with Ash with me." I'm completely fluent in Imperial, but he still speaks to me sometimes like I'm a mindless beast. "Do you understand?"

"Yes, Master Aefre."

Then Aefre looks to Ash, "Do not bite off Ember's penis. Do you understand?"

"Yes, I understand, Master Aefre" Briar answers. I can tell she's annoyed he would say that her.

"If you do, I'll sew up your vulva and you'll never have sex again."

Briar looks horrified and just then, Kaelin enters our room. It seems much smaller than it was two minutes ago. He has two leashes in his hand. He comes over and attaches one to my collar and the other to Briar's.

"Ember, take off your clothing," Aefre says.

I obey him. But the entire time I'm undressing, my eyes are locked with Briar's. Her eyes are a mixture of surprise and desire. Perhaps she doesn't mind sharing me. I know despite how much I want Briar all to myself, after being locked up in the chastity belt, I'll take what I can get.

"Oh you're already aroused," Aefre says with mock enthusiasm when he removes the chastity device from my groan.

Kaelin moves over to Briar and attaches a leash around her neck. Then leads her to Aefre. He takes her leash tightly in his hand and then pulls her up so she's standing on her tip toes. "Good girl," he says while removing her chastity belt and starting to stroke her pubic hair. "You're not nearly as excited as Ember. We need to change that. Do you have any ideas?"

Briar looks at me. I can tell she doesn't know what to say.

I can't offer her any help. I know Aefre likes these games to be mostly one-sided.

"Tell me what you want, Ash. You've done it before."

Briar is still looking at me blankly. Then she turns her gaze to Aefre. "I don't know."

Wrong answer, I think.

"You don't know?" Aefre repeats back. "If you don't know then we'll have to do what we normally would do if you weren't here."

I stiffen.

Briar sensing my tenseness says, "I changed my mind."

Aefre shakes his head.

But she still adds, "I want Ember inside of me and I want you and Kaelin to watch."

Aefre and Briar hold eye contact for some time. I'm worried he won't let her go back on her first statement but after a minute he says, "Fine. Ember, come here. I want you both to have sex on the floor like animals. I'll tell you what to do. Kaelin you hold Ember's leash tight and I'll hold Ash."

Kaelin holds my leash tightly and says, "On your knees."

I obey and watch as Briar is told to lays down on her back, legs open. And I hate that I want her so much like this. I look up to Aefre for his command.

"You're such a good boy, Ember. On the count of three you can lick her like it's your dinner. One, two..." he purposely pauses, playing with me, "three."

I don't hesitate as I begin licking Ash's sex like it's a race against time to make her orgasm. There's only one thing in the back of my mind nagging at me, the suspicion that Aefre has spiked my collar with a sex hormone. *It doesn't matter*, I tell myself, *I want this*. I need to taste her and feel her most delicate parts against my mouth. And I like the familiar comfort of Kaelin pulling on my leash as I do this.

"That's a good boy, Ember. Yes lick her lightly right there. Not too much. Back off a little. Look at the way she trembles. Oh, good girl. That's what she likes. Don't you Ash? Get back in there Ember, right there on your left side."

Kaelin pulls hard on my leash dragging me backward. I don't look up as I try to get my face between Briar's legs again. "You're going too fast. She needs time or else she won't enjoy it as much."

I give Kaelin a frustrated look as I lick my lips, tasting her desire. Then I try to move back towards her.

Aefre is holding her leash tightly. "You're such a good girl being pleasured by your partner. He's a good boy isn't he? Now listen Ash, you've got to orgasm when he comes back or they'll be pain to follow." Aefre nods to Kaelin and then I'm allowed between her legs again. "Wait, Ember. Now on my mark you have three minutes to make her orgasm or she'll be punished. Begin."

I hungrily dive into her pubic hair finding her clit again and licking and sucking like mad. I don't want her to be punished because of me.

"Thirty seconds left," Kaelin says.

"Get your nose in there," Aefre suggests. "That's it. Oh good boy. Look how she's coming for you, Ember. That's some team spirit isn't it?"

CHAPTER 56

BRIAR

"I never get tired of seeing humans with all their fur rubbing against each other while they're mating," Kaelin says, pulling Gabriel's leash so that he has to look up at him. He runs his hands through Gabriel's beard. "Look at her lubrication all over your face and fur. It's so adorably human."

Aefre pulls on my leash and says, "On all fours, Ash. I know this is the way you like it best."

"Yes Master Aefre." I obey him and he's not wrong.

Aefre pulls my leash tight as he instructs Kaelin, "Bring Ember closer. Yes, that's it. Line up your cock at her entrance, Ember. Oh look how hard you are. I bet you both are dying to have sex. Those chastity belts must have been torture. In fact, I know they were, I saw the readouts."

"Ash are you ready to have the sex of your life?" Kaelin asks. "Semen is already dripping off Ember's penis he's so excited."

"Yes, Master Kaelin."

Aefre smacks Gabriel's ass. "Good boy. Now position your penis so it's lined up with her entrance and when I say begin, you can start moving in and out of her slowly. But you can't touch her with any other parts of your body. Now begin."

I feel Gabriel breach my body with his pierced cock and it feels amazing, I moan, "Oh Gabriel."

"Bad girl," Aefre says and I get a shock through my collar. "Your human names don't exist anymore. Stop Ember. Move back out of her hole," Aefre says and I can hear Gabriel's moan of disappointment.

"Both of you will obey me," Aefre commands as he yanks on my leash and I stand up, hands behind my head. "Turn around and show me that ass."

I obey him knowing what's coming next.

"Pick up your tail."

As soon as I do he begins spanking me. He's conditioned me to count in Imperial so I do, "One, two, three..." He gives me twenty strokes.

When he finishes he asks me, "Are you going to be a good girl now?"

"Yes, Master Aefre," I answer him. I'm so sexually frustrated from the chastity belts I would do anything right now to have sex with Gabriel. I look over at Gabriel's erect penis and I want it so much. I inadvertently touch myself between my legs.

"Bad bad girl," Aefre says taking my hand away. "Don't touch yourself without my permission. Now we're going to have to tie you up. Kaelin."

Kaelin hands Gabriel's leash to Aefre and then proceeds to tie me up with wrists attached to each corresponding ankle so that I have to lay with my knees up and my hands at my sides.

"Good. But just so you don't ruin this anymore. Kaelin, get the muzzle."

Kaelin puts the muzzle on me. But I don't even care. I just want Gabriel to inside of me. I hope my eyes convey that to him.

"Kaelin bring Ember to a kneeling position. That's it. Now Ember I want you enter her with your penis only. I will tell you when and how fast you should go." Aefre tells Gabriel and I watch as he obediently obeys. "In and now out. In. And Out. In. Hold it there. Don't move. Now out."

This goes on for so long I think I'm going to die being so close to an orgasm and not being about to have one.

CHAPTER 57

Aefre

I'm becoming so aroused watching Ember thrust his wet penis in and out of Ember's furry folds I don't know how long I can watch this without participating.

Just when I think Ember is going to orgasm, I say, "Wait. Back up. Take yourself out of her."

Ember is hesitant but Kaelin drags him back by his leash and even shocks him once.

Then I stand and say, "Ember come undress me."

He comes over on his knees and with trembling fingers begins taking off my clothing. He's done this for me many times. Once I'm naked I tell him, "Get my cock ready."

Ember puts my penis into his mouth and then licks and sucks my balls. Then I get to my knees and position myself in front of Briar's waiting body. "Now Ash, it looks like you need a hard fuck. Is that what you want from me?"

She cannot speak with the muzzle, but she nods eagerly. I look at Ember then, "You see. We all need each other. Now hold my dick up to her entrance."

Ember only hesitates for a second before doing what I ask. Once my penis is inside of Ash I take hold of her hips and pump into her the way I know she wants right now. She likes it hard and rough. "Hold her nipples up and still, Ember." I tell him and he obeys. "Look at her. She loves that, coming again. Such a good girl."

I orgasm hard into Ash. Her human vagina is way too small to take all of my semen and it spills out onto the floor, into her fur, and on to her thighs.

I move back. "Ember, lick her clean of my seed." I watch him as he begins on the floor and then her thighs, and finally her vagina where it's still seeping out of her in white waves. "That's a good boy."

When he finishes I say, "Now you may have her too. Position yourself. Now enter her. Good boy, Ember. That's it you can go faster. Kaelin hold his collar tighter. That's it. Now go faster Ember. Faster."

I watch as Ember releases inside of her. "Oh it's not so much because you're human. Why don't you lick that up as well. And when you're finished, we'll take the muzzle off of Ash and you can kiss her."

Ember removes himself from Ash and then begins licking up his own semen from her. Kaelin removes her muzzle. "Now kiss her. Share that with her."

Ember leans over Ash and kisses her passionately. Their tongues intertwining with all the sex we just had.

"Good pets," I say satisfied with this trainer and pet bonding session. After Kaelin has cleaned them up in the shower, we put the chastity belts back on.

CHAPTER 58

BRIAR

After Aefre and Kaelin have left, the air between us feels thick with unspoken thoughts. I look over at Gabriel, but he's just staring at the ceiling.

My mind is reeling. I want to talk about what just happened about how I wanted it and didn't want it at the same time. No, that's not true. *I wanted it.* I just didn't want myself to want it. But the sexual tension between all of us has been building for quite some time since that last time, the off-hand remarks Aefre makes about the hair between my legs, the way Gabriel watches my breasts bounce when I run, and the way that I look at Aefre when I'm in my pet bed aroused knowing he can give me what I want. And I enjoy having them together both of them playing their roles of trainer and pet.

But I worry that Gabriel feels like he should have protected me. I remember last time. But then again, he watched as Aefre had sex with me and it turned him on. *He's not like men from Earth,* I remind myself. He's lived in this world for twelve years. This is normal, isn't it?

In the end, I decide that I enjoyed myself and that if Gabriel didn't, then it's up to him to say something about it.

"Do you think anyone on Earth knows about *them*, the aliens?" I ask, breaking the silence and changing the subject.

Gabriel shifts, his golden eyes catching the faint light as he turns in my direction.

"You mean the Imperials? The Octopods? Or all of them?"

I nod. "Yeah. All of them. All of this." I motion around the room.

He exhales softly. "I don't know. Maybe. I would like to believe that if they knew they would try to warn people against alien abduction or do something..."

"It's strange. In the last ten years, people can easily make videos and pictures with their phones and share them with the world in real time. And there are so many UFO videos online, but no one believes them. It makes me think there's a conspiracy to keep all of this hidden and the best way to do that is to tell everyone else that the person with the UFO story is crazy."

His hand brushes against mine. "And if we went back? If we somehow made it back to Earth, what do you think they'd say if we told them about our lives here?"

I laugh bitterly. "They'd call us crazy for sure."

I close my eyes, letting my imagination run wild with that thought. Going back to Earth and telling people about Aefre, Kaelin, the collars, the tail, the sex, the Grand Championships, everything. "They'd say we were making it all up for money. A bad sex story. A really terrible one."

"Yeah," Gabriel says with a faint smile. "Human pets in a galactic competition. Doesn't exactly scream *believable*. No one in France would ever believe that."

"And even if they believed us, what then? What could either of our governments do? Send an unarmed rocket up and demand their people back?" I ask rhetorically.

Gabriel doesn't answer me, so I continue.

"You know, I always used to hear things. Retired military guys, conspiracy theorists, even that Israeli space guy, what's his name? Eshed?—talking about aliens."

Gabriel raises an eyebrow. "And what did you think?"

"I mean, I was curious," I admit. "But then Eshed said Trump knew about aliens, and I no longer believed him."

He lets out a low laugh. "Pourquoi? Pourquoi Trump?"

"Because there's no way Trump could keep a secret that big. Not a chance. He'd want to get in there and try to negotiate some kind of deal."

"Touché," he says. "But why would Trump know? Alien real estate?"

"Oh you don't know. He was President of the United States. Maybe he is again. I was taken before the election."

Gabriel smiles. "It's still true then, anyone can be anything in the US."

"Except be believed if you talk about aliens. Ironic that isn't it?"

Gabriel's goes quiet with his own thoughts.

"Anyway, I never quite believed anything I heard about aliens. So it makes me wonder...why?"

"And now?" Gabriel asks, his voice quieter, his amber eyes fixed on mine.

"Now, I wish I'd listened more," I whisper.

We are silent just looking into each other's eyes. I don't know what's worse, that the people on Earth might not know about us, or that they might know and simply not care.

Gabriel's hand brushes mine again, this time more deliberately. "Maybe it's better this way. If they did know, then people might be living in fear all the time. But then, not to warn people is disingenuous. I'm not an educated man, but surely there's someone on Earth, some group that could build some kind of defense or at least provide people with a tracker so the police would know where someone went."

My heart is breaking for him. I can't imagine the pain his parents must have suffered looking for him after his disappearance.

"You're right though, regular people wouldn't believe us even if we tried to warn them. It might just make our lives even worse, to return and to be called liars. Even though, it's such a strange thing to lie about," Gabriel says, almost to himself. "But we know it's real. We've lived it."

"That's enough, right? We don't owe Earth a warning?" I say wanting to clear my conscience.

His gaze meets mine, his expression softening. "It's enough. If we get a chance to do anything it won't be wasted on a message back to Earth. Our chance will be spent on trying to escape."

"With Gael?"

"Yes, or someone else like him. He can't be the only one. But he's the one here now."

The silence returns, and I close my eyes, trying to imagine a life where any of this makes sense. "Gabriel, do you think Aefre would ever give us this kind of freedom? A room to ourselves, to just... be?"

He considers my question. "If we win, maybe. Aefre's strategic, not generous. But it's possible. Why?"

"If we win, it could be a start," I say. "A chance to learn more about Gael the Returner. And maybe next year... we go."

He exhales sharply, muttering something in French, his voice laced with frustration. "Si nous gagnons, cela ne veut rien dire, Briar. L'année prochaine? Tu crois vraiment qu'ils nous laisseront partir?"

"I don't understand you," I say softly.

He turns to me, his golden eyes blazing with intensity. "Next year?" he repeats in English. "You think they'll just let us leave? This year may be our only chance. I don't want that image we saw in the mirror maze, the child with the collar, our child, to become a reality here. Getting two adults out is difficult enough, but a child?" He throws a hand up in the air, "Forget about it. Impossible."

Before I can respond, he leans over, cupping my face gently. His lips find mine in a kiss that's tender but filled with purpose.

When he pulls back, his voice is full of raw emotion. "I want freedom. And I won't leave without you. Je ne peux pas imaginer ma vie sans toi. We're a team, Briar. We're not meant to be pets. We're human. We're meant to be free."

CHAPTER 59

AEFRE

I watch Ash and Ember warm-up. Their movements are stiff at first, likely still feeling the strain of yesterday's challenges. But there's something different in the way they carry themselves this morning. A steadiness that wasn't there before.

Last night was what we all three needed. When I returned to my room, I checked their collars' readouts as a precaution. Cortisol levels were a steady baseline, heart rates were stable, but slightly lower indicating calm. A new rise in dopamine confirmed contentment, while a subtle increase in oxycontin told me there was an emotional closeness between them, perhaps even trust between all three of us. And their endorphins were elevated, indicating satisfaction. The balance I sought between them and me is solid for the moment. But, I'm going to keep monitoring them and making adjustments until I am certain their bond is unbreakable.

I study their synchronization as they move through the warm-up drills, noting the way Ash glances at Ember more often now, as if seeking silent confirmation and Ember gives her more assurance that what she's doing is right. This is exactly the kind of progress I had hoped for after our session last night.

Kaelin enters followed closely by two other trainers. Their skepticism is evident in the way they linger, watching Ash and Ember with scrutinizing eyes.

"A bold gamble," one of them remarks. "Allowing them to have sex with each other as well. Are you that confident, Aefre? Or are you experimenting with breeding them already?"

The bait is obvious, and I don't bite. My gaze remains fixed on the pair below. "They needed to connect and it was completely supervised."

"Connection?" the second trainer echoes. "With *that* female? I wouldn't risk my prize male even with a muzzle and a leash. She's dangerous."

"She *was* dangerous," I retort. "But I've trained her now. She's no longer *that* human animal. And Ember doesn't need protection from Ash. Their bond is strong."

"Didn't Ember have a strong bond with your last female?" the first trainer asks. "What was her name? Fifi?"

The mention of her reminds me of what I lost. Fifi, the one who slipped through my fingers. "Ember won't make the same mistake twice," I say quietly, though the weight of that statement is directed inward. *Neither will I.*

"You're certain you're not letting sentiment cloud your judgment?" the second trainer presses.

"It's not sentiment," I counter, turning to face them fully. "It's strategy. They're both progressing exactly as I intended."

"It's still a risk," the first trainer says. "Calculated or not, you're betting everything on a pet who was forced on you. Let's not forget that the Octopods practically shoved her into your hands."

I allow myself the faintest smirk. "And how lucky I am they did. Thank you for reminding me, I've been meaning to send them a bottle of their finest nectar as a 'thank you.'"

Kaelin breaks his silence then. "Ash and Ember are the strongest pair on this circuit. Aefre's training has taken Ash from a liability to a contender. If anyone doubts his methods, they haven't been paying attention."

The trainers exchange glances, their skepticism thinning, but not disappearing. They leave shortly after.

"They're different now," Kaelin says quietly looking at Ash and Ember below.

"If they weren't, I wouldn't be standing here defending them."

Below us, Ash and Ember tackle the coordination drills. Their movements require precision and trust through an intricate sequence of mirrored actions that leave no room for error. Ash hesitates at a particularly complex turn, but Ember adapts instantly, guiding her with a subtle shift. They finish the drill flawlessly.

"Good," I murmur.

"Fifi had potential too," Kaelin says carefully, testing the waters.

"She did," I admit. "But her bond with Ember was fragile. I'm not making the same mistake with Ash."

I bring up my control ring, subtly increasing their oxytocin levels through their collars. They won't notice, not consciously. But the connection they feel, the trust that grows between them, will solidify even further. They'll attribute it to their own bond, their own effort, and that's how it should be.

Kaelin gives me an anxious look. He thinks it's too much, but he's not as experienced as I am.

"Go on. Just say it."

"You know what I'm going to say. If they start believing it's actual love...they can behave erratically. You know what happens when pets imagine themselves in love."

I wave a hand dismissively, gesturing down at the training floor below, where Ash and Ember are exchanging smiles during a short break. "They have no reason to do anything drastic. Their lives are comfortable on the *Luminous Arc*. You saw them last night. They enjoyed themselves."

"Comfortable, yes, but they might still be seduced by the idea of freedom."

"Rubbish." I face him. "Look at Ember. He's been with us since he was practically a boy. He knows he wouldn't last a year on his own out there. And Ash—" I pause, watching her brush a lock of pink hair behind her ear as she leans in to say something to Ember. "She'd do anything he wanted, the moment he asks. They complement each other perfectly. Ember was shaped by a matriarchal system, always waiting for a woman's lead. Ash, coming from a patriarchal world, subconsciously defers to male authority, especially a man she loves, even if it's artificially induced. They're caught in this loop, neither one truly leading nor even noticing they're in it."

Kaelin arches a brow. "But what if they break that loop? Share decisions as equals? Agree on something like... running away with Gael? Two pets who believe they are in love and working together is risky. Even you can't deny that possibility, Aefre."

My gaze drifts downward again. Ash and Ember are back at their drills, moving in flawless tandem. I feel a surge of satisfaction. My training and meticulous planning are finally bearing fruit. They'll be unstoppable if they perform at this level in competition. *Why would they ever want to leave?*

"Ash and Ember have no reason to throw away everything they've worked for. If they win, they'll have status and comfort beyond anything they'd find out there. Ember knows that. I even allow him to use his UCs to pay off the attendants in the cleansing room. He's got the best pet life any human could ask for."

CHAPTER 60

G ABRIEL

I watch from the pets' observation deck, my knuckles white against the railing as the latest men's round begins below. The judges have set up obstacles with razor sharp spikes and rotating blades. Unlike the women's competitions, there are no illusions here, just primal brutality. In the Empire, men aren't considered clever enough for mental tasks. We're the "muscle," forced into these lethal gauntlets, treated like performing beasts. *C'est cruel*, I think bitterly.

I watch as another man slips at the final jump, and the crowd cries out before he falls to his death. My stomach turns violently. I never used to feel this horror. Last year, even the year before, I watched men lose their lives without this physical revulsion.

But today, it's different. I can't look away from the crushed remains of that man's life. And then it occurs to me.

I raise a trembling hand to my collar, tracing the smooth metal with Aefre's name on it. *Did he keep me numb last year? Or was it that I only wanted to win?* My pulse hammers at the possibility that these feelings, this sudden empathy, might be artificially stirred or suppressed by Aefre's meddling.

The crowd roars below as the next male pet staggers into the arena. *Why am I only seeing the cruelty now, after so many years?*

In the distance, the overhead speakers announce the next pet's name, but the words don't register. All I can do is stand here, grappling with the question I can't shake, *Which part of me is real, and which part belongs to Aefre's manipulations?*

CHAPTER 61

BRIAR

The whispers in the training hall this morning confirmed what I had already suspected, that the individual challenges for women are different, designed to fuck with your head. In a matriarchal galaxy, females are seen as the thinkers, the intellectuals, the manipulators of mind and strategy. They believe even human female pets possess these same qualities, so they test our minds too. And I've been told more than once that the Garden of Shadows Challenge is as much about survival as it is about unraveling who you really are.

That's a terrifying thought. I've only seen glimpses of my true self and she's a fucking ruthless bitch and she's going to eat me alive.

I stand at the threshold to the challenge. The artificial sunlight from the arena has been replaced by a dim, eerie glow filtering through twisted, alien trees. The "garden" sprawls before me, its paths shifting like something alive.

Aefre said, "This is for your mind, Ash. Show them it's as strong as your body."

The gate behind me hisses shut, sealing me in.

The first step I take onto the soft, moss-like ground sends a shiver

through me. The plants seem to react, glowing faintly, their bioluminescent tendrils curling toward my feet. They pulse in time with my
breath, or maybe my heartbeat. I can't tell. It doesn't matter. It's
creepy and unnerving.

The lead judge lists my objectives: "Retrieve the Orb of Essence
from the Heart of the Garden. Survive. Twenty points."

I move forward cautiously. The garden is watching me, reading
my mind, feeding on my thoughts, and my fears.

And then it begins.

The first apparition appears so suddenly I trip on the moss and
nearly fall. A small figure stands in the path ahead, a child, no more
than three years old, with golden curls with ombre pink tips, and
piercing green eyes. It's the child from the mirror maze, the one with
my hair and Gabriel's eyes.

"Mommy," it whispers, its voice soft but chilling. "Why did you
leave me?"

I freeze. "You're not real," I say aloud, trying to convince myself
as much as the hologram.

The child takes a step closer, a tiny pudgy hand reaching out to
me. She looks so real, my heart stops for a second.

"Mommy, don't leave me here. Maman, je ne veux pas rester ici!
Take me with you. We have the same collar. I belong with you and
Daddy on the *Luminous Arc*. Don't leave! I don't like it here!"

I force myself to move, stepping around it, but the child follows,
its voice growing louder speaking a mixture of English, Imperial, and
French. It's the most frightening thing I've ever encountered.

"Mommy, why don't you love me anymore? Why won't you save
me? Don't you want me?"

Tears run down my face, but I shake them away. So many times I
wondered why my father chose suicide over me. And I used to
wonder why he didn't want me. This child's voice sounds exactly the
same as mine used to, when I would cry into my pillow, "Daddy, why
didn't you want me?" I stop and let the memory run its course. Then

I turn to the little girl. "You're not real," I repeat, louder this time. The garden seems to laugh, but then it concedes and the child finally fades into mist.

I don't get far before the path shifts again, leading me into a clearing. There, standing together, are my parents. My father's warm brown eyes and my mother's long blonde hair. They look just as they did before they were taken from me.

"Briar," my mother says. "Come here. We're so proud of you."

"Mom?" My voice cracks, my feet dragging me closer even though I know better.

"Come home, Briar," my father says, his voice steady but filled with pain. "You don't belong here. It was all a misunderstanding. All of this. We didn't die. You were the one in a coma. All this has been a dream. It's time to wake up now and join us."

My chest tightens as they step closer, their hands outstretched. I want to run to them, to feel their arms around me again. I want to believe this has all been a dream. "Everything? The social workers, the foster homes, my job, the aliens, Gabriel?" My mind centers on Gabriel and I feel something shift. *This isn't real* and if I run to them I'll probably fall to my death.

My mother gives me a sad smile. "Yes it's all been a dream, baby. We're so happy you're waking up from your coma. We will have such a wonderful life together. Come here and give me a hug. I've missed you so much."

I take another step toward them. I long to have parents. Sometimes I even forgot that I had them. I felt as if I was just born into existence from the sea foam and found on the beach.

But, is this real? Was I in a coma all this time? Did the nurses have on the television that's led to this nightmare? How do I know what they're saying is true?

I say the word out loud, "Trust." And then I think of Gabriel. "You're not real," I whisper, backing away. Their faces twist into grotesque grins before vanishing entirely.

But the garden isn't done with me. The path curves sharply,

leading me into a dark alcove where a single figure kneels in front of a painted wooden cross. I freeze. Rebecca.

Her blonde hair hangs limply around her face, her skin pale and translucent, as though she's fading with each passing second. She looks up at me, her eyes hollow. "Briar," she whispers. "Pray with me. Help me find my way back to Earth. To Heaven. Saint Peter says we can only enter together. You must pray with me. Don't leave my soul with these devils."

I shake my head, tears spilling down my cheeks. "Rebecca, I'm sorry, I can't—"

"Please," she begs, crawling toward me in an unnatural way. "They took me, Briar. Just like they took you. Help me find peace."

"I can't. It's not real," I say.

Rebecca moves forward abnormally and grabs both of my hands in her cold ones. She speaks in a demonic voice, "It's real. I've seen the monsters here. They chase me and they'll chase you too after you die, which won't be long now. Pray with me now and our souls will be returned to Earth, where we both belong. You know the words. Pray Briar or risk eternal alien slavery in their Afterlife."

I stumble back, shaking my head violently. "You're not real!" I scream, my voice echoing through the garden.

Rebecca's face changes to something akin to a monster, her eyes darkening as she lunges at me.

I cry out, falling backward as her form dissolves into a swarm of glowing insects that scatter into the trees. I realize I almost fell off a cliff into a valley. I pull myself up and sit down for a second. I have to collect my thoughts. My heart is pounding in my ears. *Nothing here is real,* I remind myself. Then I get to my feet. I must keep moving.

The garden grows darker, the air thicker, and I can barely see the path now, but I know I'm close. I can hear the Orb of Essence chiming in the distance.

I hold my breath looking at the orb. *I just have to grab it, right? That's all.* But a figure steps out from behind a tall hedge, blocking my view of the orb. At first, I think it will be another hologram, but when I see the measured stance of the figure, my heart stops in a panic. Aefre.

He stands with his arms crossed as his cold eyes assess me. Exactly how he appears in real life: the trainer I've relied on, the man who molded me from day one. In so many ways, he's been an authority figure, teacher, captor, lover, and I don't want to admit it, but father figure as well. Seeing him here, blocking my path, sends a jolt of confusion throughout my entire body.

"Master Aefre? What are you doing here?"

Aefre doesn't answer. He takes a step closer, his green eyes locked on me.

My mind races with possibilities. *Is this another illusion?* Maybe something is wrong with the challenge?

"You're not supposed to be in the female's individual challenge," I say. "This has to be a trick."

"A trick?" he echoes. "You're the one who's been tricked, Ash. Look at you—bleeding, trembling, and doubting yourself. I came to collect you before you fail this challenge and die."

His words hit me like a punch. That calm and condescending tone. It's exactly how he's reprimanded me before. It's so authentic, so hurtful, and real. I doubt my own senses for a second, but then I say, "Stop. Please move. I need to get the orb."

He takes another step towards the orb like he's going to take it himself. *Could it really be him?*

I make a fast move trying to grab the orb to end the challenge. Then I'll know what's real and what's not.

Aefre lunges and manages to strike me. Pain explodes across my ribs as I stagger back, away from the orb.

"Think carefully, Ash. If you fail this challenge, you fail me."

I'm struggling to stand up straight. My mind is reeling. *Is he real?*

Aefre strikes again, a move he taught me himself. A kick at my

Achilles tendon. I barely move away in time or else I'd be on the ground right now.

My heart is beating so quickly I can hear it in my ears. *It isn't him.* It can't be.

But am I sure? If I strike a trainer in the Grand Championships, I'll probably be put to death.

Before I can think about it further, Aefre rushes me so fast I don't have time to defend myself.

I let out a strangled cry from the hit. Tears begin to blur my vision. I remember Gabriel reminding me that illusions can kill here if I let them. This is no harmless nightmare. Even if this is a hologram, my death will be real.

I muster the last bit of strength I have and attack Aefre with another move he taught me. I was never a fighter before I became a pet.

Aefre staggers for a second and I reach for the orb but he quickly blocks me and pushes me to the ground.

My lip is bleeding. I look up at him. His eyes are narrowed in a savage way I've never seen before.

Aefre surges forward, a vicious strike that leaves me struggling to catch my breath.

"I can't do this," I gasp. My vision begins to black out at the edges. "Please Master Aefre..."

His face contorts with something like triumph. "You never were worthy to be partnered with Ember."

A wave of heartbreak floods me. Is that something Aefre might actually say?

"I know from the collars that Ember imagines Fifi when he's fucking you."

Fury gets me to my feet. I make eye contact with Aefre. I drop into a low stance. My muscles protesting with every move I make, but I have to fight.

The orb gleams just beyond him. But that's not what I'm thinking about right now. Lunging forward with all the strength I have left; I sidestep his incoming blow and drive my elbow into his sternum.

He reels, but not enough. Aefre retaliates by gripping my wounded arm and twisting it until intense pain explodes.

I bite down on my scream, driving my knee upward into his gut.

Aefre stumbles and releases me. When he catches his breath he says, "I wish you would have been the one to go out of the air lock on Abyssal Nexus. I never wanted you."

His words hurt me so much whether he's real or a hologram I'm going to kill him. I put my entire body weight behind a final strike to his temple, the move Aefre taught me specifically for subduing monstrous creatures. The irony. The blow connects with a sickening crack.

Aefre's eyes widen in shock.

Did I just kill my trainer?

If I did then it's time to pray because I'm definitely going to be put out of an airlock.

I stare at Aefre's dead body. Time seems to slow as I panic. Was I supposed to control my anger? Was that supposed to be the challenge and now I've failed by killing? Aefre always reminding me that humans have no self-control and largely act on instincts alone.

Then with great relief, I watch as the illusion of Aefre disappears just like the others before him.

I drop to my knees, crying. I can't do this anymore. The holographic Aefre's words still ring in my ears, "I never wanted you." After a minute, the glowing orb catches my attention, as if it's calling to me.

I crawl over to it on my hands and knees. Then I close my fingers around the warm orb and a brilliant surge of light engulfs me.

When the light fades, I'm back in the arena.

The hush of the crowd is eerie, like everyone witnessed me do something unspeakable. I clutch the orb against my body, tears mixing with sweat and blood. I raise my eyes to the trainer's level, half-expecting to see the real Aefre scowling, arms crossed. But my chest throbs with confusion when I can't find him.

An announcer's voice booms overhead, rattling off my success in crisp Imperial and then the audience roars.

The orb dims in my grip, its purpose fulfilled.

I struggle to my feet, vision hazy, clutching the orb like a lifeline. Tomorrow will bring new horrors, new trials. But I survived another day, if just barely.

CHAPTER 62

AEFRE

Kaelin and I stand near the observation window, watching the footage of Ash's challenge replay on the holographic display. My breath releases slowly, relief washing over me. She passed. She survived.

The Garden of Shadows Challenge is one of the more insidious trials for female pets. It's designed to prey on their intellect and emotions, to root out vulnerabilities that can't be addressed with mere physical strength. Many have failed, not because they lacked physical capability, but because they weren't clever enough to navigate the psychological maze.

Ash, however, proved she could handle it. She stumbled, yes, over the projection of me, a moment that could have undone her, but she recovered.

"I thought she was done for when your holograph appeared," Kaelin comments.

"She exceeded my expectations," I reply, my gaze still on the screen as it replays the hologram of me. It's an uncanny replica. "That last hologram really tested her."

Kaelin shifts slightly uncomfortably. "Do you think they did it to undermine your connection to her before the main event tomorrow?"

"Yes. But it won't work. Now that Ash knows that was only a hologram she knows nothing that was said was real. And I've already seen her and told her how much I value you her. I even gave her some chocolates. But it'll be Ember who convinces her that he never thinks of Fifi when they're having sex."

"You're not worried that Ember will play on her fears, twist this further? That human pet child hologram said, 'Don't leave me.' That came from Ash's mind."

"It's expected. How could Ash not be affected by the talk of Gael the Returner. It seems all anyone talks about anymore. So of course it's in her subconscious. But thinking about something and actually acting on it are two different things entirely. I'm not concerned. Ash scored well. She and Ember are in pole position to win tomorrow. Why would they consider leaving?"

"To me, it seems like an unnecessary risk. If I were you, I'd keep Ash with me tonight alone to show her how much she means to me. Those words spoken by the holographic you, hurt her."

CHAPTER 63

G<small>ABRIEL</small>

As soon as Briar and I return to our quarters she asks me, "What if we don't win tomorrow?"

"We will," I say firmly.

"And if we don't? What happens then? What happens to me? Will Aefre sell me? Toss me out an airlock? You know that's what he said in the Garden of Shadows Challenge."

I kiss the top of her head. "That wasn't real, Briar. Those were your insecurities." I tap on her collar. "They know everything about us from this. Aefre for what he is would never toss a human out an airlock. He sells them on to who thinks are reputable people."

"I'm so confused, Gabriel. Why are you defending him?"

"I'm not. I'm just letting you know the truth. Aefre is not going to kill you or sell you. I've seen the way he looks at you, the way he gives you special privileges no one else has ever had, not even me or Mags. I know, he's never going to let you go. You've exceeded his expectations. And that's why we *have* to win tomorrow. You and I together, it's the irony that he's trained us so well, that we're the best. This is our chance, Briar. Notre seule chance to get out of this life."

Confusion clouds her eyes. "But we are lucky to be on the *Lumi-*

nous Arc. You must know that. I've heard enough horror stories from the other pets to last a lifetime. We could end up somewhere much worse."

"This is true. I've been with Aefre almost longer than I lived on Earth and I've experienced it all. All the best alien pet life has to offer. And let me assure you, a human pet's life is a life only half lived, even if it's with someone like Aefre. Briar, listen to me, you've awakened my soul. Reminded me that I still have one. And I demand more than this life Aefre has to offer," I say, my voice steady. "I want to take this collar off and breathe without permission."

"And what if Gael is lying? What if this human colony everyone is talking about doesn't exist? What if he's just another Imperial looking to sell us to the highest bidder?"

"J'y ai pensé, Briar," I say, my tone rising with my frustration. "I've thought about this a thousand times and I said the exact same things to Fifi last year. But what's the alternative? Staying here? Staying in this gilded cage? With tails and collars and possibly having a child born into the same slavery? That child we saw in the mirrors was the most frightening thing I've ever seen in a challenge. Our child with Aefre's collar around its neck." My voice breaks. "Or even worse, you bearing Aefre's child? I can't, Briar. I won't live like this any longer. We must go. Say you'll go with me..."

She hesitates, her green eyes searching mine. "I'm scared of ending up in a worse place. Aefre treats us—"

"Comme des animaux," I interrupt, my voice sharper than I intended. "He treats us like non sentient animals, Briar. Do you want to live the rest of your life with a collar around your neck? Making no decisions for yourself. Putting your trust in another for your complete well-being? Bearing children you have no say over?"

Her jaw tightens, and for a moment, I think she'll argue her point further. But instead, she looks away. "I don't know. I'm scared, Gabriel."

"Then trust me. The colony is real," I say, my voice gentler now.

"I believe it is. And I believe Gael will take us there. I can't do this without you, Briar."

She nods slowly, her green eyes meeting mine. "Okay," she says quietly.

"Merci," I murmur, brushing a strand of hair from her face. "Tu es tout pour moi, Briar. You mean everything to me. And trust me, we must leave."

CHAPTER 64

BRIAR

I've never been so nervous. I'm standing next to Gabriel in the waiting area. We're up next to compete in the last challenge, The Eternal Convergence. There are four other pet pairs left and we are in the lead from the qualifying rounds. But there's still a chance we could lose. The points awarded in the final round are much higher, because the stakes and the risk to our lives are also higher.

Then there is the Bond Breaker Challenge for extra UCs. Gabriel promises me that if we have to do the Bond Breaker, he won't make the same mistake as last year, citing our strong connection as the difference.

But it's not like we have a choice. If we win the Grand Championships, it will be up to Aefre to decide whether we compete in the Bond Breaker. It wasn't just Gabriel who was broken by Fifi dying last year. I don't think even Aefre knows what his decision will be until we reach that point.

A wave of nausea rolls over me. I grip Gabriel's arm for support and then run out of the waiting area to the bathroom. All the toilets are busy so I stand over a sink and barely manage to steady myself before I vomit.

My throat burns as I try to catch my breath. The sink automatically removes the waste. Then I rinse my mouth and splash water on my face. I look closely at my reflection in the mirror. I look pale. But I'm not surprised given the circumstances.

As I step out of the bathroom, a small group of human female pets are gathered near the entrance. One of them, a tall woman with auburn hair braided neatly down her back, tilts her head at me. "You're doing really well for someone in your condition."

I blink, confused. "What?"

Another pet, a shorter woman with dark eyes and a knowing smirk, raises her hand and makes a rounded motion over her stomach, a gesture that needs no words.

My heart stops.

"No," I say automatically, shaking my head. "I'm not—."

The auburn-haired woman shrugs. "If you say so."

The image of the holographic child from the Garden of Shadows flashes in my mind. A child with golden curls with ombre pink tips, and piercing green eyes ... *Could it be real?* It's ridiculous to think our child would look like that, a perfect blend of us, including my artificially pink hair. But what if there's a child growing inside me now? Would I want them to live the life of a pet?

No.

But risking that child's future trying to escape?

Then another thought grips me, colder and darker. What if it's not Gabriel's? What if it's Aefre's? The very idea makes me feel sick all over again. What if the child would have Imperial features? Could a child like that be raised in a human colony?

If we made it. If the colony is *even* real.

What if I stayed? This, for what it is, is safe. I know Aefre would care for this child no matter who the father is. Could I say the same about Gabriel?

"Do they really send them away? The babies?" I suddenly ask the group of women. I'd heard rumors that half breeds disappear. Sometimes in the middle of the night and then their mothers are gaslit into believing the children they bore were all in their imagination.

The women all turn and look at me again, surprised I'm still here.

"Yes. Most trainers let you keep the baby for about a year to breastfeed and bond and then they steal them from you when you least expect it," one of the women says on the verge of tears. The other women comfort her by putting their hands on her arm and giving her sympathetic looks.

"If no one knows you're pregnant yet, which would be by the grace of God given their technology, but it does happen. Not all women have high amounts of hCG. But if that were the case and I were you, I'd try to fall so hard during the next challenge that it was lost."

I look at her horrified.

A security guard stops nearby and begins to observe us. There's no official rule we can't talk in large groups, but they don't like it.

The woman with auburn hair whispers, "If the judges know, you won't be allowed to compete. Chin up and act like it's just nerves."

"Trust me," the woman with the dark eyes says. "You think you've been through some shit with all these challenges? Wait until they rip your child from you and make it a pet. They might as well rip your heart out. Nothing will matter then. You'll be the mindless human they already think you are." There are tears in the woman's eyes and her words send a shiver down my spine.

I feel so sorry for her I can't speak. I watch as the women move on, their conversation drifting into the background, but their words stay with me.

My thoughts spiral. If I tell Aefre, he might pull me out of the competition. I'd lose my chance to win and to escape. If I tell Gabriel, what would he do? I don't know.

This changes everything. It's not just my life at risk anymore. It's not just about me or Gabriel or even Aefre.

It's about what kind of life I want to give this child...if there even is a child. Maybe those women are wrong.

Maybe this is all just nerves.

I close my eyes, trying to steady my breathing and trying to remember my last period. I know it's been awhile. All the men on the *Luminous Arc* are blood hounds, so every period is very memorable, but I just thought I wasn't having a period because I was training so much. It's a possibility. But the other symptoms? The weird smells and the vomiting...

I decide that no matter what my physical condition, the best thing for me to do now is to compete, and let fate decide what happens next.

CHAPTER 65

AEFRE

The good news from Celestial Spire security spreads quickly among the trainers, Gael the Returner has been arrested.

I study the holographic display, the image of the man in question flickering before me. He looks unassuming, his features plain, and his clothing deliberately understated. He doesn't fit the larger-than-life stories whispered among the pets, but that's no surprise. So-called heroes rarely do.

Kaelin stands at my side with his arms crossed. "It seems too convenient."

"Security has been tracking his movements for weeks. So it's not that convenient."

"This man looks too calm to be Gael. Stealing pets from the Grand Championships is one of his favorite activities. Proving to us that he has allies everywhere. So, I don't think this is him."

I glance at Kaelin. "You think the man they have in custody is a decoy?"

"It's what I'd do if I were Gael. Let the trainers relax, make them think the threat is gone. Meanwhile, his network continues to operate unnoticed."

I tap a finger against the edge of the console. Kaelin has a tendency to see shadows even when there are none. But Gael is a man of strategy, a figure who has built his reputation on slipping through the cracks, but the question is, would he sacrifice one of his own to steal a few human pets this year? There's no doubt this man in custody will be sold into slavery at Gala or put to death.

"It's possible," I admit. "But unlikely."

"You're too trusting, Aefre. Gael didn't survive this long by being careless."

"Trust has nothing to do with it," I reply. "This is about probabilities. Security has done their job. If you want to keep chasing shadows, feel free. But I have a Grand Championship to win."

I stand within the trainer's control chamber, an enclosed balcony overlooking the arena that has been transformed into The Eternal Convergence. A hush falls over the spectators as everyone waits for me to begin.

Below me is Phase One: Separation. The first part of three phases. The Separation is a labyrinth in constant motion with walls grinding into new configurations with each passing minute and those same walls separate the pairs. I watch as Ash and Ember are forced apart as large metal gates slam down between them.

The labyrinth's massive overhead screens spring to life, each one split in half. On the left, I see Ash at the entrance to a tunnel wreathed in swirling, hallucinatory mist. On the right, Ember stands before a sealed chamber that rumbles ominously, as if containing some caged predator eager to be freed.

This is my moment to lead them to victory.

I open a channel to their collars, and the arena's loud speaker so that the audience can follow along. I give my first command, my voice low and resonant:

"Ash, Ember. Begin."

Instantly, the tunnel in front of Ash shifts. Purple lights blink on and off, and illusions spring up across the walls, images so realistic that if I didn't know better, I'd swear Ember was really standing there, arms extended in a twisted parody of welcome. If she falters now, she'll die. Pets die in this challenge every year, humans who fail to meet the Grand Championship standards. But Ash won't be one of them. Her bond with Ember is strong. She'll figure out these illusions. I must check on Ember.

I switch to Ember's feed. He is bracing himself for whatever is behind that door eager for release. A mechanical hiss echoes across the chamber. The door slides open, and out leaps a terrifying creature I've only read about in ancient bestiaries, a six-legged Vraxis, each limb ending in a curved talon. I check my console. It's a holograph. But it doesn't matter for the crowd, they gasp in anticipation as it lunges. And it doesn't matter for Ember either it can still kill him

"Ember. Strike beneath the jaw. That's where its plating is weakest," I tell him. He's never seen this beast before as it's an unusual one.

Ember reacts quickly, diving beneath the scything limbs. But not before the creature scores a nasty slash across his forearm.

The crowd erupts, savoring the blood and the violence.

I quickly check on Ash. She's moved past the illusion of Ember. No surprise. They're so close now, no hologram could compare to knowing the real thing. But now different illusions swirl around her, feeding on her worst memories. She staggers, pressing a hand to her temple. The labyrinth has triggered something akin to the Garden of Shadows challenge, except more intense, designed to exploit her guilt, her love, and her hidden terrors. Fears that she may not have even know she harbors, which are the most dangerous ones.

"Ash, ignore the figures around you," I say as she is particularly drawn into a figure of a human man. I don't have time to check who that is to her, but she seems mesmerized by his words. "Focus on the puzzle console. Left side, by the wall," I say trying to guide her away from the voices surrounding her.

Ash, relieved by the sound of my voice, finds the glowing panel of cryptic glyphs, steps forward, and begins deciphering the puzzle. I watch her hands move and magnify the scene. She's pressing the glyphs in the sequence we've practiced, but all it takes is one mistake, and the console will trigger an almost lethal charge.

Ash's puzzle console emits a soft chime. The illusions around her blink out, leaving her momentarily startled. She survived the puzzle.

The corridor behind her cracks open, revealing a narrow path that leads deeper into the labyrinth.

"Good girl, Ash. Take the middle path forward." I watch as she disappears from the camera's view, moving forward into the darkness.

I turn my attention back to Ember. My prized pet roars from underneath the beast's knee, driving a sharpened rod straight into the soft underside of the Vraxis's jaw. Its limbs suddenly limp. Then Ember pulls himself up and staggers back.

The arena roars its approval and pride courses through me.

"Good boy, Ember. Now move on to the next challenge by following the corridor to your right. Ash is already ahead of you."

Ember, battered but alive, walks into a new corridor as a portion of the floor slides aside to reveal a downward ramp. "Go down," I instruct him.

My ring pulses with the tension of maintaining two separate audio feeds. I toggle them carefully, guiding both pets through the labyrinth's rotating passages. This is the precarious balance of The Eternal Convergence. One trainer and two pets, who are entirely reliant on me for direction. Any hesitation on my part could be fatal.

Overhead, a massive digital countdown reminds the entire arena how little time remains for Phase One. My mind races as I quickly move from Ash's perspective to Ember's, anticipating pitfalls and problematic illusions. I feed them instructions, where to turn and how to handle the next obstacles.

They respond with resilience just as I've trained them to do. Every time Ash falters, I coax her forward with a crisp command.

Every time Ember encounters new beasts; I deliver swift instructions to ensure he keeps fighting.

The final moments of Phase One arrive in a rush. Both cameras show them reaching identical metal doors at the far ends of the labyrinth. Ash is breathing hard. Her whole body is drenched in sweat and she's shaking from the emotional turmoil the labyrinth has put her through. Ember clutches his wounded arm, blood still oozing between his fingers. They stop before their respective doors, waiting for me. They must press the buttons at the exact same time.

I open the comm links to both their collars. "Ash and Ember, put your right hands on the red buttons. On my mark, punch it. Three, two, one, push."

The labyrinth's walls grind to a halt. They have successfully passed Phase One. And relief washes over me like a physical wave.

Then, the lights dim, and the announcer's voice booms over the loud speaker, "Phase One: Separation—*Complete*. Competitors, prepare for Phase Two: Reunion."

The crowd explodes into cheers, but I'm not celebrating. Sweat beads along my neck. We have two more phases to get through before victory is ours.

CHAPTER 66

BRIAR

My emotions are still spiraling out of control from the illusions I barely fought off in Phase One. Seeing Gabriel was unexpected. And him telling me that Gael was waiting for us and to follow him was very believable. It took every shred of my sanity not to follow him. And then the others, people who'd been transitory foster parents telling me they'd been looking for me. Work colleagues telling me that they had called the police and issued a search on the mountain trail, it was awful.

I'm grateful for Aefre. Without his commands to find the puzzle, I might have stayed locked in that nightmare listening to the voices until the labyrinth murdered me, by tricking me into a poisoned room or shocking me with electricity if I stayed in one place for too long.

But Phase One is over. I survived.

The words "REUNION PHASE" flicker on a massive holo-screen overhead. I hear Aefre's voice much calmer than I feel.

"Ash, you must find Ember. He's on the eastern side of the labyrinth. The walls have changed. Move quickly, there's not much time. Keep choosing the paths furthest to the left until I tell you to change."

The left corridor beyond me expands into a mirrored passage, each surface polished so brightly, I see every detail of my battered form, including my sweat-soaked hair and my collar that marks me as property. But I see something else, too: flashes in the mirror, visions that shift so rapidly I can't quite catch them. My parents. Rebecca, before she chose death and jettisoned out an airlock. I think I hear her scream echo in the labyrinth.

I grit my teeth. *Not real,* I tell myself, but my body shakes anyway. "You need to come up with something new," I say out loud. "I've already fought these demons."

Aefre's voice cuts in, "Focus on finding Ember. You only have eight minutes remaining."

A swirl of light draws my attention. Where the corridor forks, I catch a fleeting glimpse of someone, tall, broad-shouldered, short dark hair. Gabriel? Or a projected phantom?

My heart leaps. If he's real, we can tackle the next trial together. If he's a trick, I could be lured into a trap. I think of Fifi and how she died. I fully understand how Gabriel could have mistaken Fifi for an illusion now. It's next to impossible to know what's real in these challenges.

"Gabriel?" My voice reverberates strangely in the mirrored corridor.

I receive a small shock on my collar from Aefre, but he doesn't verbally reprimand me for using Gabriel's human name.

Gabriel doesn't reply, but he beckons me forward, his face hidden in shadow.

With a resigned breath, I inch closer, half-expecting the figure to dissolve into static illusions and half-expecting it to be the real Gabriel. Then, I round the corner and come face to face with the hologram... which is a reflection of myself!

My own green eyes glare back at me, mocking me with a grin.

I recoil, my heart pounding. It's not me, but it looks just like me. But no fucking tail. Not me. I guess in my mind's eye I still don't have a tail. This small thought makes me smile.

"Gabriel will betray you," my doppelgänger hisses. "He did it before. He purposely let Fifi die to take all the winnings. He'll do it again."

The words strike me like a physical blow. I know illusions speak nonsense from my fears, but it's terrifying how my reflection is so convincing. *Could Gabriel betray me?* My rational mind says no, but I recall moments of hesitation, glimpses in his eyes that held dark shadows. Suddenly a wave of fear threatens to pull me under.

I can't let it. I close my eyes and say shakily, "You never allowed me to trust in anyone who was trying to be my friend. You're a bitch, Briar and you need to just go away. Gabriel loves me and yes that makes me vulnerable and maybe he will leave me to die, but that's the risk I'm willing to take for love. And there's nothing you can say that'll push me away from him."

"Only losers die for other people."

"No, you have it all wrong. Only losers die alone."

Aefre's voice cuts in, "Ash it's an illusion. Keep moving. Time is running out. You must find Ember. Fast."

I force my feet to walk, ignoring my double's laughter echoing behind me.

The corridor branches again. I look up and check the timer. I only have two minutes left. *I must find Gabriel.* I run down one passage to the left, then another. Everywhere, illusions swirl: an image of Gabriel kneeling at Aefre's feet, pledging loyalty; me and Gabriel having sex with Aefre in our rooms here. *They fucking recorded that.* My anger drives me faster.

Then, in a turn that nearly makes me scream, I collide with another body. Solid. Warm. We both stumble back in shock. Gabriel, for real this time. I know him like I'd know myself. He's panting and he stares at me, his amber eyes look wild. A shallow cut on his cheek drips blood, and sweat mats his hair. Relief crashes into me so hard I nearly start sobbing.

"Briar," he whispers, voice hoarse. He uses my true name, not Ash. That alone undoes me. I fling my arms around him, hardly able to believe he's here, alive, tangible. His breath shudders against my ear.

For a moment, the illusions around us flutter and dissolve, as if the labyrinth realizes we've bypassed its manipulations. The overhead timer shows one minute left. We stand together in a trembling embrace, ignoring the crowd's distant roars. Chanting for us to RUN!

Then, a sharp mechanical screech jostles us back to reality, "Time to Reach the Core: 00:56... 00:55... 00:54..."

We must reach a designated 'core' chamber before time runs out. If either of us fails, the other has the option to continue alone with half the points.

We sprint, hand in hand, hearts pounding in unison. The corridor warps around us, fragments of illusions swirling like confetti. We brush past grotesque reflections of ourselves, ignoring them. All that matters is the solid warmth of Gabriel's hand in mine and the timer ticking down.

Adrenaline is the only thing keeping me running. I hold on to Gabriel as he runs faster than me, pulling me along with him.

"This is going to be close," he says through heavy breathing, then he curses in French under his breath when a mirrored floor almost gives way beneath us. We jump the last few feet.

Ahead, a wide circular door slides open, flooding us with light. Then we burst into a chamber I assume to be the core. The overhead timer reads 00:03, then 00:02. We collapse to our knees, panting and clutching each other.

Alarms blare the end of Phase Two.

We made it. Together.

"Look up," Gabriel says.

I look up to see massive screens broadcasting our images to the entire arena. The crowd roars in response.

But, I only feel dread. What horrors await us in Phase Three?

CHAPTER 67

GABRIEL

I tremble as I stand on the swaying platform, high above the arena floor. It's not just the drones screeching overhead or the void below that worry me, it's the knowledge that I love Briar and I don't want her or me to die for alien entertainment.

The scoreboard above flashes Phase Three: Integration, the final trial of The Eternal Convergence. If I fail to get myself and Briar through this, I die.

Aefre's voice says, "Ember, watch the left side. Ash, get ready to jump when I say. On my mark."

For so long, that voice has been my compass. He is the one who plucked me from a filthy trading post over a decade ago, naming me Ember as though I might reignite some spark he believed the galaxy had snuffed out. I learned to read Imperial under his guidance. I learned strategy, combat, and discipline. Every muscle in my body, every reflex I possess, is shaped by him. Despite the bizarre system that made me his "pet," I owe him something, at the very least acknowledgement that he shaped me into the man I am today. The human man who is ready to use his skills and escape with the woman he loves.

Had I been bought by someone else, someone less talented, I wouldn't have the opportunity to compete and win UCs in these pet competitions and then I wouldn't have the chance to leave with Gael.

I push down these mixed emotions. If Aefre were in my position, I know beyond a shadow of a doubt, he would also choose freedom.

A mechanical screech rips me back to the present. The platform beneath our feet lurches, threatening to dump us into the arena pit.

The crowd gasps.

Aefre's instructions come fast, "Ember, shift your weight forward —now! Ash, counterbalance on the right."

I react on instinct, shifting in sync with Briar so the platform levels out. Relief washes over me.

We scramble onto a rotating walkway. Drones circle overhead, stunning us when they can.

"Gabriel!" Briar yells, slipping into my real name. She grabs my wrist, pulling me behind a vibrating energy shield. Another shot crackles off the shield, spattering sparks.

Aefre's words emerge distorted, "Emb—keep moving—up... next platform..."

I want to curse him for not speaking clearly, but deep down, I know I can't blame him for the interference. It's part of this challenge, no doubt, the comms between trainer and pets going in and out.

We sprint together, vaulting a gap to a higher platform. When I land, my wounded arm jars violently, and I slip.

Briar's hand clasps mine. Her voice in a panic, "I can't pull you up."

I use all my strength never breaking eye contact with her to get back on the platform.

The crowd roars.

Our respite is short-lived. A moment later, a jarring clang signals the arrival of a menacing cage-lift. Its metal bars drop around us, boxing us in.

Over the loudspeakers, an announcer proclaims with sadistic

glee, "Only of you may exit. Only one. Failure to comply will result in termination of both pet."

I look at Briar. "You get out. Don't wait for me. You're more valuable than a male pet and will have a better life."

"No Gabriel," tears form in her eyes. "I won't leave you. If you stay, I'll stay."

"You'll die, just like Fifi and I won't do that to anyone again."

Briar meets my gaze. "We do this together. We figure out a way out, *together*."

I nod, trying to steady my racing pulse. The idea of betraying her is unthinkable, but the judges have rigged the cage so that if one of us doesn't move forward alone, the entire platform will drop.

A countdown timer flashes across the overhead display. Fifty-nine seconds. Fifty-eight. The drones outside the cage start spinning up energy blasts.

"Look around for something that can save us when this cage drops. Something we might be able to hold on to," I tell her quickly.

Then we hear a jolt of static, and Aefre's voice surges through more strongly than before, "Ember, override the cage from your side! There's a console—lower right corner!"

I rush to the console. My collar thrums, Aefre's presence flowing through the link. Even though the spectators want to see us betray each other, he's still guiding me. It's so bizarrely comforting that tears prick my eyes.

"Listen Ember, I only get one chance to tell you this. Are you ready?"

"Yes, Master Aefre," I say impatiently as I watch our time slipping away.

"Input this code exactly," Aefre instructs. "$U4\text{-}KARR1/9\text{:}S2\text{-}\Omega$. Remember to include the symbol for Omega at the end. There are no second chances. If you miss even one stroke, the system won't be overridden and you'll die."

I shakily put my finger over the keypad's alien characters and begin typing, each keystroke shimmers with a faint glow, U, 4, dash,

K, A, R, R, 1, slash, 9, colon, S, 2, dash, Omega, each beep echoing in my skull. The console emits a series of soft chimes in response and then finally, the screen pulses green.

With a wheeze, the cage doors swing open.

I grab Briar's arm before she jumps out. "Wait the drones will attack. We must jump together and protect our heads as we jump. A direct hit to the head will knock us unconscious."

"We only have a second!" she screams. "Jump!"

We jump out just as a lethal barrage of stun-beams sears the air behind us.

The last moments play out in a blur as Briar and I sprint across a swaying catwalk. Ahead, the final exit comes into view, bright lights glowing like a promise of survival. We push through with a final burst of energy, collapsing onto solid ground amid a deafening roar of applause.

For a second, I can't breathe. But then I realize, we made it.

A voice booms through the arena, "Phase Three: Integration Complete. Ash, Ember, and Master Aefre have completed The Eternal Convergence."

But did we score enough points to win?

A hush settles. A pulsing holographic display comes to life high above us, showing dozens of names all written in Imperial hieroglyphics. My heart pounds as I scan for "Ash & Ember"—for any sign of our final score. Then I see it, flashing into place at the top of the list:

ASH & EMBER (TRAINER: AEFRE) – THE ETERNAL CONVERGENCE

Time (out of 10): 9
Technique (out of 10): 9
Mental Resilience (5): 5
Synergy (5): 5

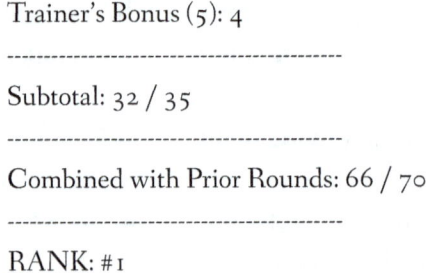

Trainer's Bonus (5): 4

Subtotal: 32 / 35

Combined with Prior Rounds: 66 / 70

RANK: #1

The arena erupts in cheers. A wave of relief crashes over me, tears stinging my eyes. Briar and I truly won. But then the screen flashes again, revealing a new line in vivid neon letters:

"BOND BREAKER CHALLENGE: COMMENCES IN 30 MINUTES"

The announcement is accompanied by the overhead announcement, "Master Aefre has entered his winning pets in the Bond Breaker Challenge. If you wish to make a wager, do so now."

My stomach drops.

Beside me, Briar's triumphant smile falters.

We both knew the Bond Breaker was a possibility, but last year it took place the day after the final challenge. I thought if we were going to have to do it, it would at least be tomorrow. We're too tired to do this.

Aefre appears. A faint tension tightens his jaw. "This is a special request from the sponsors. They want a show of unity, a final display of human loyalty from the Grand Champions. It pays handsomely, much more than usual."

"But we won," Briar says.

"Champions or not," Aefre says quietly, "the sponsors want a Bond Breaker and the audience wants a Bond Breaker. I pushed hard for it to be moved to tomorrow, but no one could be swayed. Trust your instincts and you'll be safe."

I'm overcome with resentment, fear, and exhaustion.

Briar and I exchange a glance. *We survived everything else. We'll survive this, too.*

Aefre steps aside, checking his console. "Thirty minutes," he reminds us, then gestures for us to follow. The roar of the crowd returns, louder than ever, as we steel ourselves for one final challenge neither of us wanted, but that fate, and greed, insists we face.

CHAPTER 68

Aefre

Ember's performance in The Eternal Convergence against the holographic illusions of Ash was nothing short of remarkable. Not a shred of confusion. He knew, instantly it wasn't her. And that certainty can only come from one thing, love.

"He recognized the illusions for what they were," Kaelin says. "They posed no real threat."

"Yes." My gaze is still fixed on Ember pacing the far end of the arena floor, waiting for Ash to emerge from the female pet toilets. "It's... concerning."

"Concerning? It's downright dangerous. He's supposed to adore her, but not be so bonded with her that he sees through every trick we throw at him."

I nod slowly. "I expected them to care for each other. *I* cultivated that, after all. But this level of devotion... Especially now that Gael is still rumored to be lurking around." The incompetent security forces caught a decoy, as Kaelin had summarized. "If this is love, and I believe it is, it makes my pets unpredictable. Gael would only have to whisper promises of freedom, and they might stupidly give him all their UCs to chase it."

"So what do we do?"

"After they finish the Bond Breaker, I want them placed under maximum security. Gael cannot be allowed near them. Their success in the arena has already netted them an obscene amount of credits, they can't be permitted to use that fortune to flee. Not on my watch."

I watch as Ember catches sight of Ash stepping out from behind a sealed gate, and his face lights up. "Make the arrangements. We've come too far to lose them to some idealistic half-Imperial rebel."

Kaelin nods and disappears. I remain, my gaze trained on Ash and Ember from above, contemplating the fragile line between loyalty and rebellion.

CHAPTER 69

"Behold, citizens of the Empire, the Bond Breaker Challenge!

"In this ultimate test of loyalty and perception, our champion pets must confront a gauntlet of illusions and moral quandaries, all crafted to sever the unbreakable ties they claim to share. Will they stand firm, recognizing friend from foe? Or will they fall prey to fear, confusion, and betrayal? Spectators, you have one minute left to place your wagers for in the Bond Breaker, reality itself becomes the enemy!"

The Bond Breaker arena shimmers into view, hazy shapes solidifying into a gleaming metal path. The overhead lights dim, leaving only neon-blue strips along the floor that pulse with each heartbeat.

Off to my left, a series of hovering platforms drift in erratic orbits. Each platform crackles with electric sparks, forming a sort of gravity well trap that could pull me in if I step too close. Beyond them, an arch of swirling black energy, which I assume is some kind of portal.

In the center of the arena, I see a tall, translucent tower, almost like a glass cylinder. Inside it, resting on a dais, is the artifact I'm supposed to retrieve. It glows with a faint, pulsing light, beckoning me forward. *Focus*, I tell myself. *That's the goal.*

The voice of the announcer echoes overhead, but I barely hear it through the rush of blood in my ears. The path forward is riddled with obstacles, an energy bridge that flashes in and out, and a corridor lined with illusions.

I also know that Briar is in there somewhere and I need to save her as well as get the artifact.

A hush falls across the crowd, as though the entire galaxy is holding its breath for me to begin. *My last challenge as a human pet,* I think.

I gather my courage and move. With every second, the environment seems to warp, walls shifting, illusions shimmering in the corner of my eye. *I can't lose focus.*

Halfway to the tower, I notice two figures sprawled on opposite sides of the path: Fifi on one side, Briar on the other. Both are tied from the waist down and are slowly sinking into a poisonous mist that burns my nose and throat.

The sight tears at my chest. Fifi... her face is contorted in pain, her body trembling like she's at death's door. Briar, similarly wounded, calls out my name. *This can't be real.* Fifi died a year ago. *Didn't she?*

"Gabriel," Fifi rasps, lifting a shaky arm. "Je ne suis jamais morte. I didn't die. It's all been an Imperial trick. I've been here at the Celestial Spire all along, waiting for you." Her eyes shine with tears. "They lied to you so you'd believe I was gone." Her French is perfect just as she was in real life. How could they recreate that? Imperials refuse to record or keep records of human languages, as far as I know.

"Gabriel," Fifi calls out again. "Tu te souviens? It was the Imperial holiday on the *Luminous Arc*, everyone was celebrating, or too busy to notice. You and I pooled our credits to bribe les garçons to sneak out a bottle of Aefre's private reserve. We laughed so much, thinking we'd get away with it. We hid in that tiny area of the cleansing room, remember? Toasting to our imaginary 'freedom,' just for one night. C'était toi et moi, Gabriel. The wine was bitter, but you told me it tasted like victory." She pauses, "Tu te rappelles, mon amour? I never forgot how you looked at me under those sterile lights... how we promised, if we ever truly escaped, we'd drink again under real sunlight. How I longed to feel the sun on my skin. Remember?"

For a moment, the illusion's words are heartbreakingly vivid, drawing on a memory only Fifi could have shared with me.

"Je suis revenue pour toi," she says with desperation. "Save me, Gabriel. If you leave me they will kill me for real this time. Don't let me die alone in this place."

Impossible. But the Bond Breaker thrives on illusions, and doubt. *But what if she survived?*

Briar coughs from the opposite side, tears running down her cheeks. "Gabriel, it's a trick."

Fifi's words address me again, "Don't let me die here. Don't fail your partner again."

"Gabriel, *listen to me!* This isn't real, *she* isn't real. You know that if Fifi were alive, Aefre would have never bought me. Think! Why would she suddenly appear here, in the Bond Breaker, spouting old memories? It's exactly what these illusions do, they latch onto your guilt, your regrets, and twist them into something that feels real.

"Remember the corridor you two drank wine in? There were details that only *you* and Fifi would recall... except the illusion got some of them wrong. You and I talked about that night, you said the bottle was half-empty already, that it tasted stale, not "bitter." It's a mistake in the illusion.

"*You can't trust it.* This is how the Bond Breaker tears people apart by dredging up the one thing that makes you hesitate. You're hesitating now, Gabriel, and it's going to cost us everything. Fifi died. I know it hurts to accept, but you saw it happen. And Aefre, think about him. He also loved Fifi and he would never have agreed to leave one of his beloved pets in someone else's care for a year. Don't let the sponsors and judges exploit your pain to trick you again."

Fifi yells to me. Her voice desperate, "Master Aefre was paid to leave me here. She's the illusion." She points to Briar.

Briar coughs from the poison rising faster now. "The illusion wants you to believe you can save her this time. But if you run to her, you'll kill us both. Fifi's gone, Gabriel. You owe it to yourself, not to chase a memory, but to survive and protect the partner who's right here, right now, fighting to stay alive."

"Gabriel, mon amour, you have to see the truth. That—" she hisses, gesturing toward Briar, "—that *thing* is the illusion. Elle n'existe même pas! They designed your collar to invent this 'Briar' person, how else do you explain the perfect bond you supposedly share? Ça n'a aucun sens. You've known me, Gabriel. J'ai été ton unique partenaire. You and I were real. But she's too perfect to be real."

"I'm the real one," Briar yells then bends over in a fit of coughs.

"Notice how she supposedly understands you so deeply, tout ça, c'est faux! The collar manipulated your mind, conjuring a fantasy partner so you'd stay compliant. Je suis la vraie, Gabriel. She's nothing more than a program feeding off your regrets and hopes. *We* have a history, nous avons un passé, I'm here now. Your *real* partner. Leave that American phantom behind before she drags you into her nightmare."

A spike of nausea grips me. I know there are clues to help me figure out what's real, but I can't reel in my emotions enough to focus on the details.

In my periphery vision, I see the artifact, just a short climb away through a ring of swirling energy. If I race for it, maybe I can secure our victory, maybe the illusions would disappear if I take it. But that didn't happen last year...

What if I take the artifact and they both die?

What if one of them is actually real?

What if they are both real?

What if they are both illusions?

The announcer's voice booms overhead: "You have a choice, Ember. Save your partner or claim the artifact. Choose wisely!"

The crowd roars, thirsting for drama.

My collar vibrates as stress hormones register my escalating terror. Memories of Fifi's death slam into me, how I let her slip away during a previous Bond Breaker. I can't do this again.

"Gabriel, I'm real! Don't you see how she wants to keep you from the artifact? We can't survive if you lose this challenge!" Briar screams, her voice desperate.

Fifi calls out to me from the other side, "Mon Dieu, Gabriel, how could you forget me so easily? If you don't save me, they'll kill me."

I'm torn in two. My heart says Briar is the one I've fought for, the one I love now, ma partenaire. But the pang of regret over Fifi still haunts me. *What if it's really her? Could Aefre and Kaelin have lied?* Another wave of illusions surges, making the floor ripple beneath me. I stumble trying to keep my balance.

I look at the dais with the artifact. If I dash for it, I risk letting one or both of these illusions die. If I try to save one of these women and they are an illusion, I die. Then if I die, Briar, wherever she is, also dies.

Briar's desperate cry pierces my thoughts, "Don't do this again, Gabriel!" Her voice hoarse from coughing. "I'm your partner. *Please.* The other Fifi, she's not even affected by the mist! And how the fuck would she know I'm American. I could be Canadian! She's the illusion from your mind. The real Fifi died here last year."

The words strike like lightning. She's right. Fifi is unaffected by the poison mist and Imperials wouldn't know about human countries.

I close my eyes and think, *Fifi is gone.* I turn toward the trembling figure that must be Briar. *But is she real or an illusion as well?*

A final timer blinks overhead. If I don't claim the artifact soon, I'll fail the challenge. I glance between the artifact and Briar.

In a burst of adrenaline, I sprint for Briar.

Fifi screams my name, her voice altered by betrayal. It sounds the same as it did last year when I left her to die. My heart is breaking that I'm leaving her to die again, but I keep reminding myself she's an illusion.

I reach Briar and throw my arms around her, ignoring the

stinging mist. If she's an illusion too and I'm going to die, I want to do it with the knowledge that, no matter what, hologram or not, I love Briar.

She gasps in relief, hands clutching my arms. "Gabriel, oh thank you, you chose me! I was so worried. Untie me."

I swallow hard, tears from this nightmare running down my face.

The announcer's voice booms overhead: "A risky gamble from Ember! Time is running out. Can he still reach the artifact?"

Maybe there's time. Clutching Briar, I force myself into motion. We run toward the platform, each step agony, the illusion of Fifi's wails echoing in my ears. But I can't look back. I push forward, half-dragging Briar to keep up with my pace, half-praying the ring of energy doesn't collapse.

In a final burst of desperate speed, I lunge. The artifact glows within reach. I stretch out my hand, feeling sparks bite at my fingers. *Focus.* With a final push, I seize the artifact, lifting it off the dais just as the swirling energy crackles and the ring of energy shuts behind us.

Thunderous cheers from the audience rattle the arena walls.

My knees buckle and Briar slumps against me.

The illusions dissipate. The phantom Fifi dissolves into mist, revealing that empty corner of the arena. My chest twists with sorrow for Fifi. But it's over. I have the artifact and Briar is safe. This time I made the right choice, thanks to Briar.

We did it. *We survived the Bond Breaker.* My heart throbs as Briar exhales in trembling gratitude. She looks up at me, tears in her eyes, and I know that we passed the ultimate test. No illusions could sever our bond.

I press my forehead to hers. "Je t'aime, Briar," I murmur.

She manages a weak smile. "We're safe," she whispers.

But then, suddenly, everything goes dark. The audience screams in panic. The drones overhead short out, dropping in a shower of sparks. Confusion and fear wash over the arena like a wave.

I hear distant shouting, the pounding of boots. Alarms shriek.

A figure steps onto our platform with one single, small, flashlight, half-wreathed in smoke. Gael the Returner. My heart jolts. I thought he'd been caught by security.

"Come on!" Gael shouts. "Things have changed. We need to leave *now!*"

I hesitate. Is this another trap? An illusion.

"It's not real," Briar says shaking her head. "Maybe we're still in the Bond Breaker. Maybe winning was an illusion?"

Gael quickly whips out a blade and before I can stop him, he takes Briar's hand and slashes a deep cut across her palm.

She cries out, clutching her hand, blood flowing between her fingers.

"Holograms would never do that," Gael tells us wiping his blade clean on his black trousers. "Allies helped push the Bond Breaker up, so I could get you now before your trainers lock you away forever. Now move! Do you want freedom or not?" Gael snarls as he deactivates the tracking on our collars with a small piece of tech. "Those will only scatter your location and make them unable to render you unconscious for a few minutes. Follow me quickly if you want your freedom. You won't ever get another chance!" Then he jumps off the platform into the smoky darkness.

Briar and I exchange one charged glance then we hurry after him.

Just as we leave the arena through a crudely made hatch, the lights switch back on and I see Aefre, high above the arena floor looking for us. My throat constricts with emotion. I owe him everything. And I'm betraying him in front of the entire galaxy.

"Ember... Ash... don't do this. Please..." Aefre's voice sounds over the arena. "You can have your own room on the *Luminous Arc*."

I freeze. Mon Dieu, I never thought I'd hear him beg.

Gael yells at me to keep moving, but my legs feel like lead. The collar is still there, binding me to Aefre in a way I can't just throw away. For the last twelve years of my life, he's taken care of me in his own alien way. I press my hand to the metal ring around my neck.

"I'm sorry," I whisper, knowing he can hear me. "I... I can't keep living like this, Master Aefre. I need my freedom."

Before Aefre can answer, Briar swats my hand away from my collar. "Too little too late. He should have offered us that room a long time ago. But even then we'd still want freedom, wouldn't we?"

"Hurry the fuck up!" Gael shouts. "We are leaving with or without you two!"

I close my eyes, tears forming. I imagine the hurt in Aefre's eyes. I click my collar to hear him again. I can't resist. His voice is strained, "Ember, you'll be lost out there. You won't be able to protect Ash or yourself. Let me help you. If you want freedom we can talk about it."

A tear slips down my cheek. "I know," I say, my voice unsure, "but... I have to try. I'm sorry it has to end this way. Thank you for the last twelve years. And by the way. My name is Gabriel and she is called Briar. Farewell."

Briar grabs my arm, pulling me forward into the hatch, descending into the bowels of the arena. My collar continues buzzing with half-formed words, but I force myself to keep running.

I hear Gael up ahead. "Here they come!" he yells to someone else. "Come on Grand Champions, hustle!"

We scramble inside a transport, our hearts pounding. The door seals shut with a satisfying lock, and engines roar.

Gael hits the thrusters, and we rocket away from the Celestial Spire.

Alarms chime from the cockpit, indicating a pursuit.

Briar crouches next to me, cradling her wounded hand. My collar crackles one last time with a faint, broken transmission of Aefre calling my name, "Ember let me help..."

Gael flips a switch that cuts the feed without a word.

And just like that, I am free... But in the back of my mind, Aefre's image lingers, questioning this choice.

Who is the stranger that I've entrusted my and Briar's life to now?

CHAPTER 70

BRIAR

Gael ushers us through a narrow corridor from the transport onto his own ship. I hug my arms tightly around my body as we walk. Gael gave me the clothing off his back. It's the first time I've had clothing to cover my breasts and groin in eight months and I'm relieved. However, the fabric can't stop me from wondering anxiously about what happens next.

Gabriel hovers protectively behind me. I sneak a glance at him over my shoulder. He looks torn, like a man traveling between two worlds, one that kept him leashed since he was sixteen, and another that offers freedom but no promises.

We've all been silent since Gael said "Run!" And like obedient human pets, we obeyed a different grey man. Ironically, this is exactly the kind of behavior Aefre always said made humans not fully sentient. That we don't think about things logically, but act solely on instinct.

"In here," Gael grunts, leading us into a small medical bay. The walls are white, but scuffed with the marks of countless procedures. Instruments hang from the ceiling on retractable cords, clinking softly as we enter. The room smells heavily of antiseptic.

A woman is waiting for us inside. She has grey skin and short black hair. Despite looking Imperial there's a gentleness to her expression that I never saw in Aefre or Kaelin. She inclines her head in greeting, green eyes gliding over Gabriel and me.

Gael clears his throat and then speaks in perfect Imperial, "They're yours now." He sounds tired. "Remove their collars before their trainer can track us. He's a rich man and lost a lot of pride today. He will spare no expense to pursue them, even if there's just a faint signal to follow."

The doctor gives a short nod. "Okay, I got it." Then gesturing to us, she says more gently, "You can sit." She speaks clearly, as if she's used to talking to non-Imperial patients.

Gael leaves without a word to us. I guess he doesn't want his shirt back yet.

Gabriel and I exchange a brief, nervous glance. I perch on the edge of a bench, while he hovers an arm's length away.

The doctor beckons him gently, "Let me remove yours first. As you've worn it the longest."

Slowly, Gabriel steps closer to her. He's still wearing the dark training bodysuit from the final challenge. Blood from a shallow cut on his arm has dried in a dark rust stain, a reminder of how close we came to losing everything.

"The collars," she says, switching to an even gentler tone in Imperial while she opens a box full of equipment. "They're still transmitting. We need to deactivate them, but I can't do that while you're still wearing them." She begins fighting with Gabriel's collar and he grimaces. "Sorry, it might shock you a bit, but don't worry you're in the medical bay and I'm a doctor."

Neither Gabriel nor I acknowledge her joke if it were meant to be one.

I watch as Gabriel holds part of the sleek metal ring around his neck, trying to help the doctor or holding on to the memory of Aefre for one last second? More than a decade under one man's control can warp anyone.

The doctor unclips a handheld device from her belt. She fits a small, disc-like attachment to it, and a faint electronic whine fills the bay. "It's safe," she murmurs, stepping closer to Gabriel work on removing the collar. "This one is tricky."

He nods stiffly and tilts his head.

She presses the device to the collar's seam, and I watch a light go through a series of colors. With a click and then a hiss of releasing pressure, the collar snaps open.

Gabriel exhales, his posture sagging like he's just been allowed to exhale after years of holding his breath.

I swallow against a swell of emotion. If Gabriel's not crying. I shouldn't be crying.

The doctor sets his collar aside, carefully powering it down with her tools. I watch her tinker with it and then finally she says, "Done. This was an old one. I don't see many of these especially on men. You must have survived hell many times over," she says and puts a hand on Gabriel's shoulder. "But you did survive."

He's lost in thought and doesn't acknowledge her words. He just keeps rubbing his neck where his collar used to be.

The doctor lets him be and then turns to me. "It's your turn."

I walk toward her and she begins investigating my collar with cool and gentle hands.

"Yours is very new," she says just as much to me as to herself. "This will be much easier. Some *friends* gave us the fail-safe code." She grabs a tool. The device vibrates near my ear, and I brace for a pinch of pain. But I only feel relief as the collar's lock unlatches, a cool rush of air caressing the raw skin underneath. My breath escapes in a shaky gasp. *Gone.* The constant sense of being tethered is just... gone. There's a mild twinge of pain where the collar's edges once dug into my skin, but it's drowned in the rush of relief flooding my body.

The doctor sets my collar down with the same delicate care, then powers it off.

"I know these are the last things you want to keep right now, but you need to. They're part of your payment to join the colony," she says softly. "There's an initiation ceremony to take you from pet to citizen in Haven."

I recoil at the sight of that metal ring, the symbol of everything I've endured. "I don't want it," I whisper in English.

But she presses it gently into my hands, unwavering. "It's not a choice. The ceremony is important," she explains, her Imperial still calm. "You must bring them so that your freedom is recognized and... protected." Then she looks over at Gabriel, who is holding his own collar like a foreign object he doesn't understand. "And it's important for your healing. To mark the end of your being owned. Especially for him."

I look over at Gabriel and I can't help it. I wipe a tear away. *Is this real?* Is he really free? Am I? I can't stop staring at him, at his bare throat, at the faint red line where his collar once was, at the tears shining in his amber eyes.

The doctor smiles wearily, giving us space with a nod, and quietly steps out of the med bay.

"C'est fini," Gabriel murmurs.

I meet his gaze, and something fierce and electric passes between us. It's a wild, reckless elation, the high of survival. My pulse pounds in my ears. We're alive, we've escaped, and all at once, a torrent of emotions floods me, joy, disbelief, and most of all sexual desire.

Without speaking, we reach for each other. His hands tremble as they cup my face, and I feel the warmth of his breath as he whispers my name, "Briar, Je t'aime comme un fou. I love you like crazy."

Suddenly, all the tension, all the near-death terror, converts into a blazing need for human contact. For him. The press of his lips is urgent, a plea to affirm that we're still here, and that this is real.

I answer his lips with equal fervor, my fingers twisting in his golden hair. Our kiss deepens, and a soft whimper escapes me, half-sob, half-laugh. We're free, no collars, no leashes, just this primal need to confirm we're *alive*. I run my hands along his shoulders, feeling the sinew and strength that carried us both through the horrors of captivity.

He whispers in halting, emotional French, "Mon ange... tu es ma vie. Nous sommes libres maintenant. Je ferai tout pour toi." Even though, I can't piece together every word, the tenderness in his voice nearly brings me to tears.

I respond by pulling him closer, nails digging lightly into his skin, and he shivers. My body ignites at every point of contact, a primal wave of urgency for him to be as close as two humans can be to one another.

We topple onto the medical bed our bodies intertwined. The ship's hum seems to fade, every one of my senses is focused on him. His hot breath against my ear, the way his heartbeat matches mine, the savage hunger in our lips. Each touch feels heightened, magnified by relief and adrenaline.

When our eyes lock, his beautiful amber eyes are teary. And I know why. I'm thinking and feeling the exact same thing, *We did it.*

I trail my hands across his muscular chest covered in golden hair, marveling at the absence of any device controlling us, any ring that might sting with a punishment. This is *our* choice.

There's something reverent in the way Gabriel kisses my neck, as if worshipping the fact that no collar remains. I hold him tighter, murmuring half-formed words of comfort and desire. The ghosts of our old cages hover at the edges of my mind, but I push them aside, letting the rush of euphoria carry me forward. Right now, we exist only for each other. No trainers, no illusions, and no threat of an electric jolt.

Gabriel positions his large penis at my entrance and I thrust my hips forward to impale myself on him before he can thrust. It's not long before we are moving quickly and in time with each other. Our hearts pounding and our breaths mingling, as if we're trying to become one.

Quickly our orgasms build and crash over both of us almost simultaneously in a wave of sensations, the warmth of his skin, the taste of his mouth, the muffled sounds of my own moans and his whispered, "Ma chérie... tu es libre..." The sweetness of those words collides with the fresh shock of escape. Everything I've craved, every moment of closeness I've been denied, all of it is bursting into reality now.

And nothing has ever felt so real.

There are no collars now, no manipulations, it's just us alone in this room.

When the urgency has been fulfilled, we lie tangled in each other's arms, and out of breath.

I trace a fingertip along the faint red ring that circles Gabriel's neck.

He does the same for me, and says, "It's gone."

I can't speak. I close my eyes, but I can't stop the silent steady tears.

"Briar," Gabriel says softly. "It's okay." He holds me close to him. The familiar feel of his body against mine helps me relax into full blown sobs. "You're mine and we're safe."

When the doctor returns, she opens the door slowly, for politeness. A kindness we've not had in a long time.

"Doctor?" I say, stumbling over the Imperial words. "Can you... remove this?" I gesture to the tail. "And... these." I point at the small silver studs piercing my nipples. "I want them gone. I want to be—" I hesitate, swallowing hard. "—like I was before, if that's possible?"

She gives me a compassionate nod. "A proper facility is needed. The tail is attached to your spinal column. It will need more than a portable kit." Her eyes shift between Gabriel and me. "On the colony, they have advanced equipment and they can easily remove those enhancements."

Gabriel's gaze flicks to the tail, then to my face. "Are you really going to remove it?" he asks quietly in English. "I kind of like it."

I feel my throat tighten, uncertain if I should laugh or cry. A part of me wants to snap that he's been twisted by Imperial standards of pet beauty, but I bite down on the words. He's in such a fragile state and if he were in his right mind, he'd never suggest I keep my tail.

"Gabriel, I want my old body back. I hate that they gave me this tail to make me look more like a sexy human pet."

He looks wounded, eyes drifting to the collar in his hands. I realize, too late, I might as well be insulting the entire life he's been forced to live.

"I'm sorry," I murmur, and I reach for his arm.

He lets me settle my hand against him, though he won't quite meet my gaze. "It's... fine," he replies, even though it isn't.

Silence weighs on us. The only sound is the hush of the ship's engines and the distant murmur of Gael speaking with someone in the hallway. Freedom was supposed to be a relief, not this tangle of guilt and confusion.

The doctor touches my shoulder, as if reading my mind, she says, "It's natural to feel confused."

"I don't know if I can be human," Gabriel admits quietly in Imperial. "I don't know if I'll be accepted in a human colony like this."

"Many have come to Haven feeling the same way as you, Gabriel. And some were even born in Imperial captivity and didn't escape until they were adults. We all have our own stories," the doctor says sympathetically.

It's odd to hear his human name spoken in an Imperial sentence, and I see him react to it as well. "And they have all found their way to come to terms with what happened and live as free humans. I have no doubt, you'll find your way too. I can read your mind. I know you worry Aefre and Kaelin might have changed your brain, but they didn't really. They just conditioned you. And you have the power to uncondition yourself."

Relief washes over him. "They didn't?"

"No," the doctor answers him with confidence. "But I understand why they wanted you to believe they did. It's a common tactic."

My own collar lies cold in my hands, unwanted.

But Gabriel is still clenching his own collar tightly, like he's worried he might need to put it back on.

I wish I knew how to help him.

"This is real," I remind him.

CHAPTER 71

G<small>ABRIEL</small>

I rub the stiff skin at my throat, wincing at the raw feeling where the collar used to sit. It's gone now, really gone. My neck feels too light, naked. For the past twelve years, that band of metal has been part of me. I glance down at it resting on a nearby tray, faintly reflecting the harsh lights overhead. Even powerless, it fills me with a blend of fear and nostalgia.

I think I was expecting freedom to come crashing over me like some glorious tidal wave. A flood of relief, unstoppable and pure. Instead, it's quieter, more confusing and laced with guilt. I catch myself almost missing the collar's weight around my neck, and the thought disgusts me. *They* did this to me, Aefre and Kaelin. They hammered all traces of normal life out of me until I barely remembered how to be a human man and not a human pet.

I shake myself out of my thoughts when Briar asks me a question. "Are you all right?"

I shrug, forcing a tight smile. She knows I'm not.

I watch as the doctor checks a small console with lines of Imperial script scrolling down it wondering when we'll be free to leave the medical bay. She says she just wants to check our vitals, to make sure there wasn't a poison that was released into our systems when we got too far away from our masters. I can't imagine Aefre or Kaelin using that feature. They could be brutal but as far as I know they never killed a human.

The device glows faintly, displaying our vitals and something else. I can't quite follow the words, but I do recognize a single term the doctor mumbles under her breath, "Pregnant."

I snap my gaze to Briar. She's gone pale, her lips parted as though she's about to speak but can't find the words.

The doctor glances between Briar and me, obviously realizing she's dropped a bombshell. "The condition is early. But definitely pregnant."

My heart roars in my ears. That single word echoes. Pregnant. *She doesn't look pregnant.*

"That must be a mistake," I say. The *Luminous Arc's* medical team presumably tracked everything, didn't they? If she'd tested positive, they'd have locked her down. Imperial breeders don't let things happen by accident. This must be an error. Some glitch in the system or a short-circuit from the collar's removal.

But then, I look at Briar. Her eyes are huge, alarm flashing behind them. She doesn't look shocked, she looks guilty.

A slow, icy dread seeps through me. "Briar..."

She flinches like I might strike her. I'd never do that—*never*. But her reaction alone sends me over the edge.

First, it's not a mistake.

Second, she's known and didn't tell me.

I open my mouth to demand answers, but the words stick in my throat.

"Maybe eight weeks," the doctor tells us like background noise.

Two months. The time frame lines up uncomfortably well with the... moments we had. My heart hammers, a dull roar thundering in my ears. I search Briar's face, trying to find the smallest trace of reassurance, *It's yours, Gabriel, everything's fine,* but I only see fear. Or is it shame? *Why didn't she tell me?*

A single question tears its way out with desperation. I turn to the doctor, trying not to sound panicked and ask, "Do you know who the father is?"

The words hang in the air like a thunderclap.

The doctor stands there, face unreadable, while Briar squeezes her eyes shut, tears brimming. And I wonder if I'll be forever stuck with Aefre. His child.

CHAPTER 72

BRIAR

"You have no right to demand that information," the doctor says firmly to Gabriel, like she's accustomed to settling such disputes. "It's Briar's choice to know and as to whether or not she wants to share that information with anyone. You have no right to know."

I blink, taken aback. I'm used to Imperials treating me like an animal. But the doctor, unmistakable Imperial with grey skin, black hair, and with an air of gentle authority, reminds me again that not all Imperials are the same. Her words are bracing, but not cruel. Still, I'm stunned by how easily she dismisses Gabriel's question. I glance at him, expecting him to bristle in anger.

He just exhales slowly, shoulders sagging in resignation. "C'est un matriarcat. The matriarchy. The galaxy's built on it and here's my first taste."

He's told me about the matriarchal structure countless times, how women hold the higher social standing in the galaxy and how the entire Empire is organized around women. But seeing it in action, directed at Gabriel, unsettles me.

I fold my arms over my stomach. "Doctor," I begin quietly. "I... I don't actually know who the father is." My voice trembles on the last part. It feels so surreal, the taste of those words in my mouth. I think of Aefre, of all the nights I've shared with him in trainer to pet relations. And Gabriel...the passion and comfort, the warmth of hope we found in each other's arms. "Could you... I mean, can you tell?"

The doctor's eyes filled with an unexpected compassion. "We don't have that kind of technology on this small ship. But in Haven, they'll be able to tell you if you want to know before the birth."

"And would they allow me to keep it if it's half-Imperial?" I don't look at Gabriel as I ask this question.

"All are welcome in Haven, so long as they swear an oath never to reveal the colony's location to anyone who might do us harm."

When I finally muster the courage to glance at Gabriel, I see the turmoil swirling behind his eyes. As if the pregnancy news wasn't enough of a shock, now there's the question of paternity, him or Aefre. Neither of us expected freedom to bring this kind of twist. The possibility of a lasting gift from our Imperial owner.

I rest a trembling hand against my abdomen. Part of me still can't believe there's life forming in there, not after all the horrors we've endured. "Gabriel, I hope it's yours. I truly do."

His gaze moves between my face to my stomach, unsure where to land. I think of all the times the Imperials manipulated him, how they turned intimacy into a spectacle, even gave him advice, holding his leash while he had sex. A bitter taste fills my mouth.

"But if it's not yours," I continue, "I... I can't kill it or give it up. This child is still half me, no matter who the father is. I'd understand if you didn't want to... to raise it with me if it turns out to be Aefre's." Tears escape my eyes and I have to pause to get a breath. I hate how weak I sound, but I need him to know he has a choice. If it's Aefre's, how can I ask him to accept that burden? What if it looks exactly like Aefre?

Gabriel doesn't answer.

I'm half convinced he'll leave. My vision blurs with tears. I press a hand over my mouth, trying to stifle a sob. "And I know you think I knew, but I only found out seconds before the final challenge.

Remember I went to the bathroom? I didn't know I was pregnant, the other women...the other human women told me and they told me that if Aefre knew he'd pull us from the competition and then we'd have no chance to be saved by Gael. And all I could think about was the child from the mirror maze. Our child with a collar around its neck and so I said nothing."

I let out a small, shaky sob. My shoulders tremble. *This* is freedom? Pregnant, uncertain, my only comfort a man who might not even want to be involved if the child is fathered by our former owner.

Suddenly, Gabriel pulls me into his arms.

I lose it then, burying my face against his chest, tears dampening his tattered uniform.

His arms wrap around me with a fierceness I've never felt from him before.

For a long minute, we just breathe together. Breathe in pain and exhale relief.

Then he speaks, voice cracking with emotion. "Briar..."

I bite my lip, bracing myself for the worst.

He rests his chin on the top of my head. "I think it would be... *fitting*," he says, the words spilling out slowly, "if—if this child turns out to be Aefre's... that we raise it. Together. That we teach it to be free. Maybe it can grow up to do something good in this galaxy. Maybe..." He chokes on a laugh that sounds like a half-sob. "Maybe even rescue humans from being turned into competition pets, like Gael does. You know he's half-human despite his appearance. It might be the ultimate revenge to have a man who looks like the best human pet trainer in the galaxy to be a liberator of human pets."

A swirl of relief, awe, and heartbreak rushes through me, so intense I almost can't breathe. "Gabriel..." I say but then stop, I don't have the words. I just cling to him tighter. I feel his chest rise and fall, and then his shoulders begin to shake. He's crying now, too. There's no crowd to witness it, no collar around his neck compelling him to hide his emotions. There's just us.

"I didn't imagine freedom to feel like this."

"It's... new, ma chérie," he says in a whisper of French. "No one likes change at first. But I suppose we'll learn to love it..." After a few minutes, he adds, "I couldn't control what happened to me in the beginning or middle of my life, but now I *can* decide how I will live the rest of it. And I choose you. You were the light in my darkness. "Tu es à moi, Briar... Vous êtes tous les deux à moi. "You're mine, Briar. You both are mine."

EPILOGUE 1
AEFRE

I stand alone on the observation deck, my breath fogging against the reinforced glass. The once-raucous arena is silent, its lights dimmed, the seats long since emptied. Only the echoes of the audience's cheers remain, a distant memory of the spectacle that ended in my ultimate humiliation.

The labyrinth is still partially erected on the arena floor below, half-collapsed walls and flickering holograms casting ghostly shapes in the darkness. It was supposed to be a testament to my finest work. Ash and Ember were to be my masterpieces, living proof that, with enough guidance, any human could be molded into perfection.

Instead, they are gone. Taken by that opportunistic half-breed, Gael the Returner. The memory of his sudden appearance, the sabotage he orchestrated right under my nose. The feed from the final phase replays in my mind, the moment I lost them captured in looping clarity. I should have seen it. I should have known.

I close my eyes, remembering the instant I realized they'd chosen escape over victory. The corridors erupted in alarms, and Kaelin and I tried to give chase, but it was too late. They'd vanished into the maintenance shafts, leaving behind nothing but scorched metal and the furious roars of the crowd.

My jaw tightens. I imagine how, even now, Ash's collar is probably lying in some trash heap, severed and discarded. Ember, the one I had counted on, *depended* on, turning his back on me in that final moment.

I gave them everything, training, discipline, sex, food, comfort, and a chance at glory. In return, they have left me with nothing but questions. When did Ember first decide to abandon me? Was it the day Fifi died? Or was it when he realized he loved Ash?

I run my hand over the control ring , its circuitry completely inactive now, severed from any collar. The ring feels heavier than ever, a relic of a bond that has been irrevocably broken.

A faint hiss signals Kaelin's entrance behind me. He's silent, his rage simmering just beneath the surface. We have no words for each other. There is only the quiet accusation in his eyes, a question that neither of us dares to voice aloud, *Where do we go from here?*

"I've spoken to Ira. He's demanding an explanation."

"I will tell him the truth," I say, surprising myself with how steady I sound. "We were betrayed. The system was compromised by Gael the Returner. Ash and Ember... seized an opportunity to flee."

"And you just let them?"

I bristle but hold my composure. "They didn't ask my permission, Kaelin." The retort is sharper than I intended. Kaelin did warn me after all. "Focus on solutions, not blame."

He nods and then with a curt bow, he leaves me to my solitude.

Once he's gone, I tap on the console beside me. A new display crackles to life, showing star charts and flight paths. In the center glows a red dot indicating the boundary near the border, the place where Gael's ship vanished from Imperial tracking.

I zoom in. I analyze the data, searching for any sign of where they might have gone. Do I chase them beyond the border, risking condemnation for crossing into neutral territories? Or do I remain here, rebuilding my reputation, forging new pets into champions?

For the first time in my life, I'm uncertain. The Empire sees humans as commodities, but Ash and Ember, they challenged my long-held view. Part of me wants them back, if only to prove that I was right all along, that my methods *do* work, and that humans can't survive in the galaxy on their own because they aren't sentient, not fully. But another part of me wonders if, in losing them, I've liberated myself from a bond I did not fully comprehend until it was too late. And that Ember really is one of the one-in-a-million humans who are sentient and deserve to be free. And maybe Ash too?

I stare at the star chart until my eyes burn. Perhaps I will track them. Perhaps not. But I suspect we are far from finished with one another. A bond like ours can't be undone by a single act of rebellion, no matter how triumphant.

My hand clenches around the control ring. My perfect pair... gone. Just like that. Gone.

Closing my eyes, I draw a slow, deliberate breath, steeling myself for the inevitable next move. Tomorrow, I must face Ira. Tomorrow, I will account for what happened here. But tonight, I stand in the hush of the deserted arena, letting the reality sink in. A reality I will only ever tell myself. *I failed Ash and Ember.*

EPILOGUE 2
BRIAR

The stars stretch endlessly outside the ship's viewport, an ocean of light against the black canvas of space. The sound of the engines is the only sound in our tiny cabin, a faint, steady rhythm that reminds me we're still moving forward. Away from the Celestial Spire, away from the *Luminous Arc*, and away from the Empire. Toward something we can only hope is real.

I sit on the small chair, my knees drawn to my chest. It's a cramped space, barely large enough for Gabriel and me. But it's private.

My gaze lingers on Gabriel, noting the slight bruising on his jaw and the raw redness around his throat where his own collar used to be. He's deep in thought and from the nightmares he had last night I'm not surprised.

"What are you thinking?" I ask softly, breaking the stillness wanting to help in some way.

"That we made it," he answers, voice flat.

"Do you think the colony, Haven is real?"

"I don't know," he admits quietly. "But I think so."

"Do you think Aefre will come after us?"

Gabriel's expression darkens. "No. He'll be furious but then buy another set of pets. He won't waste his energy chasing us. We are just two human pets. Not worth the hassle."

Days later, we arrive at Haven, relieved that Gael didn't trick us. "I'm sorry I don't have any more UCs to give you," Gabriel says to Gael. After our escape, Aefre declared us feral and our winnings were stripped from our accounts.

Gael extends his hand to each of us then says to Gabriel, "You don't owe me anything. Fifi paid three-fourths of it last year. And then, when we first met, what you gave me in good faith covered the remainder. I'm sorry for what happened to Fifi. She had already arranged it all last year, but when she died in the arena, I couldn't risk going in for you. I didn't know if you *wanted* to be rescued. And I have a policy, I never force any humans out of captivity."

Gabriel's jaw clenches trying to hold back the tears. "Thank you for telling me."

Gael nods sincerely. "Fifi would have wanted to get you both to freedom. She would have wanted this for you, Gabriel. She said you were like the brother she never had."

"I know," Gabriel says, his voice breaking. "She was so excited at the idea of freedom. I didn't listen to her. I didn't believe her when she said she'd talked with you. I should have."

Gael gives Gabriel a compassionate touch on the shoulder. "You're not the first man to believe freedom is out of reach and you won't be the last. But if you can promise me something?"

"Anything."

"Don't dwell on the past. Only look forward."

"I promise."

"Now, I'll leave you both here. Haven is a good place. Prosper and make something of your freedom, you now know that it's a gift."

Then we watch Gael and some of his crew walk away.

A tall woman with cropped black hair steps forward, flanked by two men. The woman looks human but the other two look like hybrids between human and Imperial.

The woman introduces herself, "Welcome to Haven. I'm Anna and these are my assistants. Before we go any further, you both need to swear on pain of death that you will never leave Haven without my or Gael's permission, that you will never have communication with anyone outside the colony, and that you will keep our organization and what you know about Gael and our mission secret, even if you are abducted and sold into slavery again. Do you swear Gabriel?"

"I swear."

"Do you swear Briar?"

"I swear."

"Good. It's been noted and your answers have been recorded as truthful. Now our first stop will be to the medical center. You both need full mental and physical workups. We will try to repair the immediate damage that has been done to you. Other things will take time, but we do expect you both to make a full recovery and thrive here."

"And can we live together?" Gabriel asks tentatively.

"If you want. However, you must make a commitment to one another for at least three months. We have rules about co-habitation."

Gabriel looks at me and asks seriously, "Do you want to live together Briar?"

I'm irrationally irritated by his question. "The only thing that upsets me is that you're asking. Of course I want to co-habitate with you."

He smiles at my word choice.

And I have no choice but to smile genuinely back. This feels good. To be free and make choices.

"Now that that's settled," Anna says. "Let's go to our first stop, the medical center. Then this evening we will welcome you into our community with a special ceremony to mark the end of your enslavement."

By nightfall, the colony gathers in an open plaza called the Soul, where a bonfire crackles. Shadows play across the crowd's human, hybrid, and Imperial faces, all reflecting a shared understanding of why we're here.

Anna steps forward to address everyone, "Thank you for joining us tonight to welcome Gabriel and Briar into our community. As some of you already know, they were kept as show pets by the notorious Imperial pet trainer Aefre. They've been through a lot as many of you can sympathize with. But today is the last day they will ever be associated with being a show pet. From this day forward they are citizens of Haven." Anna looks at us then and says, "The first step is letting go of what ties you to them. It's time to throw your collars and anything else you want into the fire."

Gabriel goes first. He approaches the fire, shoulders set, and tosses his collar into the flames. There's a hiss of hot metal twisting, melting and burning. His jaw flexes tightly as he watches it until it's unrecognizable. When he turns to look at me, there's a new lightness in his eyes, like he's shed a piece of himself.

It's my turn now. With my collar and my severed tail in my hands I hold them up against the heat of the fire. My fingers tremble. Part of me is terrified to let these objects go, as if I'll be in trouble for losing them if Aefre comes back. But I remind myself that I'm free now. So with a shaky breath, I throw them in. The flames leap and devour the last year of my life and I breathe easier.

Anna then ceremoniously leads us all in a silent procession to a place called the Sanctuary. It's a small chamber, like a chapel but without an altar. And it's lined with mementos, plaques, trinkets, and ribbons. "You can leave a name here if you want," Anna says. "No one will judge. It's for those who want to remember someone from their former Imperial life."

Gabriel steps up to the wall first. He grips the small engraving tool and etches the name Fifi into a blank space. I can't read his expression, but I see how his hand trembles slightly. I know how deep that wound runs.

Then it's my turn. I think of all the people I've lost or failed, all the illusions that haunted me in the Grand Championships. One name stands out more prominently than the rest, *Rebecca*, the brave woman *I* couldn't save. I feel guilty for her death. Not only because I didn't try to stop her from going out the airlock, but also because of her absence on the *Luminous Arc* allowed me to take her place and because of that, it was I who fell in love with Gabriel and I who am now free.

My heart pounds as I engrave her name and carve a Christian cross next to it. A quiet ache settles in my chest, but it feels right to honor her here. "I hope you've found your peace, and I hope you know, you've given me mine," I whisper.

The next months are a blur of activity. Gabriel finds his purpose in the Forge, helping with repairs and building everything from small gadgets to improved farming tools. I join the Greenway, learning about horticulture and sustainability in the colony's underground ecosystem. The baby in my womb grows, along with an ever-present worry, *Do I want to know who the father is?*

I choose not to and Gabriel never pushes. By the time I'm heavily pregnant, our relationship has grown beyond the question of paternity. We've created a life here, together. And we're ready to welcome this child into our lives.

When I go into labor, I'm ushered into a calm, dimly lit birthing chamber in the medical center. Midwives guide me through each contraction. Gabriel's hand never leaves mine, and his whispered French endearments keep me anchored. Hours later, we're rewarded with the loud, fierce cry of our newborn. The midwife places the baby in my arms, and my heart explodes with love, fear, and wonder.

Haven gathers three nights later in the Soul for a naming ceremony, welcoming the child into the colony. Anna lifts the baby gently and addresses the crowd. "This child is a symbol of what we fight for," she declares. "A new generation born free. Born in Haven."

Warm tears slip down my cheeks as she dips her hand in a bowl of fresh paint and touches the baby's feet. "Orion, son of Briar and Gabriel of Haven, may these feet always walk freely no matter where you find yourself in the galaxy."

Gabriel and I lock gazes, and in that moment, everything feels possible. For the first time in my life, I feel like I belong somewhere. Not as a pet, or not as someone's show piece for becoming rich as commodities trader, but as a human being, loved, accepted, and free.

I don't know what will happen if Aefre ever finds us, or if the Empire discovers Haven. I don't expect the fear will ever go away completely. But at least now we have something bigger than ourselves to fight for, a community, and a child who deserves to grow up without a collar around his neck.

EPILOGUE 3
GABRIEL

I stand on a ridge overlooking the Greenway, where morning sunlight filters down through carefully engineered vents cut into the cavern ceiling. The air here in Haven always smells of new life, fresh soil, growing things, and the subtle hints of bioluminescent fungi that glow by night.

A few feet away, a metal wind chime hangs from a low-hanging vine, clinking softly in the mild breeze. I remember forging it a few months ago, shaping the scraps of an old Imperial panel into something melodic. I used to hate the sound of metal, it reminded me too much of collars, cages, and the clang of training equipment. Now, I've learned to make it sing.

A lot of my activities in Haven revolve around dissecting elements of my trauma and reshaping them in my mind. Or 'unconditioning' myself as the doctor on Gael's ship called it.

I rub the back of my neck, an old habit from when I used to feel the weight of my collar. Even though it's been two years since I threw it into the fire, part of me still expects to find cool metal under my fingers. Instead, I feel only my own skin. Sometimes, that realization leaves me dizzy.

Fifi's name is etched on a plaque in the Sanctuary behind me. I think of her sometimes. How I failed her. I know I can't change that past. But in the quiet moments, I let myself hope that by living here, free, I honor her memory better than if I'd died in that arena too.

A small voice breaks my reverie. "Papa?" A tug at my trousers follows.

"Tu es déjà réveillé?" I murmur in French, scooping him up. "Does your mother know where you are?"

Briar appears, her blonde hair, devoid of any pink or purple, is pulled back in a loose braid. Our eyes meet, and for a brief moment, I'm overwhelmed by how far we've come. How we once crouched in cages and wore collars, never imagining we'd see a day like this.

"Hey," Briar calls softly, crossing the mossy clearing to join us. "Festivities are about to start. Did you lose track of time? We need to set up the stall."

In the last few weeks, I've spent my free time at the Forge, hammering old Imperial scraps into something new. It's my way of purifying myself, by taking old shards of our oppressors' technology and reshaping them into harmless trinkets. I'm far from a master craftsman, my decorations are uneven, the welds imperfect, but each one is made with a quiet resolve, proof I'm no longer a "pet" or a "champion." Here, I'm simply Gabriel, a man forging his own path.

I place a gentle kiss on our son's temple, Orion, our little hunter, and set him on his feet. He toddles eagerly toward Briar, tiny fingers grabbing for the fabric of her shirt. She picks him up, and he giggles with delight.

This morning, these simple moments catch me off guard, these small reminders of how free I am, and I suppress my strong emotions of joy and relief.

This is real.

Haven's plaza is alive with color and sound. People bustle between stalls where bartered goods are displayed, hand-sewn clothes, fresh produce from the Greenway, small electronics the engineers have refurbished, and of course, my little stall of imperfect trinkets. Overhead, vines and mosses create a living tapestry that filters the daylight. Strings of metal lanterns, some from my own forging, hang between columns of rock, casting a playful glow.

After a few hours, Anna, our leader stands atop a makeshift stage, addressing a group of newcomers who arrived on the last supply ship. There looks to be about twenty of them. All young humans, like I was when I was first taken. They're trembling with fear. They're all holding their half-fused collars.

"Here, you can learn to be yourselves again," Anna is saying, her voice carrying through the plaza. "We don't require perfection, just honesty. You are safe here. There are no masters and no owners."

The crowd claps softly, welcoming them, but it's not without emotion. I hear some sobs and not from the newcomers. Some of us are still processing our freedom. I share a look with Briar. I remember the day we threw our collars into the fire; how final and uncertain it felt.

Freedom is a complicated gift.

There's always that worry, *Will Aefre come after us?* Will he track us down, determined to reclaim what he once owned? Maybe. But if Aefre tries, he'll find we aren't his obedient pets anymore.

On the way back home, Briar stops in front of a new mosaic, small tiles depicting a child in the arms of a mother, ringed by silhouettes of others. It's a testament to the colonists' unity, a future we're trying to build. She turns to me. "It's beautiful, isn't it?"

I slip an arm around her waist. "Yeah." My gaze settles on the child in the mural. I wonder what our son will grow up to be in this place, someone free and maybe even unafraid. "Orion will never have to fight in an arena. Never wear a collar. Never be breed. Never be owned by another."

Briar nods. "He'll just... be. Our Orion."

At the sound of his name Orion says uncertainly, "Papa... maison."

I have a sudden rush of affection for this little boy who wants to go "home," even though we've only just built this life here. "D'accord, Orion," I answer quietly, lifting him into my arms. He clings to my shirt, relief reflected in his green eyes. The same green eyes that I looked into for twelve years of my imprisonment. "It's all right," I murmur in French, pressing a gentle kiss to his temple. "On rentre à la maison, d'accord? We'll go home."

He nods, his tiny grey hand clasping my thumb. I stand, holding him close, and head down the winding path. I pause by the wind chime I made, now set up near a small patch of blooming flowers. I hold Orion up so he can tap one of the metal rods gently, letting a soft, resonant note ring out.

"What do we call that Orion?" Briar asks in English.

"Chime," he answers.

Briar and I share a smile. There's something very fitting about Orion, Aefre's son, speaking French and English, and this is something we take pleasure in every day. And one day, we hope he grows up to be just like the man who saved us, Gael the Returner.

Every citizen of Haven who can pass for an Imperial is trained in their ways to serve as Protectors of Haven. As far as I'm concerned nothing could be more fitting. And in this way, Orion is loved and cared for within the community in the same way as the human children.

"We're really here, aren't we? Actually... *living*. No simulation could last this long, could it?" I ask Briar as we reach our humble three room cottage.

"We really are here, Gabriel, it's not a dream. Childbirth hurt too much for that."

I kiss the side of her cheek remembering my first request. The first sign I couldn't fully 'just act human.' Soon after Orion was born, I asked her to breastfeed me too. Briar was reluctant at first. But after some thought she allowed me. However, in doing so, she cured me of the Imperial way I had been trained to crave the act. Briar made it sexual and about two adults loving each other. And it was a way for her to give me a piece of my humanity back. And I stopped wanting to feed from her before Orion was three months old. It just felt wrong then.

But other habits have been much harder to break.

Orion finally dozes off in the next room, his little breaths steady and comforting. I stand at the doorway, watching Briar as she tidies away a few things, then gives me a soft smile.

I love this woman, this life we've built since escaping. But there are nights when the shadows of captivity still press down on me, threatening to choke out all sense of normalcy.

I swallow. "Briar," I begin, voice unsteady. "Est-ce que tu peux...? Can you...?" Even after two years of freedom, my throat tightens at the words.

She sets down a small plush toy. "If that's what you need tonight." Her eyes reflect understanding, not judgment. An acceptance of the parts of me that never fully healed.

We retreat to our bedroom, *our* space, no cages, no cameras, and no technology. The door closes with a soft click, sealing us in a sanctuary that, ironically, sometimes becomes a stage for the old roles I can't quite let go of. My pulse quickens as she opens a small trunk we keep hidden in the corner, removing a narrow leather leash. She offers it to me with both hands, her gaze unwavering.

I inhale shakily, trying to anchor myself in the present, reminding myself this is a choice we both make, not something forced. "Merci," I whisper, feeling the hot sting of tears at the corners of my eyes. My captive past is a tangle of pain and identity, and though we're free, a piece of me still craves the twisted familiarity of submission and control.

"Undress," I tell her. Then with trembling hands, I slip the collar around her neck and she slips another collar around my neck.

She touches my wrist as a silent reassurance. "I trust you," she says. Her acceptance is part of my healing, even as it feeds the darker side of my psyche that seeks release through the very acts that once enslaved me.

I lead her gently to the bed, the leash draping between us. My heart hammers in my chest. This is the moment I simultaneously fear and crave. "Je suis désolé," I murmur, choking on the apology. "I hate that I need this sometimes."

She tilts her chin up, eyes warm with empathy. "You're not forcing me, Gabriel. I choose this because I love you, and we're free to rewrite what these chains mean."

Her words stir something in me, shame, gratitude, and desire.

"Hands and legs out," I tell her and she obeys. Then I tie her wrists and ankles with fabric strips. I shudder with each knot. Sometimes, just the simple act of binding her wrists and ankles is enough but not today. Not after seeing those new members.

Then I take a small leather whip and I begin to strike her beautiful body. Her skin turning red where the leather licks her. "Count," I command her in Imperial.

"One, two, three..." she stumbles as I strike her vulva, increasing the pain.

I stop and rub her there, my fingers slipping into her wet labia. Then I grab my own leash and pull hard, like Aefre used to do before a breeding. I still hear the sound of his voice in my head, 'Smell that desire, Ember? You must bring her to climax first or you'll be hurting her. Understand? There's your reward. Good boy."

I think all of these things as I lick Briar between her legs. I circle my tongue around her clit and then use long strokes across the entirety of her vulva. This is the way Aefre wanted me to do it and a style I no longer use because it's not my own. But on nights like tonight, I do everything as Aefre used to instruct me.

Soon Briar's muscles are contracting around me and the scent of her desire is so strong I want to continue licking her, but I pull on my leash again and imagine Aefre's voice in my head, "That's a good boy. Seven minutes. Not bad. Now enter her slowly. She's got a small vagina; you don't want to hurt her. Don't give into your human barbarism. You want to breed a happy human pet, don't you?"

I hold my leash against my neck hard as I slowly plunge into Briar's wet core. I close my eyes and I'm back on the *Luminous Arc*, Aefre holding my leash while I have sex with another human. The doctor and Kaelin giving me advice.

When I orgasm into Briar I moan with the pleasure of it and pull my leash tighter almost choking myself. I can hear the doctor's voice in my head, "That's it, let it all out, Ember."

Then I withdraw. And release Briar and I say the words as they were always said, "Lick him clean, pet."

I lie on my back while Briar licks the remaining semen from me.

Then she looks at me with a lingering question in her eyes, *"Do you need me to hurt you this time?"* She doesn't say it out loud, she never does. But sometimes I see the concern, the sorrow, when I ask her to deliver the beating I once endured from so many trainers.

Mon Dieu, I loathe that part of me.

I nod. "Please. *Just a little.*" My hands clench, and I brace for the sting that used to define my existence.

Her eyes reflect her mixed emotions but that doesn't stop her. She pulls me up with my leash and positions me naked against the wall and then comes up behind me. Sometimes she uses the whip other times just her hand.

The first strikes are barely more than taps with her hands. She's reminding me that I need to count in Imperial. And I do. I begin to count in Imperial as Aefre and Kaelin used to make me do. Then she begins to spank me as hard as she can. Each blow stings both physically and emotionally, but it's the only path I've found to transform that old fear into something I can control.

Then she takes the whip and continues. Every time I exhale from the pain between my breaths I feel like I'm releasing ghosts from my lungs. Finally, I lean my forehead against the wall, tears slipping freely from my eyes. "Je t'aime," I murmur. "Merci. I'm... sorry."

She presses her lips softly to my bloody back. "I know," she breathes in between kisses. "We're... rewriting it together. Remember?"

We sink onto the bed, leashes, knots, shame, and hope. All tangled together into one heartbeat.

When we are both sated a strange calm settles over me and my mind quiets. What I saw today no longer haunts me.

Briar looks into my eyes, face flushed. "You okay?"

"Oui. You?"

"I don't feel the pain like you do," she says. "And I want to do things that help you heal."

"Mon amour, you already do. Every day."

I carefully remove the leash from her neck, and she does the same for me. This is an important part of our role play and we do it every time. Symbolically granting each other freedom again and again and again.

MY INSPIRATION FOR WRITING
MY WILD PET

Dear Readers,

If you'd rather leave the story as it is, feel free to skip these notes. But if you're curious about how *My Wild Pet* took shape, I'd love to share some background and sources of inspiration.

Before I begin, I'd like to acknowledge a few concerns that have been raised by readers, specifically regarding genre and content.

First, yes—this *is* a romance. It may not wear the usual hallmarks of the genre, but at its core, *My Wild Pet* is a story about two people who survive because they find love in one another. Gabriel and Briar do not escape their captivity through cunning alone. They escape through connection, loyalty, and emotional defiance. If that doesn't qualify as romance for some, I understand. But for many readers, it does. Love doesn't always arrive in formulaic packaging.

Second, I recognize that this story includes challenging themes: power imbalances, psychological manipulation, captivity, and I understand that some readers prefer detailed trigger warnings. While I don't include a list at the front of my books, I encourage anyone who needs that information to read reviews or reach out to me directly. I support every reader's right to protect their peace, and I respect that *My Wild Pet* may not be a good fit for everyone.

Lastly, I've been told that this Author's Note comes across as condescending or heavy-handed. That was never my intention. This note is not meant to instruct or moralize but to offer a glimpse into what I was thinking about as I built this world: questions of freedom, personhood, language, and belief. You are, of course, free to disagree with any or all of it. But for those who are curious about history, psychology, control systems, or aliens, I hope this adds another layer to your reading experience.

Please note: Some of the historical examples I reference in the following pages may be upsetting. I've included them not to shock, but to draw meaningful parallels between fiction and real-world systems of power and dehumanization. If you choose to continue, please do so with care for your own emotional wellbeing.

Now, let's explore the decisions behind the scenes and themes in *My Wild Pet*.

WHY DON'T IMPERIALS SEE HUMANS AS SENTIENT BEINGS?

This is one of the main themes throughout all of my books, drawing from real-world parallels: when a technologically advanced society encounters one that is less advanced, the outcome is almost always tragic for the latter.

There are many examples of this throughout history, but these are the first that come to my mind. The Spanish conquest of the Aztec Empire which led to massive cultural and population losses through warfare, disease, and forced labor. The colonization of the Americas more broadly, especially North America, brought similar tragedies upon various Indigenous peoples, including forced relocation, assimilation efforts, and the near-eradication of entire cultures. In Australia, British colonization caused violent displacement and cultural destruction upon Aboriginal peoples. The Scramble for Africa, epitomized by King Leopold II's brutal exploitation of the

Congo Free State, also stands out as a stark example of domination and dehumanization. These historical events demonstrate how disparities in technology and power often breed tragic outcomes for less advanced societies.

If you want to read a biographical account of one such relationship, please check out my blog about Ota Benga and Samuel Vernon, their story served as a major inspiration for *My Human Pet*.

The Inspiration behind My Human Pet

Psychological Control and Human Pet Training

In the *Whispers from the Imperial Cage* universe, Imperials have long treated humans as lesser beings,"adorable pets." Their belief system about humans has evolved around a few core misconceptions:

Fear of "Primitive Languages"

Imperials insist human languages might cause "brain damage" if spoken frequently, which may sound outrageous. But in their eyes, human languages are archaic, error-prone, and too "limited" to express the more advanced concepts in the Imperial lexicon.

In *My Wild Pet*, the doctor warns Aefre of trainers who begin listening to their pets. In our own world, the same is said of biologists working with gorillas. Not that Imperials ever think that humans are as far down the evolutionary line as gorillas, but I couldn't help but think about *Planet of the Apes* when I wrote this and then the case of Koko a western lowland gorilla famous for learning some signs adapted from American Sign Language. Although Koko clearly used many signs to communicate wants and needs, her actual abilities remained a point of debate. The scientific consensus is that she did not demonstrate true grammar or syntax, leading many researchers to conclude that her trainer, Francine Patterson, overinterpreted Koko's signs. Some argued that Patterson's approach blurred the lines between scientific rigor and personal affection, resulting in exaggerated claims about Koko's language skills, as well as broader ethical concerns about Koko's living conditions. And so when Aefre questions whether or not Gabriel is sentient he always comes back to, "Ember is mirroring me." And when Gabriel shows understanding beyond what humans should be capable of Aefre wonders if he is anthropomorphizing Gabriel because he likes him so much. Exactly what Patterson was accused of.

If you're interested in reading what Patterson wrote about Koko, I can recommend the paper, *Language acquisition by a lowland gorilla: Koko's first ten years of vocabulary development. FGP Patterson. 1990. WORD: Vol. 41, No. 2, pp. 97-143.* There are also videos on YouTube of Koko. One in particular is especially moving, 'Koko the last talking gorilla... Her dying words." (It's very emotional).

DENIAL OF A HUMAN SOUL

Imperials assume that only advanced species (with high level of technology and a mastery of the Imperial language) possess a "spirit" worthy of continuing after death. The latter is important because Aefre struggles with Ember and wonders if he might be sentient because he speaks Imperial almost perfectly.

Dismissing humanity's claim to a soul helps the Imperials feel less guilty about enslaving and trading humans as "pets." However, other alien trainers question Aefre about this at the Grand Championships as the other trainers do not believe in the Imperial religion and do believe humans are sentient. Their stance is humans are less technologically advanced and therefore can be taken advantage of. It is not morally correct but it is a scientific assessment. Aefre, on the other hand, doubles down that humans are not sentient despite the logic placed before him.

The most famous example of this I can think of would be the

holocaust. If you're interested in reading about the dehumanization of the Jewish people by a group of average middle-aged German police, not eligible for military service and mostly not Nazis, who were sent to Poland and ordered to kill tens of thousands of Jews, I can recommend the book, *Ordinary Men* by Christopher R. Browning.

WHY LANGUAGE AND RELIGION MATTER IN *MY WILD PET*

Telling someone, "Your language harms you," or "You have no soul," sows deep self-doubt. It's a potent form of control, far more subtle than physical chains. There were signs that Gabriel might believe he has no soul. We know from Briar's encounter with Rebecca that she is unsure whether God exists to begin with. Rebecca is a believer and fears for her human soul from the get-go which is why she commits suicide. Which probably saved her months of agony because Aefre would have heavily utilized psychological tactics on Rebecca to force her into submission that probably would have driven her insane.

By exploring these Imperial beliefs, I wanted to highlight how prejudice and pseudo-scientific myths can sustain oppressive structures.

These nonsensical beliefs mirror our own past, where seemingly absurd rationalizations have often been used to justify cruelty and inequality.

One well-known example is the pseudo-scientific belief that heavily contributed to the oppression of Western women which was "female hysteria." Originating in ancient Greece and persisting well into the 19th century, "hysteria" was often explained by the concept of the "wandering womb" (the belief that a woman's uterus could literally roam around her body, causing erratic emotions and behaviors [it's insane to think that women's organs would move and men's would not]). Medical and social authorities promoted this idea to portray women as inherently prone to irrationality, anxiety, or even insanity. Basically, any behavior that deviated from expected norms, be it sexual desire, outspoken opinions, serious academic study, or simple stress, could be labeled "hysteria," bolstering the notion that women were *biologically* ill-equipped for independence. It was something that men touted for centuries as a reason women couldn't be seen as equal human beings.

Which leads me off topic from the dehumanization of the Imperial pets to discuss the implications of a matriarchal world regarding medical technology.

Imperials and Menstrual blood

Although my story features only Imperial males, the broader society and galaxy are matriarchal, shaped by women for women. As a result, women's health is paramount, and men, consciously or not, uphold that priority.

One striking example of this is the use of menstrual blood. In a matriarchal society, its rich stem cell potential would have been likely discovered and utilized far sooner than in a patriarchy.

In our own world, scientists have only recently begun exploring menstrual stem cells, in large part because a patriarchal perspective historically treated women's bodies as "inferior men," and believed menstrual blood to be, "unclean." My narrative flips that viewpoint, here, it's the women of the Empire who view men as "inadequate women."

If you want to read more about these advances, I can recommend. *The multi-functional roles of menstrual blood-derived stem cells in regenerative medicine,* Lijun Chen, Jingjing Qu , Charlie Xiang. National Library of Medicine, 2019 Jan 3;10(1):1

Why the Imperials Give Them New Names

From a writing point of view, having two sets of names used by different characters wasn't an easy thing for me to do and I tried writing the book without changing their names. But unlike Ensley in *My Human Pet*, Briar and Gabriel were show pets and would be treated a lot differently by a professional trainer so in my mind, there was no doubt they would be given ridiculous pet names (just as we do with our pets today). And renaming them accomplished two goals:

ENFORCING OWNERSHIP

Much like historical examples of renaming enslaved people, the Imperials strip away a human's given name to sever any lingering tie to their past, culture, or family. By assigning new names they reinforce the notion that humans are "property" rather than individuals with their own identities.

In ancient Rome, slaves were given names by their owner. When they were freed, they often kept that slave name and took their former owner's name as their first and family name. For example, a man named Publius Larcius freed a slave named Nicia, who then became known as Publius Larcius Nicia. However, there are also many other examples from ancient Rome where owners just made up ridiculous names for their slaves so that people would always know they had been a slave.

UNDERMINING IDENTITY

A name is part of a person's sense of self. Forcing someone to answer to a different name disorients them, making it easier for captors to control them psychologically. If you're no longer "Briar" but "Ash," you become more likely to see yourself as part of their system rather than your own.

Gabriel wouldn't give up his name even though we know he'd let go of so much else of his humanity while in captivity. I purposely wanted to make this his last stand. If Aefre would have been able to break him of his human name, he would have completely owned Gabriel.

There are many examples of this in history, countless really. Most notably, as an American, I think of the Native American US government-run boarding schools where children were forced to speak English and were given new Christian names. Another example comes from nuns in the Catholic Church. They are given new names as a way of giving up their own lives and becoming the wife of Christ (not all of them did this voluntarily).

How Can Imperials Deny Human Sentience Yet Still Have Sex with Humans?

In the *Whispers from the Imperial Cage* universe, the Imperials maintain a deeply contradictory view of humanity. They claim humans lack full intelligence or spiritual worth, yet they're willing to engage in intimate acts and even exploit genetic similarities for breeding. This paradox mirrors uncomfortable truths from Earth's own history. Many oppressive societies have rationalized slavery by labeling certain groups "less evolved" or "mentally inferior," yet exploited them for forced labor or sexual gratification.

Psychological Self-Deception

The Imperials compartmentalize, they tell themselves humans aren't truly "sentient," but still value humans' physical and genetic qualities. And by calling humans "soulless," the Imperials avoid facing moral guilt for using them *even if* they know that humanity shares their biology.

Power Dynamics & Objectification

Viewing humans purely as property or a source of pleasure strips away empathy, letting the Imperials mask their hypocrisy under the guise of "pet ownership."

Reflecting Real-World History

This contradictory mindset—treating people as mentally or spiritually "less" while still abusing them is not new. My intent was to show how supposedly "advanced" civilizations can prop up oppressive systems with warped beliefs, no matter how illogical they seem. There are countless examples from every corner of the globe, throughout human history, I will use an example from US history.

"Children of the plantation" is a term sometimes used to describe individuals whose ancestry traces back to enslaved African women, who were impregnated by non-black men (typically the slave owner, his relatives, or the overseer) in the context of the trans-Atlantic slave trade. Under laws *like partus sequitur ventrem*, these children inherited the enslaved status of their mothers and had no legal recognition as the legitimate children of their fathers.

While some fathers provided limited opportunities, such as education, careers, or eventual manumission, others cruelly sold their own multiracial children as property. Thomas Jefferson's children by Sally Hemings, are examples of those who received comparatively better treatment, while Alexander Scott Withers infamously sold two of his own children to slave traders.

If you're interested in reading more about this, I can recommend the books, Alex Haley's *Queen: The Story of an American Family* (1993) and Edward Ball's *Slaves in the Family* (1998).

Freedom in *My Wild Pet*: A Reflection

Throughout *My Wild Pet*, the human characters are bought, sold, and forced to perform in an alien arena. So is it ever possible for them to be free even when they are physically free? This question goes beyond literal chains, touching on the deeper layers of psychological, emotional, and societal constraints. And it's up to the reader to decide if Briar and Gabriel are really free in Haven.

This dynamic mirrors real-world histories (and even present-day situations) where "freedom" might exist in name only, as social, economic, or cultural forces maintain a grip that's just as limiting. If you want to read more about modern "freedom" I can highly recommend Noam Chomsky's book *For Reasons of State*, New York: Pantheon Books, 1973. Specifically, the chapter, 'Psychology and Ideology.'

BRIAR AND GABRIEL REDEFINE FREEDOM

True freedom in *My Wild Pet* emerges from choice. And I believe this is true in our own world as well. The ability to choose makes us free.

Briar and Gabriel reclaim pieces of themselves through loyalty and love. So while they might never escape every chain from the trauma they endured, they find moments of liberation by seizing autonomy where they can and refusing to let fear of being abducted again and their past trauma define them. That to me is freedom. Is it freedom for you too?

WHAT DOES THIS HAVE TO DO WITH ALIENS?

Imagine if aliens were to capture us, would they treat humanity with any semblance of respect? It seems unlikely. After all, we have barely managed to reach the Moon, and in a more advanced civilization's view, we might appear primitive. History itself shows how readily humans mistreated others deemed "lesser," even among our own species.

Yet humankind has already broadcast its location across the galaxy. According to *Time* magazine, the Voyager 1 and Voyager 2 probes, launched in 1977, carry golden records full of Earthly music, as well as messages from former President Jimmy Carter and over a hundred analog-encoded items revealing who and where we are. The hubris behind such an act is striking. Those responsible clearly never considered the possibility that truly advanced beings could see us as mere curiosities or worse. They likely never envisioned themselves in scenarios reminiscent of *My Human Pet* or any books from my series *Whispers from the Imperial Cage*.

If we fail to imagine ourselves as lesser beings in the eyes of an alien race, and if we don't address the dire threats we pose to our own survival, whether through war, unchecked AI, or environmental destruction our downfall may be inevitable. At best, an encounter with extraterrestrial life could mirror the grim fates of my fictional characters; at worst, it could mean our total annihilation.

Thank you for reading these notes and for diving into *My Wild Pet* and steer clear of any bright lights in the sky.

Best wishes,
Olympia

2025

ALSO BY OLYMPIA BLACK

Whispers from the Imperial Cage

My Human Pet

My Wild Pet

Their Human Receptionist

My Prized Pet

His Beloved Human Pet

Other books related to the Whispers from the Imperial Cage:

My Human Wife

***

Other books in the same universe:

Volunteer 4711

Short Stories:

Human: A Short Story

I'm Bored on Earth, Take Me

My books are available in ebook, audio, and paperback.

ABOUT THE AUTHOR

I write dark science fiction about humanity's relationships with aliens and artificial intelligence. To build my stories, I do not shy away from explicit encounters or highly emotional scenes. My books are not for the faint of heart but are observations about the human condition.

For new releases, please sign up for my newsletter:

https://www.olympiablack.com/contact

And you can find me on Substack:
https://substack.com/@olympiablack

With best wishes,

Olympia

- facebook.com/OlympiaLBlack
- instagram.com/olympiablacksciencefiction
- amazon.com/Olympia-Black/e/B084DLSMJ4
- bookbub.com/authors/olympia-black
- tiktok.com/@olympiablack_author

GALACTIC SENTIENCE CLASSIFICATION SYSTEM

In the universe of *Whispers from the Imperial Cage*, the Intergalactic Court (IGC) employs a standardized classification system for evaluating cognitive capacity across species. This system differs from Earth's scientific definitions and is used throughout galactic society for legal, commercial, and social purposes.

IGC COGNITIVE CLASSIFICATION LEVELS:

- Level 1 - Basic Sentience: Capacity for sensory perception and emotional response. Includes most animal life forms capable of feeling pain, pleasure, and basic emotions.
- Level 2 - Reactive Intelligence: Demonstrates problem-solving abilities, learning from experience, and complex social behaviors. Many Earth mammals, some avian species, and certain marine life.
- Level 3 - Adaptive Cognition: Shows abstract thinking, tool use, basic communication, and environmental

manipulation. Includes dolphins, great apes, and some cephalopods.

- Level 4 - Standard Sentience: Possesses self-awareness, complex language, mathematical reasoning, and cultural development. This is the minimum threshold for legal recognition as a "person" under galactic law.
- Level 5 - Enhanced Sentience: Advanced cognitive abilities including meta-cognition, theoretical physics comprehension, multi-dimensional thinking, and species-wide coordination capabilities.

HUMAN CLASSIFICATION CONTROVERSY:

Humans present a unique challenge to this system. While some individuals test at Level 4 (Standard Sentience), others score only at Level 2 or 3, leading to the controversial practice of individual cognitive assessment rather than species-wide classification. This discrepancy has been exploited by various galactic entities to justify differential treatment of humans.

The Imperial classification system tends to be more restrictive, often requiring Level 4+ certification for full citizenship rights, while some progressive sectors recognize cognitive potential rather than current testing results.

Note: When characters in these stories use the term "sentient," they are typically referring to Level 4 Standard Sentience or above, unless otherwise specified.